THE WOMAN I'VE BECOME.

WHEN YOUR LIFE GOES PUBLIC, THERE'S NOWHERE TO HIDE.

SUE MACKENDER

Published by Crooksbury Publishing

ISBN 9871739647407

Typesetting services by BOOKOW.COM

For those I've loved and lost and those I've yet to meet.

FOREWORD

Other Books by this Author

The Woman I've Become.
The Chartley Girls Series
The Girl on the Hill.
The Chartley Girls Series
Accident of Fate.
First of the Liam Riley Duo
Accident of Birth.
Second of Adam/Liam Riley Duo

PREFACE

The Chartley Girls series was originally one book called "A Date in the Diary" and was reviewed by a major publisher who thought it better as three standalones. So, this is how Mia (Maureen), Grace, and Cassie got their own novels. Yes, I attended a boarding school – no, none of these events are based on fact. Is there romance involved in each story? Yes.

I wanted to write about change and challenge. From the thirty-six-year-olds they are today and how receiving the invitation to a reunion is the marker for catastrophic changes that are the catalyst for the way each deals with intolerable situations and the women they become before they reunite.

Acknowledgments

I can't believe this is my fourth novel and the second in the series of The Chartley Girls. I'm hoping book three sees the light of day, mid-2024.

Firstly, I would like to raise an imaginary glass to friendship and support, for my magnificent writing group, *The Diamonds: Denise Barnes, AKA Molly Green, Terri Martin, AKA Terri Fleming* for taking my wordy to the chopping board and, last but not least, my red penned pal, *Tessa Shapcott;* our monthly get-togethers are full of laughter mixed with the serious matter of reading our chapters and getting good honest feedback. The three, all professional authors, write in a trio of genres so there's no competition.

Next, my tireless friend, *Helen Shrubb*, who painstakingly reads every chapter and is honest with her thoughts on my current project. It also helps that she enjoys a walk with a coffee at the end of it. Thank you.

To *Zoe Hatfield*, my fabulous editor, who has polished this book ready for publication in an extremely short turnaround time. It would be amiss of me not to mention *Mal Foster*, author extraordinaire and founder of Woking Writers and Authors, bringing local talent to the fore.

Thanks to my many writing friends, on and offline, for always championing me. There are so many people

I want to thank that I could fill another novel.

Lastly to those of you who support me by buying my books. Without you my life would be nothing but a pile of words. Thank you for your continued support and posting your reviews on Amazon and Goodreads, which all authors rely on to promote their work.

Good luck to my Granddaughter, *Madeline (Maddie) Jones,* who is about to complete her first novel. I'm very proud of you.

Reference to Bruce Springsteen's *Dancing in the Dark*

The Woman I've Become

THE CHARTLEY GIRLS SERIES

SUE MACKENDER

1

Looking back it started as an ordinary day, as ordinary as you can get when trying to herd four children ages sixteen to eight complete with homework, football kits, and ballet shoes out through the door. And the answering machine blinking its tiny red light, informing me the tape is full. I hadn't bothered to play the messages, knowing most of them were from my absentee husband, Tom. I grit my teeth every time, angry with him for not ringing when he knew we'd be home. He knew our timetable—he wrote it. Instead, Tom deliberately called knowing we weren't home to deliver his news that filming was being extended… no longer than a month, he'd add. I knew the way his mind worked he'd leave a message to let me get used to the idea and then phone, hoping to sweet talk me. Not that I could do anything about it. It was all part and parcel of being married to a celebrity jungle explorer who spent more time with the tribes of the Amazon than he did with us. Or was it Peru this time? I can't recall.

We live in the middle of nowhere. Tom calls it our settlement, liking the peace when he's home, being surrounded by miles of nothingness. It's a forty-five-minute drive for the school run. Affecting not only me but our children too. After-school clubs and play dates are impossible, as the remoteness of our property means where one goes—we all go.

Tom has rules. Lots of them. He says they are like traditions—keeping order and the tribe together. One rule he makes is no radio, TV, or electronic devices before school. I agree with this, otherwise I'd never get the kids out of the house. Once Jack, Melissa, George, and Alice are in the car, you'd think that would be a relief. Not so. My second challenge is to run the gauntlet of cows crossing roads after milking, not to mention the dreaded milk float that all too often hampers our journey. Then, of course, there's the railway crossing to negotiate. All this before school even starts. So there was, as I said, nothing unusual. It was an ordinary day.

2

'Come on kids, we'll be late! Jack, for heaven's sake, have you combed your hair?' I grab a brush from the hall table, ignoring the flashing red light on the answer machine. Stuff Tom, I think angrily. He has nothing to say I want to hear. Actions speak louder than words. He should be at home with us, not extending contract after contract.

'Comb it now, or I will.' Sixteen-year-old Jack scowls, batting off the offending object.

'Not with that—it's pink, and anyway, everyone wears their hair waxed. It's called fashion.' He looks at me from under a greasy fringe, combed across one eye. The rest stands bolt upright.

'Not to me it's not. Sort it now.' I turn to see Alice kneeling on the floor, surrounded by the contents of her schoolbag.

'Alice, love, what on earth are you doing?'

'I've lost one of my ballet shoes and Miss won't let me do ballet without it and then I won't get picked to be in the—' She stops to draw breath, reloading the bag.

'Did you look inside your shoe bag?' I say, trying not to look at the clock.

'It's not there,' she says, her plaits bobbing on her shoulders.

'But did you actually look?' She drags the bag towards her.

'It's not… oh yes, silly me.' Alice throws a toothy but endearing smile and scrambles to her feet, stumbling past me to the front door. She comes to a halt, challenged by big sister Melissa who is blocking her way.

'Lissy, let me through.'

'For God's sake,' I mutter, hoping no one can hear, as it's a phrase I'm constantly chastising them on.

'All of you in the car, now, or no TV tonight. Melissa, stop teasing your sister.' Melissa folds her arms, pulling in her lips.

'Ok but when the kids laugh at her at school, it won't be my fault.' She points at Alice's backside.

'Okay. Good girl. Alice, skirt … knickers … you don't want everyone to see your pants, do you?'

The beginning of the journey is uneventful. No one's forgotten anything major and so far, we are on time and ahead of the electric milk-float. For once we won't get stuck at the railway gates.

Approaching the crossroads, I notice three men standing at the side of the road by a dark Volvo and a red Fiat. Nothing unusual about that, except, as we pass they rush to get into their cars and pull out close behind me. I catch the frown on my forehead as Melissa interrupts my thoughts.

'Charlie didn't come in for his food. That's not like him. Do you think he found somewhere else to live?'

'Well, cats are very independent. They take off when they feel like it, and Charlie's old in cat years, so he's allowed to be cantankerous.' I'm tempted to add, 'like husbands,' but there's no point in mentioning Tom negatively to them. They're victims, as much as I am. My mobile trills from my handbag in the footwell at Melissa's feet. 'Melissa, see who that is and tell them I'm driving.' She drags my bag from the floor with little urgency. When she finally unzips it, the ringing stops. 'Who was it?' Melissa scrolls to "missed calls."

'Aunty Jenny. Shall I call her back?'

'No, I'll ring her later,' As I speak, the phone gives out two beeps.

'It's Aunty Jen again. Call urgently. "Urgently" is in capitals. She needs you bad, Mum.'

'Badly,' I correct. 'Well, she'll have to wait,' I say, glancing in my mirror. The Volvo and the Fiat are still directly behind me. A tug of uncertainty tightens my gut. They are following us, but why? I'm unnerved now and speed up. So do they. I do this journey twice, sometimes four times a day. I know this road like the back of my hand. More confidently, I pull away, knowing I have the advantage. The hedges are too high for a car to see over, but not a four-by-four. The crossroads are ahead in the distance. It's car-free to the left, but the milk-float ambles its way from the right. Bloody hell, I'll be arriving at the crossroads the same time as the bloody milk-float. I rechecked my mirror and pushed my foot hard to the floor. *Christ,* is that a telescopic lens in the Volvo's windscreen?

'Yay, go, Mum,' Jack yells from the back seat.

'Shut up,' I snap, fear clawing at the pit of my stomach. 'Oh, Christ!' Swerving erratically, I narrowly miss the milk-float. Behind me horns blast and tyres squeal. I'm aware of the sound of glass smashing as milk crates slam onto tarmac. In the mirror I can see the upturned milk crates and a slurry of white. A thousand pinpricks shoot down the backs of my hands as adrenalin surges through my body. *Dear God.* The Volvo's front end is in the ditch and the Fiat caught behind the milk float. The milkman is shaking his fist after me, but I drive on. The road dips and I can't see them any longer. I breathe in slowly, calming my thumping heart – three breaths in, four out. I hear Alice's sobs. George, ashen faced, meets my gaze in the mirror. What have I done? I attempt a joke.

'How's that? Good bit of stunt driving, eh?'

I yelp as Melissa punches my leg.

'You could have killed us,' she cries dramatically, crossing her arms and slumping in her seat.

'Nonsense. I needed to get ahead of the float.' I slow the car. 'Alice, everything's okay. I'll go slowly now, I promise. Blow your nose and stop crying.'

Jack is whooping—slapping his thigh.

'That was great, Mum. Didn't know you could drive like that. Wait till I tell Dad. He'll never believe it.' With the mention of the 'dad' word, the car falls silent.

At the school gates Jack and Melissa take forever unloading their sports kit and homework bags from the boot.

'Can you hurry, please?' I say, conscious as always of the time.

There are more parents around the school gates than usual. As I dispatch my two youngest, I wonder if it's my imagination or are people staring at me? I look down. I'm wearing trousers so it isn't the length of my skirt, and there are no unbuttoned cleavage reveals. I run my hand across my face in case there's a Marmite smear as one mother nudges another who throws me a furtive glance, then turns addressing another two women. How odd. Are they talking about us the mad, isolated family? One lady shakes her head sadly as I pass.

Alice drags her Princess rucksack along the pavement. George calls out goodbye as all around heads turn from phone screens to me before hastily shoving them into pockets and bags. My face glows hot and there's an uneasy feeling flowering in my stomach. They couldn't have heard about the milk-float fiasco already, could they? I'm still receiving stares as I pull out into the traffic. At the blast of a horn my foot hits the brakes, barely missing Dan Mayne in his silver Land Rover. He shakes his head slowly and waves me on, but not before I've lipread "women drivers". Can this day get any worse?

I'm desperate for an illicit cigarette with my coffee but I don't have any, so I drive to the village shop. I rarely buy my private stash here: too many gossipers who'll frown on it, but after the sort of morning I'm having, I deserve one. Pulling up to the pavement, I spy Becky Greenway's mum Evelyn, the notorious queen of gossip, holding court on the pavement with several other women.

'Christ's sake,' I hesitate, but it's a six-mile drive to the next shop. Oh, well, in for a penny, in for a pound,' I mutter to myself.

Evelyn's eyes widen as she watches me approach, I spot her openly nudge the woman in a grey coat beside her and sense my stomach hollow.

'Oh, Mrs. Lane – Grace, dear. You must be devastated. I know I would be. I was shocked when I saw it on TV this morning,' she moves to block my path, her perfume strong, pungent. Her face molds an artificial disposition of sympathy. 'I told Becky to keep an extra eye on Melissa at school. Children can be so hurtful.'

Others gather around us pretending they aren't listening, but I know they are. Why are they all looking at me?

Why, what's going on? 'Evelyn I—'

A woman breaks through the group and squeezes my arm.

'I'm so sorry. It must be awful for you.'

My breath is imprisoned in my ribcage. What the hell are they talking about? I swing back to Evelyn, who is sporting a fake, but sorrowful smile.

'I mean, did you have any idea? Did he tell you?'

The other women shuffle awkwardly. I don't understand what they're on about. I try to push through them, almost knocking over the newsagent's 'A' board. It's then I read the headlines that brand themselves to my eyelids.

LOCAL TV CELEBRITY EXPLORER
FATHERS 17 BY JUNGLE

TRIBESWOMEN

3

I read it twice until black dots, like wine flies, filter my vision. Like a dripping tap, the words become fact. Fact becomes disbelief, horror.

'Bastard, bastard, fucking bastard.' My knees buckle. I shrink in humiliation as Evelyn takes my arm to offer support, my temper gets the better of me. I jerk it free, forcing my legs to get me to my car. Spurred on by an adrenaline hit, I pull heavily on the steering wheel into the morning traffic, oblivious to whether the road is clear for the second time this morning. My seat-belt alarm flashes and pings relentlessly, I don't care. I must get home – get away.

I glimpse myself in the rear-view mirror, a Halloween mask stares back at me, mascara runs like tramlines on my cheeks, bubbles of snot burst from my nostrils. I search my pockets for tissues. There are none.

'Oh Christ,' I cry even harder. Did I look like this outside the shop? That cow, Evelyn, will dine out on my personal tragedy forever, milking it, repeating it.

It's an age before the railway crossing gates part to let me through. *Must get home, need to think, make sense of it. 17 children?* What did that mean? It must be a joke, gutter press making ludicrous headlines to sell newspapers. My car races past the forest. Am I driving it, or the car driving me?

I'm home. I kill the engine dabbing my face with the end of my scarf.

Why's there a muddy Land Rover and a red car parked on my land? The Land Rover's door is open, the key dangling from the ignition. I hear shouting. Gingerly, I follow the sound turning into the yard.

'What the hell is going on?' I scream, blinking in disbelief. Matt Barton is standing aggressively astride a scruffy, grey-haired man in a sheepskin coat. The mans on his back, supported by his elbows surrounded by the contents of my dustbins. He catches my eye and looks relieved and struggles to his feet.

'All right, no need to get rough. I'm going. I'm only doing my job,' he says, brushing off his trousers.

'Doing your job? You reporters are the scum of the earth,' Matt growls, 'destroying people's lives. Look at you – rummaging through bins. You don't care who you hurt, do you? Now get going, or do I have to persuade you some more?' Matt steps forward, grabbing a handful of the man's coat, heaving him to within an inch of his face. The man shies back.

'Okay, okay, I'm going no need for that.'

I'm rooted to the spot, my jaw sagging. He shakes off Matt's grip, turns and takes a step towards me, taking a notebook from his pocket. Matt raises a hand and knocks it to the ground and with one stride spins the man, who I now realise is a reporter, around. He has him by the seat of his trousers and the collar of his jacket and frogmarches him out of sight to the front of the house.

My hands reach behind me for the wall of the barn, gratefully I slump against it; legs like strands of string, they can't hold me. Blood pounds and whooshes in my ears, its presence drowning out an understanding of my predicament. *17 children. Dear God!*

I can't focus. A car starts, raised voices, the crunch of feet on pea shingle. I push myself off the wall as Matt comes into view, striding towards me open-armed and breathing hard with exertion. I fall against him. He rocks me in his embrace. I bury my head in his jacket and sob. He strokes my hair, hushing me, he smells of hay and disinfectant. His body stiffens against me. He pulls away, leaving me bereft and confused and runs back to the front of the house leaving me whimpering like a puppy. Matt's voice is raised, I hear angry voices. The sound of a car pulling off on shingle at high speed. I hug myself. Matt appears in the opening, wiping sweat from his brow.

'I'm sorry Grace, the little scrote came back and took a picture of us. I wasn't quick enough to get the camera before he drove off.'

My mouth moves wordlessly. He takes me by the shoulders, we stand facing each other awkwardly. I still have my keys in my hand, he takes them from me and leads me into the house. I watch in a stupor as he drags out one of the solid oak chairs and presses my shoulders to sit. I'm dazed, shut down – my head fuzzy, seeing but not seeing.

'You're trembling. It's shock. You need a strong cup of tea.' I'm aware of him filling the kettle. I watch stupefied while he searches in cupboards for tea bags, cups, and spoons. It's an age before he places a steaming mug in front of me. My nostrils detect brandy fumes. I try to object, but he shakes his head. 'Medicinal,' he says before joining me at the table. It's awful. My head swills with unimaginable thoughts. I look at him, his eyes are full of concern, it's too painful. I turn away clasping my hands around the china mug, ironically, it's Tom's, decorated with Jungle Book characters. A present from Alice two father's days back. She'd insisted, even though Tom didn't come home. My hands tremble so much that I slop the fiery liquid as I take a sip. We both ignore it.

'Did you have any idea?'

I rub my eyes with the heels of my hands, shaking my head.

'Is it true?'

He shrugs. 'It was on the early news. Hit the papers too, I believe.' He looks embarrassed, pink tinges his cheeks. 'Look, I'll clear up the yard, give you some time to yourself.' Despite the brandy and hot tea, I'm cold. I pull my collar up around my ears and rest my elbows on the table. 'Grace, there's something else... I'm sorry It's more bad news, but in his haste to get away the bastard ran over a cat. Yours, I presume?'

A cry fills the room, I realise it's me making it. I can't think, it hurts my head. I zone in and out at some level of consciousness unable to follow the conversation. Then I'm aware of a surrounding stillness, exhaustion. Time slows. I don't know how long I've been sitting here. Through the window the sound of a shovel on cobbles, scraping metal. Something dragging – my dustbins? My mind can't visualise Matt's clean-up. I finish my drink, stand on cotton wool legs, and remove my coat. At the sink I wash my face until it looks more like a version of me reflecting in the window.

'Feeling better?'

I turn slowly into Matt's smile as he lays a steadying hand on my shoulder.

'Yes, thank you. I don't understand how you got here, and that man?'

Matt runs the tap. I step out of his way. He soaps his hands and forearms. It's strange to see a man other than Tom washing at our sink.

'I heard the news,' he says rinsing away the grimy suds.

'You and half the village, apparently.' Matt glances at me over his shoulder, shaking water from his hands. I pass him the towel I'm holding, embarrassed by the unwashed breakfast things piled high on the draining board. 'The milkman called at the farm, said there was a car in a ditch and asked if I could tow it out. He wasn't very complimentary about your driving.' That was the icebreaker I needed: I force a weak smile. 'When I got there, one chap started asking questions about you and Tom and I realised they were press. I'd seen the other car turn around and head back this way, so I followed it. When I got here, the bastard was going through your bins.'

I'm watching his mouth work, I'm not here, this can't be reality, can it? I feel stupid standing mute and drag myself back into the moment.

'I don't have the radio or TV on in the mornings, if I did, I'd never get the kids to school and I unplugged the phone last night because I was angry with Tom and expected a call, but that's another story.' Matt checks his watch. 'Sorry I'm keeping you.'

'No, no. Not at all. At least another half an hour before I need to go. Would you like me to bury the cat while I'm here?'

The room swims as I absorb what he's saying, Charlie is dead. Did I know that? The taste of vomit rasps my throat, forcing me to run to the cloakroom. I wretch until there's no more to come. Charlie dying is almost worse than what Tom's done. I'll have to tell my children, they'll be devastated. How will I cope with their grief *and* Tom's betrayal?

Lowering the toilet seat, I sob quietly for Charlie. How old was he? I don't know. Tom came home with him wrapped in an old jumper before Jack was born. Someone had abandoned the kitten on waste ground. That was well over 16 years ago. How long is that in cat years? Ninety? One hundred?

I don't want to leave the small space of the cloakroom. It's safe, comfortable. One of Alice's hair slides sits on the windowsill. It's not out of place, its normal. I come across them most days. This one's lilac and pink. Alice's favourite colours. I push myself to my feet with the reality that I must be strong for the kids. The question is, can I?

4

Part 2

Before that day

Every Tuesday is a Groundhog Day. As soon as I've dropped Jack off at his cricket match, I must race across town to collect Melissa from ballet. If my plans don't materialise, I'll be late getting the little ones from Stagecoach and Alice will sulk all evening. Jack mumbles something incoherent as he slides from the passenger seat to the pavement, dragging his cricket bag behind him.

'Bye, Love,' I shout into thin air, already edging the car back into the lines of other parents' cars doing the same. I'm on constant alert, switching my view from the road ahead to my rear-view mirror and back again. I'm taking no risks. The next mile is smooth sailing, I'm feeling smug until I get to Matt Barton's farm.

'Bloody hell Matt! You and your ruddy cows will be the death of me.' They amble across the road, indifferent to my anguish, dropping the occasional cowpat on one of their twice daily trips in for milking. Matt is at the gate; he gives me a cheery wave. I force a smile as he rounds up the last of the lumbering stragglers.

I finally reach Tapper's Dance School, rolling my shoulders to release the build-up of a day's tension and pull into the curb. Melissa is waiting outside as instructed and jogs towards the car, she's about to get in when Miss Warlock comes rushing from the building.

'Melissa, can you pop back in for a moment?'

What now? The woman's a pain. Melissa rolls her eyes at me and follows Miss Warlock inside. I'm trying not to get wound up but I'm already drumming my fingers on the steering wheel. My eyes sweep to the doorway.

'Melissa come on,' I growl. The clock on the dashboard taunts me. 'Sod this,' I say, and give the car horn a blast. Passing mothers, guiding their little darlings along the pavement, tut and shake their heads in disapproval.

Melissa reappears at the same time as the milk float rattles past me. *'SHIT, SHIT, SHIT.'* My head flops onto the steering wheel. My life is a disorganised, or is it an over organised, mess? Murphy's Law or some other buggers, and talking of buggers, bugger Tom. He's been away almost six months. I know people envy me, thinking how wonderful to have a husband who famously trots the globe, discovering lost tribes, living beyond the Rain Forest, sharing a home with a family of Tibetans or whoever. Truth is, I'm left to wrestle our children's intricate social lives. Even Alice, at seven, has more going on than me. I never have a minute to myself. If I'm not rushing here or there, cleaning, cooking, not to mention running Tom's fan club and writing the monthly editorial for World Explorer magazine. Tom never asks if I mind. Why would he? He is hunter gatherer, the provider. I try not to blame everything on him; he does after all pay for the roof over our heads, even if it is in an impossible location for a growing family and was never my choice in the first place.

When exactly was it that I fell out of love? Have I fallen out of love? What happened to the couple who couldn't keep their hands off each other? Who finished each other's sentences? The little flip in the pit of my stomach when I heard his voice on the phone. The smile that made my heart sing. The need to touch his face and run my fingers through his hair has vanished in a mire of domesticity.

I start as Melissa almost wrenches the rear door off its hinges; struggling to force a box, spewing pink and lilac netting, into the car.

'What the hell is that lot?'

She raises her brows and sighs as only a twelve-year-old can.

'It's for the autumn show Mum, *remember*, you said you'd help,' she says, accusingly.

'Yes, with your costume, not the entire cast's.'

'It's not the entire cast. Just the five enchanted nymphs, and you said you'd do it and if you don't Becky Greenway's mum will, then she'll persuade Miss Warlock to let Becky be lead Nymph instead of me. And she's not even good enough. Miss Warlock never notices, because Becky Greenway's mum paid for the new stage curtains, and says she'll provide the refreshments and the printing cost of the programs.'

I'm amazed my daughter hasn't turned blue through lack of oxygen. Instead, she sneezes, ending the conversation and within a Nano-second is on her mobile and deep in conversation. Leaving me free to negotiate the quickest route to pick up her siblings.

She's right, of course. Evelyn Grainger, or Evil Evelyn as Jenny calls her, has muscled her way into everything from fundraising, PTA, Women's Institute, and book club. People rarely say no to her, worried they'd be blackballed from the Macmillan coffee morning or harvest festival distribution. There was little to do for some mothers once the children were in school. If only I was one of them.

My thoughts are depressing, I decide, as I dawdle behind the milk float while it jangles and rolls along in front of me. I can't help comparing Evelyn's life with my own. She has the classic work-a-day husband. Home at weekends. Both play bridge, golf, and tennis in the summer. They have weekends away, go to the theatre, have spa breaks. Whereas I live a virtually single existence, without the benefit of come and go as I please, but Tom does. When he is at home, he goes to the pub, the gym – plays tennis, goes clay shooting, and lies in bed with the Sunday papers. A life uninterrupted.

When did I last go out without making commando-like plans to browse the shops in town? It's not through lack of money. We're comfortably off, as Tom never stops saying how he keeps me in a way I was *unaccustomed!* His little joke! But it annoys the pants off me. *Stop it, stop it.* I scream silently, enough is enough. Smile Grace, your family need you.

I edge the car into the tightest of spaces, twenty minutes late. Alice, red eyed and teary, glares accusingly. George's eyes are lowered to the pavement with a brotherly arm curled supportively around his little sister. He flashes a weak smile that spells relief. Alice, always the drama-queen, dabs at her eyes, her bottom lip thrust forward as she clambers onto her booster seat.

'Sorry kids, Melissa's teacher held us up.' I say, hopeful that Alice won't launch into one of her vengeful monologues, but I'm out of luck.

'Where were you? You took *forever.* People were looking at us and I got frightened and thought you'd left us and then George said you might have had an accident and I thought you might be dead, and we'd be orphans and sent to the workhouse.' For added impact, she says, 'And a strange man in a blue car tried to get us to go with him.' Each sentence is punctuated with a sniff to stress her point. Thankfully, dear sweet George interjects.

'It wasn't a strange man, it was Josh's dad, and he was only checking if we had a lift. I said the milk float probably held you up and he laughed.'

'Well, we're all safe and sound now. Everyone strapped in?' Two grunts and a sniff reply. I try to be the smiley Mummy, but—

'For goodness' sake Alice, stop sniffing,' I yell. Melissa visibly jumps and I experience a surging guilt.

'OK, George, give her the tissues, they're in the door-well. Alice have a good blow,' I attempt to make up for my outburst. 'I love you kids, but sometimes you drive me nuts.'

In the rear-view mirror, Alice is wearing her hard done by face. I soften; it's not the children's fault that

Tom abandons us so regularly, and Alice being the youngest misses him the most.

Our gruelling routine hinders my enjoyment of our children. When did I last play with Alice or bake cakes with her and George? There's never a moment to sit with Jack and talk about his school day. I've no idea how he's doing as I couldn't get a babysitter for the other three to attend his, or their parent's evenings. That's the trouble with living five miles from any form of human activity. The bus stopped at the crossroads once an hour, but the last one was six o'clock. Then a three mile trek before reaching our *tribal settlement*, as Tom insists on calling it.

I glance at Melissa, she's been teary lately, probably due to start her period and I haven't had the birds and bees conversation yet. I'm on a downward spiral and they don't deserve my grumpiness, they're lovely kids and it's my job to make them happy.

'What did you do at stagecoach?' I offer lightly. George has his headphones on so doesn't reply.

'Rehearsing,' Alice says.

'What for?'

'A musical play.'

She won't let me off lightly for being late.

'What play's that then?' I say, adding '*my sweet,*' to win her round.

'Oliver.'

'Ah, Oliver. I see. Let me guess, you're an orphan in the workhouse?' I glance in the mirror. Its game over, Alice has pushed her sulk as far as she can. I silently cheer a ridiculously insignificant victory.

'Yes, I'm an orphan and abandoned.'

I do my best to suppress my amusement. Alice has a talent for drama, I wonder if she'll follow in her father's footsteps and end up on TV? God. I hope not. Fame isn't all it's cracked up to be for the people left behind.

Three kids fed, and it's almost time to do the return journey to collect Jack. I'm putting rubbish in the dustbin when I notice a large plastic sack leaning against the step. Tentatively, I poke it. Its soft and gives under my touch. I release the elastic band and peer inside at men's tweed jackets, and an assortment of grey blankets. They smell musty. There's a bulky package with my name on it in blue biro. Curious, I drag it inside the hall to get my reading glasses from beside the phone. Bemused, I remove the contents. A single folded sheet of white paper bearing the Stagecoach logo and what looks like brown paper cuttings.

Dear Mrs Lane,

Thank you so much for volunteering to help us with our costumes for the Oliver production. Alice told me how much you enjoy doing this sort of thing. I have cut the patterns out of Brown paper and labelled each one as per outfit.

We would appreciate a fruit cake or Brownies for the refreshment table. It's so kind of you to offer. Alice said you'd also be keen to sell raffle tickets, so I've enclosed three books.

Thank you so much for your kind support. It's unfortunately a rare thing to find a parent as willing as you.

With grateful thanks

Gemma Bradley

The letter slips from my fingers, fluttering to the floor. I slump against the hall table, a pile of freshly ironed clothes topples to the ground. I'm overwhelmed.

Silent tears spring to my eyes flooding my cheeks, I can't stop. I'm trying to get air into my lungs at the same time. I begin thinking about those missing programmes featuring thousands of people who vanish from home each year. Those who walk out of the door and keep going.

Alice comes out of the downstairs loo and without looking at me offers a reprimand.

'Honestly, you're always telling me off for sniffing, but you do it. Use a tissue Alice, don't sniff Alice.'

She wobbles her head from side to side and wanders off to the playroom. The sound of my laughter surprises me, it's not a funny laugh, more a hysterical one as it occurs to me that even if I could run away; ready to abandon the car at the station and catch the first train to its farthest destination; I'd probably miss it because I'd be stuck behind the ruddy milk float.

'What's funny mum?' Melissa calls out.

Hastily, I wipe my cheeks on my sleeves in case she comes to investigate. If only I could answer her question truthfully.

5

I love working the trowel into the warm earth, uprooting weeds who stake their claim like squatters. Leaving each new plant neatly bedded in is a gratifying sensation, like fresh sheets on the bed. But whose law says that every time I plan to do something I enjoy, the damn phone rings. I begrudge the interruption, trying to ignore it. It's a wasted effort, I'm programmed to act on it. Discarding my gardening gloves and wiping sweat from my brow on the hem of my T-shirt I jog the few paces to the house, betting the phone will silence before I get to it. It doesn't.

'Hello.'

'Mrs Lane. Stephen Salt, Jack's head teacher.'

My nerves scream, preparing for bad news. My free hand slaps against my heart.

'What's happened? Is Jack alright?' I say, the rush of adrenaline making me lightheaded.

'No Mrs Lane, he's not alright. In fact, he's as high as a kite.'

'What? Kites, I'm sorry, you've lost me.'

'I'm afraid Jack's in a lot of trouble. He's been smoking cannabis. Caught with two other boys at lunch break in the art room.'

My blood pressure levels. Not injured, safe, but smoking drugs? My Jack? No, surely not. Kick a football through a window, yes, but smoke dope? It must be a mistake.

'Mrs Lane?'

'Yes. Yes, sorry. I was trying to take it all in. Are you sure it was Jack?'

'Positive. We have a strict policy on drugs. We don't accept this sort of behaviour at Bixton High.'

The way he says the word *drugs* takes my breath away. It sounds stronger, more menacing than smoking a joint or a spliff. Drugs sounds addictive. I push the word to the back of my mind concentrating on what he's saying.

'Frankly, I'm surprised at Jack's involvement, he's normally well under my radar, but we do not tolerate drug taking in any shape or form. Can you come to the school? We need to discuss repercussions.'

My head nods in time to every word he says. I need to stop and join the conversation.

'Yes, yes, I understand. Should I come now?'

'I think that would be best.'

My watch said 12.50. 'I'll be with you by 2 o'clock.'

'Thank you, Mrs Lane.'

I replace the receiver with a string of expletives accompanying my exhale. Why do I feel I'm the guilty one being sent for a telling off by the head teacher, not Jack? Tom will go ballistic. I know who he'll blame. There's no time to speculate. A tramp looks back at me from the mirror—dusty shorts above dirt brown knees. Sweat-soaked hair sticks to my neck, and what's that smell? I pluck at the hem of my T-shirt and sniff, realising it's the stench of Fish, Blood, and Bone fertiliser I was spreading on the soil. I run a juddery hand across my forehead and down my cheek, biting back a tear.

'Tom, you're never here when I need you. Why?'

It's a rhetorical question but there's no time to stand about feeling sorry for myself. Upstairs, I dump my soiled clothes in the wash basket and run the shower. The cool water soothes me as I scrub aggressively at my limbs, thinking of Tom, of his absence of responsibility. Living carefree, grinning at the TV cameras for millions of adoring fans, feeding on maize, roasted bat, or monkey. Shampoo gets in my eyes, and I wish it were Tom I'm washing out of my hair. I calculate the dates as fast as the water swirling down the plughole. Another two weeks before he'll be home expecting a champions welcome. That tah-dah moment. I swear he'd be happy if we waited flag-waving at the station with a brass band to acknowledge our hero's return. Yes, I sound resentful because I am.

Okay, Tom works hard in extremely remote places. All for us. He declared he was providing a better life for us. That was true when we only had two children and they were babies, but now, years later with the addition of two more. The only person it's better for is Tom. Right now, I hate him with a vengeance, but I could do with his arms around me and some reassurance.

'When will you stop; you selfish bastard?' I yell at a photograph of him in some tribal dress, all feathers and leaves. 'It's taking its toll on us, you shit-face. Now this. Drugs? Jack needs you and so do I. I need reassurance and the kids need their dad. Not some shit-faced celebrity basking in the public's glory.' SF, my private nickname for Tom when I'm with my best friend Jenny. At least it stops me swearing so much.

Towelling myself dry, I wonder what's suitable attire for being summoned to the head teacher at your druggy son's school. "Suitable" didn't seem the right word, I'm the one on trial here, whose parenting skills are being challenged. I run my eye along the skimpy collection of clothes on the rail. Who cares what I wear, this isn't about me. It's about Jack's drug-taking. Mr Salt said Jack's involvement surprised him, that he was normally under the radar. So, who were the other boys that hadn't surprised him? What are their names? I should know who his friends are? The question of addiction I push away, floundering, in my ignorance on drugs. How do I handle this situation—meekly or with anger?

Tom would have understood better than me. He once lived with a tribe who took a hallucinative brew that made them vomit. Spew out the devil, he'd said. I remember yawning at his elongated narrative. Perhaps I should've taken more notice.

I pull a blue button through dress from its hanger. One of the few I possess. I need little in the way of clothes. I don't go anywhere, and this dress must be at least ten years old, I wore it for the first months when pregnant with George.

'God, Tom, I can't wait until you call tonight. We need some help. I can't do this anymore.'

Out of the corner of my eye, I spot the book Jen gave me as a joke for my birthday. A self-help book entitled "HOW TO PUT UP OR SHUT UP." *A step-by-step guide to a happier you.* Perhaps I should read it, but strangely it scares me.

***

Jack mumbles as he shifts into the passenger seat.

'Stop mumbling Jack, you do that a lot lately,' I snap.

'I didn't hear you.' he says, miserably. 'What about cricket? I've a match later.'

'Cricket!' I screech. 'I get dragged to your school to deal with my pot-smoking son and you think I should let you play cricket? How do you think that works, Jack?'

'Christ's sake mum. It was one joint, a few puffs, that's all.'

'Don't you dare try to justify it? One puff or ten, it's not the amount, it's the act.'

'Yeah, yeah. No need to kick off,' he says dismissively.

'Kick off? You bet. You're grounded till your father gets home.'

'Whatever. I'm sixteen, not ten.'

'Don't you dare take that tone with me! As if being called to school wasn't bad enough, having Mr Salt ask if we were experiencing problems at home with your Dad away so much. That topped the lot.' My shoulders brush my ears. 'And who were the other boys involved? Not a nice sort apparently, bringing drugs into school and even worse knowing where to buy them, is more to the point.'

Jack rears up in his seat to face me.

'You don't know them, and if we didn't live miles from anywhere like natives, I'd have more to do, and I could choose my friends not hang around with the morons from the estate.'

I gulp down the accusation. 'So that's your excuse, is it? It's our fault because we don't live in the right place. God, give me strength.'

Jack's voice does that man-boy thing where it breaks in the middle. He slaps his hand angrily against the dashboard.

'You don't get it, do you? And it's not just me, Lissy hates it too. Our lives are full of boring crap, nowhere to go, nothing to do, stuck at home with my little brother and sisters. Do you know how much stick I get at school?' He makes shapes with his fingers to emphasise. '"Mummy's boy". "Jungle Jim", that's what they call Dad. They ask if we had snake pie for dinner or in a shortage do we eat hedgehog. I told Dad, he thought it was funny.'

I'm hoping the thrum of the engine will calm things. I start the car, but his words strike a chord. Jack is right, Steadcoate offers little for a teenager. In its favour there are clubs and activities but my older two can't attend because I'd have to leave the little ones sleeping and alone to make the twenty-minute journey each way to collect them. Steadcoate isn't a destination of choice. People live in the area because it has a railway station, and bigger houses are reasonably affordable. The area sprawls from Steadcoate Village on the West to Steadcoate Ley, to the east. Both are rural deserts.

Jack pivots his body away from me, his head resting against the window. He looks miserable. I hate rows, but this is an extreme situation. I hadn't realised it wasn't only me who hated our life. Jack is right, grounding him isn't a punishment, he is naturally grounded every day. He spends most of his time in his bedroom anyway. That's wrong and I'm the only one who can change it. He flinches as I touch his knee.

'Look Jack, we won't talk about this anymore today and definitely not in front of the others, okay? But I do have to tell Dad when he rings tonight.'

'You have to, really?'

'Of course, this is serious, and I'm sure half the village knows by now if Evelyn Grainger's got anything to do with it.'

Jack curls his lip. 'And Dad will say, you're going to boarding school, or some stupid boot camp like he always does. 'It will make a man of you,' he says, mimicking Tom's voice. 'Actually, I hope he does. At least I'll be with people my age with things to do.'

I can't refute what he's saying. That will be exactly Tom's reaction, and it appears it wouldn't be a punishment, but a joy. I don't want my boy sent away I want him happy. There's only one way to stop this downhill spiral in Jack's behaviour. He needs a man about the house, and we need to live with within reach of the village. Tom's stealing their childhood and I'm letting him. Well, no more, we owe it to our children to meet friends out-of-school hours, try new experiences. I remember my childhood playing in the street. Roller skating, cycling to friends, swimming club. Simple things like walking to the shops. Jack's right, I'd loved my time at boarding school–well, most of it. Sending him away is not the answer. Our kids are missing out. It's my duty to make it right, grow a pair, stand up to Tom. Tell him his dream isn't ours. We live it and it's horrible. We're damaging our children with this isolated life. We have to move closer to the village before it's too late. But will Tom agree?

6

With one eye on the clock, I'm waiting on Tom's call, debating what to say about Jack's escapade. The situation spins on a roundabout in my head. I suppose I could always opt out and get Jack to speak to him first. Remove myself from the shouting and blaming because there would be plenty. Tom's reaction would be epic. That's a given. But is it fair to dump on him when he's thousands of miles away? In the end, I decide to play it by ear and see what sort of mood he's in.

Jack's behaviour can't go unpunished. He's holed up in his bedroom, only leaving it briefly for meals. The rhythm of his music seeps from under his bedroom door, rising to a crescendo whenever he takes a trip to the bathroom. His isolation worries me – am I losing him, my beautiful boy, my firstborn, tugging off the invisible pull of my apron strings.

At 11. 20pm, I gave up. Tom's failing to call is nothing unusual. Sometimes, because of lack of signal or filming, or travelling from one location to another. In a way I was relieved, the worry weighed me down. Maybe I should see a doctor, get a pick me up. Perhaps that's why Jack smokes dope. He feels the same

—hemmed in. Hypocrisy pushes its way in. Me with my secret stash of cigarettes. Did that make me any better or worse than Jack? Yes, cigarettes were legal, but nicotine is still a drug and something I do on the sly. That can't be right.

Yawning but unable to sleep, my mind wanders. Tom is a man of habit. The man who even in the safety of the English countryside bangs his shoes against the wall before putting them on, in case a scorpion or some other deadly creature crept in while he slept. Ridiculous, but I'm being unfair. Tom wants to be a good father I'm sure. He probably thinks he is one. He didn't exactly have a perfect childhood himself, something we both have in common.

I pummel, fidget, and rearrange my pillows blaming myself for not paying more attention to my children's needs, but it's hard dividing yourself by four. Perhaps I am a useless mother, slash father? Struggling to fill both roles. Failing at both. I try to recall when Jack and Tom last spoke, but I can't remember. Tom's calls when they come are brief, and the little ones grab most of their father's attention. Is that part of the problem – does Jack feel overlooked, minimalised by his siblings? I can't second guess. I'm a woman. Jack needs a man to understand him, a bit of male bonding with some-one who understood about being a boy of sixteen with heaps of testosterone, pushing the boundaries.

The familiar sound of an argument wakes me. It's Melissa and Jack. I absorb one end of the conversation. Melissa's heard on the school grapevine of Jack's brush with trouble. I let them argue it out while I shower in preparation for yet another Groundhog Day.

I'm surprised when Jack takes my hand and leads me away from Alice's nosiness to Tom's study where he hands me a smartly written letter of apology to the headmaster. I hadn't asked him to, and his initiative warms me. But am I being played? Am I doubting Jack, or a doubting-Thomas?

'What do you think?' he asks, as I hand it back to him. I glance at his pale teenage face, bumfluff forming on his upper lip. The skin taught over his cheekbones. He looks as exhausted as I feel.

'It's a good letter but doesn't let you off the hook.' He surprises me by wrapping me in his arms.

'I won't do it again. I promise.' He sounds sincere and I have to – want to, believe him.

Grounding him isn't the solution, he needs to oc-cupy his time positively, and sport is an outlet. I hand him his cricket kitbag as we leave the house and I'm re-warded with another show of affection. I don't know who needs the hugs most between the two of us.

Returning from the school run, my daily routine starts in our bedroom, the room I share with Tom for a third of the year. My foot kicks against something on the floor. I bend to pick it up, realised it was a "how-to" book. It's open at Chapter one.

"Are you ready to change your life?"

Now that's ironic, if only. The shut-up and do some-thing book says make lists. The first is for anxiety. I doubt I have enough paper to write my full list, but it makes me think. If I don't change, nothing will. Baby steps. I decide to make a list of small things that won't disrupt the family and made me less of a shadow. I'll do it tomorrow.

7

Dan Mayne carries the tray of his luxury range cook from chilled produce into the village store. He doesn't normally do deliveries, but his local driver is off sick. The shop is heaving with boys in cricket whites dragging bags of kit on their skirmish for after-match snacks.

'Just my luck. I should've come earlier,' he says looking at the queue.

In front of him three boys jostle with each other. One, is a thin boy with greasy hair and an angry spread of acne pitting his face. Another is on his way to becoming obese, with badly dyed yellowy hair and a torn shirt. Even from where he stands, he can detect an odour of unwashed clothes and stale tobacco. The spotty kid elbows a third boy in the ribs, he collapses, winded, crashing into a display shelf and they laugh at him.

'Dare yer,' the spotty one says to the lad on the floor.

It sounds more like a threat than a dare Dan thinks, watching the other two move in front of the winded one, thereby shielding him from the view of the shopkeeper. The boy shoots a look towards the shopkeeper, to the boys and back again. Furtively he unzips his bag, lifts a bottle of vodka from the shelf and slides it into his holdall. Clambering to his feet, he does a double take at Dan. Dan glimpses a spark of recognition. He's seen this boy before. Was it Grace Lane's lad? His little sister Alice was Leah's friend and always at his house. Now, what was his name? James, no, it was Jack.

The three shuffle together.

'Excuse me, lads, can I get through, this lot's getting heavy.' Dan lifted the tray of goods above their heads pushing his way between them. 'Hello. It's Jack, isn't it? Alice's brother?'

Jack peers at Dan through his fringe and nods. Dan hands over his delivery exchanging a few words with Ivan. A shove from behind made him lurch forward. Jack either fell or was shoved into him. The other lads think it's hilarious.

'Sorry,' Jack says, a flash of colour forming on his cheeks.

Dan makes a split-second decision. 'Boys, stop mucking about. You'll break my bottle of booze. Come on, Jack. I know you've slipped it in your bag. Nice try.'

The spotty lad wearily backs off, colliding with the fair-headed one who turns and makes for the door. Jack stares at the floor.

'Always joking with me, aren't you, Jack?'

Jack unzips his bag, removes the bottle, and puts it on the counter.

Dan opens his wallet hands over a twenty-pound note and takes the bottle.

'Get the change,' he says over his shoulder. Walking to the door he glances at the oval security mirror and sees Jack hold out a shaky hand and accept the change. He's been caught red-handed and has no option other than to face Dan outside.

Outside, Dan looks both ways down the street, the other boys have vanished. Behind him the door pings and Jack appears, looking sheepish.

'Your friends have gone. Legged it. Probably thought the police would turn up. That was a pretty stupid thing to do.'

Jack shuffles his feet, head down, unable to meet Dan's eye, he holds out his palm full of coins. Dan ignores it and grabs Jack by the scruff of his jumper and manoeuvres him away from the shopfront and prying eyes.

'Right, you little tealeaf. What have you got to say for yourself? Did you think it was big, stealing booze? Clever, eh? Going to get smashed with your mates behind the bus shelter, were you? Classy. The big man *or* the idiot who allows himself to be exploited. Where are your mates now? I'll tell you where. Laughing their socks off because you got caught. They bullied you to do it then ran away.'

Jack shrugs, mumbling a barely audible sorry.

Dan considers giving him a ruddy good shake, like his own father would have done. Except his father had been an honourable man. Not a pratt like Tom Lane, detested by the locals who knew him.

'How old are you?'

'Sixteen.'

'Old enough to be prosecuted and get a record as a juvenile, before you've even started your life. Those idiots, they're not friends. And if you shoplift to impress them, you're an even bigger idiot.'

'I don't even like the stuff,' Jack mumbled.

Dan tilts his head. 'What? Speak up.'

'I said, I don't even like the stuff. It's a laugh, that's all. Everybody does it.'

Dan sighs shaking his head.

'No Jack, not everybody does. Some people work hard for a living like Ivan and his wife, and you stealing from them affects their livelihood.' He clicks his tongue. 'Christ's sake, you steal something you don't even like! What sort of muppet are you?' He releases his grip. 'What's next? A car? Quick joyride?'

Jack scuffs his trainer across the pavement. 'No, I wouldn't.'

'You would. That's what these things lead to. What about your Dad? Is he home?'

Jack eyes widen. 'No. Why? You won't tell him, will you?'

Dan assesses the situation. The lad looks scared at the mention of his father. And what about his mum? From what he could see she had enough to put up with – always the lone-parent with the kids in tow, looking stressed and exhausted. A lovely woman, by all accounts, although they'd never spoken properly.

'You don't think he should know that his son is a thief as well as in trouble for smoking wacky baccy? Yes, Jack, nothings secret round here. I think I should tell him. Someone needs to give you a firm hand.'

7

'Honestly it was a one off,' Jack shoots back, a tremor visible to his jaw.

'And was this?'

'Yes. I won't do it again, I promise. Please don't tell my dad, he'll blame Mum and it's not her fault.'

The crack in his voice isn't lost on Dan, he remembers his own man-boy stage. The bit where you think you can conquer the world but still want your mum to tuck you in. I bet he has a strange old time, stuck out in the middle of nowhere. It must be hard to fit in.

'Don't you get pocket money?'

'I wouldn't buy booze. I told you I don't like the stuff. It was a one off.'

'No Jack, it was a one off with consequences. So, what do you do with your pocket money, have you a hobby or something?'

'Some, I'm saving up. Dad goes by the less is more thing.'

I bet he does. With his idealistic views on life, Tom often preached in the pub.

'What are you saving for?'

'A guitar,' he says adjusting his shoulders.

'Like music, do you? Is this all practice then, drink, drugs, and rock-and-roll?'

Jack quirks his lips. 'No, I want to get into the music industry – study properly. Go into recording– something like that – and if I'm good enough, write music for screenplays. There's an academy in Manchester, the BIMM.'

'And that stands for?'

'British and Irish Modern Music.'

Dan dips his head appreciatively.

'So, you *have* got plans for a career then?' Jack looks up. 'Good for you. That's even more reason not to cock it up before it even starts. Now, how are you getting home?'

'Mum's picking me up. You can't tell her – please,' he says, the gravity of what he's done banging home. 'She's already mad because of the spliff. Look, I get bored, there's nothing to do around here. And they're not my mates.'

'No excuse to steal. What about a paper round, or a Saturday job – something to earn some money and get skills for the future, before you get to college?'

'I can't. We live too far out for a paper round and there aren't any Saturday jobs in Steadcoate. Please, Mr Mayne, I won't do it again. It was stupid.'

Dan scratches the side of his nose and looks away. Had he put the fear of God up him? Would this be the end of it? A memory of him pinching an orange from outside the greengrocers caught him unexpectedly.

'I tell you what, Jack. I think you're a likeable lad and I don't think we should worry your mum about your latest brush with crime, but it must stop. Don't let others lead you astray. Your mum relies on you to be the man of the house while your dad's away. She doesn't need this.'

Jack's eyes fill with tears. 'I know. I'm sorry,' he says, rubbing the cuff of his cricket shirt across his eyes.

The lad isn't all bad, anyone deserves a chance- a firm hand and something to occupy him, that's all.

'Okay. I believe you. Here's what I think we should do. How about you come and work for me on a Saturday? Mick passes by your drive about eight. He could pick you up and drop you back to the end of your lane.'

Jack straightens his shoulders; his brows rising in surprise.

'What sort of job? Doing what? Sorry, I didn't mean to sound – you know, rude.'

'You can help in the packing department, feed the cider press, or help with the harvest. There's plenty to do in the summer holidays and if your mum says so, we can teach you how to drive the tractor, perhaps even the forklift. Or work in the bakery. Definitely *not* on cider production, though.' From the corner of his eye, he sees Grace's car approaching. Hastily he hands Jack a business card. 'Talk to your mum, see if she's okay with it and call me. That's if you're interested. Seven pounds an hour.'

A broad grin rides Jack's mouth. 'Great. I'm interested. Thank you. I'll ask Mum. And I am sorry, honestly, I won't let you down.'

Dan climbs into the driver's seat of his car and hears a tap on the window. Dan lowers it.

'Mr Mayne. Your change.'

'Call me Dan and put the change towards saving for that guitar. I'm relying on you to make a clean start.'

Grace pulls into the curb. Dan raises an arm out of the window and waves before pulling away. He's thinking about what just transpired. Tom Lane was an arrogant attention seeker. He wouldn't be too pleased if he knew what his son had been up to. It might affect his bullshit PR. Now there was an idiot, who left a lovely looking woman alone for months on end. God knows what she ever saw in the obnoxious twerp, but if she were my wife. I'd want to be with her.

8

Dan Mayne waves as he pulls away from the curb. On this occasion he's not mouthing "women drivers". I don't know him very well, not at all actually, but on the rare occasion I'm in his orbit he always seems to have a gaggle of women around him. I think about the noun, it's perfect to describe the way women vie for his attention. Fluttering lashes, pushing their bosoms before them. It's pathetic the way they undermine themselves, clamouring for his attention like it's a competition. Dan plays to his audience a complete flirt. I've seen him giving the odd wink here, a lazy smile there. I hate men who think they're God's gift. Tom may be some things, but he's no flirt.

Jack buckles up. He smells of sweat and cut grass. I'm thankful that today it's the right sort of grass. The car is unusually quiet. Alice is falling asleep. I suspect she read long after she should've last night. George has his comic open, for a moment, peace reigns and then Jack swivels to face me, dragging the curtain of fringe away from his eyes.

'You look pleased with yourself, did you win?' I say.

'No, we played abominably,' he says in a way that implies he doesn't care.

'You don't seem too unhappy about it?'

'It was predictable. They've got three fast bowlers compared to our one, and he's pretty rubbish. Anyway, I don't care about the cricket, Mr Maine's offered me a job.'

'My foot hovers over the brake pedal. This is unexpected news, and I wasn't sure how I felt about Jack working for Mr Gigolo.

'What sort of job? He realises you're still at school?'

'Yes, yes, of course he does. It'll be weekends and holidays.'

'Doing what exactly?' I say, attempting to veil my suspicion.

'All sorts, working on his food production line. Packing, that sort of thing. Apple pulping for cider production. All sorts. You will let me, won't you? Mum. I need something to do for a change and earn some money of my own. Even Dad couldn't moan at that.'

He's right, Tom had done the full range of paperboy, shelf stacking, dishwashing, and bar work to make his way through college. He couldn't object, could he? This could be the making of Jack, get him away from bad company, but as fast as my hopes rise, they plummet – shot to smithereens by the thought of another journey to add to my rota.

'I don't know Jack. Being purely selfish, I could do without another regular journey back and forth. Weekends and holidays are the only opportunity to see friends or potter in the garden not haring around the countryside.' I tap his knee. Our eyes met briefly.

I'm aware of youthful excitement bubbling keen to wipe away any barriers I created.

'No, Mum, that's another brilliant thing, one of his workers will pick me up and drop me off. He lives our way. Please say yes, I really want this.'

Melissa had been gazing out of the window with her earbuds in, but she'd obviously been following the conversation.

'You'll have to wear a hairnet. They all do. You'll look a right Wally.'

Jack snaps his head round to face her.

'Not if I'm driving a tractor, I won't.'

My stomach turns. 'Tractor. You didn't mention driving dangerous machinery.' Thoughts of Jack mangled in a field flash before me. He must have registered the look on my face and begins backtracking.

'Not at first but when I'm trained up. You know, all the health and safety stuff. That probably won't be for ages.'

'Jack Lane, I'm not an idiot, so don't treat me like one. You can ring Mr Mayne later but—' My Son's sigh accompanies an eye roll. 'Before you start, I'd like a list of the things you'll be doing. What sort of machinery you'll be using, that sort of thing.'

'He'll probably be sticking labels on boxes for months.' Melissa says, trying to goad him.

Jack leant around the headrest.

'I don't care what I do. Anything to get me away from you will be good. I can't take the boredom of you and Darwin prison any longer.'

'That's enough. No more arguing,' Jack mumbles something and I throw him a death stare. 'Right, when you call him ask what you should wear. Do you need shoes with toe protection, that sort of thing, or does he supply whatever you need?'

'Yes, Mum. I can speak for myself you know. I'm not stupid.'

'Nah, just a junkie,' Melissa says. 'That's pretty stupid.'

Amazingly, Jack doesn't bite back. A minor miracle.

Without realising it, we are home already. I can't even remember the railway crossing. Perhaps the car drives itself nowadays, God knows it knows the way.

Around me doors opened and slam with a rush and bustle towards the front door. George, as usual, is last. Tucking his comic under his elbow, he ambles through the door stepping over the jumble of shoes and sits on the stairs to take off his and places them neatly side-by-side. I often wonder how I'd got a child so different from the others. Jack, Melissa, and Alice feisty and competitive. Not so George, he's shy and takes life at his own pace.

I click the tension from my neck and collect six abandoned shoes from along the hallway and place them in pairs beside George's. While I am unlacing my own, I feel a pulse of agitation. Out of the corner of my eye, the answer machine's light is blinking. It can only mean one thing. Tom's called while we were out, not an error on his part, he knew we'd be out collecting Jack.

'Cowardly bastard,' I say with gritted teeth, wanting to grab the bloody machine and hurl it at the wall. My lungs expand as I stuck in a cool cleansing breath ignoring the red light and walk away, smiling to myself 'Sod you Tom.'

9

Alice appears in front of me, wearing an expectant expression.

'Was that Dad? When's he coming home?'

I'm tempted to say long enough to pick up his clothes after the divorce hearing, but don't. It isn't Alice's fault she has such a conceited, egotistical, self-centred git for a father, who left messages rather than face the music. Well, two could play that game. I'll listen in my time.

'Oh, he'll be home soon enough.' I lie, sifting through the day's post, most of which has found its way under the hall table, shot to its destination no doubt by the pile of ironing bound for a selection of bedrooms.

'Okay.' Alice says, ' I wanted to tell him...'

I'm distracted by an envelope addressed to Grace Denning – my maiden name. I'm poleaxed No one's referred to me as Denning for almost seventeen years. It's been redirected. A rare gesture of kindness from my impossible mother. Biting down a smile I shove the other post under my arm. I'm peeling back the flap —.

Alice rushes from a doorway. 'Mum - Mum, come quick, George has one of his nosebleeds.'

I blow out my cheeks. The letter feels special, but it will have to wait.

'Alright Alice, I'm coming.'

'Well hurry. He might bleed to death. It's so red Mum.'

I sigh. 'Blood usually is.' Reluctantly, I slip the letter into my jeans' pocket. Although I'm still furious with Tom I decide not to tell the children that their father has once again chosen not to speak to them personally even though he could have. Tom always delivers bad news by message. Well, he can wait. Perhaps my letter will be some sort of compensation. The first bit of intrigue in my life for years. But for now, I have to focus on a bloody nose.

George and I are alone in the kitchen. He looks like a Walrus with plugs of tissue rammed up his nostrils.

'It's our homework project,' he says. 'We have to say where we were born and how we got to live in Steadcoate.' He looks at me expectantly.

'Okay, that's easy. Jack and Melissa were both born in Balham. That's in London. It's spelt BAL HAM.'

'You and Alice were born here, in Steadcoate.'

George frowns pushing his glasses further up the bridge of his nose. While he's writing that down I carry on sponging down his school jumper.

'And how we came here – well, because of Daddy's job being on the television. He had what is called an entertainment agent and a specialist solicitor who sorted out his contacts and things. That person was

Auntie Jenny, long before you were born – and then we moved here.'

He rests his hand against the side of his head grim faced.

'To this house?'

'Yes, that's right. Why the grumpy face?'

'Cos, we have to draw a picture of it, and I'm pants at drawing.'

'No, you're not,' I say squeezing his shoulder. 'You did a lovey card on my birthday.' He doesn't look convinced, 'Tell you what, let's go and ask Jack if he'll help.'

Clearing away the last of the tea things I remember a giggling Tom, hiding something behind his back. We moved from the Balham flat to a two up two down when Melissa was born. Tom was away a lot, but we were financially secure. I remember the excited look on his face, how animated he was, flapping a paper in front of my face. I can't help smiling at the memory.

'*Come on, Gracie, guess what it is.*'

'*I can't guess. Stop teasing me.*'

'*Try,*'

'*I can see its paper. A cheque? A contract?*'

'*Duh! Better than that.*' He'd made a tah-dah sound before handing me estate agent's details of this house. The one I'd never seen. '*It's the one I looked at with Robin, I've bought it.*'

'*What! But it's huge. Can I see it first before we commit, and can we afford it?*'

'*Course we can. It's cheaper than London. Imagine the country life for Jack and Lissy. Playing in the fields, climbing trees, a garden for you. In fact, several acres of garden. No traffic pollution. You're going to love it.*' He'd jiggled his feet in a little dance and listed more of Steadcoate's virtues. *Jenny and Robin up the road and Todd and Lily. Lunches at the golf club. Wait till my father sees this.'* He'd reclaimed the paper. *'That'll make him sit up.'*

I doubted anything Tom did would make Roderick Lane sit up. For everything Tom achieved Roderick found a negative to bash him with.

As I recalled that bit of our history – what the *Shut up* book called, "A Pivotal Moment", a marker of my acceptance of his wishes over mine. Tom bought the house for all the right reasons and although it was still Tom's way, he thought he was doing the best he could for his family. In those days he wasn't SF the shitfaced husband. He was dear Tom, or poor Tom, not sod Tom or bugger Tom. How proud he'd been, thinking it was the best surprise ever and how I'd loved him so much that I hadn't say it was a horrid house and that I liked the convenience of Balham. The park nearby, a place to feed the ducks, playschool for Jack. My yoga classes and friends, my NCT baby group but at the time it felt like the right thing to do. To follow Tom's dream.

He never understood my loneliness, or the way I was slowly shrinking. Vanishing from the person I used to be, like Alice In Wonderland—down the rabbit-hole, pulled along by Tom's aspirations, abandoning my own. The shrinking liquid in the bottle marked DRINK ME.

10

The envelope taunts me from the coffee table, waiting. Its pull like radiation to a Geiger counter. Everyone's in bed and with my slippers discarded and a large glass of wine, I settle to read my letter. The one addressed to the person I once was, Grace Denning.

The box of pink netting catches my eye.

'You will not make me feel guilty. I'll do it later, after my letter. The Oliver costumes, they can wait until tomorrow, and I'll clarify with the teachers that it's positively the last time. Evelyn Grainger can do the lot. I've run this sweatshop long enough.' I shut my eyes praying for something magical to be inside the envelope, I thumb my nail under the corner of the envelope. 'Please, please, be something exciting.' Flattening out the enclosed pages my fingertips tingle. 'A reunion! December, how wonderful. I can go, Tom will be home. I'm so excited I want to share my news with Jen but its late so I gabble to the cat whose woken from his nap in the armchair. 'I can go Charlie! How fantastic, something to look forward to. Brilliant, brilliant, brilliant.'

A vision of Maureen flashes before me and what that girl endured. I bite my lip remembering, but I didn't tell. I kept our pact. I push away a vision of her tear-stained face.

'Don't go there.' I tell myself, deliberating on what I should wear and deciding it would be something new. My scalp itches, unused to rare moments of excitement. So much so that I want to rush from the house and go right now. I crushed the letter to me, addressing the cat.

'I wonder who'll be there, Charlie?' Charlie yawns flashing a raspy tongue and sharp white teeth. He arches and stretches out his paws, unimpressed. But if anyone had been here, they would have witnessed my grin grow wider by the second, as memories of my schooldays flood back.

'Something for me. Only me. I so need this. Thanks Dad, thanks Hannah,' I shout skyward. 'You got God to give me a break.'

For the next hour I drink, refilling my glass before it's even empty, thinking about the four of us as girls. Wonderful, warm, caring, but ditsy Cassie. Annoying diminutive Sophie, like a scurrying mouse, and Maureen. Oh God, Maureen – Miss Vinner, and what I'd been party to. My mood plummets.

Miss Vinner always popped into my head whenever there was mention of child abuse or pornography. Was I the instigator of the break in to her flat, or was it Cassie? My recent joy stagnates, I wonder if Maureen felt damaged. Did she carry that invisible sign that said *victim*. Would she want to return to see her old friends or not? I hope so, but I could understand it if she wanted to forget.

'What will they all look like now?' I ask Charlie. 'Oh, God, what about Phillida O'Riley?' My cheeks glow recalling that awkward moment in the boot shed. 'Ugh! God, I hope not.'

Inelegantly, I get up swaying towards the mirror. The sparkle in my eyes fades. I look older than thirty-sex, almost thirty-seven. My browny-grey hair hangs either side of my jowls. I nod my head up and down, side to side, examining my profile, my chin, the frown marks hiding under my fringe. Certainly not pretty. My mood flat lines, so I open another bottle of wine and return to the couch.

'Perhaps I won't go after all. I bet they all have happy lives and have married men with an interesting sur-name that can be double-barrelled with Jones. A man who likes hugs more than sex and has nice shoes and beautiful skin and no tattoos, and a lovely mum and attractive feet. Lane Denning – Denning Lane. Crap. Best I let them remember me as I was not as Grace Lane, mother of four. A nobody. Around here I'm not even that. I'm Tom bloody Lane's Wife. Wife of Jungle Jim.'

I've got hiccups, I hold my breath – no good and I can't scare myself. The TV remote is on the arm of the sofa. I press its buttons. It's on Sky plus showing a repeat of Tom's earlier series, *Wild in Peru*.

'No way am I watching that bastard grin his stupid grin on my TV tonight.' I press random buttons and …Ah, Hyacinth Bucket that's more like it. A re-run of *Keeping up Appearances*. At least she knows how to get what she wants.

I'm sleepy now, I have to keep waking myself up. The second bottle is empty. So is my glass, but it has sediment in the bottom. I study it, turning it this way and that, wondering if I can read it like tea leaves. I can't. Water, I need water.

'Hydrate yourself Grace,' I weave my way to the kitchen seeking more wine. 'Tonight, I will go with the flow. Tom and his messages can get stuffed.'

By the time I've got to the kitchen I can't remember what I came for, so look up at the cupboard that houses empty cake tins and remove my stash of cigarettes and a lighter.

'I'm a good mum. I never smoke in front of my children.' Tom hates smoking. 'Well sod you Tom I'm gonna live a little.'

I'm giggling, with a cigarette dangling from my mouth and a glass of water in my hand. Hyacinth has finished. I fall back onto my seat and pick up the remote - flicking back and forth until I find what I'm looking for. Sated when Tom's face appears on the screen. Ha-ha, so funny. I raise my glass to the screen in a salute. 'Fuck you, Tom. Things are gonna change around here.'

11

The invitation is behind the toaster, along with school timetables, requests for money for school trips and junk mail I've been too lazy to take to the recycling bin. But no matter how hard I try, I can't ignore it as I move about the kitchen clearing breakfast things. Jenny will tell me I should go. I'd become a Jen project; she'd remodel me like on those make over shows but then she has enough confidence for both of us.

I focus on the weather outside. The chalk blue sky promises a clean fresh day. The view from our kitchen is panoramic, reaching to the horizon are acres of unspoiled fields. A jigsaw of greens meets slim Silver Birch trees that line one side of the hill, flanked by tall pines on the other. The only thing on an otherwise perfect landscape is a farm building. The roof is long gone, as has much of one wall. The wooden door gapes and tall grasses grow up against it. I wonder what use it had in earlier days before it was abandoned to the elements.

'Abandoned like me,' I murmur.

'Mum, you're actually talking to yourself?' Melissa tugs at freezer drawers, tutting, poking then slamming them shut.

'Not so rough Lissy, you'll break them. What are you looking for?'

She throws up her hands. 'Chicken pieces. You know, arms and legs of dead birds. God mum, where have you put them?'

Her words boil my anger.

'Don't be so rude, young lady. You wouldn't speak to me like that if your father were here.' She doesn't even look up, dislodging packets of peas and fish fingers.

'Fat chance of that. Becky Greenway's mum says Dad probably has the time of his life away from us, and it's a good job you're so homely.'

HOMELY, the word stings. I'm stupefied with rage.

'Homely. Is that what she said? She's got a nerve. The spiteful busybody. At least I'm not the village gossip.' I reach for the kitchen roll, tear off a piece, wipe away an unexpected tear. Melissa surges forward, almost knocking me off my feet, locking her arms around me.

'I'm sorry. Sometimes I don't think. I shouldn't have said that.'

Her warm breath on my chest is comforting. I kiss the top of her head, taking in the aroma of citrus shampoo. She tilts her head up to look at me.

'Don't be sad Mum, Dad will be home soon, perhaps we can talk him into a holiday.'

'I'm sorry, love. I'm a bit tired, that's all.' I wish I could be honest with her – explain that several bottles of wine are probably more than responsible for my current mood.

'We don't have any chicken, do we?'

Guilt spreads like Marmite, thick and sticky.

'No, we don't. I haven't shopped. I didn't know you needed any.'

She peels herself away, striding to the toaster, pulling out a yellow piece of paper and disturbing the rest of the detritus that slides across the worktop.

'I gave it to you last week. You said you'd have it ready for me, and I need a red and green pepper too.'

Another account of my failings pushes through my ribcage. I quash it, slapping on the mask of a smile.

'No problem. TROOPS.' I bellow and Charlie shoots through the cat flap as if scolded. 'Everyone ready now!'

Remarkably, and in record time, we are in the car and on our way. Approaching the crossroads, I spot the milk float trundling along from my right. It can't get ahead of me. My children are oblivious to me lowering my window and raising my arm, curling all but one of my fingers in the float's direction. One to me, I think.

Driving home I relish the peace and quiet, unable to decide what my priorities are for the day. The weather's warm, the sky a forget-me-not blue. I'd love to feel the sun on my skin and potter in the garden, hopefully, uninterrupted by irate teachers. The flowerbeds need attention and if I don't pick the last of the runner beans they'll go woody, but before I get out there I've got admin to do. George brought home a reminder about payment for his history trip. Then there's stuff I needed to do on Tom's fan club, and then there is the invitation. I won't decide if I'm going until I've caught up with outstanding correspondence.

My keys jangle as I dump them on the console by the phone. The flashing red light is demanding. I may as well get it over with. Tom's voice breaks into the silence of the hall.

Hey. Er, called in for supplies and managed to get a landline. Stroke of luck. Hope you are all okay? Gracie, this has been an amazing trip. The producer's so pleased, we're going to press on and shoot another six for the next series. Brilliant, eh? Anyway, must go, so see you. Ah, now let me see, it won't be the end of August now, probably more like December.'

He cough's and pauses.

'I've got a bit of a dodgy stomach. Must be the stew we had last night; God knows what was in it. Oh, and by the way, can you go to the school fund raiser that awful woman runs. Must keep up the old celebrity status with the natives. Thought I'd be home for it but obviously not. They won't expect a speech from you, but I suppose I could dictate something for you to read out. I think you could manage that.'

I suck my teeth in agitation.

'Condescending bastard, you can't string two words together. I write all your bloody speeches – yes and the jokes.'

I listen to the rest of tape with growing indignity.

'Sort out a couple of my survival books and box set of DVDs for the auction. Only one though, I'm not made of money. And don't bid on anything over fifty quid. Tell Mrs whatsit, I'll do a personal appearance in the new year – they'll love that. Well, must go. Don't miss me too much. Love to my little tribe.'

A rapid sequence of disbelieving blinks blurs my reflection in the hall mirror. I'm waiting for the message to end with a succession of lip-smacking noises, and I want to throw up. Self-promoting orders.

'Shit-face you-you, shit-face. I needed to speak to you, not a bloody machine. Well Fuck you and your self-promoting orders. I'm not gonna wait for the "king of the jungle" to make decisions I'm capable of making for myself and if you want so much done, hire a bloody secretary.'

I spend the next few minutes slamming anything that's it's possible to slam. The calm that falls over the house when the children are at school, I usually find welcoming, but right now it annoys me. Dark oppressive thoughts ambush me. They're not new or unusual, they're squatters sitting somewhere on my sternum, immovable objects, except today they're stronger and may squash me. I sink a glass of water then pile everything that needs doing onto the kitchen table, including the pile from behind the toaster, and settle myself to work with my mug of coffee. Charlie is asleep on the chair next to me.

'Hello old boy.' Old and bad tempered Melissa says, when he won't let her pick him up like she used to when he was little, when he would good-naturedly tolerate her dressing him up. My hand runs along the ridges of his spine. 'Charlie, you need a bit of fattening up. I'll poach you some nice fish later. How about that?'

Robin, my best friend Jenny's husband, is our vet. He recently checked Charlie over and said he was fine but he's just very old.

11

'Well, Charlie, should I do what I should be doing, or what I want to do?' he sleeps on and my mind wanders to the front flowerbeds crying out for pansies to see us through to the autumn and brighten up the bleak exterior of Darwin house. Tom's choice of name of course. I much preferred Chester Farm, its original name. I glance longingly out of the window then back to the table and drag the toaster pile towards me.

'Pizza delivery? I think not.' I toss it into the waste bin strategically placed to my right. 'Pizza to go. Ha-ha Grace, you're bloody hysterical.' Seed catalogues and buy now get two free stickers and a gym membership. 'If only.' Next is a flyer advertising an evening with Rosa Moon Clairvoyant. 'Too late for you now Rosa, I should have met you years ago before I married SF.' I drain my cup of my now cold coffee, rise, and stretch. The sun's still taunting me through the window. If I complete what needs doing, there may still be time for a bit of gardening. Tom has a stand-alone computer in his study that I often use when he's away. His space gives me the creeps with its carved tribal masks and graphic photos. My eye catches a cobweb stretching from its frame to the curtain rail I only dusted yesterday.

'Well, you can bloody-well wait cobweb, grow as long as you like. See if I care.' I press my lips together thinking how much I've taken to talking to myself. It's quite comforting to speak the words out, as opposed to them floating around my head. First sign of madness apparently.

The reunion invitation remains in its envelope awaiting its fate. Next is Tom's RSVP to Evelyn Grainger's annual fund raiser. Apparently, it's a good do. Tom goes every year. I've never been. I doubt I'd be welcomed with four kids in tow. The preamble to the event always made me mildly embarrassed. The way Tom swanked about at these functions.

"The blue shirt, I think Grace. I must look my best. My fans expect it. Did I tell you how many people wanted to speak to me last year? Taking selfies, I swear my face ached from grinning. It must be nice for them having a celebrity who so obliging."

My head shakes unasked, he acts more Tom Cruise than Tom Lane. Well Evelyn you're gonna be disappointed, you'll have to find another C-list celebrity.

The remnants of my coffee are stone cold. I slide out the reunion invitation from its envelope as if it were some ancient, delicate, document; avoiding Tom's fan club and accounts stuff that needs preparing for the accountant.

'Chartley. Memories good and bad. Friends I should have kept in touch with but didn't. It would be so nice to go. Something pre-Tom. Dare I?'

My phone vibrates and shifts around the table like a demented insect. It's Jenny and before I can greet her, she's already talking.

'Morning, my lovely. How's life?'

'Better than last week but do you know that cow Evelyn Greenway told her daughter I was homely? Homely, for God's sake. That's worse than being dead, and to prove how flunking right she is, I'm spending my day tackling a backlog of paperwork, like a dutiful wife.' I make a Grr, sound. 'But I may just throw it all in the bin. Anyway, how are you?'

'You do make me laugh with your flunking's and flucks.'

'I know, but it's the only way I can stop myself from saying the alternative.'

'Anyway, lunch today. Golf club. I'm in need a bit of a chat.'

'Why. What's up?

'Tell you when I see you.'

'Sounds ominous.'

'Mm don't get your imagination flowing. I take it SF isn't around to police you, he's not back till July, August, isn't he? The paperwork will still be there when you get back, but you'll be in a brighter mood to deal it. You can do your circuit for the kids on the way back.'

'Its December now. He left a message.'

'All the more reason to make the most of it. Come on, let's lunch. Don't procrastinate, do it. You're growing old and musty and before you know it, or perhaps Evelyn's right.'

'Oh, nice. Thanks a bunch.'

Jenny let out her spiky laugh. 'C'mon girl, you know it makes sense – see you at twelve.'

'One,' I protest. 'I have to wash my hair.'

'Stick it in a scrunchie. Twelve-thirty.'

'No arguing with you, is there?'

'Nope. See you later.'

Bugger, she's right. 'I grab the family laptop and switch it on. I do need to get a life. In haste I pay for George's field trip. Happy that I've achieved at least one of my tasks. Everything else can wait. I'm going out. Time off for good behaviour. Tom's taking the rise, I wonder where he is today. Probably in some mud hut eating snake or bats. Rats would be more appropriate. Wait till you get home at Christmas, matey. Things are going to change. And flunking Evelyn Grainger, I'll show you who's homely. SF is in for a shock. He has disappointed us for the last time. Your time's up Tom, and mines just starting.'

12

Jenny climbs from her black Audi Coupe looking stunning in skinny jeans, a yellow cropped denim jacket and navy top sat higher on her neckline than usual.

'Well done for escaping Colditz,' she laughs, dragging me in for a hug. Her oversized silver disc of modern jewellery is cold against my chest. Arm in arm, we stroll towards the entrance to Green Lawns, Hotel Golf and Spa resort, parting inside the entrance as three cups of coffee send me off to the ladies while Jenny goes to claim our table in the restaurant.

I love Jenny. If I didn't have her in my life well … Jenny's vibrant. Her chestnut hair swings across her perfect shoulders and her smoky-grey eyes sparkle above the smattering of light freckles dotting her nose, but it isn't only her looks. It's how nothing ever bothers her and even if it does, she'll poke fun at it. That is Jenny.

Although I did ponder about what she wants to talk about. I know she'll eventually get around to it. If it's something serious, she's hiding it well. Always does, so annoyingly self-sufficient. Perhaps she wants a moan about Robin, he's a constant worrier, but Jenny does enjoy the control, she wouldn't have it any other way.

She's mock fanning herself as I approach.

'Phwoar, good job I'm happily married. I bumped into Mr sex-on-legs Dan Mayne. He certainly is easy on the eye.'

Sitting opposite Jen, I think I must look drab by comparison.

'He's offered Jack a job actually,' I say, bending to put my handbag on the floor. 'After-school, weekends, that sort of thing.'

'Lucky you. I doubt Todd would consider doing anything so grown up.'

'At least it will keep him away from the cannabis crew,' I say hopefully.

'Seriously though, I wonder what his secret is?' she says dreamily.

'I presume we're still on Dan Mayne, not Jack? Must he have one?' I say, pouring iced water into our glasses.

'Yes, of course. I love a man of mystery.'

'I don't know him very well. Actually, I don't think we've ever spoken. He's always surrounded by swooning women, looking pleased with himself. Lord of the Manor, country gigolo.'

Jen doesn't comment but rouses herself enough to pluck the menu from the middle of the table giving it the shortest amount of attention. As she lunches here several times a week, she doesn't need to.

'I think I'll have the asparagus and hollandaise. Salmon for you? Or are you going to be daring and go for a Caesar salad?'

'Am I that predictable?' I say, shaking my head. She doesn't reply and checks her phone. We order our food and a delicious bottle of crisp white wine and chatter and laugh mainly at Robin's expense with his endless list of things to worry about. Jenny's anecdotes on life as a vet's wife are priceless.

There is something different about Jenny, I can't put my finger on what but examining her closely, I notice dark semi-circles she's attempted to conceal under her eyes and her laugh is forced, causing tension lines on her forehead. Before I can ask what, she wanted to talk about, she's ambushed the conversation and is talking about Lily wanting to change her options at school.

It's good to be out and being me. Jenny's right, I need to do more of this, relaxing and enjoying myself. Life is short, as well I know. God, Hannah, I miss you so much. All my life I wanted to be like you, my lovely big sister, make you proud. I didn't care that you were Mum's favourite. Then suddenly you're gone and Dad too. I never had the chance to say goodbye. But I'm getting maudlin. I can't change the past, but I can have a damn good stab at the future.

'So, what's new in your world, my precious. When's SF coming home, December did you say?'

I'm horrified that I instantly well up.

Jenny leans across the table placing her hand over mine.

'Hey what's this. I didn't mean to upset you. I'm sorry hon. I won't call him SF again I promise,' she signs an imaginary cross over the silver disc dangling above her dinner plate, while I sniff into my napkin.

'How embarrassing,' I say looking to see if anybody's noticed. You're right my life is shit. I've been so down lately Jen. I can't lift above it, perhaps it's an early menopause. That would about sum up my luck.'

She lifts the wine bottle from its icy case emptying the last of the Chablis into our glasses and eyeing me with a tilt of the head.

'Come on, spill, this has been brewing for ages. What's going on?'

My thoughts and self-pity pour forth until I run out of steam, relieved to air my feelings from their stagnant casement.

'I'm not going to slag him off, that won't solve anything. Even though he is an arrogant, selfish, self-centred git. Sorry, I know he's yours and you love him but life can't be all about Tom. There are six of you.' I nod agreement, through sniffs of woe. 'I'm sorry to be tough on you but it's true. You've got to learn to live your life, not his, and as big as a shit as he is, you've let him get away with it.' Her fingers comb the air as she searches for words. 'Your destiny is in your own hands. Perhaps that's harsh.' she says, softening. 'You know what I mean. Tom will never change unless you make him. Come on perk up. You're an escaped maiden an urban warrior. Well, for now at least.'

'Well, I've made a start. I've been reading that "Put up or Shut up" book. I know you bought it as a joke but some of it is quite inspiring.'

'Then use it as your Bible.'

'I'm trying,' I say meekly. 'Anyway, let's not spoil a lovely lunch. What did you want to chat about?'

Jenny's expression changes in an instant, she breaks eye contact her brows bunching together and reaches for her phone, checks the screen and sighs, laying it face down on the table.

'Jenny?'

Her lashes flicker. 'Stop looking at me like that.'

I cross my arms above my chest, and I throw her a schoolmarm's glare.

'So, it's right for me to unburden but not you?'

'There's nothing wrong. Drama Queen,' her eyes flit anywhere but on mine.

'Would you tell me if there was? Only you must've checked your phone at least fifteen times since we've arrived. What are you waiting for that's so important?'

'What's this, the third degree? Everything is fine. By the way, did you get that leaflet for the clairvoyant?'

'Don't change the subject.'

'I'm not. That's what I wanted to talk about. I've got us tickets. Rosa Moon – look into my eyes, deep into my eyes.'

I shake my head as she curls her hands into the air.

'That's a hypnotist nutter. Not a clairvoyant.'

'Whatever. It'll be a laugh. It's all organised. Lucy will sit your kids.'

I fix her with a suspicious eye. 'You're hiding something. I know you, Jennifer Maxwell.'

She leans forward propping her elbow on the table and resting her hand on a curled fist if I am, Rosina whatshername will out me.'

We both laugh and I look out across the manicured greens where two men are putting on the 18th with others watching. There's a ripple of applause followed by some back slapping. I sigh turning back to Jenny decisively.

'You're right, I should get out more but there's always something that needs cleaning, ironing, making, and mending.'

'Then get someone in for a couple of days a week. Old SF will eventually get used to the idea.'

My wine glass is empty, I fancy another but I'm driving so I sip my water instead.

'Not a tribal thing, apparently.'

'Rubbish, in a tribe they all muck in. I've watched his series. It's about the division of labour. The men dance about and hunt. The women cook, wash in a muddy river, and have babies. I think he likes the fact that you can't get out much. It keeps you out of the way of lurking Romeos like Dan Mayne.'

Tutting, I shake my head in disagreement.

'No, that's not his reason—it's the risk. He thinks they will leak stories of our life. Kiss and tell, what the housekeeper saw. He wants to keep us private. I can't blame him for that, he lives in a fishbowl most of the time.'

Jenny barely stifles a wince.

'I remember the days working with entertainers was a challenging job. Tom was a nice bloke on the way up and you can't knock his achievements, he's elbowed that Bruce Parry, Bear Grylls and that oh, you know Steve someone – all into touch. I don't know how he does it, but he takes the prize for a being top a class presenter. I often check on his ratings, old habits die hard. He pushes the limits.'

'Yes, mine.' I say bitterly.

'Grace, you are an absolute Saint, old SF doesn't know how lucky he is.' Jenny swipes at her phone screen and I hear a message ping to my phone. 'Right. I've sent you the number of my ironing lady. You drop it off and pick it up when it's ready. Use her when he's away, you can save hours and he'll never know, it will only be yours and the kids' stuff. Without his boxers, it's of no interest to the front page of any tabloid.'

'If, like you, I only had my two eldest to deal with life would be a doddle, don't you think I'd love to be a lady who lunches. You always had Lucy, first as a nanny when yours were small and then you turned her into a housekeeper, clever move that was.'

'You make me sound a right lazy bitch. She only works at home part-time; she mainly works for Robin doing all the admin and accounts for the veterinary surgery.'

'Only after she's ferried your kids to school and done the all the mundane stuff, leaving you to turn up at the more interesting events looking stunning.'

'I'm not gonna win this argument, am I? Jenny says tipping water from her glass into the lone Gerba that's bowing over the condiments.

'No, but when I grow up, I want your life,' I say smiling.

'Be careful what you wish for. You could change your life, Grace. Destiny is in your own hands,' she said, in a mock Mystic Meg voice.

We ask for the bill and while we wait, I open my mouth to ask again what she really wanted to discuss. It's rare to see her in such a ponderous mood but she beats me to it.

'So, if SF isn't back until December, he can't be guest of honour at the fundraiser.'

'Nope, that's right. Evelyn will be livid,' I say with a conspiratorial wink.

'Great, then no argument.' She grabs the bill before I can. 'You're going.'

'I'm not and it's my turn to pay.'

'Shut up. Who's counting. Right, bring Alice and George to ours for the night. I'm sure Jack and Lissy can get a sleepover somewhere. That's final, you're coming with Robin and me.' I give up as my excitement settles at gas mark two. I'm tempted but my confidence wains. Can I actually go? My social skills are rusty, perhaps I should polish them up a bit before the reunion at Chartley.

13

Jenny's words resonate as I return home after the school run. The slamming of three doors jolts me back to reality. Melissa beats me to the kitchen, grabbing the laptop before Jack can claim it. They could do with one each, but Tom won't hear of it. Part of saving the planet. Funny how he has every new gadget going.

'Hey! I'm using that,' I say.

Melissa pastes on a winning smile.

'Homework comes first mum. Anyway, you can use Dad's computer. We're not allowed.'

What can I say, there's no arguing with that.

The Shepherd's pie has defrosted so I pop it in the oven gathering up my to-do pile from the table and go to Tom's study. While the computer loads, I flip through what's left of the pile of papers. Despite the heat outside it's chilly in here. I rarely come here unless it's to flick a duster and vacuum. My bottom settles into the soft leather swivel chair. It makes a sound like a sigh as I shuffle back. The home screen populates, and I notice a shortcut folder marked Photos and click through pictures of a younger us, in happier times. Long before Tom became famous, when he worked at York Uni as a guest lecturer. Bluffing mostly, he'd said laughing, holding a finger to his lips "but don't tell anyone". The next is Tom looking handsome in his dinner jacket. His hair was thick then. Jenny at his side, she's hardly changed at all. It had been some red-carpet bash she'd taken him to. Dear Jen, my lifesaver, and if Tom hadn't been in entertainment I'd never have met my almost sister.

'Ah, my beautiful babies, look at you.' I settle on an image of Jack in my arms, newborn, Tom proud as punch leaning over the bed. Lissy, adorable at two, or was it three? Dressed as a fairy, holding Charlie under his front paws, his body dangling the length of hers – the reluctant cat wearing a tiara. Another, of Tom holding Lissy up to blow out birthday candles and George on his first bike, a plaster over one lens of his glasses, to correct his squint. Happy times. The next makes my smile widen – a rare occasion Tom and I on a date at a cheap Italian – was it an anniversary? The waiter had taken the picture.

'We were happy then, weren't we? I even looked worn out back then. Flunking-hell, I still have that blouse.'

I can't remember what we'd eaten. Or if the food was good or not? Did we care? Air whistles through my teeth. Those were the days when lovemaking wasn't confined to the bedroom. Where we bathed together washing each other's backs. The days when no one knew who Tom Lane was – before he learnt to complain loudly at shoddy service or expect a buckshee bottle of wine and embarrass me in a restaurant. Neither of us feature as a couple in any of the later albums.

Was that the point where it all went wrong? When did we last say "I love you" and mean it? My hand hovers between the gym membership flyer and the Chartley invitation.

'Sod it. I'm going.' Before I can change my mind, I type out my acceptance including my updated details and click send. My hand hovers over the gym membership. It's an excellent offer but Tom will balk at the price. All the more reason, I think defiantly. Tom already has a membership package that covers the gym, spa, golf, and a discount for rooms in the hotel complex. I've only ever lunched there with Jen. Raised voices float down from upstairs, Jack and Melissa are rowing. I swivel to face the open doorway.

'For Christ's sake, shut up you two. Good job we don't have neighbours, noise you make. Can you please stop arguing?'

'He's got the laptop charger Mum. I need it.'

'I haven't got it dimwit, its downstairs. You had it this morning. Der!' Jack shouts.

'He's right. It's in the kitchen. You put it there. Now shut up both of you,' I say.

'Dimwit,' Jack jeers.

'Don't call me a dimwit. Moron.'

'Melissa enough!' I bellow before clicking open another folder marked Photos, there are few marking our wedding day. A sad grainy image taken on a throwaway camera, scanned into the computer years later. Tom's parents: his mother in a borrowed suit one size too big and his father Roderick, with his jaw set in a hard-line and his expression chequered with disapproval. Thankfully, my mother didn't come.

She couldn't bear the shame of people knowing her brazen daughter had sex out of wedlock. Shotgun wedding. Only it wasn't, we loved each other and if Tom had wanted a chance to escape from me, that was his chance. I'd offered a way out as soon as I knew I was pregnant.

My forehead ridges beneath my fingertips as I concentrate on another file I've opened that's marked Family, only it's not our family. It's of babies held by bare-breasted tribeswomen. Outstretched hands clutching grinning coffee-coloured toddlers. Dozens of them. I presume they are mementos of his job. Closing the file, I set about replying to his emails and paying bills. I log out, tired and stiff and thinking about an evening with Rosa Moon, where Hannah and Dad both send messages. 'In my dreams,' I say stretching my arms above me. I'll tease myself with the idea of going with Jenny and Robin to the fundraiser for another day.

The shepherd's pie has browned nicely.

'Kids, supper's ready.'

Four bottoms fill the seats at the table. Melissa picks out the meat.

'I'm thinking about going vegetarian,' she says.

I zone out of the conversation on global warming that ensues. Even George has an opinion on it. Jenny's words hover in my mind. What was it? Something about overseeing my destiny. Put up or shut up. She's right, I must get a grip, take my life by the throat, and give it a damn good shaking. Friendly advice, but is Jenny's life all tickety-boo? I suspect not. Something is going on behind those big grey eyes that's worrying her.

'Mum what's a Clavi...oi... ant?'

'A what, love?'

Alice waves the flyer she'd been copying advertising Rosina Moon mystic services.

'A Cl... Clario voi ant.'

'Oh, that's a Clairvoyant... a person who tells fortunes.'

'Fortunes? Like magic and seeing into the future, a Psychic?'

'Yes, that's it.' I'm about to add talking to the dead, but decided against it, Alice has an overactive imagination.

'Mrs Berry talks to the ceiling peoples.'

My lips press together suppressing a giggle. Alice hasn't noticed she's busy chasing peas around her plate.

'The ceiling peoples? What do you mean Alice?'

'Well, when Mrs Green comes into our classroom and asks Mrs Berry, "why haven't you done this? Or why haven't you done that?" And Mrs Berry says no one told her, and after Mrs Green goes she talks to the ceiling peoples and says, 'does she think I'm psychic?'

'Ah yes, the ceiling people, now I know who you mean.' Course I do. I've been speaking to them a lot recently. Bless Alice's take on the world it gives me a surge of love.

'Perhaps we could ring Rosa Moon and ask her when Dad's coming home?' Alice says innocently. That jolts me into realising that he still hasn't phoned. I hold back on replying that if I had my way it would be soon, and long enough to tell him his fortune.

Dinner over I decide to call Jenny. Robin answers, inwardly I groan knowing he will insist on telling me his worry of the week and a two-minute call will end up being twenty and I must finish the costumes tonight.

'Robin, it's Grace. How are you?'

'Ah the lovely Gracie. I'm fine, worried about these gypsies who've parked near the common.' My eyes roll, 'Could ruin our house prices and they leave rubbish everywhere.'

'Yes, well, I expect the police will move them on. Er, can I speak to Jen please?'

'Hang on a minute.' The background noise of a TV drops as if a door closed.

Come on Robin, it doesn't take that long to find her. Or have you discovered a burst pipe or gas leak on the way to worry about?

'You still there?' He says eventually.

'Yup.'

I can hardly hear him. 'Robin, speak up I can't hear you.'

'I can't it's about her birthday, I want to plan a surprise.'

'Okay, what did you have in mind?'

'I thought London—a show, dinner, that sort of thing. I had thought of a cottage in Cornwall, but it might rain and then there's all that driving and always accidents–'

'Go with the show idea, she hasn't seen Le Misérables and wants to.'

'Oh? I was thinking of Cats.'

Course, he was, he's a vet, bless him.

'I'd go with Les Miz. Er anyway if I could speak to her.'

I listen as Robin carries the phone, progressing through the house. I visualise each room as he passes through it.

'Ah there you are, enjoying the garden.' I hear him say.

'Hardly it's more of a backyard.' Jenny complains. 'Even the lawn looks bored.' She's right. Their garden is a square patch of grass, a privet hedge one side and a bleached wooden fence marking the other two boundaries, easily livened up with a few planters. That gives me an idea. 'Who is it?'

'It's Grace. I was telling her about…'

She cut's him off mid-sentence. Perhaps I hadn't chosen the best time, Jenny sounds in a grim mood.

'Then stop waffling and give it here.' There's a muffled sound as he hands over the phone.

'Missing me already?' Jenny says brightly.

'Yep, and keen to report that since I left you at lunchtime, I've phoned the ironing lady, joined a gym and accepted an invitation to my old school reunion.'

'Blimey, no stopping you once you get going.'

'I know I'm late for new year resolutions but in future I'm going to be more less doormat, more matador.'

'Bravo,' Jenny cheers 'about time.'

'Anyway, baby steps.'

'Old SF won't know what's hit him.' Jenny snorts.

'Indeed. Anyway, I forgot to say, about Evil Evelyn's fund raiser, swimming pool, roof, or something. I will come.'

'Thank God for that I thought we'd have to kidnap you to get you there. You'll love it. Everyone goes, I mean the whole bloody village. Our kids don't even attend that school but we wouldn't miss it. I can't believe you've never been.'

'Thanks for reminding me, how I'm always Cinderella.'

'Ha-ha. Perhaps this time you'll meet your Prince Charming.'

'One man's enough for me thanks. So, tell me more, I should go?'

'Yes, it's a must. Evil pulls out all the stops. It's the show off night of the year in Steadcoate. No one wants to be labelled stingy, they virtually vie for an opportunity to look generous. It's an absolute scream. It's worth it alone to see what creation Evelyn's squashed herself into. Thinks she's Dolly Parton. So, what you are worrying about?'

'Well, I wasn't sure I was looking forward to it until now, but it sounds like I'd be an idiot to miss it.'

'Sorted. Let the kids have a sleepover, there's no school the next day anyway. Lucy can put up tents and they can camp out. We'll be back by about ten thirty. It's never a late one.'

'I might just treat myself to a new outfit.'

She makes a whistling noise. 'Dare-devil.'

***

Could it be pre-children since I last browsed the shops unbridled? I don't feel an ounce of guilt and I don't care that SF hasn't rung for almost a week. It's empowering.

The stylist holds up a mirror to show me the back of my head. I can't resist smiling, I hardly recognise myself, my new colour is called Conker Sheen, there's not a grey hair in sight. I touch my cheek, the way it's cut frames my face and even with my outdated lipstick my skin looks warmer, fresher. I keep looking at myself in the mirrors on my way towards the payment desk. The price is exorbitant, or am I'm out of touch?

My next stop is a department store, where a young girl with the most perfect eyebrows gives me a makeover. I'm a mug and purchase a full bag of products. I've spent a lot, so much I must be eating into this month's housekeeping allowance, but quash the guilt until after I've got something new to wear. Inspired by my sassy unfamiliar look I enter a pricy boutique and leave half an hour later clutching a shiny black bag, containing a deliciously bold red dress. The top is a little lower than I normally wear but I don't have anyone to criticise me buying it, so what the hell. I have some sparkly jewellery somewhere that will complement it. The Chartley reunion springs to mind. Tom can't complain if I wear the red dress to both events, "Cost per wear" is what Jenny tells Robin. I wonder if that would work on Tom.

***

Head held high I pretend I'm off to one of Tom's red carpet events in my new red dress and matching shoes.

'Mummy, you look like a princess,' Alice says with a toothy grin,' you can borrow my red hair band, if you like.'

God, I love that child.

'Thank you, Alice, but I think I'll pass. Now, will you be a good girl for Lucy?'

'Yes. And will you bring me something home from the party?'

'It's not that sort of party honey.' I kiss her soft skin, then pop my head around the lounge door.

'Ready everyone?' George picks up his Buzz Lightyear and a book. The look on Jack's face tells me he'd rather stay at home, but they all rally into their various seats and buckle up.

I know I've got it wrong the moment I see Jenny in white slacks and a slash-shoulder pink top. She looks gorgeous. The pink weirdly toning in with her Chestnut hair.

'Oh, Christ, I'm over-dressed, aren't I?'

Jenny purses her lips appraising. 'Not wrong, you look fab, colour's great on you and the hair gorgeous, and you've really toned up.'

'Hardly, I've only been to the gym twice.'

She nods. 'The killer heels have to go, we're in a marquee on wobbly ground and –'
'And?'

Jenny fingers my sparkly necklace. 'Get this lot off. Hang on a sec,' she says nipping upstairs and returning with a pair of beaded cork Mules in one hand, and a chunky multicoloured necklace and bangles in the other. 'Here, swapsies.'

Restyled, I smile into the mirror at the transformation.

'Okay, Gok Wan. You win. Good job. I feel much more like myself now, thanks.'

'Relax, just be yourself. Robin is driving so let's party,' she says doing a shimmy.

'Hang on a sec,' I say, nipping around the side of the house to see Lucy. The four older kids are checking out each other's phones, the little ones are helping Lucy with the tent.

'Lucy thank you so much. You have the Grainger's telephone number, don't you?'

Lucy gives me a confident grin. 'Go and enjoy yourself and yes, I have the number; but I won't need it. Now go and have a good time.'

'I will,' I say, my eye scouring the south facing plot. It would be easy to give the garden a makeover for Jenny as a birthday present. With the help of the children, we could do it the weekend Robin takes her to London. Simple to plant shrubs with all year colours. Put up a trellis for climbers, perhaps an arch. Do something with the patio. Rope in Todd and Lily for ideas. The idea of making something for Jenny gives me a warm feeling as I join her at the car ready for Robin to drive us to the fundraiser.

14

Robin leads the way from the field earmarked for parking, towards the marquee enveloping the Grainger's garden. I'd been there many times before with Melissa but never actually got out of the car. I hadn't realised the grounds were so show-off grand.

'Goodness, the entire village is here and you two seem to know everyone,' I say to Jenny.

'You know some of them.'

'A few mums from the school gate, that's all.'

Her brows scrunch mockingly. 'That's because you're a hermit,' she says.

'I won't be. I'm feeling brave.' It's a lie. Inside, a battle rages between my fresh look of confidence and ugly self-doubt. The one who shouts loudest, saying this isn't for me. You're homely. You shouldn't be here.

Jenny lifts two glasses of wine from a tray and hands me one. I gulp it down.

'Brave, are you? In that case I dare you to go up to at least two men and make conversation.'

'What about?' I grin. 'Only joking. No problem at all.'

'Go on then,' she demands.

'When I've finished this glass. Is that beef bourguignon I can smell?'

Jenny makes a clucking noise in my ear.

'No, you'll make it last all night. This is for your own good.'

'You can be a bitch sometimes.'

'So, sue me - off you go.'

My glass is already empty. I grab two more from a passing server. The palms of my hands are damp with stress. I make my way across the marquee. The hum of conversation over the music from the band is deafening. Across the sea of heads I spot the infamous Dan Mayne sink my wine and head his way. He'll do, I can thank him for giving Jack a job. As I get closer, I notice he has one hand resting on an upright above the head of Juliet, a teacher from Alice's school. She's laughing and from the way she's looking at him I bet his words are flirtatious. Hm, perhaps I won't choose him as my first challenge. Ah there's Matt Barton.

Dan gets a last once over from me as I pick my way towards Matt. Okay, Dan is easy on the eyes and yes, he's nice and tall – muscular, broad shouldered. Problem is he knows it and is such a flirt. I wonder which of the unknown women is his long-suffering wife; I presume he has one. Look at him giving that woman with the stylish highlights a wink over Juliet's shoulder. Perhaps that's the wife, and he's winking to keep her happy. Tom has faults, but thankfully flirting isn't one of them.

Damn. Where the hell's Matt gone? Feeling like Billy-no-mates I join a group of mums I recognise and join the conversation on the proposed tourist caravan park. Wilma; a loud, flashy American sets me in her sights.

'Tom not with you?' she says scanning the room.

I wave at a server and exchange my empty glass for a full one.

'No.' I say without explanation.

'It must be so exciting being married to such a famous man.'

I hate her accent. 'Probably.' I say, realising that's not the correct reply. I don't want to talk about Tom. I'm a person in my own right and this is my night. A pause in the communal conversation allows me to break free. I've run out of platitudes and the heat from so many bodies is overbearing. I need air and weave my way towards the opening, passing Dan en route. His hand is on the arm of a petite lady in a halter-neck dress. Silly bitch is gazing up at him, hanging on his every word. 'Yep, a real player. A man-tart.'

Outside, my head lolls back. Sucking in a breath of cool air I gaze up at the reddening sky. Red sky at night. Will it bring us the much needed rain tomorrow I wonder? Then remember my bet with Jen.

'Right, get back in there or she'll think I've chickened out,' I say. 'I will find two men to approach, if it kills me.' Something shifts in the shadows. 'What the hell?' I freeze. I shouldn't be out here on my own. A dark silhouette moves towards me. I gulp.

'Sorry Grace, didn't mean to startle you.'

'Oh, Matt it's you,' I say shakily. 'Why are you skulking about in the dark?'

'I could ask you the same,' he says raising a querulous brow. 'Who are you hiding from?'

'Hiding? I'm not hiding, I came for a cool off.'

'Whatever floats your boat,' he says drinking beer from a can.

'Anyway, delighted you joined me.'

'Quite a do, though, isn't it?' I say relaxing.

'I should think so, the price of the tickets. I'm not one for this sort of thing but it pays to attend, for the farm shop expansion.'

'So, its PR incognito?' We share a snap of laughter.

'Yes, I suppose it is. I haven't seen Tom. Where's the great explorer? Holding court as our famous Celeb of Celebs?' Matt rocks on his feet, 'I'm sorry, that was rude.'

'No apology needed. If he were here, that's exactly what he'd be doing, playing to his adoring public, and I'd be home with the children.' The wine's making me bolder. 'You don't like him very much, do you?' A flash of red appears on his neck. Or perhaps it's a reflection from the sky, I'm unsure.

'I don't know him, so it would be rude to pass comment. All I know is you're on your own a lot with the children,' he smiles. 'Oh, what the heck, just because I find him egotistical on a personal level, doesn't make him all bad. I'm a huge fan of his programmes. He puts the others to shame. It's so interesting, the people. Lost civilisations, weird insects. And it's on before bedtime.' He cocks his head. I notice the weathered lines ingrained around his eyes, are they weathered or laughter lines? Am I flirting? I've never been this close to him before. He's nice looking but you're homely a voice says in my head.

'So where is he?'

My facial muscles contort to sneer.

'Oh Borneo, or rainforests, living with Pygmies, swimming with tigers, who knows? I watch the telly with the kids when he's on. Reminds us of what he looks like. Sorry, I didn't mean it to come out like that. I'm a bit fed-up of late. This is the first time I've been out on my own in years, it feels very odd and I'm devoid of social skills.'

'Nonsense, you're very amusing.' We mirror a look. Matt clears his throat, squints, and checks his watch. 'That's it for me, I'm rubbish at late nights and if I don't go now, Elsa will give me hell.'

'Elsa? I didn't know you had a lady friend. You kept that quiet.'

Matt's jaw cracks and he roars with laughter. He has nice white teeth. We are back at the entrance to the marquee. The noise and heat hit us. He's still chuckling.

'What's so funny? I'd love to meet Elsa.' I say.

He wipes a laughter tear from his eye.

'You probably already have. Elsa has four legs, is black and white, and is my best milker.' He gives an apologetic smile. 'If I'm not at that gate at 4am she sulks, and as she's the only female in my life, I can't afford to upset her. Sorry Grace it was funny. Anyway, I'm not stopping for the sit down I'm ready for my bed.'

We re-enter the marquee. The heat hits us like a slap to our faces. Matt is blotting his forehead with a napkin. Inwardly I groan. The dreaded Evelyn is in our path and she's with dastardly Dan.

'Oh, here they are - naughty people. I thought you'd found us boring and sneaked off. Or were you having a naughty five minutes outside in private?' Evelyn coos.

She gives a coy but knowing look and I want to punch her.

'No, afraid not,' I say, 'we're having a great time, it's a shame that with so much put into the evening you didn't think of fans. It's baking in here.'

A tight-lipped smile appears on Evelyn's face accompanied by a flush of annoyance. Somewhere in my head I think I hear a cheer. My confidence is soaring even if it is wine fuelled.

'I was telling Grace the only woman in my life is a heifer called Elsa.'

'You need to get out more.' Dan says, sliding in closer.

'If I had your life Dan, I would. Some of us have to work for a living, we're not all cooks and gentlemen farmers,' he says, laughing. 'How's Kate doing by the way? I haven't seen her in ages.'

Dan's smile melts away. I see something in his eyes that's unreadable. He coughs a recovery.

'Oh, you know Kate, probably having a ball in America while I take on the perils of the school run.'

That explains his behaviour. No wife to give him that "you've overstepped the mark" look.

'Well, send her my best when you speak next. Right, I'm off. Hope you raise lots of money.' Matt doffs an imaginary cap and moves away. I wish he hadn't as the dynamic shifts. Frantically I try to think of something witty to say, but inspiration has buggered off.

'I don't think we've been introduced,' Dan says. 'Unless I count you trying to run me over?' He holds out his hand. It's cool. I meet his gaze agreeing that yes, he has nice floppy hair and a sort of lopsided smile, and his build is very commanding.

Evelyn gives a polite cough.

'Sorry, how rude of me, this is Dan Mayne. Dan, Grace Lane and, should I add, wife of the famous TV explorer, Tom Lane.'

'I'd rather you didn't,' I bristle. 'I am a person in my own right and find it extremely condescending being referred to as Mrs Tom Lane.' Is that three nil or four, I'd lost count? Dan grins. Is he mocking or cheering?

'Delighted to meet you Grace and are you as infamous as your husband?'

A familiar flush of annoyance prickles my collar-bone, along with the desire to volley back an insult. I don't because this is the man who'd given Jack a step away from trouble. I move closer, fixing my smile. He is at least a foot taller.

'No Dan, I'm not. But how about you? Are you married, single, attached to a celebrity? It's annoy-ing being perceived as insignificant and someone else's shadow.'

'Well, actually he is quite famous.' Evelyn twitters. I blank her. It feels empowering.

'I mean, do you have a wife, a significant other? A famous father or mother, perhaps? Or maybe a per-sonality in your own right?'

'Ouch, I think I may have touched a nerve,' he says. 'Now let me see,' he strokes his chin in a comedic man-ner. I'm determined he won't charm me. 'I once had a girlfriend who was on Blue Peter, does that count?'

It's hard to contain my twitch of amusement.

'Touché, very droll and on that note, you must excuse me. I need to find my table.' I go to walk away, Evelyn blocks me. Her sickly condescending smile reminds me of a picture in the Red Riding Hood book I used to read my children. A wolf in Grandma's clothing.

'Such a shame Tom's not here, he normally does the welcome speech – always so charismatic. So good at getting people to part with their money,' she says, resting her hand above her amble breasts tortured into the tight-fitting bodice.

'Does he indeed?' I prepare for her next cutting remark.

'Mm, sorry he can't be here. How long has he left you for this time?'

My lungs fill as far as they can. My out-breath ready to explode in her face.

'It must be difficult what with so many children.'

'Good God,' I say. Her face slackens. 'How funny Evelyn. We're wearing the same dress.' Her eyes goggle as a glance confirms it. 'The blue didn't suit me. A bit too pedestrian for my taste much better on a more mature woman.' There's definitely cheering inside me now. Yeah, take that you gossiping old bat. Do I add I didn't realise they did it in larger sizes? 'We must confer in the future, can't turn up in the same outfit too many times, you know how people gossip.'

Dan angles his body away, but I can see his shoulders quaking.

'Indeed.' Evelyn says, a sour expression darkening her eyes. She raises a regal tilt of the head, taking Dan's arm.

'So, Daniel, will you do the honours in Tom's absence?'

I notice how subtly he disengages her grip. Bit too old for you Dan?

'Er, um not my bag Evelyn, nice of you to think of me but there're others better placed at public speaking.'

'If you'll excuse me,' I say. Am I imagining it or is Evelyn, all five-foot-four-inches fluttering her eyelashes at him? This is too funny for words.

The music has stopped. Jenny is waving but my route is gridlocked. A hand touches my shoulder. Dan.

'Well, you're a surprise. I can't believe you put Evelyn in her place. I wish I'd been the one to point out the dress thing. Priceless.'

He smells of lemony cologne . I decide that's probably the most agreeable thing about him.

'I would have thought with your experience of women, words never fail you. Or is it only chat-up lines you're good at?'

His eyes drill into me.

'Hey, unfair. I think you've got the wrong impression of me.'

'Oh no. I've definitely got the right one.' I say schooling a smile. 'But I'm sorry. I haven't thanked you for giving Jack a job. It was kind of you. He's loving it.'

'He's a likeable lad and a good worker. But Grace, you've got me–'

With my pathway clear I re-join Jenny at our table and raise a salute.

'Mission accomplished. Two men detained. One escaped, the other I've released back to his hareem.'

'Bravo,' Jenny says pointing to the stage. 'Looks like Evelyn's been hunting too.'

Robin is red faced and looking uncomfortably out of place as Evelyn drags him onto the stage.

'Oh No,' I say.

'Yup. Now he really has something to worry about,' she says recharging our glasses.

Next is the auction where testosterone fuelled men bid against each other. My cheeks burn when Tom's lot only gets one bidder offering a tenner, until Dan's now familiar voice doubles it and cajoles the other to stop being so tight. The bidding rises to forty pounds, Dan crests at eighty. It's all about being impressive. Or worse, does he feel sorry for me? Well, I don't need his pity or condescending actions. I may be drunk but he's an obnoxious pig.

When I next spot him, he's engaged in conversation with a petite blonde in an intimate huddle. Dan's arms around the back of her chair, and I can only imagine the tinkle of laughter as the woman puts a hand to her mouth.

'Dan's wife's away, apparently. What a flirt. Look at that silly woman. He pays her a bit of attention and she's putty. How does Kate put up with it? I'll make sure I give him a wide berth in the future. Thinks he's God's gift.'

'What are you mumbling about,' Jenny says, thrusting a book of raffle tickets at me as Craig Grainger waits patiently. Jenny scribbles my name on the back of several strips of tickets and I hand Craig a twenty-pound note.

'Can we go soon please,' I hiss. 'This social lark's not all it's cracked up to be. Tom's welcome to it.' Actually, I'm quite lucky when I think about it smugly. There's my husband tucked away in a village somewhere far from civilisation. Not flirting outrageously behind my back. One thing in Tom's favour- he's a one-woman man. Some women are so gullible.

15

PART 3

The After

It's hard to take in what's going on around me. I'm aware of the constant ringing of the phone, the change in tones of voices as the answer machine clicks in. I can't answer it, the stone that was once my heart spreads its icy fingers through my veins. Voices float on air. I wave them away clutching my stomach, rocking like someone demented. I am that someone.

Jenny's face appears in front of mine, with out-stretched arms that I can't let encircle me for fear my pain will puncture into the air and poison everything in its path. My hands raise to fend her off, she backs around the table and sits. Lucy comes into view, fussing with kettles, filling the dishwasher. Practical, like when someone dies.

'Grace, talk to me, love. I'm so, so sorry.'

Numbly, I raise my head. Jenny has tears in her eyes. I feel an urge to comfort her, but I can't move. I'm both dust and stone. I blink.

'I'm okay,' a voice I don't recognise says.

'This is dreadful,' she says as we breathe in the silence of unsuitable words while Lucy tidies my kitchen and Jenny places her hands over mine. It seems an age before Jenny clears her throat, rousing my senses.

'I don't know what to do Jen. How could he do that to us?'

She shakes her head, exchanging something telepathic with Lucy, who turns away. I free my hands from under hers and pull up my legs, resting my chin on my knees and hug into myself. A chair scrapes the floor and Jenny's arms encircle me. I sob quietly until I remember my kids and wail.

'Oh God, the kids. I must go to them.' I make to stand but my legs refuse me and I fall back onto the chair.

Jenny talks softly. 'Here's what we're going to do. Lucy's going to pack some things for everyone. You're coming to us until this blow over. We've plenty of room and new surroundings will be a distraction for the kids. You're too isolated here.'

My life is being organised around me, and with relief, I let it. My shoulders drop and curl as she unwraps herself. Strands of wet salty hair stick to my cheeks. I run my palms over them, tucking them behind my ear.

'I don't know Jen. I can't think straight. Everything's such a... a blur.' I say wiping salt and snot from my face onto my sleeve.

'Exactly, and that's why you need to get away from here. You need time to get over the shock.'

'But will I? How long will that take? All those children. He's ruined our lives!'

Jenny rubs the top of my arms. 'Come on love, you can't deal with this on your own.'

'I don't want to uproot the kids,' I say, 'It's going to be bad enough for them. Oh God, what must be going on at school, my poor babies.' A raft of tears ride my cheeks as Jenny folds me into her arms and I cling to her. 'Jen, what shall I do?'

'I know darling it's awful. Try not to think too much, there's nothing we can do right now apart from keeping you and the kids safe and making the best of a horrid situation. You're in shock. We're going to get you out of here before the media circus begins. There's a TV crew setting up at the end of the drive.'

'Dear God, I can't take much more. My poor kids and, oh my God. Charlie.'

Jen looks at Matt who I hadn't noticed is still here. Of course, it was him who let Jenny in.

'I've buried the cat near the old orchard.' I nod a thanks. 'I've left you my numbers on your pad. Call me if there's anything I can do. Perhaps your two eldest might like to spend some time on the farm helping with the stock. It'll be hardest on them and it would be a distraction.'

With Jen's help I get up and step towards him, taking his hand in mine. He mistakes the gesture, thinking I wanted to shake it. We fumble awkwardly and I pull him closer and kiss his cheek.

'Thank you, Matt, that's kind of you, and thank you for your help. I don't know what I would have done if you hadn't been here.'

He smiles, raises a palm, and backs away. Lucy slips out behind him. The stairs creak as she climbs them.

'I must help her,' I blurt out, feeling I should do something.

'She's fine. How about washing that face. You'll feel better for it.'

'Okay, but then there's something I have to do.'

'I can do whatever it is. You rest.'

'No Jen. Thanks, I have to do this on my own.'

The kitchen door swings shut behind me and I'm alone with the blinking red light of the answering machine. I glance up the stairs and shudder. Jen's right. I can't sleep in that bed – the one we shared and can't bear to see his clothes in the wardrobe. The ones I want to stamp on, tear to shreds, burn.

On jellied legs I go to the cloakroom and splash water on my face, refusing to look in the mirror. My hands fumble with the pink and blue towel. Is it today I normally replace it with a clean one? What a stupid thing to worry about at a time like this.

A flash of lightning illuminates the hall, swiftly followed by a clap of thunder and the sound of rain pelting against the windows washing away the cloying air. The letterbox never shuts and lets in the rain. I visualise it running down the dark wood onto the door mat, but don't move to do anything about it. Instead, in the hallway I lower myself to the second rung of the staircase, raise my knees and cover my face with my hands, clearing my thoughts and breathing deeply. When I'm ready, I open my eyes and fix them on the ancient answering machine. The one that's followed us from house to house ever since before we married. In those days my tummy flipped with love at the little red light, because it held loving messages. Snatched calls to hear each other's voices. Ten minutes between lectures where Tom sang "I just called to say I love you" by Stevie Wonder, an oldie, but a goodie. Or Phil Collins, Two Hearts. When Tom worked away, whenever there was a moment, he'd call, telling baby Jack to look after his precious Mummy for him. Then later came Melissa. Was that where it ended? Seventeen more babies.

Anger gives me strength. There are dozens of messages, one will be one from Tom. In slow motion I press the play button, shrinking at the harsh tones of my mother. There are no niceties. No support. That would be too much to expect.

'You should have listened to me. What a disgrace he's made of you. I warned you, but you knew best. Like you always do. I told you he was no good and you let him have his way with you. Couldn't be decent like your sister, could you? As for him, a wicked sinner like your father and that woman. Men like them can't keep it in their trousers. Don't think you can come here to hide. You've brought enough trouble to my door. I won't have reporters hanging around my house. Hannah would never have brought shame on the family. You made your bed—'

Delete.

I don't need to listen to the rest. My mother has aired her views and disappointment of me a hundred times over the years. I don't need more of the same.

The next calls offer some respite, offers of help, sleepovers for my children – they talk of safe havens. Dan Mayne saying he was sorry, and could he help?

Delete.

The next voice raises bile in my throat. He's engaged in a conversation with someone in the background before he speaks his message. *Roderick Lane,* my father-in-law. Bossy, demanding, and a cruel bully. The only person who could bring Tom to tears and thrive at the pleasure of his humiliation. It said a lot.

'*Grace, what the devil is going on? All this nonsense and lies about our boy. Call me back immediately. Immediately do you hear?*'

'His boy?' His lying, cheating bastard of a son.'

Delete.

My breathing is erratic as I listen and delete half a dozen messages from the press, offering vast amounts of money for my story.

'This is unbelievable, it's like a terrible dream or a sick joke.'

Mr Salt, Jack's head teacher is next, suggesting it would be better for Jack, Melissa, and the school, if they stayed away. He stutters that it's almost summer break and they've finished exams. "It would best suit everyone." There's a similar message from the junior school.

At the sound of Tom's voice, my stomach clenches tightly and slides painfully up under my ribs. I don't want to listen to him, but I must.

'*Gracie, it's me. I can't seem to get hold of you. I must talk to you. In the meantime, if anyone tries to tell you lies about me, don't listen. I'll call later. Er, love to you and the kids.*'

A bubble of bile and snot bursts from me at the smacking sound of his kisses. I rest my head against the newel post balancing the tape machine on my knees, waiting.

'*Grace, I've got to talk to you. It's important. I'll call again at eight o'clock your time. Make sure you're in.*'

'Still calling the shots, "make sure you're in", aren't I always? Looking after our children, funny how you can suddenly find time to call now you bastard.'

'Grace, stop playing around. Where are you? Pick up the phone. We must talk.'

'Oh, no we don't, sonny boy.' The cesspit of anger swells, I'm sure I'll explode at its power.

Delete.

'Grace, listen, please. I know it's upsetting, but it's not true, the babies aren't mine. Believe me? Ring me back on this number. I don't care what time it is. I need to hear your voice… please Grace I'm begging you.'

Pressing the delete button means nothing now, I'm numb. Then I remember the pictures on Tom's computer. All those tribal women, some pregnant or holding up half naked babies. It made sense now. His family album. His babies. The twisted knife of betrayal pierces my soul. Did he ever truly love us?

'Grace, it's me. I'm coming home. Don't meet me at the airport; there'll be too much press. If the tabloids turn up, don't give an interview. We'll pack a few things; drop the kids at Mum and Dad's and go somewhere nice together, till this thing settles down.' He pauses, my hand hovers to delete. *'I love you, my Gracie. We can get through this and be stronger. I must go now. I'll ring you from arrivals. Please remember, it's you I love.'*

I don't want to hear anymore. I erase the last message and unplug the machine. For a while immobilised, drained. My head swims and every ounce of energy seeps away.

A floorboard creaks at Lucy's footsteps above me. Alice's room. I listen to drawers and cupboards opening and closing. I should help, but I can't. I'm too damaged.

I will go with Jenny and take solace for now at least. Make decisions tomorrow. See Tom when he gets here, of course, but only when I'm ready to talk about the end of our marriage. Ready to pick it over like a crusty scab until it can heal. Till then, well, Jenny wasn't Hannah, but she's the next best thing. I don't know if I can ever recover from so much heartache, but I'll try for my kids they're my priority. What will the future hold for any of us now?

16

It seems a lifetime ago that the joys of life were small, anticipa
longed for, hard earned and inconsequential. But that
was then, now daylight forces dawns glow through the
window, chasing away darkness. Birdsong chatters
through the open window. Yesterday's storm was the
climax. The end of my marriage. The night out, the
new dress, now irrelevant.

Melissa mumbles in her sleep. Alice is spread-ea-
gled, claiming most of the double bed. The single
that's mine has only a small dent in the duvet where I
sat. There's no imprint on the pillow. The creaks and
groans of Jenny's house have kept me company while I
watched over my sleeping daughters. The events of the
previous day flash through my consciousness. They no
longer have that gut-scaring effect, they've eroded to
numbness.

Jenny had forced copious amounts of alcohol down
my throat last night and my mouth is dry and sour.
Careful not to wake the girls, I close the bedroom door
behind me. The familiarity of Jenny's vast kitchen is
comforting. The solid wooden table could give up so
many secrets. Endless cups of coffee and glasses of

wine, celebrations, and commiseration's. The latest, devastation sinking through the soul of its surface.

Jenny doesn't have a jug of water chilling in the fridge, she has a watercooler that glugs and gurgles when I refill my glass. The water quenches cold down my windpipe.

'I thought you'd be up. Did you sleep at all?'
I clasp my chest. 'Jen, you scared the life out of me.'

'Why, who else were you expecting?'

'No one I suppose,' I say, feeling silly. 'Did I wake you?'

She strokes a soft palm across my shoulders as she passes to fill the kettle.

'No, you didn't wake me. I'm a bit of a light sleeper lately and I drank far too much wine last night. I came for water but now I'm up I fancy a cup of tea.'

'Me too.'

'Who can blame you. How did it go with the kids, was it awful?'

I wrap my arms around my body hugging myself as she pours hot water onto teabags and slips into the seat across from me.
'Pretty much as you'd expect,' I say, drawing my hair off my face then letting it fall. 'I don't know if what I said helped or made it worse. They all had their own potted versions, care of the village gossips who'd done their worst long before I got to them.' I grip my mug to warm away the chill in my spine. 'How do you explain that their dad has been busy siring seventeen half siblings across half of South America?' Jen nods and smiles, probably at my unexpected humour. 'Melissa

took the worst. Bitchy comments from mothers re-layed by twelve year olds.' I stretch my arms above my head and yawn. 'Alice on the other hand thinks it's marvellous. Can you believe she's excited at the prospect of so many brothers or sisters? She actually asked if they'd be visiting. I almost laughed.' I roll my eyes, 'and George, well George is refusing to accept anything he doesn't understand. He carried on as if nothing has happened, that's quite a worry. Jack, well he boiled in white knuckled silence. He didn't wait for the full story, whatever that is and stormed off. He came back an hour later. I think he'd been crying but would never admit to it. He needs to express anger somehow. Perhaps he'll talk to you or Robin.' My stomach rumbles loudly.

'You didn't eat anything last night.' Jenny says, pushing herself up from her chair.

'Please, no Jen. I'll be sick again. I can't keep anything down.'

'That was yesterday. Today's a new day. Boiled egg and soldiers will do the trick.'

I'm too fatigued to argue.

Jen stands over me as I eat my egg. The act itself is comforting. Pushing my plate away, I'm tempted to turn the empty shell upside down and smash it like my children do.

'Where did it all go so wrong Jen? You knew him when he was starting out. You're his solicitor for God's sake – you knew all his secrets.'

Jenny purses her lips studying a space above the door.

'In those days Tom's secrets were confined to not telling you when a cheque was delayed. Or filming date put back. Nothing like this, but being under a camera lens changes you. It happens. That's entertainment,' she shrugs. 'No matter how hard you work to carve a career – and we can't take that away from him. He put in the hours, did the weird jobs to pay the rent. Did his homework, researched his next job. That's why he's so good at it but fame chips away at you. It's hard enough in a day job to come home to the wife and kids and play Dad. The one who puts the bins out, unblocks the sink, but to be away for months at a time absorbed in discovery while you are safely out of sight. He's the star who signs autographs in a taxi. Features in magazines, gets on talk shows. Opens supermarkets. His head swells. You believe the hype; the PR. God, remember the bare all calendar for prostate cancer. What did he do? Got a wax and a fake tan? That was the last we saw of the old Tom. He believes in his own importance; his own PR. Flattery got him lost in the make-believe. The real Tom, he got lost in the process.'

My palms prickle with indignation.

'So that makes it okay does it, to shag women in every tribe you happen to pass through? To break your marriage vows, ruin your kid's lives. The destruction of our family? Poor hard done by Tom struggling to cope with fame.'

'Sheesh, keep your voice down. It's not an excuse Grace but you asked the question. I know what it cost for you to give up your dream career to support his. You're his backbone, his steady rudder.'

'Oh, please, spare me the analogies. You'll have me sobbing in my tea for him next.'
Jenny's chair squeaks as she leans forward.

'Look, you're angry and this seems like the worst thing in the world right now, but you're stronger than you think. Remember the fundraiser, you saw off Evelyn because she called you homely. Christ, think what you could do with all this anger – use it. You said you were going to change. Do it. Don't be the victim Grace, be the victor.'

My chin hits my chest. 'I can't do it, I'm not strong enough.'

Jenny slams a hand on the table.

'Crap. You can and you will. If not for yourself then for those four sleeping through there. People are facing bigger problems in the world you know.'

'Yeah, yeah. Next, you'll be saying nobody died.' Jenny flinches looking like I've just struck her. She stands and gathers up the crockery.
'And hopefully nobody will. Anyway, I'm going back to bed. Can I trust you?'

'What do you mean?' Her expression is guarded, then it's gone. 'Trust me with what?' I say as she tugs the lapels of her silk dressing gown tighter across her chest.

'I meant can you be trusted to be alone in a kitchen full of sharp knives?' She mimes a slashing motion across her wrists.

'Angry, I am – suicidal, I'm not.'

'Great fighting talk. That'll get you through. Now I'm off to my bed, hopefully without waking Robin or he'll think his luck's in. Help yourself to anything you want, what's mine is yours.'

She blows me a kiss and vanishes and I'm wondering what she's keeping from me, because there's definitely something.

***

The house fills with the sounds of a new day, of bodies moving overhead and voices. I feel better for a shower and pull on fresh jeans and a pink striped shirt. Melissa pads into the bedroom barefoot, her dainty toes painted a coral pink I don't remember being there yesterday. Perhaps Lily did them for her last night.

'You okay, Mum?'

I open my arms; she falls into them and we sway together.

'I'm fine, don't worry about me. It's going to be okay.'

'Is it? Promise?' she says leaning backward, eyes searching mine, her bottom lip wobbly.

'Promise?' I say, knowing it's something I can't guarantee. 'What are you doing today?'

'Lucy's here, she says she'll take us swimming, but I don't want to leave you on your own.'

'Lovely idea, and I won't be on my own, Aunty Jenny's here. I might even go for a run.' *Another lie, I've no intention of leaving the house.* Melissa seems satisfied and wanders off. Music filters from along the hall. A door slams to shouts of goodbye. Lily and Todd leaving for school. The sound of Robin's car backing out of the driveway. I can't hide in here all day.

The letterbox rattles and I head towards it, picking up the Times. I'd rather it the Daily Mail, but this will have to suffice, anything to distract me even if it's to fill my head with politics. As I'm straightening there is a gentle tapping on the front door. I'm apprehensive. Have the paparazzi found me? I look through the spy hole, it's Matt. I let him in. He's silent as he steps past me and heads to the kitchen. I follow. He stops and looks around like he's confused as to how he got here. His face buckles and for a moment, I think he might cry.

'I'm sorry, Grace,' he says, thrusting a tabloid newspaper into my hand. I gawp at it in disbelief. 'Filthy trashy bastards,' he says, rubbing his temples. 'They turn an innocent act of comfort into something sordid.'

My eyes swing from Matt back to the front page. The photograph is unmistakably us, below it the headline.

JUNGLE FATHER OF 17's WIFE SEEKS COMFORT WITH GENTLEMAN FARMER.

17

I follow Matt to his car mumbling apologies even though none of this is either of our faults. He drives off. I need a moment before I go indoors and wander around the bland space that pretends to be a garden. I'm muttering to myself when Jenny comes up behind me.

'What on earth are you doing out here? God, you look awful, worse than yesterday. Come inside.'

She manhandles me indoors, each step a marathon, and presses me into a chair. Her wet hair brushing my cheek. She must have been in the bathroom and didn't hear our voices of anger and despair.

The newspaper's still on the table, face down. I reach across and turn it over. Jenny's pupils widen, she looks from me to the paper and back again.

'Oh, shit.'

'How could they, Jen?' I say, shaking with anger.

'Fuck.' Jenny says with a shrug. 'You couldn't make this up.'

'Poor Matt scandalised for what, helping me? Fodder for the gossips the likes of bloody evil Evelyn, she saw Matt and I outside at the fundraiser and implied we'd been up to something. No doubt she'll say she already knew – that we'd been at it for years. Tom's scandal will be yesterday's chip paper. Isn't that what they say? Forgotten. Like my image of being homely. Lock up your husbands, Grace Lane is on the prowl. God, it makes me sick to the stomach.'

Jenny wriggles her closed lips. 'I'm glad to see you've got your sense of humour back.'

'I don't know how. Matt's devastated. Poor guy only came to help, ended up burying a cat and becoming front-page news.'

'He'll survive and he won't blame you.'

My fingernails dig into my palms. 'Fuck you Tom, you bastard.' Tears gloss my eyes. 'He did love me once, didn't he? When we first met. We were both so young. Full of dreams and plans for our lives ahead. I knew he was going on to better things. His dream was to be an anthropologist, and I was going to be a travel journalist, exploring the world together. But along came Jack, and give him his due, he didn't back off. He was the one that insisted we marry.'

'Hey, stop this, he's not worth your tears. Of course, he loved you. Probably still does. He let his ego get in the way. It happens.'

'Do you think so?'

'Look. I don't know what happened, what went wrong, or if it's a thing taken for granted amongst the show biz worlds. Infidelity I mean, but don't under-sell yourself. You were part of his success. You supported him through the roughs in his early career. I remember you told me you glued toy guns together as a homeworker, bringing in extra money to support you both.'

'I did,' I say rubbing my forearms. 'Fancy you remembering that. Piecework, it paid a pittance, but it helped. A baby in a bedsit. Not the best way to start married life.'

Jenny moves to the counter pressing the plunger on the cafetière. 'Talking of glue,' Jenny said, 'you were the glue that held it all together.'

I nod. My headspace filled with a time when Tom and I were a couple who fought the world together. Neither his father, nor my mother approved of the marriage. Roderick hadn't lowered his voice when he told Tom I would hold him back, stifle his career. But my mother was right about one thing; Tom is a womaniser, but not in the traditional sense.

'Penny for them.'

'When the children came along, Tom was the best Dad ever. Jen, he was like a child himself. Once when Jack and Lissy were quite small he came home from a trip. He was working as a travel journalist then. The job I'd always dreamed of. He built a huge wigwam in the garden out of bean poles, covered it with a bedsheet and the three of them slept huddled up on the lawn the size of a postage stamp in our two-up two-down in Balham. The kids idolised him.'

'Is that why you stayed with him?'

The question smarted.

'What?'

Jenny ran a hand across her chest.

'We both know dozens of people divorced for far less trouble in their marriage than yours. You always took second place, everyone saw that. Sorry, that's harsh.'

I put my coffee mug on the table. 'No, go on.'

'Tom grew that monstrous ego, treated you like a skivvy, a second class person to run his glossy magazine home life. And you let him – when anyone could see he was nothing without you. He gave you so much to do so you didn't have chance to think about leaving him. He even bought a house in the middle of nowhere. I remember Robin saying at the time he wondered why Tom wanted to keep you so isolated.'

I narrow my eyes, taking in what she's saying. The summing up of my marriage hurts.

'You're saying this is my fault, that I let him use me?'

'No, of course not. I'm saying he was jealous of you. God, look at his column. You write it, he takes the credit. Who endured his rules, instructions, orders, his way, or no way? He pushes you, all the time testing your love.'

A burst of amusement has me throwing my head back and laughing.

'Well, he's certainly done that, with knobs on. Testing my love, where did that come from.'

'I don't know,' Jenny says, vigorously scratching her nails through still damp hair. 'Fifth grade psychology classes. But —'

'But what?'

'What I can't understand is why you didn't leave him?'

Cornered, I examine my fingernails. 'Perhaps I was happy with things that way.'

'Bullshit.'

'Okay then. Perhaps, I had nowhere to go. Perhaps, I didn't have the money. Perhaps I didn't want to break my children's hearts.'

Jenny lets out a deep sigh. 'Well, perhaps, it may have been kinder than what they're going through now. And you could have found the money somewhere Tom would have had to give it to you.'

You will not cry Grace Lane, I repeat the mantra in my head, biting my lip.

'Sorry I'll take that back. That's harsh. But don't you see. He didn't want you to grow. He wanted to keep you away from the world, under his control. Away from anyone who might steal you, entice you to be yourself, to become… oh, I don't know… the first space woman… anything. God, I know you're going through hell, but perhaps now's the time to tell you what everyone else sees. And as your best friend, I'm the only one who dares. There I've said it. Now you can hate me as well as Tom.' She walks around my chair her nimble fingers work their magic on my neck and shoulders. 'Look, all that's in the past. It's what you're going to do in future that counts.'

'I'm still in shock, I haven't had chance to take it all in, let alone plan what's next.' Her fingers work my shoulders. 'Right after breakfast, we'll make a list.'

'Like a plan of attack?'

'No, a plan for the future. I'm going to show you that inside of that beautiful, loving, supportive wife and mother, is a woman who can grow a pair and kick arse.'

***

Lucy interrupts our rhetoric; she has her arm around George's shoulders. His dressing gown wrapped tightly around his bent frame. His face is wet with tears.

'Grace, I found George in the playroom, he's a bit upset.'

'George darling, what's the matter?' He falls into my arms sobbing. Jenny and Lucy leave the room, giving us privacy. 'Darling, what's wrong, you can tell me?' George can't speak because he's crying so hard. He's a big boy but still, I drag him onto my lap. 'Is it Dad?' He shakes his head. I force him to look at me, cupping his chin in my hand. 'How about you whisper it?' He nods and I offer my ear, feeling his ribcage heave and quake against my own.

'I. I. wet the bed.'

I feel his shame for not wanting to tell Lucy and sigh out the breath I'm holding.

'Oh sweetie, is that all. It's alright. It doesn't matter. It's a strange house, not what we're used to. Anyone could have done the same.' It's rare I see him up close up without his glasses and my heart stretches out to him. He looks at me, his little face blotchy, his breaths hitching.

'But Alice will t-t- tell everyone. Call me a b-b-baby.'

'Alice won't know, it's our little secret. Where are your pyjamas?'

'Under the b-b-bed.'

Poor little bugger, he hasn't wet the bed for years. There had to be some sort of reaction. Poor George, poor all of us.

'This is what we're going to do. You have a shower and I'll see to the sheets and your pyjamas. I'll remake the bed, and no one will know. Okay?' He nods, his hair tickling my chin as he threads his arms around my neck. My sweet boy. 'And don't worry about Alice, we'll make sure she doesn't find out. Come on, let's do it now.' He slides from my lap and looks up at me.

'Love you Mummy.'

If I weren't already heartbroken, I would be now. I swallow back the lump his words trap in my throat.

'I love you too,' I say, truthfully. 'Very much.'

He cranes his neck to look. 'To the end of the counting?'

'Oh, much more than that,' I say pulling free, so he can't read the emotion on my face. 'How about after you shower, I make pancakes for breakfast?'

'Yes, please.' His face lights up and he scurries out of the kitchen.

Now where is Alice? I need to be sure little miss nosy is out of the way.

Jack and Melissa are practicing backflips on the lawn. The playroom is empty, but I can hear a voice coming from the dining room.

'Alice what on earth are you doing?'

The eight dining chairs are lined up along the wall, throw cushions from the lounge rest upright next to them. Followed by the cushions from the back and seats from Jenny's sofas. Alice's Mary-Jane doll, and George's Buzz Lightyear completed the row. 'You can't go pulling Aunty Jenny's house apart.'

Alice is still in her nightdress. She gives me one of her looks. The one that says I'm a simpleton. Her hands rest on her hips.

'But I haven't got enough dolls!' I frown, confused. Alice's shoulders rise and fall as she huffs, 'For all of us. I need twenty-one, Jack added it up for me.'

17

'Twenty-one dolls?   Alice, what are you talking about?'

She rolls her eyes. Waving open palms up and down to stress her point.

'For all my brothers and sisters in the jungle silly. This is Timothy,' she says walking over and touching the first cushion, 'Jason, Harry, Rosie, Bertram. I know that's not their proper names, but it will have to do.'

I feel sick but equally amused at Alice's ability to accept seventeen new siblings as normal.

'Alright,' I say, trying to be understanding, 'but you can't go moving people's furniture.'

'Well, I did. Uncle Robin said I could.'
'Did he now?'

'Yes. As long as I didn't scrape the walls or break anything.'

'Well, make sure you don't. I'm making pancakes, I'll call you when they're ready.'

'Okay and can—'

'No.' I say firmly, anticipating her question. 'I'm not making twenty-one pancakes.'

In the kitchen I rub a finger against my temple.

'Christ sake. We need some normality all of us. If you were here right now Tom Lane, I'd slap your face. No – actually, I'd probably stab you with one of Jenny's kitchen knives but then I'd be done for flunking murder, or would it be like the French, a crime of passion?'

I gasp as Alice surprises me.

'Who are you talking to?' Alice climbs onto the booster step to get a glass out of the cupboard and goes to the water cooler.

'The ceiling people,' I say. 'Drink that here. You're not to slop it around the house.'

'But –'

'No buts. Drink it up or pour it away.'

'It's not fair,' Alice strops, forcing out her bottom lip. 'Everyone at the tea party is thirsty. Sometimes mummies are horrid. They don't understand how hot it is in the jungle.'

I flatten my lips together, cracking eggs satisfyingly into flour and beat the hell out of them.

18

We wave off my three youngest, they are all happy to be going swimming for the third day in a row. Jack is working at Dan's.

'I feel guilty not going too,' I say.

'Nonsense you need some you time without worrying about them,' Jenny says massaging my shoulders. 'God, you're tense. Knots like pickled onions. You could do with a spa treatment, but that's probably not a good idea.'

'Definitely not. You can guarantee I'd bump into bloody Evelyn.'

'Too negative! We're going to forget about the Evelyn Grainger's of this world today and make plans. You need to move forward, stop focusing on gossips and newspapers.'

We carry our coffees to the garden, settling on the rattan furniture in the sunshine.

'You forgot to add seventeen children, and that everyone thinks I'm having an affair with Matt Barton.'

'That's in the past. This is about your future.'

Easy for her to say, but how?

'I know, Jen, but I'm still overwhelmed by it all, and I can't do anything until I know what finances Tom will allow me.'

I know that came out wrong. Jenny's grimace is one of intense frustration.

'*What Tom will allow you?* Do you know how pathetic that sounds. Don't you have your own money?'

'No, only the housekeeping account Tom pays into. He said years ago he'd put the house and car in my name for tax reasons, but I've never seen any paperwork. The house is mortgage free that's about all I know.'

'And I bet he said you don't need to worry your pretty-little head. Blimey Grace, as a modern woman you're such an innocent. Well, it's time to find out exactly what your position is. Where does he keep the important stuff?'

'In a drawer in his study,' I say, heat rising up my neck, knowing any moment she's going to say I should know what's in there. 'Tom was strict about his privacy,' I add lamely.

'And we know why. Do you have any proof you own Darwin House?'

'Until this lot hit the fan, I'd no reason to doubt it. Am I that stupid? Is that how people see me?'

'No, darling, I'm just playing. But you need to know what your financial position is. Tom's idea of keeping you in the dark is so 1950.'

I'm feeling uncomfortable with this conversation, probably because no matter how unpalatable her words, it's the truth. Once I was strong, I took no prisoners. I had my own ideas. I was fun, and dammit, I had a voice. One that Tom has eroded over the years. And the only person to blame is me for letting him.

'It was one of the few things he didn't delegate. I'd enough to do dealing with the day-to-day stuff. Tom did the big things involving accountants, solicitors, and financial planning, to be honest I found that side boring. I never actually asked. Christ, what an idiot.'

We lapse into silence, sipping our drinks. Jenny's staring at a bald patch of grass, her eyes zigzagging across it. I can tell she's working something out, but will I like it? The numbness inside me is fading. It's a slow process and until I see Tom it will stay there.

Glancing around the scorched lawn, my thoughts roam to the garden makeover. It's the least I can do to repay her and Robin for taking us in. With the kids' help we can make it an oasis of colour. Something Jen can enjoy, perhaps a water feature or something restorative. Other people's marriages – no one knows what goes on behind closed doors. On the surface Jen looks in control but the tension lines on her forehead are deeper. My mind wanders and her drinking is worrying, but I've given up asking what's wrong as it rattles her. I've caught Robin watching her too, so I know I'm not imagining it.

'You need a plan,' Jenny says, getting up and going inside and returning with a notepad and pen. 'We'll assume the house and car are yours, but we need the paperwork to prove it. If that's correct, at least you have some decent assets to be going on with, and awesome bargaining power.'

My eyes flicker. I feel childishly inadequate at dealing with something I don't understand. I want to be organised and full of fight, but I'm as guilty as Tom's absences and infidelity. I'm equally to blame for my naivety, I realise with a sinking feeling how Tom managed me, and how I let him. That stings. I can't help my sorrowful sigh. Jenny places her hand over mine.

'Come on, chin up. Let's plan.'
'Other than killing him with one of his shotguns?'

'That's more like it. Use that humour as your shield. I won't push you, but how about a trip to Darwin House – today?'

My shoulders rise. 'I can't, Jen, the very thought of being smuggled in under a blanket again is horrendous. I can't do it.'

'I thought I overheard Jack saying they'd gone.'

'Lissy said she'd asked the milkman and he said they weren't there when he passed by. But that doesn't mean they're not there now.'

'Ah, but I've a cunning plan,' she says, tapping her nose with her middle finger. 'We'll take the kids' back-packs, drive to Barton's Farm. Leave my car and walk the rest of the way across the fields.

'It's a fair old hike,' I say with pessimism. 'But we both could use the exercise.'

'You cheeky bugger,' she says, nudging me. 'Go change into shorts and trainers. We'll be two girls out for a hike.'

***

We park in front of the farm shop and cross the road, taking the footpath that cuts several miles off our journey.

Matt's cows watch us with suspicion. One objects loudly leaving me wondering if that one's Elsa.

18

There isn't a cloud in the sky. Since the storm, the land has returned to fresh leafy greens. I spot wild poppies, cornflowers, and columbines. A rabbit skits across our path. The fresh air is cathartic, like a drug that allows me to wallow in its addiction.

'Thanks, Jen. I needed this.'

'You're not alone. I'm enjoying the walk too, it's sort of cathartic. Makes you look outside of yourself.'

'How funny, I thought exactly the same.'

The track widens, enabling us to walk side-by-side. Jenny drapes a lazy arm around my shoulders. We bump along in silence until we're laughing, ungainly clambering over styles and splashing through replenished streams. We reach the wood, relieved to be out of the blistering sun, breathing in the intoxicating scent of the pine forest, overlooking Darwin House. From here we have a bird's-eye view and make out a gaggle of people at the entrance to my property.

'There you go. We've outsmarted the buggers,' Jenny laughs.

'Hurrah for that,' I shout, starting downhill past the abandoned building to the gate that leads to our property.

The sensation I get when I step over the threshold isn't alien to me. Cold pricks my skin with a familiar dread, tempting me to turn and run. A gentle push from Jenny gets me over the threshold.

'Come on, let's get to it. He's not here and you're not staying – we're here to determine your future, so let's get started.'

We untangle ourselves from the webbing of our

rucksacks, ignoring the amount of post trodden underfoot on entering. I hover in the doorway of Tom's study, nausea rising. This is the room I scurried in and out of, flicking the occasional duster, on strict orders never to move anything.

'I'm parched. I'll get us some water,' Jenny says, pulling a face at the shelf full of TV awards.

Carved masks leer at me from the walls. The crude musical instrument, gouged from some vegetable, hangs by a leather thong above the desk. His favourite, a brightly painted drum, settles in the corner beside a spear decorated with a black snake curling its way to the point and ringed with feathers. I shiver, recalling how Tom said he'd speared a monkey himself, delighting the hunting group he'd been out with. I imagine bare-breasted women bobbing and jiggling in celebration with spear-tapping men before Tom, like he's some sort of demi-god.

Tom's photo gallery spans the wall to my left. Him in a canoe in tribal dress. Him with his face and hair red with mud. Bile enters my mouth as my eyes settle on him laughing, surrounded by half-naked women crushing maize on a stone. Were these the women who'd shared his bed, carried his children? The last is a black-and-white photo of him waving a club with a hunting group, a limp animal stretched on sticks between them. My gut rolls with disgust as my eyes settle on that very club displayed on the shelf above the desk.

Jenny passes me a glass of water. 'Took ages to get it clean out of your taps. It was muddy to begin with.'

The cool water slips down my throat. I don't want to do this, but I must. Stepping in, I pull out Tom's chair, sit and lower my head, pinching my eyelids between fingers and thumbs. I will not cry as I face evidence of my sham marriage.

'Sooner we're done, the sooner we're out of here.' Jenny squats on the floor touching my knee.

I nod, opening the first of four drawers. No surprises, just cheque books, a stapler, a paper knife, envelopes – nothing unfamiliar. From the next, I hand Jenny life insurance policies, disappointed there's no lurking secrets. Jenny puts them with the car logbook, MOT, and insurance documents.

'That's it.' I say with a mix of disappointment and frustration.

'I'm not giving up yet,' Jenny says, getting to her feet and stretching out her back. 'Come on, keep looking.'

Diligently we investigate every drawer, wardrobe, shoebox, sock, and underwear drawer, checking nothing's taped beneath like some second rate crime movie.

'I'll put the kettle on,' Jen says, giving my arm a squeeze as I climb down from the loft ladder.

'Nothing up there either,' I say despondently, following her downstairs like a stranger in my own home.

Jenny makes black coffee, the milk in the fridge is sour. I make a list of things the kids might need, including passports.

'Have you seen our passports Jen?'

'Yes, in a bag somewhere. I meant to bring them down, back bedroom, I think.'

'I remember.' Relief comes in a rush. 'I'll get them before we go.'

Jenny places hot coffee on Tom's desk. My fingers itch to put it on a coaster but deny the temptation. Jenny crouches, resting back on her heels as she loads our booty into our rucksacks. My jaw aches because my teeth have been clenched the entire visit. I don't feel well. A pounding batters my ears, my throat dry from rushed breathing. I grab the back of the chair as a primeval cry spews from my lips. I jerk violently clawing at the photographs, the glass trophies, smashing them to the ground. I hear Jenny's gasp, but I can't stop. Tugging, ripping, bending everything I can, discarding it to a grotesque heap on the carpet. The club is next. Jenny jumps out of the way as I swing it at the drum. It hits with a dull thud. I do it over and over until Jenny locks her arms around me.

'Enough.'

Sweat runs stinging my eyes. I slump against the wall. She steps towards the drum, its skin split and flapping, and wrestles it to its side, tearing away the remaining hide she turns to me with a beaming smile.

'Jackpot. Woo-hoo.'

I gasp for air. My heart cantering against my ribs. From inside the drum Jenny pulls out a folder wrapped in a T-shirt of Tom's I haven't seen for years. Next is a handful of memory sticks. I should rejoice but I can't. I can't bear it. Who was this man I shared my life with? What a fool I've been. It's another slap to the face. I can't acknowledge Jenny's find and rush from the room shouting that I'll get the passports, leaving her to sift through. I don't want to look, it's too painful. I'm not ready to swallow another dose of Tom's deceit.

Upstairs, I collect the passports and add them to the pile of things Jack needs, remembering I promised Melissa I'd get her shampoo. Someone has pulled the plug on a sink of dirty water and not rinsed it. Jack or Alice, I suspect, both are equally untidy. Hating myself, I grab the cleaner and cloth from the under-sink cupboard. Jenny's right, the water's been sitting in the ancient pipes too long. I let it run. She's shouting something up the stairs. Dropping the cloth, I grab a towel and lean over the landing rail.

'Sorry, couldn't hear you.'

Jenny comes into view.

'You're never gonna believe this. He has five bank accounts – four in his name only. It's only the house-keeping account that's joint, but…' she says with a grin that's so infectious. I smile an upside down one back at her, 'it's not all doom and gloom. This house *is* in your name. Solely.'

'Great.' I say, gathering up the pile from the landing that I've collected of our belongings to take. 'It was something to do with assets and tax.' I push everything into a carrier bag and go down to join her.

'You own a boat too. A 47ft sailboat. Sleeps six, apparently,' she says, wide eyed.

'You're joking me?' I say in disbelief.

'Nope. And guess what it's called?'

She's clutching the papers against her chest, giggling like a kid.

'I can't guess, give me a clue.'

'Humphrey Bogart.'

'Not African Queen?' I say in disbelief.

'Close, very close,' Jenny says, teasing a piece of paper in front of me.

'I give up. Come on, what?'

She bends double exploding with laughter.

'Only bloody African King. Can you believe the ego of the man?'

I'm laughing too, it's too crazy for words.

'How come he's never talked about it, and we've never seen it?'

'Probably because it's berthed in Kinsale, County Cork.'

'Ireland?' We've never been to Ireland. Well, Tom has. He often flies in via Shannon, says it's cheaper.' A lightbulb moment shines clear. I'd never questioned his dates or times. I wouldn't know if he spent a week or two sailing in Ireland, and I can't imagine Tom sailing on his own. So, who was he with?

Suddenly the hall phone rings loud and unexpected, we exchange glances.

'Don't answer it. It could be the press.'

I ignore her warning. I can't keep shying away from things.

'Hello?'

'Grace, what the devil's going on up there? I told you to call me.'

I bristle at the order, mouthing *Roderick* to Jenny.

'What's happened to my boy. You and this farmer fellow, what's going on.'

I make a fist with my free hand, mimicking an upper-cut punch, Jenny covers her mouth, stifling a cackle.

'Roderick, shut up and listen.' I shout, surprising myself at my boldness. 'Firstly, I don't take orders from you, and now, thankfully, not from your son either. The son you say you care about, but bully to tears at every opportunity. I, for your information, have done nothing, with anybody or to anybody. But the temptation to strangle Tom has crossed my mind. You don't like me. I don't like you. Thankfully, my children don't even know you. We need never speak again. If you want the creep, too bad, I neither know nor care where he is. Don't ring again.' I slam the receiver to its cradle and do a running on-the-spot dance.

'Yes, yes, yes. Oh God, that felt good. All the years I've wanted to say that. Right, that's him told. Now what was I doing? Oh yes, sod the cleaning.'

Jenny picks up the sturdy straps of her rucksack and struggles into it. I stoop to mine, finding a pocket for the passports while everything else goes inside. So I own the house, the car, and a boat. Toms' deceit has backfired on him.

'Christ, that was funny. Come here and give me a high five,' she says. We slap palms mid-air, laughing. 'Ready? Let's get out of here. We've got what we came for.'

I don't argue and five minutes later we leave the house by the back door, retracing our steps up the hill. Jenny hums Rod Stewart's *I am sailing*. I break into the chorus, belting out *stormy waters*, disturbing a murder of crows who take indignant refuge in the tops of the pine trees.

'Thanks, Jen.' I say, taking her hand.

'What for?' she says.

'Everything and more. I don't want to be the woman I've become, and you're showing me I'm better than that.'

'Blimey, or should I say hallelujah?'

'Everything and more. I don't want to be the woman I've become,

19

The house is thick with silence. Lucy has spirited George and Alice away. Melissa's at a friend's, Jack at work, and Jen's taken Todd and Lily to visit their grandparents. It's like walking on eggshells with everyone tiptoeing around me.

Tom's train arrives in forty-minutes, hopefully without the press on his heels. That's all Jen and Robin need, is them camping out on the pavement. And that's another thing. I could have sworn Jen had been crying this morning, but when I asked her, she said she'd got shampoo in her eyes. She can't fool me. Her mission to help me through my current situation is the only thing she's enthusiastic about. She's like a clam, a secret keeper and I know no matter how many times I try to find out what's worrying her, she won't tell me. Her parting words today were to glam up and show Tom what he'd thrown away. I've been in two minds about that, but it would be something to do.

In the bathroom I open my drawstring make-up bag. Most of the items are from my recent trip to town, some feel awkward in my hands. I brush on grey-green eyeshadow, forgetting to use the primer first so it sits badly. I'm hoping it won't appear so heavy once I've done my lashes, but the black and gold wand is clumsy and slips from my grasp into the sink, leaving an ugly black smear.

'Damn, is this how this day's going to go? Another fine mess, I've got myself into.' At the second attempt my hand's so shaky that mascara ends up on my eyelids. I grimace and wipe it off. 'That's better.' I apply my new lipstick, pressing my lips together. 'Beautiful, you're gorgeous. You're ready.' My tanned skin glows against Jen's cream top and tangerine, and taupe chunky necklace. Even though I fought hard against Jen's idea of a makeover. 'This is what you've thrown away Tom Lane.'

Acid indigestion bubbles in my windpipe as I pace like a caged lion. How am I supposed to behave? No one gives you a rule book on the etiquette for these situations. Perhaps I should write one myself. I need something to focus on other than being the wife of a man who fathers umpteen kids, but would it have hurt any less if it had only been one? A vision of Tom making love to a naked brown body makes me retch.

'Stop all this crap,' I shout into the void of the hallway, my voice echoing. 'You're better than this. You need to be practical. Make plans for a future without Tom. What do you think about that, ceiling people?'

There's no knowing what today bring, but one thing is for sure, we are never returning to Darwin House. The kids love being in Steadcoate. I've no way of visualising the alternative. Perhaps it will be clearer after our meeting. The word meeting sounds so formal.

The low rumble of a train in the distance warns me Tom will arrive shortly. I laughed at his melodramatic text, saying he was arriving by rail, as he had less chance *of being intercepted.* He's hardly David Attenborough but that is Tom all over.

My mouth is like blotting paper dry. I make time for another visit to the bathroom before I kick off my flatties and take out the pair of Lily's mules I'd worn to the fundraiser, not to make me look more attractive but so he can't look down on me.

My nerves scream as the knocker hits the hardwood door. I smooth down my top, stretch my spine and stroll to open it calmly but my fingers fumble with the catch.

Tom blusters in, swinging a holdall from his shoulder to the parquet flooring.

'Christ, that was a helluva journey,' he says, removing his baseball cap and sunglasses, and with a confident smile reaches for me. 'Come on, Gracie, how about a hug?'

I'm horrified and back away. I don't know what I'd expected, but certainly not this. Not a scrap of shame or remorse.

'I'm sorry about this mess,' he says as if what's happened is minor, 'but we can sort it out.' he huffs, attempting to corner me, but I step out of range.

'Christ's sake, Tom.' I say, in disgust.

His eyes narrow momentarily, unfazed by my rejection, he gives a nervous laugh.

'Come on old girl, if I can't have a hug at least get the kettle on,' he says rubbing his hands, 'you know how I love a cuppa when I get home. I'm sure Jen has some Earl Grey hidden in that labyrinth of a kitchen.'

For want of anything better to do I stride to the kitchen. Obediently filling the kettle, and wonder why the hell I'm making him tea when I'd rather it was arsenic – questioning why I turn into an obedient moron when he's around? My head continues its argument while I stir and place two mugs on the table, patiently waiting for the floaters disturbing my vision to clear. My tongue feels far too big for my mouth, will my words be trapped inside? Grasping the handle of my mug I slop hot tea onto the table and get up for a cloth. The sound of the toilet flushing in the hall alerts me of his return. He casually pulls out the chair opposite and reaches for my hand.

'Really Tom? I don't think so.' I say swapping politeness for fuck off.

He shrugs. He's unshaven and the lines around his eyes have deepened. My nose picks out the musty smell of travel emanating from him.

'Where are the kids?'

'Out. I didn't want them here. They've seen and heard enough.'

'Come on, old girl, don't be like this. How've you been coping with all this malarkey?'

My blood pressure peaks.

'Malarkey? Is that what you call it? Malarkey is a bit of fun in my book, not the total humiliation of a family.'

'Okay, terrible choice of words. I'm sorry about the fuss, it will die down.' He picks up his cup, hovering it at his mouth. 'You don't have to be difficult.'

It takes several breaths to ward off the crushing sensation in my chest and the urge to throw scalding tea over him.

'Difficult? You think I'm being difficult? You turn our lives upside down, father seventeen children, and all you can say is, *I'm* being difficult? Have you no remorse?' I don't want to do this, I'd promised myself I would be calm; listen to whatever his excuses were, but his attitude—it's all wrong. I meet his eye waiting for him to say something – at least try to apologise but he looks down and sideways, like he did when his father Roderick scolds him. This time the little boy lost act wouldn't wash with me.

'Gracie let's not do this. Think about the children. I know you're angry, I'm sorry, I can't say any more.' His eyebrows raise behind the steam from his drink.

'Thanks for mentioning the children Tom but whose exactly, your seventeen, or my — sorry our, four?' My words fire with such force that my teeth crunch together. I want to cry, instead I swallow it away, frustrated with myself. Tom's eyes soften and for a moment, he's my Tom, the man I'd loved and obeyed.

'Why Tom, why? Make me understand. Did our marriage vows mean nothing to you? Haven't I been a good wife?'

He flexes his fingers wide then closes them, something he often does when challenged.

'It's not like you think. Honestly. It's part of my job to keep the natives happy. I go along with their traditions, and part of that tradition is to accept their hospitality, and not offend them by refusing what's acceptable in their culture – to share everything. It's expected. You don't know how hard it is, they aren't all pretty and nubile.'

My laugh follows through mixed with spit.

'You weren't in bloody Tahiti, Tom, one of the mutinous crew of The Bounty. Next you'll tell me it's in your contract.'

His features contort.

'Well not exactly, but that's how it works. If a tribal elder, or a chief, offers you one of his wives, or daughters, refusal isn't an option. It would give offence and jeopardise the show. That's what makes the programme a winner. I get so much out of them.'

'Obviously.' I say bitterly. 'Babies for a start. Do you know how fucked up this is? Alice wants to know their names and their birthdays.'

His face moulds a grin, that fades as quickly as it came.

'I don't like you swearing and it's not what you think. I don't love these women. It's not like us. Not like what we have.'

It's my turn to look amused. 'What? A farce of a marriage? You're digging a bigger hole for yourself.'

He ignores the comment, waving his arms above his head to silence me.

'But that is how they let me into their lives, it's their ethos. I realise it's hard for you to understand, but it's just part of my job.'

The sack of anger I've been carrying rips apart in a screech of fury.

'Your job? It's part of your job, that's it? That's the excuse for ruining our lives, for making us hole-up in Jen's like criminals. For our children getting suspended from school because you've made them into – what's the cliché? A laughing stock? Oh, come on Tom, you can do better than that.' I pushed my drink out of the way, resting my forearms on the table to steady my spiralling anger. My eyelids blink like morse code, hoping to banish the light-headedness I'm experiencing.

Tom slurps his tea unaware of anything but himself.

'Look, it's not love, it's sex. It's not what we have.'

'Had. You don't seriously think I can still love you after this? How would it have been if it was me seeking sex elsewhere. What's good for the goose.'

'Now you're being silly. You're overthinking things, like you always do. Anyway, we're going around in circles, I didn't expect you to be so argumentative. Once we can get back home, you'll forget all about it.'

Am I having a stroke? I wonder as a prickling sensation builds from the base of my spine. A scream building, the pressure, whooshing, rising. My breaths puffy, shallower, more frequent. The knife rack is so close. His mouth moving. Words, more words.

'It's not that bad. I don't think it will damage my career. I've already been approached to write a book. That could end up with film rights, sky's the limit.' Tom raises his hands, waggling his fingers to show quotation marks.

'"My life, with the women of the jungle." The money they are talking about would set us up for life.'

'Shut up!' I scream, banging my fist on the table. He flinches, surprise scouring his eyes. 'Stop it right now.' I can't get the words out fast enough. 'You're unbelievable. It's like you think you're some amazing sex God – a stud. You 're actually proud of it. You don't know how far you've pushed me. I could take a knife right now and stick it in you.'

Tom pushes his chair back, the wither of a scowl deepening.

'Don't overdramatise. I meant that financially it could do us good. No such thing as bad press. We have to calm down, ride it out. Got anything to eat?'

This is the Tom I recognise, bored with being challenged and a great one for a dispersal tactic to shut me up.

'I'm starving.'

He gets up rubbing his stomach. The wind has gone out of me. Dazed, I watch as he tugs the fridge door open, taking out butter, cheese, and tomatoes, opens the bread bin, takes out a loaf – turns to me. 'Want one?'

I'm done. I shake my head sapped by my outburst. Silently I study him, his thinning hair. Tom was never fat but has developed a paunch. My jaw clenches as he cuts into the loaf then dips the bread knife into the tub of butter, a habit I abhor. As annoying as the fact that he never rinsed the sink after shaving – always leaving his mess for me to clean up after him. What did I ever see in him? I stare as he bites into his sandwich, chewing hungrily as if nothing's happened and slides back into his seat. A trail of crumbs drop disrespectfully onto Jen's floor ready for me to clean up after him.

'I'm sorry, what more can I say. I know it's upsetting for you, but it's good that it's out in the open. It'll die down. We'll take the kids away for a break, I thought Scotland. We could hire a lodge, or something till the press get bored?' He looks at me expectantly. Then pulls out his mobile, as if that were an end to the conversation.

My hands grip the arms of the chair at his dismissal. I deserve his full attention. With one swift lunge, I shoot my mug across the table. He rears back alarmed as it crashes to the floor.

'Shut up, fucking shut up. Listen to yourself. Who the hell do you think you are?'

His mouth forms an O. I close him down with the flat of my hand.

'I think you'd better let me do the talking. That is, until my solicitor takes over.'

Spittle forms at the corners of my mouth and I wipe it away with the back of my hand. 'We won't be going on a trip to Scotland. There's not a chance of reconciliation, no anything. Just a divorce.'

His face reddens, then creases, he gives an awkward boyish grin, almost submissive, but an agitated hand fingering coins in his trouser pocket says otherwise.

'Calm down. I can't believe you're behaving like this, you're usually so, so —.'

'What? Compliant? Complacent? Well not anymore, I—'

The door bangs and we both turn.

'What the—' Tom attempts to defend himself as Jack rains angry blows on him. Tom is displaced from his chair.

'I hate you—I hate you. You dirty bastard,' Jack yells.

Tears of anger stream down Jack's tortured face. It takes all my strength to pull him off his father. He spins into my arms, sobbing.

'We don't need him, Mum, don't take him back, please. I can look after you. He's a worthless piece of shit. A fucking embarrassment and I hate him.'

He says the words with such venom and I should reprimand him for swearing, but I don't.

'Hush now,' I say, locking my elbows so that we face each other, 'I'm not taking him back. Everything will be alright.'

Tom scrambles to his feet, straightening his dishevelled clothes.

'You cut my lip.' He wipes a trembling hand across his mouth, blood seeps between his teeth.

'I think it's time you left.'

He ignores me, turning to Jack.

'Jack, son, I know how it looks, but we can sort it out. I love your Mum. Love you all. If you were older, you'd understand.' His chin quivers, do I spot the glint of a tear?

Jack veers towards him, but I hold him fast.

'If I were older, I'd have thrown you out like Mum should've years ago. I've seen those kids' photos on your computer. You sick pervert. Shame you didn't stay in the jungle with them. We don't want you,' his eyes radiate hatred. 'Fuck off and leave us alone.'

I push my son behind me. 'Tom. Get out. Now.'

'Jack come outside,' Tom says, stepping forward without his usual swagger. 'Let's have a walk around the garden, man to man. We're mates you and me. A chip off the old block.'

Tears spill from Jack's eyes. He's boy and man-child rolled into one, and I love him for wanting to protect me.

'We're not mates,' he growls, clenching his fists. 'You don't even know me. I put up with you. We all do, except for Alice, because she's a silly kid you can bribe. She'll hate you too when she's older. Do us all a favour. Fuck off and ruin your jungle kids' lives. Leave us alone. You're pathetic. Everyone around here thinks you're a joke, a wanker.'

Jack's words hit home. Tom flexes his chin, angered by the insult.

'Stop swearing and don't speak to me like that. Have some respect. I'm your father. Apologise,' he demands, nostrils flaring.

'No, he won't. Jack,' I say, stepping across his path. 'You've nothing to apologise for. Get out, Tom, and don't bother us again. The only thing I want from you is a divorce.' I watch a flash of uncertainty cross his face. He recovers, a supercilious grin spreading from his lips.

'A divorce?' he says, throwing his head back with a raucous laugh and widening his stance. 'You won't enjoy living without the luxury I provide for you. Nor you, Jack. If you think I'm agreeing to that, you can think again. You won't catch me paying a fortune to keep you sweet. Do you think I'm going to walk out and give you everything I've worked for?'

My spine flexes with the sensation of growing taller.

'Walk out? You were hardly here in the first place. You always had one foot in the jungle. That's what I used to say. Silly me. If it had only been a *foot,* we wouldn't be in this mess.'

The look he throws me reminds me of his awful father, Roderick.

'Oh, very droll. How long did it take you come up with that one? No wonder I prefer the tribal way of life.'

I blink the sting of his words away as Jack tries to get around me. I back him up against the fridge.

'Monogamy is very over-rated,' he says shaking his head cockily. 'You won't like the repercussions of living on a small budget.'

'Really, Tom.' I say, my fury settling and my inner strength growing, 'I think little will change, the courts will see to that.'

'You won't get away with it you bitch, and to think I actually felt sorry for you.'

He strides to the hallway. I follow, Jack behind me.

Tom starts pulling open the drawers of the hall dresser.

'You can't do that. It's not your house. Tom, what are you looking for?'

He moves to the coat rack, tapping pockets.

'The keys to the Range Rover, are they in your handbag? Get them. I haven't got a car.'

'Tough, you're not having it.'

He huffs a laugh.

'I bloody well am.' I sense a shift in him, a regret. I can't fall for it.

'No, you're not and if you try to take it, I'll call the police. It's one of the many things in my name – like the house. Remember, for tax avoidance: ah, and I've also discovered I own a yacht berthed in Ireland as well.'

Tom rocks on his heels. His face crumbling with discomfort and loss. He stares past me to Jack, who's pallid and shaking, his eyes wet, red rimmed. I glance back at Tom, who looks hopefully at Jack. For a moment I think he's going to have one last try to get Jack on side, but he doesn't, instead he lowers his voice addressing me.

'Don't cross me, Grace. You're nothing without me, I looked after you. Remember, I didn't have to marry you. I felt sorry for you because of Hannah. You'll regret this, trust me.'

He wrinkles his nose in a sneer. 'Let's see what the courts say when they hear about you playing cosy with Matt Barton, he's been sniffing round you for years. I have friends in high places, no one can be that squeaky clean. You obviously kept good company whilst I was away earning a living to keep you. I notice you've finally done something with yourself.' He looks me up and down. 'For his benefit, was it?'

With a strength I didn't know I had in me, I open the front door wide then lurch at him, both my hands grab at his clothing, and I manhandle him out of the door slamming it behind him. Jack's swiftly by my side. I make a grab for him but miss as he pulls the door open. I step out behind him; worried what Jack will do. Tom hasn't got as far as the gate, he must have lost his balance, as he's sitting on the path, looking stunned.

'Here.' Jack yells. 'Take your crappy disguise with you.' He flips his wrist like throwing a frisbee only it's Tom's baseball cap. It sails past Tom, landing in the road.

Tom's jaw drops, ugly tears, and bubbles of snot trail to his chin. Jack holds up Tom's sunglasses, snaps them in two and hurls them into the air.

'What's up Dad, you look upset. Not crying, are you? You told me tears were for cissies. Don't bother, nothing's going to change. Tosser. Oh, and mind you don't trip over your ego as you jog on.'

Tom looks shrunken, he's openly crying. His despair isn't at what has been said but in our rejection of him. Something stirs in me, not satisfaction, more like a feeling of loss, not mine but Tom's.

Jack takes my arm and leads me indoors. I'm aware of the door slamming as my knees give way. I slide down the wall, into a crumpled heap. Today should have brought the nightmare to an end, instead it started a new one. He hankers down beside pulling me too him. My head falls to his chest. We sit and cry for an age until Jack's heart stops pounding against me and I run out of tears.

'He didn't mean those things he said Mum.' Jack says softly.

'I know, but it's still hard to hear. I'm sorry you had to witness that. Why did you come back?'

'The packaging machine broke and…'

'It was a good excuse to come home?' I say.

'I wanted to make sure you were okay.'

He stands holding out his hand and pulls me to my feet, engulfing me in a hug. I feel small against him, he's at least six inches taller. A recollection blooms of my father holding me when someone, or something, upset me, *probably my mother*. It's comforting.

'I'm fine.' I say, pulling away. 'I'm glad he's gone, but darling, I don't want you to hate him. He loves you all.'

'Really? He's a funny way of showing it.' Jack rams his hands in his pockets, 'Mum, I know you want it to be right, but it never was. Not since I was about five or six years. I can't miss what I've never had. I've talked more to Dan and Mick in the last few weeks than Dad in the last five years. Living here, and seeing Robin with his kids, Dan with Leah, doing things together. That's a Dad. We never had that, and it's not your fault. He chose his job over us and sorry Mum, but now we know why.'

I don't want to have this conversation with Jack. I want to protect him, instead he's looking after me.

'You might be right,' I say, 'and thank you for coming to my rescue, but honestly, the result would have been the same. I want him out of our lives too. Together, we'll make a better one.'

'Oh yeah,' he says with a grin, 'and when can we go out on the yacht?'

'Guess we'll have to learn to sail first.' I say, forcing a grin.

We move to the kitchen and while I clear up Tom's mess Jack pours us both a glass of water.

'So now that Dad's gone, can we move back home?'

'Lets, leave it another day or so. In case that's where he's gone.'

'He can't unless you let him. You own it.'

'I do, but he may put up a fight. Wait a few more days, till I get the legalities in place.'

Jack nods.

'I suppose, well, I'd better get back to work.'

'Thought you said the packing machine broke.'

He throws me a guilty grin.

'I lied. It runs in the family. You sure it's okay for me to leave you?'

'Positive. I think I'll go for a walk and clear my head.'

'Good idea,' he says kissing my cheek before he leaves. I'm so proud of him. His words of wisdom stay with me long after he's cycled off. He's gone from grumpy teenager to my rock in a matter of weeks. I suppose I have Dan to thank for that, but that's another man I've decided isn't trustworthy.

20

Dan waved Jack off outside Jenny Maxwell's home. He'd known Jack was lying when he made some paltry excuse to bunk off that morning. Later, when he returned with red, puffy eyes, Dan understood. Jack hadn't elaborated but said his dad had paid them a visit and there'd been some sort of altercation, but that Tom had now left.

Dan liked Jack. He was a good kid, and a good worker. What Tom Lane had done to his family was despicable. He was surprised he'd returned to Steadcoat at all, but then Dan didn't have Tom's ego. Jack is a credit to his mother, he thought. Nothing at all like his show-off father. Giving Jack a job had turned out to be a bit of a life saver. It kept Dan's mind occupied. Jack had opened up about how hard it'd been growing up in Tom's shadow. He didn't know the rest of the family, still doesn't, except that Alice and Leah were in the same class at school and good friends, and occasionally did sleepovers.

The village store was his last drop off. That was it for the day. He dreaded the emptiness of the farmhouse, Leah was on a playdate cum sleepover and Flora was visiting friends. It was a nice evening for a walk across the fields to the Three Doves. Some company and a pint would serve as another distraction. He couldn't seem to switch off and avoid the inevitability of Kate's prognosis.

He set off, crisscrossing his land through open fields along narrow tracks following the river, working up a thirst.

Tourists crowded the pub garden, their excited children running about ignored by their parents who knew they couldn't come to harm in the fenced off play area. Dan breathed the scent of dry thatch and roses as he followed the path and ducked under the arched doorway where the hoppy aroma of beer and food took over.

The bar area wasn't too busy. Roger, the landlord, greeted him, his face the rosy shade of a drinker.

'Haven't seen you for a while Dan. Usual, is it?'

Dan nodded straddling a barstool. 'Been busy Roger. Trying to get ahead ready for my Christmas ranges.'

'Christmas?' Roger said, setting down a pint of bitter on the bar towel. 'Give us a break, we've not finished summer yet.'

Dan raised the glass to his lips and took a swig, the point of his tongue licking away the head of foam from his lip.

'Looks like you've had a good one so far. I see you've added more outside tables.'

'Didn't have a choice. Tourist trade always wants to sit outside in summer and expects a roaring grate in winter. Sal and I make the most of it while we can. 'Yes, sir, what can I get you.' Roger said, moving off to serve another customer.

Sally, Roger's wife, came out from the kitchen fanning herself. She was a rotund, jolly woman who gave the impression of being a pushover, but anyone who thought so was mistaken. There was a lot more to her than her excellent food and cheerful smile. Dan witnessed the smile slide from her face as a noisy group of men entered, settling on the table directly behind him. He didn't turn, continuing his conversation with Sally, relieved she'd not enquired about Kate's health. Not for lack of caring, he knew that. Sally was a lady who noticed things without being told and however kind others' sympathetic enquiries about Kate were, replying to them exhausted him.

The group behind him became rowdier, laughing and loudly exchanging anecdotes. You didn't need to be Einstein to know they were the reporters who'd been hanging around Darwin House.

Roger handed Sally a food order to fill.

Sally tutted.

'Why people want hot food in this heat I'll never know,' she said heading for the kitchen.

Dan lifted his glass, then put it down again. One voice stood out of the huddle.

Ruddy Tom Lane.

'Honestly, you don't know how willing they are, and nimble as fuck… I've always preferred a little dark meat to—'

'For Christ's sake!' Dan growled standing to face the group.

'Frankly, I'm surprised it's only seventeen,' Tom continued. 'I've had more than that over the years.'

Dan closed his eyes at the lack of respect Tom had for his family.

'Know what I mean?' Tom said with a knowing wink.

Dan fumed, his anger building as he stepped closer and stood over Tom.

'So, you're back. I'm surprised you've got the nerve to show your face round here after the grief you've caused your family. But then again, you've done the world a favour now everyone knows what a fuckwit you are.'

Tom pushed himself to his feet.

'What's up Dan, not getting enough yourself?' he sneered.

The assembled press group sensed something worth recording was about to go down and scabbled for note-books, mobile phones, and adjusted camera lenses. Their action stopped Dan from punching the little shit in the face. It would only give him more publicity.

'Pathetic,' Dan sneered. 'Think all those women makes you more of a man, do you? You're a tosser if you believe that. You always were a sad excuse for a human being.'

Tom held a smug grin, his head turning from his audience and back to Dan, relishing the attention. He gave a slow clap.

'Very good Dan. Sounds like jealousy to me.'

Dan clenched his fists to his sides, his jaw tightening.

'You think anyone would be jealous of you? Trouble is, you believe your own publicity. Everybody round here thinks you're a joke, a loser, pathetic. Your wife,

Grace, is a lovely lady whom we all have great respect for, and she's a great mum, so be more respectful. As for your Jack, he's been working for me. Nice lad, real credit to his *mother.*'

Tom's eyes narrowed; his lips thinning to a hard line.

'Sniffing around you now, is she? Understandable, now everyone knows Matt Barton bats for the other side. You do know that don't you?'

Dan squared his shoulders ready to grab Tom by the lapels but caught sight of Roger coming around behind him.

'Well, you're welcome to the frigid bitch.'

Tom flinched as Roger slapped a heavy hand on his shoulder.

'That's enough. I won't have this conversation in my pub,' Roger said. 'We have a great deal of respect for your wife, and for that reason, I'd like you to leave.'

Tom gave a half laugh. 'You're joking?'

Dan stood fast, watching the colour drain from Tom's face.

'I'm deadly serious. I suggest you go of your own free will, otherwise, Dan and I will toss a coin to decide who knocks you out first.'

Tom looked to the gaggle in his group for support. He was unlucky. Heads were down, busy studying their phones or examining their drinks, stifling giggles. Humiliation flushed Tom's cheeks. He downed the remains of his drink and placed the glass on the table.

'See ya, boys. I'll be in the Rose and Crown if you want to join me. Never liked this crappy pub, anyway.'

Dan side-stepped to let Sally pass, carrying a bowl of chilli and a sandwich. Dan's jaw collapsed in shock as Sally shoved Tom sideways with her shoulder, sending him sprawling onto his backside. She stood over him and purposefully let the bowl of chilli empty onto Tom's crotch.

'Oh, dear Tom. I'm sorry, how clumsy of me. I must have lost my balance.'

For the second time that day Tom scrambled from his elbows to his feet, chilli sliding down his trousers. The group guffawed in delight, slapping thighs and shaking with laughter. Others raised cameras, snapping frame after frame.

Dan leant forward, retrieving Tom's baseball cap from the floor.

'Not nice being humiliated is it Tom? I'm wondering what headline this lot will produce for tomorrow's tabloids. Something like, *Jungle Explorer who Fathered Seventeen gets a Chilly Reception*. You couldn't make it up.'

Tom snatched his cap from Dan's hand and pulled it on.

'You lot haven't heard the last of this. It's assault. I'll sue.'

A male voice from the assembled group muttered 'prick', as Tom headed to the door leaving a trail of food behind him.

'I wouldn't go to the Red Lion if I were you.' Roger shouted. 'They've a strict rule about bringing unauthorised food onto their premises.'

The press group roared with laughter.

Roger threw Dan a wink.

'Another pint, Dan? On the house, I think. I've been dying to chuck that idiot out for years.'

21

I let myself in as quietly as possible, but Jenny is already up and dressed, car keys in hand.

'Good run?' she says, checking herself in the hall mirror.

She looks drawn, worried. Something's hidden behind her eyes, if only she'd let me in.

'Lovely,' I say, 'just me, the birds, and the elements. Where are you going at this hour?'

Her eyes avoid mine.

'Dentist.'

'It's six thirty in the morning Jen. Has your dentist moved or something, like to Edinburgh?'

Her eyes sweep the floor furtively.

'I've had a row with Robin and I –'

'It's okay,' I say placing my hand on her arm. 'You don't need to elaborate.'

Her shoulders drop and she hovers about to hug me but I step back.

'Don't, I'm stinky and sweaty.'

'Yes, you are,' she says as if seeing me for the first time. 'Laters' she says, closing the door behind her.

Robin's the first to appear in the kitchen, a frown etched on his forehead.

'Have you seen Jenny? She's not upstairs.'

I'm always surprised that a woman as attractive and engaging as Jenny chose a man like Robin. He's tall, with fair hair receding at the temples over a flat broad forehead. He wears his signature corduroy trousers come rain, or summer heat. His long fingers worry his chin, it aggravates me. It shouldn't because he's been incredibly kind, but I always find him strangely annoying.

'Dentist I think.' I can't say I know for definite because I'm sure she was lying. Robin checks the corkboard plastered with appointments, school notes, diary dates and routines.

'There's nothing on the board.'

'Perhaps she forgot.'

Robin stares at the back of his hands.

'Do you think she's okay? I'm worried about her.'

I ought to agree, but this is Robin we're talking about, who can't get through a day without finding something to worry about, it's his norm.

'Yes,' I lie, 'she looked fine to me.'

He heaves a sigh. 'I don't know Grace, something's worrying her. Every time I ask, she gets cross with me. I mean you hear about women going through a midlife crisis…'

His grey eyes settle on mine.

'You girls talk about all sorts of things. You would tell me if something was wrong?'

So, I'm not the only one who thinks Jenny's hiding something. I must say something to make him feel better.

'It might be us. I mean, five extra people is bound to change the dynamic. We won't be in your hair much longer. Can I make you anything? Coffee, tea?'

'Not for me, I'll have one at the surgery, thanks.'

He plucks his keys off the hook, passing George in the doorway who rubs his eyes sleepily. His hair's wet and he's combed it slick against his head. The usual strand of hair stands bolt upright on his double crown. He squints, tucking the arms of his glasses behind his ears.

'Morning Sweetpea.' He rewards me with a hug. 'Egg or pancakes?'

'No thanks,' he says, reaching for Rice Crispies.

Lucy laid the table for breakfast the night before. I make coffee listening to music filtering from Lily's room competing with a gaming device from the boys' room. George is happily slicing a banana into his cereal.

Our bedroom is empty, the bathroom isn't. I'm dismayed to hear a bath running, Melissa will be ages. Resigned to the wait, I go back into the bedroom.

The carrier bag of post retrieved from Darwin House is propped against the side of the wardrobe, and as I've nothing better to do I straighten the duvet and empty the contents onto the bed, separating official stuff like utility bills from the other mail. I wanted to go paperless, and it surprised me that Tom was against it, since he likes to be known as an eco-warrior. Saving the rainforest and all that. The rest is an assortment of coloured envelopes, obviously cards of some sort, but it's no one's birthday and not Christmas so I'm both intrigued and daunted at the same time. The first I open is a card with kittens on the front. Inside it says,

I wanted to tell you how sorry I am that you and your children have had to suffer at the hands of yet another unfaithful man. Yours sincerely Margaret Sullivan.
The next is a typewritten. *I'm sorry for your troubles. Please use the enclosed to treat your children to something nice.* The cheque is made out for two hundred pounds. A lump expands in my throat. Other people's pity is more than I can bear.

Alice wanders in, forcing me to paint on a smile.

'Come here, my lovely, where's my cuddle?' I open my arms and she climbs onto the bed, leaning into me.

'Love you, Mum,' she says, giving me a squeeze.

I rearrange a wispy curl by her ear. 'I love you too, Princess.'

Alice sits up stroking her overgrown fringe from her eyes.

'Why aren't you dressed.'

'Lissy's holding me up,' I tell her, visualising Melissa neck-deep in bubbles thinking she has all the time in the world. 'I can't go out all smelly, can I?'

Alice picks up a cream envelope from the pile.

'It's not your birthday, is it?'

'No, darling, not my birthday they're letters.'

'About Dad?' she says hesitantly, prompting a flashback of his visit the day before.

'You know Daddy has a fan club. And we get lots of letters from the people who like to see him on television.'

'Not this lots,' she says peeking into the bag.

'Not this many,' I correct.

'Okay, see you then,' she says sounding bored, and bounces to her feet.

The moment she's gone, I shove the unopened mail into the corner before Melissa can see it and give me the third degree.

***

The knocking is louder than the whirring of my hairdryer. I switch it off, opening the door to Jenny who's jiggling excitedly in the doorway.

'I've made coffee. You're never going to believe what I've got to tell you. It's made my day,' she says, her hand playing like a violinist's bow into the V of her jumper. A habit I've noticed she's gained of late.

'What's happened?' I'm suspicious yet inquisitive because she's so animated.

'I'm not telling you. I need your full attention. You're going to love this.'

She moves away throwing a *hurry up* over her shoulder.

'Let me get dressed first.' I pull on a pair of cropped jeans and a sleeveless linen top.

Jenny is seated at the kitchen table, two steaming coffees placed on coasters- not instant, fresh ground, marking it as some important event. The aroma's enticing. Jenny's brought iced covered pastry's, one each. I lick my lips and take a seat.

'Called into the farm shop, did we?' I say, pointing at the pastries.

'Couldn't resist,' she says.

Simultaneously, we pick up the lovely buttery treats of icing sugar, cinnamon and plump sultanas, a delicious treat for my taste buds. Jenny's bouncy, revving up to spew out whatever her "must tell" is. Judging by her delight, I'm guessing it's Evelyn up to her old tricks.

'Amazing you can eat so well afterwards.' I tease.

'Afterwards?' she says, licking a flake of pastry from the corner of her mouth.

'The dentist?' Her face is blank, she makes a quick recovery by taking a gulp of coffee. 'You were very cloak and dagger this morning, Jennifer Maxwell. Row with Robin? If I didn't know better, I'd say you're up to no good. With that dentist, is it?'

She laughs a genuine laugh.

'You wouldn't say that if you knew him. Anyway, you'll never guess what.'

I sigh. 'No, I probably won't, so tell me.'

'Well,' she says, leaning forward, her eyes wide, 'Tom.' I groan. 'He was in the Three Doves with a stack of newspaper guys. Something got said, not sure what, but Dan Mayne got involved.' She halts to pick up her pastry but doesn't take a bite.

I roll my eyes and sigh. 'Why does everything have to involve that man?'

'That man,' Jenny says, 'the one who gave Jack a job and…' I wait while she swallows her mouthful, 'came to your rescue.'

'Like he does, or would, with any female he thought he had a chance with. While the cats away,' I say sarcastically.

She throws me a weird look waving a hand to shut me up, bursting to reveal all.

'So, Dan and Tom have a stand-off. Roger, the landlord gets involved and asks Tom to leave. Then,' she picks up her mug then puts it down again, 'then

Sally comes out of the kitchen, knocks Tom off his feet and…' She reaches to the next seat pulling out a tabloid and lays it in front of me. 'She only poured a bowl of hot chilli on his crotch. I hope it was boiling hot. That'll calm his sex drive down,' she shrieks with laughter.

Something stirs in me as I read the headline. CELEBRITY JUNGLE FATHER OF 17 GETS A CHILLI HOMECOMING.

'Isn't it a scream?' I'd love to have been there,' she says rocking back in her chair.

I'm not laughing. I swallow the mush in my mouth too soon and it wedges in my gullet. Pressing my palms into the table I stand. Jenny's laughter falters.

'What?' she says, folding her arms across her chest, 'don't you think it's brilliant?'

My words escape in a growl.

'As a good friend Jenny, I can't believe you actually thought I'd enjoy Tom's humiliation at the hands of Dan Mayne, or anyone else. Don't you realise whatever happens to Tom reflects on me and the children. It's yet another bit of humiliation heaped on them. Ridiculed for the dad who once came home like a conquering hero. Who they believed in. What Tom did or didn't do is not for the Steadcoat Mafia to meddle in. You actually thought I'd join in the name-calling of my husband and enjoy it?' I tug at the back of my hair. 'Can't you see how shaming it is for me – for us. Whenever they involve Tom, be it in fame or demise, it reflects on us, and I have to protect my kids from the pain of it.'

My voice hitches. I push away my half eaten treat and storm out. Jenny doesn't come after me. I've no idea where I'm going but cross the road walking with purpose. I've only gone a short distance when I hear the hiss of hydraulics. The blue Hopper bus linking the villages pulls in, I climb aboard, pay for my destination and take a seat midway down. There are only three other passengers, thankfully I don't know any of them. I stare blankly from the window trying to absorb another nightmarish situation.

We're almost at the roundabout where the bus will take the first exit and carry on its journey. I ping the bell and get off, standing on the grass verge I become momentarily distracted by a sparrowhawk riding the thermals.

'As free as a bird,' I say, crossing the road to make my way along the footpath. It's overgrown in parts and nettles sting my ankles. I limp along in search of a Dock-leaf to rub on the hives. I'm relieved to reach the farm track which forks in two directions. If I keep to the main one, I'll exit close to the entrance to Darwin House. If I take other, it takes me up the hill, the route I took with Jenny. I chose the first path. If there are reporters lurking, so what? I'm not hiding anymore. I've sat around wallowing in self-pity for too long. Everyone, including my children, are wrapping me up in cotton wool that feels like a straitjacket.

The gateway is deserted. Calmly, I make my way down the drive, wishing I'd brought a cardigan. The summer sun is weakening and a chilly breeze stirs the air. The house looks as unwelcoming as always, with its cold grey facade. Some houses look like they're smiling and happy, with upper windows like eyes. A porch or a front door, a nose and mouth. The side windows I imagine as rosy cheeks, but not this one. Darwin House glares back, reminding me of my mother's sour disdain.

The bunch of keys jangle in my hand. I select one, hesitating as I turn it and push the door, barely opening it. Dank air seeps through the crack and settles on my skin. Why am I doing this to myself? I tug it shut feeling cowardly. I can't bear to enter on my own, no matter how strong I feel making promises to myself to take control. The very thought of going in makes me nauseous.

My car is parked in the same spot from that day. The day my world imploded. The day I read the newsagents board, and listened to Evelyn's pitying, only to discover Matt with a reporter in our yard.

The smooth leather of the steering wheel is a comfort – independence. It feels good to be behind the wheel again, and I realise with a jolt I now make my own rules. At the end of the drive I turn left, instead of right, purely because I can. Who cares if it's an extra couple of miles to get back to Jenny's. I don't have anyone to answer to anyone, or do I? I think of the letters waiting to be opened back in my room. It throws me, the kindness of people who think they're helping. Tom's face while he stood on the driveway, broken and tearful. It makes me realise something I hadn't thought of before, that Tom needed us, because he wasn't anyone without us. We were his achievements, his trophies, the things that defined him with his successful career. In his mind, a brilliant husband and father who was raised by a bully to believe he wasn't good enough. Self-absorbed people only think about what makes them feel good. They don't have respect or regard for anyone. It's not in their makeup and his control eventually wore me down.

Once, my life was full of friends, a social life, with or without my children. Moving to Steadcoat hadn't been about country life as Tom had insisted. It was about control. He had manoeuvred me, taken me away from my friends, placing me at a purposeful distance away from where I could make new ones and enjoy life, while he was away working. He couldn't allow me a life without him. He had to be the centre of it. If I planned to go anywhere and he was home he'd pop out on some lame excuse, only returning after it was far too late for me to go. I'd accepted his flimsy apologies, until recently I did everything robotically, as requested. I wore my hair the way he liked it, dressed mumsy. Was that to keep male predators at bay, so no one would compliment me, and I'd be kept in my place?

His own ego eventually needed more feeding, horny sex, whatever. He took advantage of the situation. Was he all nudge, nudge, wink, wink with the film crew? Look at me, what a stud.

If the papers were to be believed it's seven years since he fathered his first jungle child. To Tom it was something that substantiated his maleness, his fertility, and for all of my swollen resentment I'd still loved him. He'd been my world until he made it harder and harder, and I ceased to be me.

My breath catches in my lungs, I feel like I'm drowning, gasping like a dying fish. I can't be part of his loss or his grief. I can't let him back into my heart, my life. I expect he'd agree to moving house, or anything I requested, in order to have his place in this world rebuilt. How easy it would be to forgive him. I always do. Always, but not this time.

22

I'd been enjoying the clarity of my thoughts until I turn onto Jenny's drive and spot Melissa. She doesn't look up. Her knees are raised, and she's hunched against the fence dissecting a leaf – something she often did when little, trying to get the perfect leaf skeleton. Her face is blotchy post crying and I prepare my icy spine for more bad news.

'What are you doing sitting out here, has something happened?' Melissa shrugs, her face crumples in misery.

'I hate it here.'

Her bottom lip trembles. I open my arms and she falls into them with a sob. I rock her gently, stroking her hair.

'No one wants us here. I had a row with Lily.'

'Oh, I see,' I say.

'No, you don't see,' she snaps, stepping away. 'She's such a bitch.'

'Darling, that's—'

'Don't you dare say that's not nice. You didn't hear her.'

She turns her back to me. I can't let her walk away without knowing what's going on.

'Why don't you tell me,' I say in a soothing voice.

Melissa's hands fly to her hips, challenging me not to interrupt. I lean against the car, waiting.

'She was on the phone, talking to her posh private school friends.' I nod. 'She said how she couldn't have anyone on a sleepover because they still had the jungle perv's squatters staying.' Tears river down her cheeks. 'I hate it here. When can we go home? I don't care if it is miles from anywhere, I want it to be us again.'

My shoulders squeeze in ugly shame. I've been so self-absorbed, so cosseted, that I failed to notice my children's misery. I've let them down. They're hurting too. I can hardly blame Lily, and Jack and Todd aren't natural friends. They share a bedroom but skirt around each other and George is still wetting the bed, and Alice? She's living in la-la land.

'Tell you what,' I say, sweeping away her tears with my thumbs. 'Let's get in the car. I'm not ready to go indoors yet either.'

The safe space of the car brightens Melissa's mood, she's singing along to the odd song on her favourite radio station. We talk a little and somehow for the second time today, I'm approaching Darwin house.

'Oh, look at your lovely flower beds, they're all dead and weedy.'

I sigh saddened at the parched flowerbeds.

'It's been hot and they haven't been watered.' We both look at the front door. 'Do you want to go in?'

'Of course,' she says cheerfully, walking ahead.

Only an hour ago I had the key in the door but couldn't go in. Melissa senses my hesitation and takes the keys from me. The door is stubborn. She gives it a hefty shove with her shoulder. The first thing to hit me is the smell.

'Yuk, what a stink!' Melissa says, pinching her nostrils. I'm on the threshold. 'No Mum, stop,' she says staring at her feet.

The doormat is spongy. Water pools and squelches into our sandals. Recent post floats along the hallway. I give her a gentle nudge and we move forward, rubbing the tops of our arms for warmth. The smell is mushroomy, rotting, dank. We paddle forward, the sound of running water drawing us in.

'Oh Christ. Lissy.'

Water is pouring out from a hole in the ceiling, down the architraves of the door to the rubble and detritus of wood and plaster. We stare up to the clear view of the bathroom. The source of the flood visible, as water cascades from the sink. I feel like I've been whacked behind the knees with a cricket bat. Melissa grabs my arm as my legs buckle.

'Lean on me Mum, It'll be okay, we can fix this.'

Her voice has a quaky confidence and I realise that I'm allowing myself to be cared for again. I take her hand.

'It's okay, love. A shock, that's all, but it's only water.' She looks doubtful, sidesteps me, and climbs the stairs. 'Lissy no, be careful, the rest might collapse.'

'It feels safe if I keep near the wall,' she says, suddenly appearing through the hole and edging a path to the sink. 'There's a cloth blocking the plughole and the tap's still running.'

There's a loud gurgling from the S-bend. Melissa rings out the cloth and the stream of water slows. I experience a mental flashback of me cleaning. Did I turn the tap off when Jenny called me, or was it when I'd taken the call from Roderick? I can't remember. Either way, the disaster is of my making and any thoughts of returning home for now are firmly on hold.

The house is old. The floors are uneven causing the water to be deeper in places. We wade up to our ankles, making waves that slosh against the walls. A glance into Tom's study tells me he's been here because his computer's missing and of the photographs, only the broken glass and frames remain as witness to my outburst. The hunting club, spear and drum are nowhere to be seen. He'll know we found his hiding place. In fact, I may have the only originals of his true finances.

'Mum, careful, it's deeper here and the floor's slippery,' Melissa flinches and screams.

'What?' I say, worrying it's a rat or something.

She clasps her palms over her mouth and giggles.

'Honest, Mum, I'd have sworn it was a snake,' she points to a buoyant runner bean, 'It's like one big stew.'

Looking at it like that, it sure did. The vegetable basket's collapsed. Carrots bob on the surface along with onions, paper, an odd sock. The stench is worse closer to the freezer. The electrics have shorted. I tug at the door, the weight of the water making it harder. I retch and clasp my palm over my mouth and nose. Everything is a liquefied putrid sludge. I dread looking in the larder.

Melissa hooks an arm through mine.

'And to think we wiped our feet on the way in,' she says grinning. 'Come on, Mum, there must be a funny side.'

She raises her hands and shoulders in a '*what?*' gesture. It breaks the tension. I ease away and rally into action.

'Let's not going make a drama out of a catastrophe,' as they say in the adverts. 'Right, let's clear up – organise a builder, get things fixed, sell the damn place, and find ourselves a new home. The sooner the better.'

'You mean we haven't got to move back here?' she says, eyes sparkling.

'No. We won't. We'll find something to rent and sell this ghastly place.'

'Yay to that,' Melissa throws me a high five.

I rack my brains about what to do next.

'We might have to take a sledgehammer to the back door to let the water out but let's try an alternative first. If I push from this side and you pull from the other, it might work. Our feet are already wet, but we'd be better off in Wellington boots, at least they'll be dry.'

The back door opens after considerable effort. The water subsides. We jam the door back with Jack's football kit bag. I avoid looking at the cat flap as the water level sinks and the destruction reveals itself. I hadn't been quick enough to lift the wicker laundry bin so whatever was inside soaked up the same stagnant smelling water. We both set to work. I can't believe my girl, she's incredible, wielding the yard broom and shovelling detritus into bin liners. What came from upstairs has reduced to drips.

My address book is in a drawer unscathed by the flood. Pete the plumber's number is there. I've used him before for minor jobs. He tells me he'll get to us as quick as he can.

Melissa has her head half covered with a tea towel knotted gangster style, cleaning out the fridge.

'Good job?' I say.

'We'll never get rid of the smell even with all the windows open.'

I wrinkle my nose, 'It is bad.'

'Gross. Even bleach won't kill that stink.'

Cautiously, I unplug the fridge freezer and between us we manhandle it outside. Melissa keeps up a running commentary. I appreciate it's to take my mind off the situation.

We never spend time together without the others around. Out of bad comes good. I haven't appreciated her inner strength. I'm proud of how amazing she is, putting on a brave face and cracking jokes. It reminds me of how Hannah had done the same when she knew she was dying. God how I missed her. If you're up there, Hannah and Dad, please whisper in someone's ear and make our luck change for the better.

With Jenny's nagging, I had transferred exactly half the money from Tom's accounts into a single one in my name only. It was so easy. I could have cleared him out, but still I wanted to be fair. Like it or loathe it, this house was one of my few assets, and although I was desperate to be rid of the place; I would have to put it right if I was going to sell it.

Later, it occurred to me that when Jenny and I left that day, Tom's study and its contents were here, so he had come here after we'd left and he could have turned off the tap and stopped the ceiling collapsing. I bet he laughed. A payback for my rejection. The narcissist in him had to have the last word to assuage the loss of me and his career. Anything remotely that remained of fond memories, I swept away with the dirty water today. There's nothing more he can do to us.

Pete arrives with a generator and sets up blowers to dry the place out. His brother, known as Chas the Chippie, is upstairs checking out the damage.

'You need a new boiler for a start,' Pete says. 'They stopped making parts for these antiques years back. I'm sorry, Mrs L, but it's not a minor job.'

'Oh dear,' I say dejectedly.

'None of your white goods have survived, and the cabinets need replacing. Doors, architraves, the lot. Pretty expensive. Word to the wise,' he says, tapping his nose with his pencil, 'I'd say you were on holiday, for the insurance.' He flashes a wink. 'The quarry tiles might survive, but that lot—' He nods towards the aged oak cupboards that I waxed with loving care, now crudely warped. We stare at a dark plimsol line several inches above floor level, 'sorry, but there's no saving those.'

I draw in a deep breath. I can't dwell. I must move on and take responsibility.

'Can you give me a rough idea of the cost, and when you can start?'

'I'll get you a price by tomorrow after the electrician's been to see what needs fixing and what can't. Got kids, haven't you? Three?'

'Four. Please don't ask me about Tom or anything else, I might cry.'

His brows squeeze in sympathy.

'I'm sorry, I can't make you tea or anything.'

'I have a flask, so no worries. You were lucky we were local. Don't worry, we'll soon get it sorted. I'll get my boy to help too. But you best get on to the insurance. They can be tricky devils if they don't see it when it's bad. Me and the missus are sorry for what you and the kids have been through.'

I nod a gratitude and move away to take advantage of a moment to myself. Melissa's in her bedroom changing into fresh clothes while I'm full of pent-up frustration. The cream and brown plastic message machine arouses the demons inside me. It represents so much of the bad that's happened.

Outside in the shed, I pick up a club hammer, bringing it down in a rain of blows on the plastic casing until it's a mess of plastic fragments and wires. The little tapes, although wiped clean, I set on fire. I'm not leaving anything around that can be turned into yet another headline.

Melissa's at the kitchen sink, her back to me washing something. I peek over her shoulder, it's Charlie's bowl.

'Come on love, that's enough for today,' I say, fearing she'll get emotional, and that I'll join in.

'I want to wash this so it's nice again. I know Charlie died. I hope it was quick, and he didn't suffer. But I couldn't bear to chuck his bowl away.'

My eyes sting. 'Oh darling. How did you find out?' I say, moving closer in case she needs a hug.

'I overheard Uncle Robin talking to Auntie Jen,' she shrugs, and I let my hands slide down her arms. 'I'm okay, Mum,' she says, turning to reveal wet lashes.

'Oh darling, I'm sorry.'

'I've had time to get over it now and he was old in cat years. Uncle Robin said it was a blessing that Charlie went when we weren't here. I suppose he's right.'

I lean forward, kissing the top of her head.

'I'm sorry, but what with everything, I couldn't tell you.'

'It's okay, you had enough problems, without me and the cat.' She plucks a tea towel from the drawer. 'Perhaps one day we'll get a kitten and call it Charlie, Mark 2.'

'Or Charlotte?'

'Possibly, and Mum – can we not tell the others. He was really my cat, Jack never played with him like I did, and no one's even mentioned him since we left.'

'Deal, and I think it's time we got out of here. Let's get home, ring some estate agents. Everyone will wonder where we are.'

We're both quiet on the journey home. Somethings shifted, not only the dynamic between myself and my daughter, but that no matter what Tom throws at me, I'm stronger for it. I think in an odd way, he's done me a favour.

23

Jenny and Robin are safely on the train to London. Robin was all smiles, and full of joie de vivre, but Jenny had worn a gallows-like expression. I wasn't surprised, the previous evening I'd heard muffled voices, sharp retorts and the sound of drawers slamming above me. I tried to ignore it as I worked on researching costs and availability of stone, wood, and shrubs for our garden makeover. We have until Monday afternoon to construct Jenny's birthday garden. It will be a great distraction for everyone, and I hope that the four eldest-Todd, Lily, Jack, and Melissa, might bond and make the rest of our stay a happy one. A team strategy might do it.

George is in on the surprise, but not Alice. She wouldn't have been able to resist the temptation to drop clues. I waited until Jenny had left before we shared our secret.

The plan is laid across the kitchen table and I've created a mood board comprising of old seed catalogues and magazines. I'm aiming for a mix of textures, colour, and trelliswork to mitigate bare brickwork with hues of blue and silver grasses along with a bark screen that will block out the ugly view. Azaleas and Hostas,

Dwarf Acers in lime green and rust. I want to create a cottage garden corner, where Jenny can sip her coffee.

Jack mentioned our plans to Dan, who offered an old sundial from a derelict cottage on his estate. I could hardly say no when a farmhand kindly dropped it off and said it would make a pleasant feature.

I prayed that the trip away and the revamped setting will bring back the old Jen, who has been drinking more than is healthy. I could have killed Alice when she asked within Robin's hearing why Auntie Jenny looked like she'd been crying all the time.

Jenny hadn't much in the way of gardening tools but that didn't matter. I had plenty at Darwin House and I'd planned to pop in today to see how the work was progressing. From Tuesday, I would embark on "Operation: Find a home" and see how soon I could instruct an estate agent. There's something else of great importance on my list, the need to drop into Barton's Farm. I need to see Matt and apologise for what he'd been so publicly dragged into after the tabloid article.

Entering the bedroom I swear under my breath, stooping to pick up a white blouse I'd ironed for Melissa a few hours earlier, now discarded on the floor.

'Why do I bother?' I say out loud. 'I only wasted fifteen minutes of my life ironing it. "But it didn't go with my jeans",' I say in a squeaky voice, imitating Melissa. 'No, never mind my darling daughter, I've nothing better to do.' The discarded hanger is on Melissa's unmade bed. 'Why don't I hang it up for you?'

I'm unaware that Alice has entered the room.

'Mum, who are you talking to, is it the ceiling peoples again?'

'Goodness Alice, you made me jump. No poppet, not the ceilings people, I was moaning about your untidy sister. Are you ready to go to play scheme?'

'Yes,' she says, clambering on the bed. 'George doesn't want to go. He says he'd rather watch the repeats of *Bake-off*.'

'Did he now? We'll see about that.'

I think it's sweet that cookery programmes fascinate George. I tear him away from the TV and drop him and Alice off with packed lunches to the half-term play scheme. Alice is smitten, George not so, but he never causes any fuss.

24

Approaching Barton's farm, my stomach muscles tense in my pelvis, as I wonder what sort of reception I'll get. I'm hoping Matt will be pleased to see me, but I can't blame him if that's not the case.

There are several cars in front of the farm shop. I whistle out a breath of relief that I don't recognise them. The last thing I need is a nosy, or sympathetic villager to corner me. There's a suitable space next to a battered Volvo estate car. I switch off my engine and clamber out, my eyes blinking shut when I hear my name. I can't hide the groan that escapes my lips. It's Dan ruddy Mayne. He's walking towards me smiling, balancing a triple tray of eggs and dressed in the uniform of the men in the area — flat cap and checked shirt, with sleeves rolled up to the elbow that reveal his tanned muscular arms. I try not to focus on his bare flesh as something flits through my head unasked — a memory of intimacy, skin on skin and I wonder if I'll ever feel that again.

'I heard that,' he says, grinning. 'Finding it tough going? Or is it only me who makes you groan?'

I raise my chin. 'I was hoping to avoid anyone I knew, and yes, can you blame me? I'm gawped at everywhere. People are so nosy; they think because it's in the media they can ask the most personal questions.'

His face softens.

'I have to admit the small-minded in the village enjoy a good scandal. I've been the subject on many an occasion.'

'I bet you have,' I say cheekily, remembering what Jenny said he'd called Tom.

'Whoa, I know that look.'

He hesitates, pretending he's affronted.

'What look?' I say a little too flirtatiously. Immediately colouring at my forwardness, I look away, slipping the strap of my bag onto my shoulder.

'The one that says, I bet he deserved it. Well, I didn't. You don't know me. Well not yet. We got off to a poor start.'

I smile up at him.

'You're right, I don't know you. But I suspect you're trouble and that's the last thing I need.'

'Never trust first impressions, you could be wrong. Anyway, bugger Evelyn and her mob. She'll get her comeuppance, as will Tom. You should rise above it. You're much too bright a lady to be aggravated by such fools.'

He indicates to the farmhouse with a flick of his head.

'I think someone else has stolen the gossip limelight.'

We both glance towards the milking parlour.

'Oh, don't, it's my fault. Matt came to my aid and now his private life has been jettisoned into the public domain.'

I struggle to cloak my emotions, staring at Dan's laced brogues, that shift towards me. I jump as his free hand cups my elbow, the trays of eggs wobbling precariously.

'At least you picked the farmer not the gamekeeper.'

'Pardon?'

'D.H Laurence. Lady Chatterley's Lover?'

'Of course,' I say, the corners of my mouth widening.

'Good, that's better,' he says, taking his hand away. 'Look, don't let the buggers get you down. I mean, if you want to raise two fingers, and I'm sure you do, then let me buy you dinner. We'll have all the sad and lonely of Steadcoate on Twitter, Facebook, or whatever it is they do.'

I smile, I can't help it and look straight into his deep blue eyes, pressing my lips together and glancing away, deciding we've considered each other a little longer than is wise. My shoe locates a pebble, I shift my attention rolling it back and forth under the sole of my shoe. I used to be great at delivering one-liners, but anything witty escapes me nowadays. Another thing to blame Tom for.

'Thanks for the offer, but I have higher priorities than getting one back on gossips. By the way, thank you for taking Tom to task, after ... well, you know... at the pub.'

His smile shrank away.

'We don't have to speak about that. No one should be put through what you have. I've experienced humiliation myself and it's not nice.'

He pauses, placing the eggs on the bonnet of his car, his arm brushing my elbow. I step sideways, disturbed by the closeness of him. His hand drops and I miss its comfort.

The sound of beep, beep, click, makes us both turn as a nearby vehicle unlocks and a rangy man in his sixties approaches. I don't know him, but he and Dan exchange a greeting.

'I must go,' I say, 'I've a lot to do today, and thanks again.'

'My pleasure, and I mean it. If you ever change your mind, fancy a bit of male company. I truly am a nice guy – kind to animals and women in distress, despite what the gossips say. 'Remember, it's a small village. Everyone gets their turn. Even lizard-tongued Evelyn will get caught out one day.'

He steps to the back of his car, opening the tailgate and retrieving the trays of eggs from the bonnet to the boot. I notice his long, tanned fingers as they pull up the tailgate.

'And if you're looking for Matt, he's in the dairy. I saw him go in while we were talking.'

I nod my thanks as Dan climbs into his car and starts the engine. I stand there like an idiot, waiting for him to reverse and wave goodbye. He does and I pick my way towards the farmyard, dodging cakes of khaki green cowpats, disturbing the ugly flies clustering on their surface. The sweet scent makes my nose wrinkle as I wonder what I can say to Matt and realise there's nothing that will put this right. The damage is already done.

Matt's sweeping a cloudy mix of water and disinfectant into a central drain as I enter the dairy.

'Hi. How are you?' I say cheerily. He straightens leaning on the broom, his cheeks patch with colour. The fact that his eyes are downcast confirms his discomfort, but I'm here now so I need to make the best of it.

'Smells nice,' I say. He glances my way out of the corner of his eye. *Why did I think this was a good idea?*

'What is it you want Grace? I'm busy.'

His voice is tight, measured. I blanch with embarrassment, realising I have alienated a good friend.

'I'm sorry. I shouldn't have come,' I say turning to leave.

'Wait, please,' he says, 'that was rude of me.'

My shoulders droop as I face him. He scratches the back of his head, eyes focused somewhere beyond the window.

'Please don't apologise, I couldn't bear it. You've every right to be upset after what Tom did. We both know he's behind the press digging into your past.'

We stand facing each other, our eyes flitting anywhere but on each other's faces.

'If you hadn't helped me that day, you'd never have had your private life raked over.'

There's a beat of silence, his eyes sweeping to mine then away.

'Don't blame yourself, Grace. It wasn't my greatest hour as I'm sure you can imagine. I hoped I'd escaped all that rubbish the rags printed about me years ago, but obviously not. There's always money in other people's misery. But then, you know that.'

'But if you hadn't come to my rescue, they wouldn't have been able to—'

'Out me.' He coughs out a laugh. 'I don't blame you. In a way it's time – time to re-evaluate my life. Smuggling in friends, afraid someone will guess, is no way to live, as if being gay is a crime.' This time his laugh holds humour. 'You've done me a favour. I've spent too much time trying to keep "my gender preference" he makes inverted commas with his fingers, 'under wraps.' It's time I came out of the cowshed.' He smirks. 'Sounds better than the *closet*, doesn't it?'

A gentle breath eases its way through my lips, and his smiling eyes meet mine.

'At least it stopped that awful Greenway woman trying to match-make me with every single female.'

'God, no.' I stifle a giggle. 'Well, that's a bonus I suppose. Look Matt, your sexuality makes no difference to me. I like the person not the label, and I hope you can forgive me for getting you dragged into my mess.'

He's smiling and shaking slowly from side to side. 'Grace, stop apologising. We're both victims here and I'd do the same again if it were needed. I didn't deserve it–you didn't deserve it, and your children certainly didn't deserve it.'

I glance down at my hands, humbled by his kindness.

'But what about your family—do they know?'

'No, thankfully. They were never great TV watchers, and Dad only read *The Times*. They missed it altogether. Twelve years ago, it was a dynamic front page for the local rag in Cranleigh, and even *The Sun* ran the story. I was worried my parents would get to hear, but thankfully not. Neither are alive now, and my sole sibling Alistair lives in Auckland, with his wife and two kids. If it was Tom, he's done me a favour. No more living a lie. I moved away from Surrey to escape the bigotry. No doubt I'll get the odd comment at the rugby club, you know, the jokes about soap, and showers, but I can take it. Those who have a problem, and I suspect I already know who they are, can get on with it. It was only because we had a vicar on the board of governors who insisted it was detrimental to the morals of the college and blew out it out of proportion.'

He drops his weight to one hip, hooking his thumb in the pocket of his work coat.

'But what about you? What are your plans? It's okay for me, I'm on my own, but you have children.'

We stroll out of the dairy and across the yard to my car.

'My lot are quite resilient, 'I say. 'The two eldest took it the worst– kids at school, or their bloody parents. They will be fine once we have sold that lumbering-great house and its horrid memories. The kids are enjoying a better life being closer to the village. They need their friends and a healthy childhood full of playdates, clubs, and sleepovers. It'll make mine easier too. I might even get a job, who knows?'

Matt touches my shoulder.

'I heard about the flood. I'm sorry, as if you haven't got enough on your plate.'

I shrug. 'It was a shock at first but it's all under control now. I'm going there next to see how the builders are progressing. The house will fetch a better price once the repairs and modernisation are complete.'

We turn at the unexpected roar of a motorbike as it sweeps around the bend by the farm entrance. The rider slaloms his body across the machine following the camber of the road as it curves and climbs the hill.

'Daft bugger, he'll end up in a ditch if he's not careful.'

'Or kill some innocent crossing the road,' I glance at my watch, realising the day is getting ahead of me. 'Well, I'd better be off,' I say. 'We're remodelling Jenny's garden while she and Robin are in London. It's a surprise.'

'Is she okay? It's not a hospital visit, is it?' he says with a frown. 'Round here, that's what most folks go to London for, and I didn't think she looked too well when I saw her last. When poor Ka—'

'Oh no, nothing like that. It's a birthday treat. She and Robin are taking in a show and staying in a lovely hotel. It will do them good to have some time on their own together.'

We stand by the open door of my car, and I'm surprised when Matt locks eyes with me and pulls me close.

'Come here,' he says warmly. 'We both deserve a hug, and this time, no one can accuse either of us of anything untoward.'

He wraps his arms around me. It's a comfortable hug, a reassuring one, better than the day my world fell apart. The smell of him is familiar now. A hint of amber on his jaw, the sweet smell of hay and the faint tinge of disinfectant. His hands slip from my shoulders, settling on the tops of my arms. He flexes his elbows, holding me at arm's length.

'Grace, you're such a lovely lady, you deserve better. I hope you find happiness with someone who'll treat you right. God knows, you deserve it.'

'I'm sure there's someone for both of us, Matt,' I say, swallowing the lump of emotion his brief speech has instigated.

'Perhaps we need to wise up, be braver? Thanks for stopping by Grace. It's appreciated.'

Driving away I catch myself thinking, what a waste of a good guy. But that's wrong. It's not a waste of anything. Matt deserves to be with another equally good man who'll appreciate him. It's a cliché to say there's someone for everyone, that's what people keep telling me, as if it's a sort of prize. They don't understand how in a way I've won too. I've got the chance to be me.

A realisation hits me, shocked, I pull myself up. Half an hour ago I was flirting with Dan Mayne. What on earth came over me?

25

The makeover team- Jack, Todd, Melissa, Lily, and me are busy working, while George and Alice chase each other with water guns. The crescent shaped bed surrounding the sundial feature is quite perfect and should be a glory of colour once everything's bedded in. Jack and Todd are busy planting red and green acers–two, a dwarf variety that will give ground cover, and two taller for shade and depth. Todd has fixed the crisscrossed trellis to the uninspiring brick wall where we have planted climbers in large tubs. By next summer it will be a wall of colour. Melissa approaches linking her arm through mine.

'I can't wait to see Aunty Jenny's face; she's going to love it.'

'I hope so. I know she won't mind but it is a bit of a cheek.'

Melissa shakes her head.

'She won't be cross with you. Who wouldn't like those,' she says pointing to the tubs of yellow petunias.'

While we admire our work Lily appears balancing a tray with a jug of juice and beakers and sets it on the patio table, then approaches me with her arms wide open and envelops me.

'Thanks Auntie Grace. This will cheer mum up. She's been a bit down lately.'

The catch in her voice isn't lost to me.

'Yeah, nice one,' Todd adds, leaning on his spade and wiping his sweaty brow on his forearm.

'We all worked very hard,' I say. My two youngest stop their game joining us to get a drink.

'It looks pretty,' Alice says, holding out her beaker for Jack to fill. 'I hope it stops Auntie Jenny crying all the time.'

Sometimes I could murder that child. I open my mouth to speak, my eyebrows shooting practically to my hairline, but with Jack's quick thinking he changes the subject.

'So, what's next Mum?'

'The Banner,' George says, jumping up and down, his glasses bouncing on the bridge of his nose.

'That's right, George. Can you organise that in the morning, girls?' Lily and Melissa nod. 'Good. The little ones want to help with that.'

'We can paint butterflies on it,' says George.

'Great idea. Right,' I say, aware of my rumbling tummy. 'Hands washed, change of clothes and let's go find somewhere for dinner. Any preferences?'

'The Three Doves do great ribs,' offers Todd.

'Erm, let's go somewhere different for a change,' I say, trying not to grimace at the mention of the Three Doves, where chilli-gate took place.

'Or the Mucky Ducks at Camborne, Todd offers. 'It's a bit of a drive but they have a bouncy castle that the kids will enjoy.'

My inner voice cheers. A place that Tom would never go to because it's "Child friendly".

'Perfect Todd. Right let's get moving.'

It's past nine when we get back to Jenny's house. Everyone's exhausted from their efforts and trundle off to bed without argument. It's been a lovely day ending with an enjoyable meal without one single argument. Everybody got on. Alice kept her foot out of her mouth throughout the journey *and* the meal. God that child will be the death of me. Will she ever learn what not to say? I massage my forehead with my fingertips, hoping the night away and that the garden makeover will lift Jen's spirits; be the beginning of peace in this household and whatever's bothering her, be it the menopause or their marriage. I hope they return a happier couple.

***

The kids hover around the house waiting for the London train to come in. George is on lookout at the gate. He puffs into the kitchen.

'They're coming. Quick!'

'Places everybody,' I say, and we pile outside. Lily and Melissa spread out so that the banner stretches taut between them. It had been George's mission to find two stout sticks of the same length to support it, it reads *Happy Birthday xxx* with an arrow pointing to the words *Surprise this way*.

I get my camera ready to capture the moment, lowering it as Robin and Jenny approach. Neither are smiling. The children yell, *welcome home.*

Alice steps forward, 'Surprise! we made you a gar-' Jack puts his hand over her mouth, only releasing it for her to join in the Happy Birthday song.

I pick up on the body language immediately. A glance passes between Jenny and Robin that holds no warmth and the knot in my stomach tells me all is far from hunky-dory. They craft a smile as their son and daughter lead them through the back gate. We follow and I try to relax as I hear cheers and clapping. Jenny's eyes are full of tears as she hugs her children.

'What a fabulous surprise,' Robin says, 'now we have the best garden in Steadcoate.'

'It was Aunty Grace's idea,' Todd says throwing me a grateful smile.

'Nonsense you did most of the work. Right, photo time,' I say, a little over cheerfully, expecting Jenny to glance my way. She doesn't. The children gather round. Robin joins the group laying a stiff arm around Jenny's shoulders, and I didn't imagine Jenny taking a sidestep causing Robin's arm to fall to his side. Both produce plastic smiles for the camera, leaving me wondering what's happened over the course of the weekend. Jenny and Robin need some room to breathe. Something is going on that Jen doesn't want me to know. But what?'

26

Jenny has the top off a wine bottle before I can take off my shoes. We disperse the combined total of our children around Jenny's Tardis of a house to talk uninterrupted.

'I'm going back to London tomorrow for lunch with some of the old crowd, from KIT PR. If I'm lucky, there might be something for me work wise. I need a project—a distraction, even if its copywriting. My grey matter needs some stimuli,' she says, twirling the stem of her glass between two fingers.

'Swap you,' I say. My hand hovering between kettle and wine bottle. 'Mine's on overload, what with the flood.'

'You can stay here as long as you like. You know that.'

'No Jen, I can't. We both know it. The kids are falling out. School starts again in a couple of weeks. Jack has his A levels. We all need some stability.'

'Fair enough, but I'm not pushing you out. Anyway, you'll have the house to yourself in a few days. We're taking the kids to Cornwall. Not that I'm looking forward to it. If it rains, I'm stuffed. Six hours in the car with Robin and—'

The sentence hangs mid-air.

'Do you both good to get away? All that fresh air, and open beaches.'

'But no spare room to escape to.' Her gaze settles mid-stare, and she shudders. *Can things be that bad between her and Robin?* Jenny lifts her feet and hugs her knees. 'Don't look at me like that. You must admit, after zillions of years of marriage, the sex is a bit like cleaning your teeth. Trouble is, Robin still thinks it's something to do twice daily, it's bloody tedious.'

I sip my wine, trying to remember if Tom had been like that *ever*. Then blink it away, it's too painful.

Jenny's interest lies more with opening another bottle than continuing our conversation. Our normal easy chatter is stilted. I study her face; she's lost in her own thoughts, but her lips are moving in private conversation. I sigh, saddened by her remoteness.

Robin's absent from the dinner table again tonight. Jenny fills the silence with chat about the proposed caravan park and how Evelyn's started a petition, but she didn't think she had a hope in hell as local shops would benefit from the trade. Dan's mentioned as the proposed site backs onto his land.

Jenny is infamous at shoehorning intimate secrets from almost anyone, but the other way around it's impossible to drag anything out of her if she doesn't want to. Whatever the problem, I hope she'll tell me in her own time. She's been my best friend since the day we moved to Steadcoate.

I zone in and out of the conversation with a modicum of guilt that I haven't shared everything myself. I'd not mentioned my encounter with Dan, or that he'd asked me out to dinner. A flush touches my cheeks at how forward I was. The man certainly has charisma, and it was probably the conversation about Matt that made me let my guard down. It *had* only been a polite exchange and Dan probably only asked me out of pity and who wants to go on a pity date? Dan does come over as kind and generous. But the fact that he brazenly asked me out when he's married speaks volumes. I should be ashamed of myself, poor Kate, I bet she wouldn't be happy if she knew that her husband went around asking women out on dates.

Jenny bends and rubs her toes. 'God, my feet ache. I've walked miles looking for that top Lily wants for her birthday, can't find it anywhere, not even on the ruddy internet.'

'What's it like?'

'The same as her blue one, that I accidentally shrank. Now she wants it in cream, for her party. She loved that top and I promised her, that and new boots. Boots were easy—the top's a nightmare. I took the shrunk one around at least six stores. You'd think a fourteen-year-old wouldn't get sentimental about clothes.'

'Where is it? Show me.'

'The top?' I nod.

'You won't find it anywhere. Robin's mum brought it for her in Milan.' Jenny pulls out a blue carrier bag. I turn the skimpy top inside out laying it flat across my lap.

'This is simple to make, and the material will be easy to find. I'll make her an identical one. You cut out the designer label and it sew it in the new one. She'll never know the difference.'

Jenny tears up.

'What would I do without you?' She rushes to her feet, almost suffocating me in a hug. 'Luv ya.'

'Love you, too. And it's more like—what would I do without you? I'll sort this tomorrow, after I've met Pete the plumber.'

'Wish life were that easy,' Jenny says, her smile fading.

I seize the opportunity.

'Jen what the hell's wrong? I know something's bothering you.'

Her jaw clenches.

'God. I was only thinking out loud. Stop being melodramatic. Perhaps I have a secret. A lover,' she says in a fake French accent.

'No way. That you couldn't keep to yourself.'

'Am I that readable?'

'You are to me.'

'Then I'd better watch out. And on that note, I'm off to bed.'

I sit for a while pondering our conversation, deciding none of it sits right, but short of torture what can I do?

***

Jenny left for London early this morning and I had expected her home for dinner but it's past ten o'clock. I decide to wait up for her. I don't bother to switch on the lamp and settle into Jenny's armchair. I know I should probably go to bed but I'm comfy and too lazy to move. I must've dozed off because I didn't hear the door open. A hand cup's my breast. I cry out snapping my eyes open and Robin's features form through the darkness, I knock him away watching him as he falls backwards, banging his head on the hearth. I don't care if he's hurt. I kick my legs for momentum and stand.

'What the *hell* do you think you're doing?'

He rocks forward, hands on his thighs. Without a second thought, I bring my palm down hard across his cheek.

His hand shoots to the spot.

'Ouch, that hurt. Grace!'

'It was meant to. What on earth do you think you're doing? And don't pretend you didn't know it was me.'

'I-I. It's dark, I thought you were Jen.'

'Liar.' I widen my stance, hands on hips. 'You knew it was me,' I spit out in fury. 'Thought I'd be up for it, did you? You're no better than Tom.'

Robin's eyes dart to the door and back, he holds a finger to his lips.

'Shush, keep it down. Lucy's in the kitchen. It was a mistake. I'm sorry. You're in Jenny's chair.'

That was true, and convenient but... I narrow my eyes.

'I don't believe you. What gives you the right to think you can grab a handful when it takes your fancy?'

Robin hangs his head like a troubled child and shuffles to his haunches.

'Sorry. I've had too much to drink. Honestly, I thought you were Jenny.' He stands. 'Do you need a bit of a cuddle. You're in shock.' He sways and I catch a whiff of beer breath.

'You come any closer and I'll slap you again.' I wheeze, winded by shock and adrenaline.

'I thought you might have been feeling a bit —'

Anger pumps at my chest.

'A bit of what exactly?'

His lips are moving, searching for words.

'I think the word you wanted was horny. Was that it, Robin? So you thought, well, she must be desperate. I'll have a quick grope?'

'We're friends, Grace. That's all I meant.' He backs away. 'Look, I'm sorry, it was a mistake. I thought you were Jen. Okay, I was out of order. We can forget it, can't we? I mean, Jen doesn't need to know, does she? No point in her getting upset over nothing, is there?'

He lowers his chin.

'I'm sorry. It won't happen again. Jen and I—she hasn't been herself lately, she—'

His bottom lip trembles. I can't bear it; he's going to cry. I push past him, determined not to let him entirely off the hook.

'If you are going to say your wife doesn't understand you, think again. There is no excuse, and no, it *won't ever* happen again, you sleaze-ball. I won't mention it this time, but only for Jenny's sake. And another thing, after Tom, I can smell a liar a mile off.'

Robin clutches his stomach as if I'd punched him.

'Grace, I-'

'Goodnight, Robin.'

In the sanctity of our bedroom, I close the door and fall against it in trembling silence.

God, I can't take much more.

My girls are fast asleep. Alice turns, kicking back the covers to expose a grazed knee. Melissa's arms are flung above her head, a strand of her long blond hair is caught between her fingers. It's a calming scene and I wonder if I should give Robin the benefit of the doubt. It was dark, and I was in Jenny's chair. One thing's for sure, apart from George and Jack, I need a man free zone. But where do I find the money to buy something? Until I've sold Darwin House, I'm pot less, but now, I can't wait that long. I'll have to rent in the meantime. I can probably raise enough for the deposit and a few months' rent.

I lie down on my bed and stare at the ceiling. *Come on God, are you up there? Hannah, ask him to give me a break. I'm running out of ideas and money. God must have a plan. If he has, can he please hurry and get it moving?*

'So,' Jenny enthuses. 'Attack would be the best form of defence. There's not a woman in the country who doesn't consider Tom a total shit. The girls at KIT UK thought it a brilliant idea.'

I look around, concerned that my children are in earshot.

'It's okay,' she reassures. 'They're all out, or under Lucy's control, and they'll have heard worse at school anyway.'

I'm floored. I don't know what to say, Jenny and her lawyer friend Kellan Grove have come up with the idea of a tell all magazine piece. Rubbing the tops of my arms, I move to the window, a cloud of worry trailing me.

'Come on Grace, say you'll do it.' Jenny badgers, stretching her ponytail tighter. 'You're not listening, are you? For goodness' sake – get a grip. This is damage limitation.' Her shoulders rise in exasperation, even though she's resting on her mammoth sofa, with her legs arranged at a perfect angle. If only I had her poise —her confidence. 'We could go for something clean, comfortable, above reproach, like a magazine or morning TV show. With coaching, it could work for you.'

'Better suited to some trashy rag more like.' I say with venom, 'You can't come back from an overnight in London and expect me to bare all to the press. No one will be interested. I mean, the only person I've ever shagged is Tom.'

'It's not a kiss and tell and think of the money.' She gets up and pads towards me, her feet sinking into the rich carpet pile, and scoops an arm around my waist.

'That's more like it, a sense of humour is what's needed.'

'Is it? You don't know what you're asking of me. A revelation of my life with him. Do I want it dissected and raw for everyone else's titillation? And what about my children? I want to protect them not force them into the limelight open to ridicule. No, I can't. It's not me.'

'You can and you will. Your kids will be proud, and the money will be useful. Come on,' she says, squeezing me in tighter until our hips touch. 'Set the record straight. I'll be with you every step of the way. God knows, I need the distraction.'

Before I can probe at what she meant by that, Jenny's banging on the window. A startled tabby cat shoots off through the bushes.

'Bloody cat. Go do it in your own garden.'

My face creases to a grin remembering my dad doing the same thing when Hannah and I were little. It's strange I can sense the comfort of his presence and in my vision, he's nodding in agreement. Telling me to take a risk.

'Alright, alright. I'll do it,' I say, raising my palms in surrender. Jenny's eyes are bright with excitement, more so than I've seen in months.

The churning sensation in my stomach refuses to still as Jen shoves me through the revolving doors of 'In View' magazine. My outfit, a tailored grey dress with matching accessories selected by Jenny, does little to make me feel less vulnerable. I wish I'd put up a fight, worn something more casual? I'm too dressy, too neat, too contrived, an imposter, but Jen's in her element and pushes past me, striding towards receptionist. Before I know it I'm in a lift rushing towards the eighteenth floor with my tummy growling like an indignant teddy-bear.

'Blimey,' Jenny giggles at my reflection in the mirrored walls.

'I think I'm going to be sick.'

'You're not. It's nerves. Try to lighten up – you've a face as long as a call centre queue.'

'I don't think I can do this. It's a bad idea.'

Too late, the lift halts with a silent sliding of its doors. She tugs me forward by a pinch of material from my jacket. The ceiling to floor windows overlook the Thames. The light reflecting through the glass makes me blink.

'Look at the view. Imagine working here every day,' she says.

My shoulders roll releasing me from her grip.

'Stop being such a tourist,' I hiss, noticing a young woman with Gothic makeup and holes in her chequered tights approaching. Her face is hard, but she cracks a half-smile and gestures the way to a large inner office. My forehead puckers into tight rows. I'd expected a mature woman in ball breaking heels and a business suit, not this. She leans against the door to let us pass, offering a bony hand in greeting.

'Hi, I'm Roberta, but I prefer Bobbie. Please take a seat. Can I get you anything, water, tea, coffee, juice?' I decline, but Jenny says yes to water.

Friendship bracelets compete with silver charms for space on Bobbie's wrist. She has the hint of an accent, Australian? Canadian? I can't place it. We sit at an enormous redwood table. The surrounding chairs are a mesh of metal and blood-red leather. I lower myself onto one, surprised how comfortable it is despite its cold appearance.

Bobbie takes a seat at the head of the table. I glance at the stack of tabloid papers with their alarming headlines in front of her and flinch. Bobbie notices and moves the latest edition of *In View* magazine over the offending images.

'Sorry. No panic, we bought the rights from the reporters. Tripod Newspaper Group has enough muscle to shut this down, that, and a magazine has a longer shelf life.' She picks up a silver pen. 'Right, shall we move on? I've a tight schedule. How are you feeling about doing the interview?'

'Well, I'm—.'

'Good, good,' she repeats, over me. ' I know you are used to writing Tom's column, but I thought we might not get the best of you. It might end up over-edited if you write it yourself. This is great stuff, real human interest. We're not here to sensationalise. So, let's do the interview and run it in the next edition. If it gets the response we expect, we can go from there,' she says, pulling a folder towards her.

The stack of images I realise are of me.

'The photo session worked well. The camera loves you. Ever done any TV work?'

I'm struggling to follow the conversation and realise that's the intention.

'A little. Not much, the odd thing with Tom.'

'Elaborate,' she says, pen poised above an A4 pad.

'Er, a game show about wives whose husbands had unusual jobs. We were contestants.'

'Great. This could be lucrative for both sides. I was thinking of the cover image.'

Bobbie pushes the photographs towards me, and I peer at the bright, air-brushed images of me.

'We'll run a mailbag page in the following issue issue —a cross between a Q&A and an agony aunt. That should attract wronged wives and girlfriends.'

Bobbie eyes the document in front of her, drawn up by my now solicitor, Kellan Grove. 'I'm happy with the contract. It's not our intention to set you up, Grace. This is a serious piece of journalism.'

'It had better be.' Jenny chides.

Bobbie shoots her a sharp glare.

'Approaching us was your idea,' she says in an acid tone, before returning her attention to me. The harshness in her voice softening.

'Sian will take it from here.'

There's a light tap on the door and a mousy blonde appears clutching a notebook. She gives me the warmest of smiles and I instantly like her.

'If you'd like to follow me,' Sian says from the open doorway. Jenny attempts to follow, but Bobby directs her to the break-out area. Sian leads me to a small but cosy office, where Silver-framed magazine covers line the crimson walls. It's more like Melissa's bedroom than a journalist's office and I sense my body uncoil.

This is less troubling than expected. My tale of life with my jungle celebrity pours out of me. I'm conscious not to sound like a moaner or too needy. My answers are honest and talking to a stranger makes me reflect as I seek the exact point of when things changed between us. Was it before he was successful, or after another two additions to the family? Hard questions, but sitting in this unfamiliar place, having my life dissected isn't scary – it's cathartic. The burning knot between my shoulder blades, my constant companion since the day reporters chased us and I read the newsagent's board, dissipates. My hands lie limp in my lap. Until now, no one's asked how it felt to discover Tom's secret life. Has it scared me? What was it like before the newspapers unearthed Tom's double life? How did I tell my children? Had it changed me – them? I disclose how I was using Tom's computer.

'The file said *family*, ours I thought but when I opened it, it was a group of tribal women holding their babies. The ones I now presume he'd fathered.' I take a sip of water. 'I'd no reason to check on him or snoop. He'd never been a flirt or a womaniser.' I'm chagrined at my naivety. All this talking is exhausting but if I'm ever to move forward, it's essential. 'Tom's commitment to his work was extraordinary. He put it first. Above our marriage and children. When we met after the bombshell, I expected him to be humble and want forgiveness. At least try to make amends or have regrets. Not so. He was cocky, revelling in his notoriety. He said it was part of his job to have sex with those women. Gifted by tribal elders. It's laughable that he thought I'd take him back after a quick holiday to Scotland. He said that being caught was good for his career. He got that wrong too.'

'You always had a beautiful home and enough money. Some would be envious of the lifestyle he created,' Sian says.

'How to reply to that. Um. It was never our choice. Tom was, well, very much, Lord of the Jungle in our house. That makes me sound wimpy, but when you have four kids and live in the middle of nowhere, you become accustomed to it. I'd swap it all for a two-up two-down, a nine-to-five dad who had more interaction and love for his family.'

'Are you suggesting he never loved you or the children?'

'Ouch, that one hurt,' I say, winded at her bluntness. Moistness finds its way into my eyes.

'I'm sorry I upset you. That wasn't my aim,' Sian says, allowing me a moment to compose myself. I glance at the ceiling searching for a sincere reply.

'No. At first times were tough, we were pretty skint but content. As Tom's career grew, so did our family, and he was a wonderful dad... and then he became famous.'

'Was that when events went awry?'

'Not initially,' I say, uncrossing my ankles under the table, 'he was home less regularly and his ego sort of took over.'

'In what way?'

'Gosh, this is hard. It's all so long ago, but the little things, like writing his column. It got a huge response and bags of fan mail. Tom wasn't good at putting together anecdotes. He made me promise never to tell I wrote them.'

'Did you mind?'

I take a second to reflect, rubbing my chin.

'Yes, I suppose I did. It's like I was growing skills wise, without progressing. Because no one knew I was capable of anything. Tom took the credit. Sorry, I'm coming over lame. I hadn't considered it until now. Tom promised a big house and money aplenty when he made it. A dream we had when scrambling to find somewhere to live in the beginning,' I hesitate. 'We were kids ourselves, us and our baby Jack learning to be parents. Tom kept his promise,' I force a laugh. 'Be careful what you wish for. Isn't that what they say?'

Sian aligns her pad with her pencil. 'Thank you, Grace, we've covered a lot.' She rises while I strive to collect my thoughts and stand. I extend my hand, then retract it as Sian goes onto tiptoes to give me a hug. It's awkward but I accept the gesture, wrinkling my nose at her overpowering perfume. She shifts, lowering herself to her flat pumps and levels her gaze. I dwarf her but feel like a child taking advice from a parent. Sian has morphed from a twenty-something wise old sage.

'Try not to worry. You are brave. None of this is your fault.' Unsure how to respond, I pull back as she releases her grasp and fist-taps against her chest. 'You're a fantastic mother and you'll grow stronger with this experience. Trust me, I have a sixth sense about these things.' The urge to giggle is overbearing. I can't look at her. I dip to the floor, retrieving my hand-bag. The doors open. Sian is already waving goodbye to Jenny, who is sitting in an enormous turquoise chair surrounded by carrier-bags.

'What?' Jenny says, looking guilty as I stare at the glossy array. 'Well, I had to do something. You were hours, and I don't get up to London often.' She drains her wineglass and attempts to get up. 'Bloody chairs.'

'It isn't the chair's fault, Jenny, you're pissed.'

'I know and it's free,' she says, giving an appeasing smile and pointing to the wine chiller. I pull her to her feet, laughing, noticing the amount of airline-sized empty bottles in the bin. 'Let's go home, and if Robin blames me for the destruction of his credit cards, I'll deny all charges.' That is a husband-and-wife argu-ment that I won't be party to as the glossy carrier-bags look expensive enough for a marital breakup. Jenny pouts as I lead her towards the lift. 'I doubt *he'll* even notice,' she slurs. Halting, I raise an eyebrow. 'What?' She challenges, 'So you assume everything is rosy in my garden? *Hic.* Crap let's say it needs pruning now and again. Robin needs to be more understanding. I've lots on my mind.' Gathering her things, Jenny links arms with me. 'Come on, home James, and don't spare the horses.'

It's an effort to get her in and out of a taxi and up the escalator at the railway station. I've never seen her this incapable. It's a struggle, but I get her onto the train and seated. Her head nods with the momentum. Within seconds, she's asleep, giving out the occasional snort. I stroke her soft hair from her eyes. The woman opposite gives a disdainful glare over the rim of her glasses. I move my dear friend's head to lean against my shoulder, fixing the woman with my own icy stare. I'm not having anyone judging Jen, she's been the dearest friend. I'd never have got through this without her.

The swaying of the train and quiet compartment envelops me. Feeling contented, I gaze out of the window, watching the city slide from focus and fields replacing out-buildings in villages with spiky church towers. It's time to stop relying on everyone else. Jenny's comment about Robin not noticing worries me. Are the cracks in their marriage expanding because of the houseful of people? Us?

28

Dan hadn't been going that way but seeing Jack worrying about his home life made him offer him a lift, convincing himself it had relevance, that he might bump into Grace. There was something about her he found intriguing. He sensed her vulnerability. If only he could convince her to go out with him, then he could discuss ways to help her.

He pulls up onto Jenny's drive, wavering about whether to get out and invite himself in. Playing for time, he turns to Jack.

'So, how much longer are you living with the Maxwells?'

'No idea,' Jack said, unclipping his seatbelt. 'The old house needs a lot of work. The flood unearthed woodworm and the electrics were ancient, so it's costing Mum a pretty penny as the insurance won't cover that.'

'Good job you're earning then,' Dan said. 'You can chip in once you've got that guitar. How's the band coming on?'

He was rambling and hoped it would it make Jack to invite him in. Jack's hand rested on the door handle.

'Yeah, it's okay, but we need a vocalist.'

'Good luck with that. Not sure Steadcoate's brimming with budding talent. Apart from you, of course.'

'Thought you said it was a racket?' Jack says, laughing.

'No. I said it was a bit of a racket. Just like that row. What on earth's going on?'

Dan unfastens his seatbelt and steps out of the Range Rover on the pretext of helping Jack take his bike off the roof-rack. Laughter and screeching emits from the back garden.

'Sounds like a water-fight,' Jack says grinning. 'I wouldn't go back there if I were you.' He gestures to the back gate. 'Thanks for the lift.'

'Pleasure. Bye.' *Bugger.* He watched Jack unlock the front door and vanish inside, then lured by Grace's infectious laughter, intermixed with the children's screams of delight, he tiptoes towards the gate, cautiously peering over the top.

Grace is wearing a black bikini and has her finger over the end of the hose, chasing the children with the spray. He watches with a burning envy. He'd have preferred a big family and a son. Spending time with Jack made him realise how much he needed family too. He wanted Leah to feel a bond like he had with Kate, but Kate was thousands of miles away, fighting her battles without him.

A void sat where his happiness should be. He can't help but smile, delighted to see Grace enjoying herself. What an Idiot Tom Lane was. Look what he'd lost. Dan would cherish a woman like Grace.

He ducked out of sight as water arched towards the gate, eager not to be seen and embarrass them both. He doubted she'd be thrilled to spot him gaw-ping at her in a bikini—one that she looked so damn hot in. She already thought he was somewhat of a Don Juan. She didn't need to add voyeur to the list.

Dan drove away, wondering if there was anything he could do to change her opinion of him. There had to be.

29

Yesterday was the best yet, watching my children morph to a normal family unit. Laughing, teasing, experiencing a sense of release at having had the house to ourselves; and not one with other people's rules and personalities where we trod carefully. Hours of playful water fights heightened by Jack completely soaking me, and homemade burgers that, if I so say so myself, rivalled any celebrity chef, topped off the day. As dusk fell, we sat together listening to Jack play guitar. It was a wonderful moment of calm.

The following morning, we are all in the car driving to Darwin house and a brief hiatus returns. I thought showing them the work in progress would be a good thing, but not for everyone. George is last out of the car, the others already out of view entering via the back door.

'Come on, slowcoach, don't you want to see what everything looks like?' I say.

George shakes his head. Peering over the top of his glasses, his gaze slides from the front door, up and across to his bedroom window. I squat down beside him, trying to see the facade from his perspective.

'Can't I stay out here?' he says, placing his small hand on my shoulder.

'It's only a house George, there's nothing to worry about.'

'It feels funny. Can't we get a new house, Mum – one that Dad has never been in?'

I wobble on the balls of my feet, touching the ground to steady myself. How could I have missed George's pain? He hides his feelings well. The others react with anger or, in Alice's case, interest but with George it goes deeper.

'Of course we can,' I croak. 'We've just come to see what the workmen have done. We are not going to live here again. Ever.'

His thin arms encircle my neck. 'Promise?' he says into my hair.

'Promise.' I say, 'and if you don't want to come in, that's all right too. Why don't you check out the swing?' I feel him nod against my skin and release his hold. He ambles away as I wipe a stray tear from my cheek and push myself up, heavy with an overbearing sense of my failure at his pain.

The pre-publication advance has come through, but it won't last forever and if Tom carries on playing silly buggers, our divorce will be lengthy and expensive. Jenny has sown the seed about me having my own career, and I'm feeling more confident that it can happen.

No one seems to want to stay long at our old home and the chatter returns to normal as soon as we turn out of the driveway.

After lunch I get on the internet, searching for a property close to the village. There are few on the market but not large enough for the five of us so not an option, nor is a purchase until I sell Darwin.

The following morning I'm pacing the kitchen waiting for Jack to return, feeling nervous for him on GCSE results day. I did offer to drive him, but he wanted to cycle with a group of friends.

A cosy warmth fills my breath as he walks through the door, all smiles.

'Three A's and seven B's,' he says, his eyes bright with pride.

I move towards him, my arms wide.

'Oh, well done, Jack. That's brilliant, your dad will be—' *Shit.* My hand flies to my mouth. How could I be so insensitive? 'Sorry,' I gasp, hoping I've not deflated Jack's cheerful mood.

'No big deal. But I won't be calling him. You're the one who nagged me to do my revision. I know I kicked off but look at my results. That's down to you, not him.'

I squirm a little, wondering if I should have spoken up for Tom, but it would ruin Jack's moment of celebration, so I hold fast.

'Okay Einstein – so what's the going rate on the street?'

'*On the street.* Mum?' he pulls down his mouth at the corners with his thumb and forefinger to make a sad face.

'Okay, humour the ancient parent.'

'Fifty pounds a pass,' he says, forking his hand through his over-long hair.

'Nice try. How about I top up however much you're short for that guitar?'

He raises his hand in a high five and we tap palms.

'Now that's a deal. Don't suppose you want to check in for a new amp as well?'

'Don't push your luck,' I laugh, hugging him to me and for a while, the world seems a happier place.

With time on my hands, I endure a gruelling session at the gym feeling energised by Jack's good news. Sweaty and glowing, I make my way to the changing room, deciding to shower at home. I find the experience of confident naked women challenging to my saggy bits. I'm searching through my kitbag for my makeup and hairbrush to make me look less fearsome – neither are there. I could swear I packed them, then recall being distracted by the postman, they're probably still on the dressing table.

The mirrors are unforgiving. My face is a blotchy red from exertion and with my hair tied back my ash-grey roots are more visible. I shrug at my reflection, swinging my sports bag to my shoulder and leave the changing room, stopping at the noticeboard to read the timetable for the classes I'm considering taking.

'Well, well. We seem doomed to be together.'

I squeeze my eyes tight shut. *Not him again.* I turn, Dan leans forward. Before I can stop him, gives me a peck on the cheek.

'So, how's your world today? Busy spinning or stretching?'

He's wearing a white sports shirt with the collar turned up, and white shorts. Handsome as hell. I force myself not to look down.

'Sorry, I . . . '

'You were looking at the class timetable,' he says, flicking his head in the direction of the display board.

'Oh, yes, I see.'

Shit, not only do I look a wreck, but a stupid one at that. Of course, he's referring to the timetable. We're in a bloody gym, for God's sake.

'Actually, I was debating on doing the bums and tums class or Pilates.' Instantly I regret my words, wishing I could suck them back as his gaze drops to my rear.

'Well, both look pretty good to me.' I bristle in silence. 'Look, do you fancy a coffee? My squash opponent had an emergency and cancelled.'

'Sorry,' I say with a tight smile, anxious to get away. 'I'm terribly busy – another time perhaps.' I step away, moving towards the sliding doors and the car park, tugging my jogging top across my chest. He starts to step in time beside me.

'Busy, what sort of busy?' Dans scoops his floppy Hugh Grant hair back from his face. 'Come on, Grace, we know that's an excuse.'

The wind changes its touch against my skin.

'Give a bloke a chance – just a quick drink and a chat. Whenever we meet, you're always running off. I'm getting a complex.'

We reach my car. I open the back door and sling my sports bag across the seats.

'Look, it's not an excuse, I am busy. I'm grateful for what you've done for Jack, but I don't have time to spare for social niceties.'

I slide into the driving seat. He drops his bag on the tarmac, standing between me and the open door, extending an arm above me to rest it on top of the door frame.

'Doing what exactly?'

Who does he think he is? My spine tingles with something – indignation?

'Dan, please. I don't have to explain my actions to you. I hardly even know you. Now please, let me go.'

He drops his arm, swooping and bending musketeer style. I note the lingering shift of confidence in his eyes.

'Grace, I'm sorry. I'm not being pushy or creepy or anything like that. I thought I could be of help after the flood and everything. It's tough being single and I —'

Although I sense a vulnerability, I still snap back.

'For God's sake, is nothing private around here?'

'I'm sorry. Jack told me. I wasn't being nosy. I hoped I could be of help. Alice could come for sleepovers with Leah after summer camp. They'll love that. But there must be some other way I can help *you*. It's hard being on your own. I know that too well.'

Huh, I don't think so. You're constantly chatting up half the village behind your wife's back. Hardly alone.

'I don't need help, thank you,' I say a little pointedly. 'The builders sorted out the flood damage.'

'Oh, that's good, so you can move back in soon?'

'No, we're not moving back. So, unless you can magic up a buyer for my house and find me somewhere I can afford with room for five, because that's a problem. I'm sorry if it offends your male ego, but I can manage on my own.' My thoughts flip to Robin and what I think of as *the incident,* because I'm not convinced it was an accident or another male chancer trying his luck. I'm shaking inside. 'Please Dan. I may be manless and homeless. And as I've already said, you have been great with Jack. But I don't have time to drink coffee. I have to go.' I switch on the engine and force a smile. 'Mind your feet I don't want to crush your feet as well as your ego. Bye now.'

His eyebrows shoot up in surprise, although his mouth displays mild amusement.

'Grace, I think I might just—'

I don't give him chance to finish and shove the gear-stick into reverse, give a wave and drive on.

'Take that Mr Gigolo,' I say pleased with myself.

***

Dan stood stark still watching Grace's departure.

'I was going to say I can help with the house sale. I have contacts,' he says into thin air, chuckling. 'God, what a woman. Talk about a challenge, feisty as hell, but I can't blame her after what she's been through. Better give her a wide berth for a while. That's if I can contain myself.'

***

Jack is on the doorstep waiting as I haul my gym bag from the car.

'Hi, love,' I say smiling, until I notice his taut jaw and knotted frown. 'What's up?'

'The magazine called; they want to speak to you.'

His eyes reflect a worried concern.

'Do you have to do the magazine thing? It's embarrassing.' I dump my bag on the mat and close the door behind me, studying him. Jack has had to mature in a rush. Everything that's happened to us has changed him. Although in the main for the better, as it's brought us closer, but I wonder if the responsibility he's adopted has been good for him. He's taken it upon himself to monitor his siblings. I take in the shadow of bumfluff marking his top lip. Working at the farm has built up his chest and arm muscles and I almost wish he was still my boy in the untidy smelly bedroom, playing deafening music. I hold out my arms.

'Hey, come here. I think you need a hug.'

He slouches towards me, allowing my arms to encircle him while his remain stiffly by his side. He smells of fruit. I guess he's been working in the bottling room. The moment I loosen my grip he ducks under my arm and lollops to the kitchen. 'So, what's bothering you, Jack? Please don't walk away.' I follow him.

Jack leans against the draining board, arms folded and head-flips his overgrown fringe into place.

'It's – well, this magazine thing. Things have settled down at school. I mean, it was bad enough the stuff about dad with all those kids. Then it was all about you and Matt and that picture and—'

He breaks off, dropping his chin and stares at the floor.

'But Jack, I thought you were coping best of all. Why didn't you tell me how you felt?' I rub my wrists. 'I'm so sorry, darling. Has it been awful?'

29

He jerks his chin up. His Adam's apple sinks then rises in a gulp.

'That bad, huh?' There's the slightest quiver to his lips. I can't bear to see him so unhappy. 'Talk to me, Jack. Please.'

His hands grip the worktop.

'Stuff like texting me pictures of black babies asking if we're related. They make Tarzan noises at me and when the picture of you and Matt appeared, they said crap stuff about you. I hoped it might stop when the papers said he was gay and some kid on the football team tried to hang himself, which took the spotlight off me.'

'He what? That's awful.'

He nods. 'I can cope with most of it but the magazine thing – well, I'm worried it will all kick off again.'

'I'm so sorry. I had no idea. You were coping so well.' Exhaustion wades in, accompanied by tears, I reach out behind me locate a chair and flop on to it. 'God, what sort of childhood am I giving you? No one should go through this. Sod the papers and sod the bloody gossips.'

I cover my face with my hands until he forces a sheet of kitchen roll into them and lays an awkward hand on my shoulder.

'Sorry, Mum. I didn't mean to upset you, but I wanted you to know how I felt.'

I blow into the tissue. When I look up, he has a teapot in one hand and a bottle of wine in the other. He quirks an eyebrow, a cheeky smile decorous on his youthful face. I can't help but grin.

'Er, that will be tea, please.'

He flips the switch on the kettle and takes two mugs from the rack.

'Most of them are idiots with mothers who get their buzz from Evelyn Greenway's book club.'

'So not all bad?' I say, trying to add some humour to the conversation.

'Well, I suppose when you put it that way, it may have some pluses.' Jack's smile melts. 'But I don't want it to kick off again.'

'I can understand that, and I promise I'll try to keep any awful stuff away, but the magazine thing, it has helped me. It was different talking to a stranger who hasn't got a hidden agenda. They've promised it will be an accurate account, not a sensationalised piece. As they said, the gutter press has done its worst, now it's time to put it right, with the facts. Trust me Jack, and I promise to be more aware in the future.' He nods a reluctant agreement. 'It's a pact. I promise things will change for the better. Now make the ruddy tea while I make us a sandwich.' I run through what I've looked at so far, property wise, explaining that there's not much on the market that's big enough. We all need our own space, even Alice.

'I'm glad you said that,' he says, making way for me to get to the breadbin. 'Aunty Jen's acting like a right weirdo since they got back from Cornwall. And another thing – Lily has a crush on me and there's no way I'm being around on Saturday for her birthday, so don't ask me to.'

'You should be flattered.'

'No. I shouldn't. She keeps cornering me and she's always trying to get me on our own. It's gross.'

How had I missed that bit of interaction?

'I'll get us out of here soon, I promise.'

I'm crossing my fingers as I speak. School resumes next week and then I have to worry about Christmas. Something must come on the market soon, even if it means another long commute. We have to get out of here.

30

With the children back at school I spend hours scouring the area for a suitable home, to no avail. To make matters worse, Mayburn Primary is putting on their production of Oliver tonight. To be honest I'll be glad when it's over, we're all sick to death of the songs as Alice bursts into them from the moment her eyes are open. I'd tried every conceivable excuse not to go, but Alice is relentless.

'Please Mum, if you don't, I'll be the only one in class without someone to watch them.'

I cup her little elfin chin. 'Alice, look, I love you very much but ...' but what? *But the whole school will be crushed into one place staring and whispering about me.* I panic every time I think of the nudges. How many sets of eyes staring at me and shudder at the thought.

'But not enough to come and watch,' Alice narrows her eyes scornfully. 'You didn't even make the costumes when I'd said you would.'

I swallow my driving guilt and tilt my head back, wondering where the ceiling people have gone when you need them.

'I know I didn't and I'm sorry. Come on now, be my big girl and try and understand. Jack will take my place, and I expect Lucy will as well if we ask her, so you will have someone there.'

'But it won't be the same,' Alice says sulkily. 'Brothers and nannies aren't as good as a Mummy or Daddy.'

There's no arguing with that. I stroke her wispy fringe from her face and shrug. What sort of an example am I setting cowering away. If we're going to stay local, I have to stop hiding at some point. So why not now? Alice is right, a brother is not the same as a mother, and I don't want her to suffer any further parental indignities.

'You're right, Alice. It's not the same. You win, I'll come.'

Alice's small arms encircle my waist and squeeze.

'Oh Mummy, thank you. You will have a lovely time. I'm very good. Look out for me and wave, won't you? I might be hard to spot as our faces are all dirty. It's because we're poor and don't have any soap.'

Alice skips off happily and I go in search of George. I find him in his bedroom dressed smartly in his school uniform. He's at the mirror, comb in hand, focusing on finding his hair parting and my heart swells, he's such a lovely, undemanding child who's never caused me a moments anguish.

'Hey, sweetie.'

He turns, frowning.

'Mum. I can't get my hair right. This bit.' He indicates to the rear of his crown, where a spike of hair stands vertically. 'It won't lie down. See?'

'Tell you what,' I say, in hushed tones. 'Let's pop into my bedroom and use a bit of hairspray. No one will know.'

Behind the lenses of his glasses his eyes widen.

'That's for girls. I'll smell of girls.'

'Okay then, run your comb under the tap and wet it, that should do the trick. Although you do look more like a waif and stray like that.'

His slight shoulders lift.

'You mean Oliver? Do I have to go Mum? I hate it, and no one would miss me. I don't have a speaking part – please Mum?'

I squat on his duvet, taking in the scraped knees and missing teeth. God, I love them all so much.

'And my costume smells funny, and it's itchy.'

I take his hand in mine. I'd given in to Alice. It's only fair George got his wish too.

'Okay, but it's our secret.'

His face lights up.

'I can pretend I have a tummy ache. Actually, it does hurt a bit.'

He gives it a rub. I throw him a sidelong glance – deadpan.

'Perhaps you should be in the play after all. You're a magnificent actor.' He looks perplexed. I reach out and ruffle his hair. 'Joking! Now go and wet that comb, and remember, it's our secret.'

***

The steering wheel is slick with sweat from my palms. I pull into Mayburn Primary car park. I turn off the engine and take a swig of water from my bottle. The night air is damp. Drifts of fog hug the exterior lights in a ghostly fashion. I'm wrestling with walking in and ignoring the stares or waiting until the play's about to start. But then I'd have to find a seat, and that might bring unwanted attention.

'Stupid, stupid, woman. You can do this. It's a school play for Christ sake.' *Right. head up – shoulders down. Go.*

There's standing room at the back. I shuffle along until I can see Alice and hopefully, she me. And from here it's a quick escape route for when it's over.

Alice's teacher fusses the children onto the stage and the music begins. They all look cute in their rags and tatters and dirtied faces. Leah and her explosion of dark curls stands stiffly beside Alice, who is very involved in her part and when not singing, beams at the audience.

I'm bobbing up and down on tiptoes hoping she'll look this way, but her attention's rooted to one area and I wonder if she's blinded by the stage lights and can't see to the back.

The performance is enchanting. I'm glad I came. I've been laughing and clapping and hadn't realised how quickly they got through the first half. I hadn't accounted for an interval.

An invisible voice announces refreshment are being served. Head down I shuffle towards the door amid the crush of parents. I catch my breath as a hand grips my elbow, propelling me into another corridor, angrily I swing around.

'What the hell do you think—' Dan shakes his head and holds a finger to his lips.

'Not here,' he says, his grip steers me past a classroom of children changing costumes and outside to the playground.

As soon as we're out of earshot I spin on my toes and shake free.

'How dare you?' I make to move but he steps in my way. A rage so strong clouds my vision. 'I've had enough of you. You *will* leave me alone.' I raise my hand to slap his face, but he ducks the blow.

'Grace listen, I'm not making a pass, it's Tom.'

I struggle to understand, blinded with rage.

'Tom? What the hell are you talking about?' I say, lowering my hand.

'He's here. In the front row. I thought you needed warning. Less embarrassing, and all that.'

I clasp my hands to my head searching for clarity.

'But. But he never comes to anything the children do.'

'Well looks like he's changed his mind. Knowing Tom, it's probably some sort of publicity stunt.'

'You are sure it's him?'

He makes a must be joking face.

'I am hardly likely to forget what he looks like.'

'No. Right.' I turn away and then back again. 'I don't know what to do?'

He rests a hand gently on my shoulder. 'Look, if you want to go back inside, I'll come with you, but do you think it's wise?'

'What do you mean?'

'Well, he does rather like taking centre stage. I wouldn't put it past him to make a scene or throw some crude inuendo aimed at us. He certainly would have a ready-made audience.'

My teeth indent my bottom lip.

'Why not go home. He expects you to be here. I doubt it's a sudden rush of fatherly affection, not with the number of kids he's got.'

I flinch at the comment. 'Thanks for that Dan.'

'I'm sorry that was badly put.'

I can't think straight. 'I can't run out on Alice – she begged me to come.'

Freezing fog swirls around us, biting at our ears. Dan turns up the collar on his coat.

'Look, it's not my call but personally I think it's better for her if you do? Did she see you?'

'I don't know. She said she'd wave, but now I know who was stealing her attention.'

'Well, that's the first thing to put right. I'll wait until they come off stage, tell her you thought she was brilliant, but you have ...oh I don't know – a migraine or something?'

'But how will she get home?'

'Don't worry about that. If it's not in Tom's plans, she can come with us. I'll drop her off. If there's a problem, I'll call. I have Jenny's number.'

He's waiting for my answer. I can hear the parents going back into the hall for the second half. 'Thank you. If you could.'

'Thanks. Not accepted,' he grins.

'Dan I'm not in the mood for games. What do you mean?'

'I mean; you can thank me by letting me take you out to dinner.'

I blow a harsh breath. 'Not that again. I don't think so.'

'Lunch then?'

'You don't give up, do you?'

'Nope.'

'Coffee?' *I owe him that.*

'If that's the best you can offer?'

'It is,' I say, rushing toward the car park, my hands rummaging through my bag for keys.

Dan yells out behind me.

'We're not all the same.'

'Pardon?' I say turning and walking backwards.

'Men. Don't let Tom put you off. Some of us have good intentions.'

'If I believed that, I'd be the one with seventeen children.' I shout into the darkness.

'Drive carefully, there's black ice about.'

I raise a hand in acknowledgement. Thanking God for his intervention, he did seem genuinely concerned. He is still a married man who doesn't wear a ring. I wonder about the mysterious Kate, is she still away or has she actually left him? Either way, Dan saved me from humiliation. And what is Tom playing at? He's entitled to the children and they him but there have to be some rules. If he'd let me know he was going, Alice would have been more than happy. Why does he have to play such annoying games?

31

I hear a full-blown argument coming from the kitchen, it's Jack and Melissa yelling at each other, while Alice wails and I go to investigate.

'Enough. What's going on here?'

Jack throws me a defiant look. Melissa moves her attention to her cereal. George sits owl eyed, and Alice red faced, with tears and snot snaking down her face as she continues to bawl.

'They...st-started it, Mum, all because I said Dad's buying me a pony.'

Jack flips his jacket from the back of the chair and launches it to his shoulder.

'Alice, if you take anything from that lying shit, I'll never talk to you again.'

'Jack. Don't talk to your sister like that. Apologise.' Melissa joins in.

'Why should *she* get a pony. I've wanted one for years, and he always said no! It's not fair.'

'You're stupid Melissa,' Jack sneers. 'Can't you see he's trying to buy her off because she's just a silly kid who can be manipulated?'

'I'm not a silly kid, Dad loves me. He says I'm special.'

Jack thumps curled fists on his scalp.

'I can't take this rubbish. Yeah, you *really* are special Alice. Out of all his twenty-one kids, you're the special one.'

He shoves past me. I try to grab his arm but he's too quick for me.

'Jack please, I didn't know he was going to be there. Do you think I'd have gone if I had?' My words flail, crushed out by the sound of the door slamming behind him.

Melissa puts her cereal bowl in the dishwasher and comes to hug me.

'Sorry Mum. It's so unfair.'

The jigsaw of muscles in my neck grip painfully.

'Listen, all of you. It's no good us fighting each other. Daddy was wrong to say you could have a pony, Alice.'

Alice looks up, her dark lashes defined by tears, and to my surprise, stops crying.

'I'm looking for somewhere for us to live. But it won't be large enough for a pony. You can forget that. I can't stand all this in-fighting. Do you understand? I know this isn't ideal but I'm trying. Alright?' It's not Alice I'm worried about, it's George. He becomes motionless and silent when there's something beyond his control. I think of the boy at Jack's school trying to take his own life. Mental health often the unseen slayer. I decide to ring the school and voice my concerns – get them to keep an eye on him. Is he like this at school or just when he's with us?

32

The call from Bobbie at the magazine is a long one as she chats through aspects of the article, my chest flutters with nerves, publication day is looming.

'What if the article antagonises Tom further, and exposes more of his dirty tricks?'

Bobbie is resolute, 'Men are like mongrel dogs. They shit on their own doorstep. You Grace are a pedigree who steps elegantly away from the mess. The way the article's pitched can only be good for you and your family and the millions of cheated women like you.'

I can't argue with that.

***

The clock says eight-thirty, so plenty of time to sort out priorities and another day of searching for a home; especially as Evelyn has taken to finding excuses to pop in unannounced.

Surprisingly, it's Robin who comes up with the solution.

'Uh, Grace. I was thinking, yesterday, a client came in called Mrs Finch, with her Corgi Nellie. She mentioned a house near her that might be coming on the market.' He shuffles his feet awkwardly. 'I know the house, it belonged to the Winters, I was their vet some years back.'

I hang on his every word.

'Is it for rent?'

'I don't know. It's easy to find out though, the owners bro –, damn.'

His phone both rang and vibrated on the worktop. 'Excuse me, must take this.'

I wait for him to complete his call, a convoluted conversation about a dog. I'm keen to know more about the house but I'm picking up on the urgency of the call from the concern in Robin's voice.

'Sorry Grace, emergency, got to go. Oh yes, I was saying, the house – I'd consider it if I were you. Here, I'll write down the address.'

'Thanks, Robin, I'll take a look.'

An hour later I drive out to Steadcoate Ley, locating the property with ease. It's sprawled sideways across a neat plot, promising spacious rooms. There's plenty of garden for the kids to romp around in and it's close enough to the village. I get a feeling about it, like the house is smiling at me. That we're drawn to each other, like a pair of shoes.

On the gravel drive is a red van. A lad of around twenty comes out of the open door wearing painting overalls.

'Hi, I was wondering if you could help me. Do you know who owns this house?'

He nods, turns his head and yells. 'Ted.'

A chubby face appears briefly at the window. Seconds later, he joins us. His thinning hair stands in tufts from an almost bald pate and pebble-dashed with splashes of emulsion paint.

'Can I help you, lady?'

He looks a bit grumpy, and none too happy to have been summoned from his task. I hold out my hand, dropping it to my side when he fails to take it.

'Yes, I hope so. Do you know who owns this house? I hear it may be coming on the market?' 'Who wants to know?' He says grumpily.

I give out a nervous giggle.

'Well, me actually. I want to know if it's going to be available to rent. I need a property with at least five bedrooms. I've quite a large family.'

The lad is staring at me. I pull my coat closer around me. Alarmingly, he suddenly clicks his fingers.

'Got it! You're that jungle bloke's wife ain't yer? I seen you in the papers.'

I look away. Thankfully Ted notices my discomfort.

'None of your business Danny, now get me a bit of paper, so I can take down the ladies' number.'

Danny opens the passenger door, head hung low, and produces a screwed-up sandwich bag. He flattens it against his chest then hands it to Ted, who takes a pencil from behind his ear, taps it on the tip of his tongue and hovers it over the paper.

'Name and number?'

'I'm Mrs Denning,' he writes and takes my number. Danny continues to stare at me as I walk back to the car. One last glance at the house makes me sigh. It did look like the perfect home for us. Dare I get my hopes up?

I catch Tod and Lily whispering in the hallway. They draw apart when they see me but not before I overhear the word 'houseful'. Since Robin's pass, Jenny has become more distant daily.

I'm passing Robin's study and overhear a hushed argument. I hurry past but catch the words *somewhere else to live*. I want to scream, *I'm bloody trying*. I'm sick with worry, we have long overstayed our welcome especially with my kids arguing. I don't want to lose my best friend, but I'm cornered at every turn.

Locked in the confines of the bathroom, I run the taps and allow myself the luxury of shedding a few tears. Letting the water rumble down the plughole, I dry myself and blow my nose, take a deep breath and unlock the door. Melissa is hovering outside with my phone in her hand.

'A man just rang about a house in Steadcoat Lea. He said he'd meet you there at three o'clock tomorrow if you are still interested. I said you'd call back if it weren't.'

'Thanks, Lissy. What was his name?'

'Er, don't think he said. Just said okay to view at three,' she looks about conspiratorially. 'Mum, Auntie

Jen and Uncle Robin had a blazing row, I couldn't help overhearing some of it —.'

I put a hand on her arm to stop her saying more.

'I know, I don't think it's helping their marriage, us being here. Sooner we're out the better.'

'It'll all work out fine mum. Stop worrying,' she leans in, dropping a peck to my cheek 'night Mum,' she says handing me the phone.

Tiptoeing into the bedroom, my mobile pings. Alice's shoulders are out of the covers, I tug them up and settle myself on the wicker chair then swipe the screen, groaning as I read it.

Collecting on my IOU. Coffee at the golf club 11.00 tomorrow. Failure to attend could ruin your future. Be there! Dan

None the less his text makes me smile. Yes, he's annoying but I owe him for the school concert debacle and quick coffee wouldn't hurt, would it?

***

I'd waved off the last of my children when Jenny comes into the kitchen. It's unusual to see her without makeup. Her jaw is set, her hair unbrushed, I can almost hear her brain whirring.

'Morning lovely. 'Coffee?' Jenny is busy emptying the contents of her handbag onto the table. 'Hello, anyone in? Coffee? Mars Bar?' Her eyes flicker. She looks surprised, as if seeing me in her kitchen was unusual. 'Jen, you alright?' I move closer and lay a hand on her shoulder. From her swollen eyelids it was obvious she's been crying. It was easy to assume they hadn't made up from their row the night before, judging by the way he'd slammed the door when leaving for the surgery. 'Come on Jen, cheer up, it can't be that bad.'

She steps away and slides into a seat.

'You making coffee?'

'I just offered you one,' I say, locating another Espresso cup and saucer.

'Black for me; I have a helluva hangover.'

'You sure it's a hangover, not something you're hiding?' My stomach turns cold. Had Lucy overheard my outrage at Robin's wandering hands and told Jen? Was that what the rows were about? The temptation to ask is great, as is the worry that if this isn't the case it will make matters worse. I change the subject.

'I was going to stick some toast in, do you want some?'

'No ta, no time. I'm going to Cambridge today; few things I have to do.'

'Shame I've got stuff on otherwise I'd have joined you.' I pass my hand across the table at the handbag spillage. 'So, what's all this then?'

Jenny looks at the mess and starts shoving the invasion of perfume sprays, lipstick, tissues, and receipts back into her bag.

'I was looking for a phone number. I thought it was here but it's not, must be in another bag. I'll check in a moment.'

'Jenny, I know I keep asking what's up and you keep saying no, but I know when you're lying. What is it, Jen? We used to be able to talk.'

She snaps the bag shut. 'For Christ's sake, will you stop going on. You're as bad as he is, badgering me all the time. You've enough problems of your own. Now drop it, or we might just fall out.'

My jaw drops. This was so un-Jenny. I stutter an apology.

'Jen I'm sorry I—'

She's red faced. 'Forget it. Just drop the inquisition.' An unconvincing smile tweaked her lips. 'So, what are you up to today? Isn't it tomorrow the magazine comes out?'

'Nice change of subject, and yes.'

'You must be excited?'

I give a theatrical shudder, hoping to lighten the conversation.

'Hope I've done the right thing. Jack is apprehensive about it.'

'He'll survive, there are bigger problems in the world than your mum being in a magazine.'

'I know but —' I walk away and feed bread into the toaster.

'But nothing. You've seen a draft, haven't you? I thought you were happy with it?'

I'm pleased to be able to turn away. It's like having a conversation with a stranger.

'Yes, and I'm quite proud of it. But well, do I trust them? I mean, they could show me one thing and print another. I am at their mercy.' My toast pops. I butter two pieces, adding lemon marmalade and pull out the chair opposite Jenny, who sticks out her arm and grabs a piece.

'Hey, you didn't want any.'

'Well, I changed my mind. It smells good, and I missed supper last night.'

I stop mid chew. 'Jen, you would tell —'

'For fuck's sake! Just because I missed supper, don't be so ruddy dramatic. Just drop it. Anyway, I expect you heard Robin and I arguing. No big deal, we do it a lot lately. Don't try and pretend you didn't hear. The walls aren't exactly soundproof, and we did rather go at it. He makes me want to scream. He's gone all clingy and weird. Keeps pulling me about. Grabbing my boobs and coming up behind me. I'm just not interested and the more he paws at me, the more I pull away. Bloody men. Think they have open house on your body once you're married.'

I can't help but frown, noticing Jenny has her hand down the front of her jumper again. A thing she does a lot lately.

'Anyway, what did you say you were doing today?'

'I didn't, but I am meeting Dan Mayne for coffee at the golf club this morning. After that, I've a viewing at a house in Steadcoate Ley. It looks perfect.'

She doesn't comment on the house, but a smirk tweaks her lips.

'Dan Mayne, eh? Very hunky, and quite a catch. All those good looks and a great cook to boot.'

'Really?' I say wrinkling my nose. 'Not for me, and in case it's slipped your mind, I'm a bit anti man at the mo. Me-thinks he tries too hard, he's a bit too over-confident for my liking. Men like that scare me stiff. Shame about Matt, I liked him. As for Dan, I owe him for warning me about Tom, that's the only reason. And another thing, he's married, and I've had enough gossip thrown my way to last a lifetime.

I can tell she's zoned out and busy scrolling through her text messages. She gets up from the table.

'Sorry babe, got to go. Enjoy your date.'

I go to object, but she's already left the room.

Dan waves a greeting as I walk in. I file away thoughts of how attractive he looks, dressed in a pale-blue shirt with upturned collar and I spot a navy jumper resting on the arm of his chair.

'You came, how wonderful. And looking as stunning as ever.'

I doubt that, I'd dressed modestly for the occasion, but it was flattering to get a compliment. Dan stood tall, broad shouldered above me and kissed me on both cheeks. His closeness stirs something inside that scares me.

'I've ordered coffee; shouldn't be long.' He rubs his hands together. 'Damned freezing out there today.' I agree, removing my gloves and lowering myself into the leather buttoned chair opposite him.

He certainly is laying on the charm, and if I'm not mistaken, by the way his fingers rub at his cuff – a tad nervous?

'Sorry, I didn't think to ask if you want a pastry, or scone, all freshly baked this morning.'

I shake my head and he smiles his twinkly eyed smile, making me fidget by tugging my jacket more firmly into place and buttoning it up. Is it just because we are alone together that makes me feel wrong footed?

'That's good then. If you get hungry later, I might get to have lunch with you after all.'

I grin stupidly. 'You really are incorrigible. Just coffee. I owe you that for saving me the other night. Thank you again, it could have been awful for Alice.'

'And pretty uncomfortable for you. Was she alright when she got home?'

'Yes, thank you, apart from that Tom promised to buy her a pony and it caused a war between her siblings.'

A waitress approaches delivering our coffee. My thoughts scramble for something to talk about, other than myself, waiting for her to finish placing coasters.

We both speak over each other, 'How's your business, I...'

'It's crap being talked about, I...'

'You first.'

'No, you please.'

'I was just going to say I admire the way you have coped – gossip can be destructive in a small village.'

'I'm getting pretty thick skinned nowadays, even a rhinoceros would be envious, but I think Jack had it worse.'

'Mm he told me, but he's got beyond that,' he puffs out his chest and makes a strong man gesture with his arms. 'What is it they say, it's all character building?'

So Jack had confided in him. That was a good thing, wasn't it? Him talking about things, not bottling it up. *Perhaps he sees Dan as a father figure, or Uncle? That's better. Uncle's less creepy, more arm's-length.* I add milk to my coffee and pass the jug to Dan, who wraps two chilly but strong hands around mine.

'Rhinoceros? Never. Feels pretty smooth to me.'

33

Attempting to pull back, the warm milk spills onto my knuckles. He lets go, apologising. *Oh, yuk-yuk. Cheesy or what?* I'm about to say so when Dan stiffens, his eyes darkening. The china clinks on the table as he nudges it with his knee in his haste to get to his feet. I turn gasping as a grinning Tom approaches.

'Well, well, well, Dan. You didn't waste much time sniffing around, did you? And you, my love. You seem to have found a replacement for that poofter Matt quick enough. Shame my mobile's in my locker, you two holding hands would have made a lovely snap.'

I attempt to stand but my crossed legs seem locked together. I make fists and push up, my anger growing.

'How dare you!' I screech, 'It's not like that Tom, and you know it. We are just having coffee.' He doesn't even look at me, his eyes burn into Dan's, who glares back contemptuously.

'I bet you are, and a little something for afters no doubt.'

'Don't judge everyone by your disgusting standards. Just go away. Haven't you done enough damage?' I growl.

Dan steps in front of me protectively.

'He's not worth the breath Grace. Leave her alone. Try speaking to someone you can't bully. You think you are such a big man.'

A chill sweeps my spine. I can almost smell the testosterone as they square up to each other. Dan is almost a head and shoulders taller. I don't want to be a victim, I can stand up for myself. I'm about to get closer and slap Tom's face but a gathering crowd subdues me.

'Knight in shining armour, eh? New tack? What's up Dan, run out of single ladies? Made it easy for you being away so often, didn't I? Well, you're welcome to my leftovers.'

I cough out a sob at his cruelty, lurching towards him. But Dan's stride is faster and his reach longer, he grabs a fist full of Tom's shirt.

'You despicable pile of shit.'

'Going to whack me, are you?' Tom says, 'brilliant for the tabloids, a nice shiner.'

Dan tightens his grip. 'You're a wanker. A disgusting excuse for a man who doesn't give a shit about what he's doing to his family. Why don't you just go back to the bloody jungle and stay there.' He pushes his face to within inches of Tom's, who has dropped his cocky stance. I watch his Adam's apple yo-yo with uncertainty.

'Oh yes that's right, you can't, can you Tom? No wonder you're trying to make a living from the gutterpress. Your visa's been revoked.'

Tom shakes himself free, slack jawed. 'How do you know that? It's not public knowledge and if I hear you repeating it, I'll—'

'You'll what, Sue me? Go ahead. I think you'll find that as I can establish it's the truth, you'd be wasting your money. You're not the only one with friends in high places.'

A voice from the onlooker's shouts. 'Sort him out Dan or I will.'

My face burns, I angle my head away to hide my shame.

'*That's enough.* Stop making a show of us Tom. What about our children? Don't you care?'

My knees bang against each other, my body collapsing in on itself. I can't breathe. Stumbling and weaving around the furniture I make for the exit. Dan calls out to me. I don't stop until I reach the sanctuary of my car, my thumping heart pummelling against my ribs. I reverse out of my parking space at speed, driving a random route until I reach a quiet spot near the entrance to Cranford Woods and pull in.

The stillness of the wood calms me. I breathe in the smell of fresh pine and listen to the hammer of a distant woodpecker. My breathing levels and I get out and open the tailgate, swapping shoes for Wellington's.

The ground is soggy underfoot in places. The occasional snap of a twig startles me. The woods thin out and I cross a field, and many fields beyond it to an open plain, stopping to take a breath and admire the tapestry of copper, greens, and the browns of ploughed furrows. The wind changes direction, washing over my face. I'm thirsty and glance at my watch, I've walked for a few hours. It's time to turn back, time to think of my future and keep my appointment in Steadcoate Ley.

I catch sight of myself in the car window. I'm a mess. Retrieving my bag from the boot, I drag a comb through my hair. It takes a lot of spit to remove my smudged mascara and I must make the right impression with the house owner. If he listens to gossip, he might not want us as tenants. I'm aware that I'm staking so much on this meeting, but my luck has to change some time, doesn't it?

34

The house is as impressive as when I'd first seen it. I take in more detail- the many windows, so I expect it to be light and airy, unlike my former home. I'm fifteen minutes early but curious to see the back of the house and follow the winding paving. Flowerbeds take up the length of the wall to the right of the plot, but as it's winter it's hard to know what secrets sleep below the soil. It's a large, secluded garden with a children's swing and trampoline in one corner. I can imagine George and Alice playing and happy laughter.

The rear of the house formed an L shape, with double doors in two locations. One opening onto a raised patio, the other leading onto a covered walkway – a lovely place to sit in summer.

The sound of a car driving in hastens my pace back around the front. The smile slides from my face.

'Please Dan, I can't do this now. How did you know where I'd be? Did you follow me?'

He scratches his head, looking as surprised as I did.

'No. I didn't. I have a meeting with a viewer, a Miss Denning.'

'But that's me, and you're not Mr Winter?'

'It's my sister Kate's married name. It's her house. How am I supposed to know you call yourself something else?'

Did I hear right?

'Kate's your sister? Not your wife?'

Dan isn't smiling. In fact, his face is scornful, he gives a grunt I assume to be a yes, unbuttons his coat and produces a set of keys from his pocket.

'Denning's my maiden name,' I say keen to put things right.

'Ted only took down the number, I *didn't* recognise the name, why would I? I left a message with someone, yours, or Jenny's daughter I suppose, and for the record. I'm *not* married, never have been.'

I'm caught wrong footed, mute as he turns the key in the lock, pushes the door open and stands back to allow me to enter.

My lips roll over each other worrying about his changed persona. He stands back, I step past him. The atmosphere between us is changed. He probably thinks I'm a bunch of trouble after our encounter with Tom earlier.

'You seem bent on getting who I am confused with who you think I am,' Dan says flatly. My sister and her husband John are living in New York. Kate's been unwell so for now I'm raising my daughter without her help. I'm a lone dad and estate agent. We hover in the hallway. 'I was ordered to attend the school concert or else. I do as I'm told between Leah and my housekeeper. Anything else you want to know?'

'I've been an idiot. Your sister? I'm sorry, Dan. I got it wrong.' My face slicks with colour. How stupid

I'd been in my assumption. I allow my eyes to roam over the expansive hallway, momentarily distracted as I imagine piles of boots and school bags dumped in the corner.

'Yes you did and if I'd known you had reverted to your maiden name, it could have saved us both the trouble. Anyway, we're here now.'

'Trouble?' Does he mean he doesn't want me to be Kate's tenant. I search his eyes, but they avoid mine. There is something deeply sad in them. I rub a spot behind my ear, suddenly apprehensive.

'I only meant we could have met here instead, and you wouldn't have had to go through – well, Tom.'

I brush away the vision of Tom's gloating face.

'Please, Dan, can we forget it? I am sorry you had to be subjected to his disgusting mouth. Can we please look at the house? I think it's lovely.'

'Don't apologise for him. But the house,' he heaves a breath as if conversation is an effort, 'if you remember, I did tell you I could help, but you were so damned stubborn.'

'I'm not very trusting of anyone. Can you blame me?'

'No, of course not. Sorry, I've a few problems of my own so I need to get a move on. Right, let's start at the top and work down. I guess the size of the bedrooms is important with your little army. Please, lead the way.'

Thank Goodness, he didn't say tribe.

We climb the stairs to the first-floor landing. The lack of creaking stairs and floorboards is joyous. My nostrils twitch with the smell of fresh paint. Every-thing is bright, clean, and painted in delightful neutral colours. The rooms are airy, and large. Even Melissa couldn't complain about wardrobe space. There are two bathrooms at either end of the landing as well as an en-suite off the master bedroom. Bliss. No more rows and hammering on doors in the morning. If he lets me rent it.

Our communication becomes easier as we discuss the domesticity of the house and make our way down-stairs. Dan leads off the hall.

'Playroom,' Dan says halting at an open door, 'I know yours are a bit over the Lego stage, but there's room to chill and mess in. Leah used to spend hours in here, dressing up and putting on endless plays that we were compelled to watch.'

His grumpiness is fading but on the rare moments he attempts to smile it doesn't rise further than his cheekbones.

'Lounge,' he says moving on. It's a lovely ob-long space with low windowsills giving complemen-tary views of the gardens. A central formal fireplace juts from one wall with deep alcoves either side. I'm clenching my fists with excitement, and perhaps I had been wrong about Dan. He does seem such a caring person. What must he have thought of me, blowing all hot and cold?

I'm feeling very comfortable in his company again, he's so considerate. I succumb to the vision of a roar-ing winter fire in the grate with our furniture arranged around it.

'Jack's a nice lad,' he says, interrupting my thoughts. 'A real credit to you. You have great kids. I gather

Melissa's theatrical. Next is George? I've had the pleasure of Alice's company on many occasions. She's almost as scary as Leah.'

'So how do you manage without Kate?'

'Flora. She's our housekeeper – been with us for years. She's a sort of Nanny McFee.'

'Is Leah an only child?' I ask, admiring what I take to be the dining room. Dan picks at a paint splash on the window.

'Must get Ted back to have a proper clean up. There are paint specks everywhere. Leah, oh yes, she's a one-off alright and growing up a right little gossip. He glances at his watch. 'Sorry, I have an important call to make. I don't mean to rush you. Shall we move on to the business end of the house?' Briefly, we glance into other rooms- a study, and finally the kitchen. Dan approaches the French doors near a long oak table. My lips form a silent "Wow".

'You get a nice breeze through here in the summer. It cools the house right down. It can get a bit hot with so many windows. I shouldn't tell you that, should I? Or you might not want to buy it.'

I start. 'Buy it?'

'Yes.'

Disappointment slumps my shoulders and my mood with it.

'It's perfect, but you said buy.' It's difficult to get my words together without becoming another blubbering mess. 'I thought it was for rent. I can't – I'm not *able* to buy anything until I sell my house. I'm sorry. We've both wasted our time.'

Dan pinches his chin between thumb and forefinger, thoughtful.

'I see. Well, Kate won't be coming back here, and they are keen to tie up loose ends. A short rental in the interim could be an attractive offer. I don't think they've even considered it. I'll find out later when I speak to John.'

My recent optimistic energy leaks like gas from a balloon. I won't ever find another place like this one. I love it. This was to be our new start, now it's dashed by the tombstone round my neck that is Darwin House.

'Don't look so sad,' he touches my arm. I glance at his long, neat fingernails. 'I'll speak to them. Don't panic. I can see how much you love it.' He leans against the wall, crossing one long leg over the other. 'Is your house on the market?'

I shake my head. 'I was waiting for all of the Tom stuff to go away, but I can't stay at Jen's much longer. I was hoping to find somewhere to call home before Christmas, but that's looking unlikely.'

He purses his lips. 'Look, my advice. Put it on the market now. Use its notoriety to market it. It could work in your favour.'

He removes his mobile from his jacket pocket and scrolls through numbers. My phone vibrates in my shoulder bag. 'There, I've sent you Brian Weller's number. He's an old friend. Also, one of the best agents in the county. He won't rip you off either.'

'Thank you, that's most kind.' I'm beginning to wonder how I got him so wrong, and Matt for that matter. But then, I'd once trusted and loved Tom with a passion. What does that say about me? My gaze sweeps into the rooms of the house I had dared to think of as home. 'Thanks for showing me around.'

He checks his watch once more, this time with a sense of urgency.

'Look Grace. I have to go, but you can stay longer, browse some more. Slam the front door behind you.'

'No point. I'll just get all excited and then find I'm out of the running.' My mood flips self-piteously. I blurt out. 'Every route I take or try to bring stability for my family is full of dead ends, and I'm sick of it. I won't delay you any longer.'

'I'm sorry Grace. I don't mean to be rude. It's Kate I have to call. It's important, and I'll do my best to put your case. I understand your frustration but trust me.'

He buttons his coat. I'll show you out.'

***

Dan watched her drive away. Her disappointment felt personal. She loved the house and he wanted to help her but the phone call he'd had before he'd driven here about Kate's worsening condition was devastating. It wouldn't be the best time to be discussing things of a business nature with John. His fists pummelled the steering wheel with juggling split loyalties.

Whenever he saw Grace, he had an overwhelming urge to protect her. It was farcical that she'd thought he was a married man. His thoughts slip back to his dying sister, another woman he couldn't save. How he wished he could be at Kate's bedside or bring her home for one last Christmas, but it wasn't an option. The feeling of helplessness was overbearing. He saw how Grace looked in Kate's kitchen, could visualise her preparing dinner for her family. Understandably she wanted to get them settled, one less thing for her to worry about.

His phone rang on the seat beside him. It was John's number. He didn't want to answer it but must. He filled his lungs with air, preparing himself for the worst of news, and pressed answer.

<h1 style="text-align:center">35</h1>

Alice steps in front of me outside the bathroom door, arms folded.

'Mum, you were shouting stuff in your sleep. You woke me and Lissy up. Now I'm tired and won't pass my spelling test.'

'Did I? Sorry darling. Course you'll pass your spelling. We practiced last night. Now go and hurry George up or we'll be late and yes, that's my fault.'

I brush my teeth, my dream still vivid. Hannah and I dancing together. Her hands clinging on to me. The Chartwell girls, Cassie and Sophie were there too. I'm shivering, my feet are sopping wet but theirs aren't. Dad had driven us. We were all young again. At tea-time Jenny announced she was going to Honduras with Evelyn Grainger. What a weird dream. I'm trying to recall what I ate for supper when there's a banging on the bathroom door.

'Mum, George says he's not getting up, he says he has a tummy ache.' I spit out the residue of toothpaste into the sink.

'Well, you go and tell him from me, tummy ache or no tummy ache, he's going to school.'

'Ok.' Alice stomps away I can hear her shouting my words to the letter before the footsteps return and there's another thump on the door. 'Told you. He says he feels sick as well.'

My frown deepens at yet another drama to start the day. Tightening the belt of my bathrobe I swap the warmth of the bathroom to the chill of the hallway. George is facing the wall, his covers a tangled heap. A hand moving back and forth across his tummy beneath him.

'George, come on, get up. I know its games day and you hate it. We all hate doing some things but still have to, now out of that bed.' He doesn't budge but I catch a whimper. 'George don't make me cross, we're late. Please. Get up, now.'

George rolls onto his back. The first thing I notice is his flushed cheeks. Beads of sweat glistened on his forehead. Pain registers in his glassy eyes. His skin is hot to the touch.

'It hurts mum.' His bottom lip quivers and fat tears run backwards towards his ears. I rub the back of my neck.

'Okay, darling, it's probably a bug. I'll bring you some tablets to make it better. Have you been to the toilet a lot?'

He shakes his head. 'No, but I feel sick, and my tummy hurts.'

My tongue clicks against the roof of my mouth.

'Don't worry poppet, we'll soon have you feeling better, I'll be back in a minute.' The mass exit of children, bags, and lunchboxes are making their way out of the door. A chorus of bye's thrown to whoever's listening.

Alice drags behind in last place. I hug her to me. She tilts her head back, her small brow creased with concern.

'He will be alright, won't he Mummy?'

'Course he will darling. Now off you go and catch up with the others and mind how you cross the road.' Closing the door behind Alice I notice that my car is the only one on the driveway. Where is Jenny at this time of the morning. Another mystery, but it isn't my problem; George is my priority. Stepping into his bedroom with a glass of water and painkillers I try to get him to sit up and take them, but he bursts into tears in such obvious discomfort.

'I think we need to get you to the doctors. I'll be back in a moment.'

'I'm sorry Dr Shaw has a full surgery until 12:30 and we already have three emergencies booked in,' the receptionist tells me.

'Is there anyone else who could see him, even the surgery nurse?'

'I'm afraid not, but if he's in a lot of pain I'd try Cambridge A&E if you are sure it's an emergency.'

With some difficulty I manage to get him sponged down, out of bed and dressed. Each step closer to the car he grows paler, a shine of sweat clings to his skin. I support him as best I can but he's too big for me to carry. I'm sick with anxiety myself, apologising for every bump in the road. Seventy minutes later, with George whimpering, his knees drawn up with discomfort, we arrive at the hospital.

It's rare to locate a vacant space so close to the entrance, but I'm in luck. George shuffles along bent double into the A&E department. Luckily the place was quiet and we were shown into a cubical straight away.

My heart tugs. George is trying to be brave as the doctor examines him. His lips press together, eyes screwed shut, his small fists clenched to his side.

'Well young man,' the doctor says. 'I think you most likely have appendicitis. It's a little wriggly thing that gets a bit angry at times. We'll pop it out and you'll be good as new.' He turns to me. 'Okay Mum, I'll give him something to help the pain while we run some bloods to be sure.'

Half an hour later I wave goodbye to my sleepy child as a porter pushes him through the swing doors to Theatre 3. I grit my teeth defying tears to fall. With time to kill, I make my way to the cafeteria treating myself to an herbal tea, in the hope it might calm me, and a scone to bridge my yawning hunger. I pick up and flip through a dogeared magazine, imploring God to bring George through this ordeal safely.

Sipping my watery beverage, I wonder if I should let Tom know. It was the right thing to do, having an operation was a big thing, something they should face together for George's sake, but would that encourage him back into our life? Until a few weeks ago I'd have informed him of every snuffle and graze. My forehead pinches as I cogitate. It's not about me. Tom's absence had taken its toll on George. Did the stress bring on the appendicitis? No, that's a ridiculous idea. I can't make Tom responsible for everything bad that happens. Jack has had his say. Melissa too, and Alice had seen him, but George had been left out altogether. Of course, I must tell him. It would be good for George to wake up and see us as a united front. I pat my coat pockets looking for my phone, it's not in my handbag either. I must have left it in the kitchen when I rang the surgery. Cursing my stupidity I go in search of a payphone, quashing my personal thoughts on speaking to Tom. I'm doing it for George. Anxious to get it over with, I negotiate the myriad of corridors, remembered I'd seen a phone booth near the entrance.

Ahead of me to my right is a bank of lifts and standing in front of one is Jenny. I do a double- take and call out her name. She turns and I'm sure she's seen me, but by the time I draw level the lift doors have closed and she's gone.

'How odd.' I can't recall her mentioning anyone being ill but then Jenny had left early. I shrug and walk on. A round wall clock alerts me. All thoughts of calling Tom vanish. George should be out of surgery.

The nurse greets me. 'He's a bit sleepy, but fine. He'll be going down to the ward shortly and will be a little sore. You might want to have a few minutes with him then nip home and get him some pyjamas, most boys hate being in gowns.' I glance at my watch.

'It would be a good idea to get home and let the rest of the family know what's happening, his little sister was worrying this morning, she has a great imagination that's prone to over-exaggeration. Oh, and George will need his glasses too. Will you tell him I love him, and I'll be back as soon?'

'Of course, here,' she hands me a leaflet. 'These are directions to the children's ward – visiting hours are pretty flexible, he'll be sleepy for a while so don't rush.'

For the first time that day, the tension slackens in my neck and I began to relax, breathing in the fresh chilled air. My relief, however, is short-lived. Attached to my windscreen is the yellow and black square of a parking ticket. In my haste to get George seen, I missed the Pay & Display sign.

'Crap. That's all I need.' I'm tempted to go back to the parking office and explain, but I've more important things to worry about than a stupid parking ticket. Weaving my car along the arrowed route to the exit, I spot Jenny's Audi. *So, it was her.*

36

Alice is on the doorstep the moment I pull in and runs to hug me.

'Where's George? Did he die?' she says solemnly.

'No, he's fine, let's get inside. Melissa puts the kettle on and Jack gathers plates and packets of biscuits together, allowing me a moment to freshen up. When I return Alice is seated, tapping her fingernails on the table. A habit inherited from Tom. That and being single-minded.

'So, you left him there?' I nod, sipping my tea. The emotional charge of the day squashing my energy. 'But he's all on his own. We need to go there *now*.' Alice abandons her seat and rushes to the hall.

'No Alice, wait. He's alright. He's had a little operation and is fast asleep now. I'm going back soon. I came home to pick up my phone, his glasses and pyjamas, and to see if you're all okay.'

'Mum, you don't need to worry about us,' she says in the voice of a maiden aunt. 'George is the one who's been cut open.' I wince at her description. 'Will he have a big scar? And what exactly did they take out?' I reach out and Alice moves close, I lay a hand on her back, giving it a light rub.

'I haven't seen his tummy yet, but I don't think it will be too bad. It's a normal operation. appendicitis is very common.' Alice sucks in a deep breath ready to launch into another volley of questions. Melissa steps in.

'Ali, we'll see him tomorrow, won't we Mum?'

'Yes of course. He'll be up for visitors by then, and you can make him a get-well card.'

Alice considers this. 'Okay then.' Her attention flips from me to her big sister. 'Lissy, will you play with me when Mum goes?' Melissa caught Jack's look of encouragement.

'Okay, but only for half an hour. I've got homework. What do you want to play?' I had already guessed before Alice reappeared moments later carrying a box.

'Let's play this,' she places the board game '*Operation*' on the table. 'I want to see where the upendasthingy goes.'

'Alice you're so predictable.' Melissa says, laughing and scooping her arm around Alice's shoulders.

Jack had his head in the fridge. 'Lucy's made a casserole, so only the spuds to do. I think I can manage that before I start my revision. Don't know why they give us this sort of stuff to do so close to Christmas, we'll have forgotten it by the New Year when we need it for our mock A's. I'll go and change.'

'Please Jack, shut the door and sit down. I need to talk to you.' His eyes reflect a hint of fear.

'Is it more serious? Is George alright?' He runs his fingers through his hair. I throw him a reassuring smile.

'Yes, he's fine love, it's about your Dad.'

Jack's lips thin to a tight line.

'What's he done *now?*'

'No nothing like that. I was thinking I should tell him about George?'

He shrugs. 'Will he care?' I search his face, bathed in disappointment. Was Tom remotely aware of what he'd lost?

'Of course, he'll care. He loves you all.' Jack rolls his eyes.

'And the other seventeen no doubt.'

I push myself up, filling the space between us.

'Try not to be so bitter. He's still your father. Put yourself in George's shoes. If you were sick in hospital, wouldn't you want your dad to come and see you?'

Jack loosens his school tie. 'Me? No. But George is still little, so probably. It's a tough one. Why don't you ask Aunty Jen?'

'I would, but she's not here to ask.'

'Then do what you think is best Mum. If it makes George feel better, do it. But not when I'm there okay?' I agree and start to clear the table, but he stops me. 'We'll do that, you get back to George, you look beat.'

The holdall ready. I leave Tom another voicemail, my fourth. In the last message I told him the ward, visiting times, and George's condition. I can't do more than that.

Jenny is parking up as I'm leaving. Todd and Lily emerge from the back of her car, wrestling with violin cases, hockey sticks, and school bags. We meet half-way up the path.

'Hi sweetie, you alright?' Jenny says, pausing to rummage through her bag. 'I can't wait for a G&T.'

'Why, bad day?' I prompt, waiting for Jen to make eye contact.

'Nah normal, traffic and kids.'

'So, you haven't been anywhere interesting?' She looks away. 'It's just…I saw you at the hospital. George has appendicitis, well did. It's out now. I'm just driving back with some of his things. So, what's up with you?' She avoids the first part of my question.

'Oh, poor love. Is he alright?' She dangles her keys, but her eyes remain lowered.

'Hope so. I haven't seen him since he went into theatre. He was still in recovery when I left but should be on the ward by now.' I'm determined not to let her off the hook. 'So, you didn't say why you were at the hospital?' She hitches her bag up her shoulder.

'Not me. Must have a doppelganger?' She blinks away the lie as our eyes meet briefly.

'In a purple suit, the same as the one you're wearing?' Her reply was lost to the sound of gravel under rubber as Robin pulls his Land Rover in beside Jen's car.

'Off somewhere nice?' He says,

'Not exactly, George had his appendix out today.' Robin's face puckers with concern. 'Poor little bugger. Is he alright? Bit sore I expect?'

While Robin converses with me, Jenny slips inside. I'm pleased when my mobile rings, Robin gives a wave of the hand and leaves me to my call.

'So, you do answer your phone eventually then?' My breath hitches at the sound of Dan's voice.

'Wha—, sorry, I saw I had missed calls but didn't recognise the number. A bit of a family emergency, George had appendicitis.'

'Poor little chap. That must have been awful, how is he?' I go to reply but he's still talking. 'I had mine out when I was ten, hurt like hell. Still have the scar to prove it,' I struggle with the imagery of Dan's taut stomach and a faded scar. 'Anyway, you probably want to get off, so I won't keep you. It's good news, the house is yours. I'll get a contract drawn up and terms.'

'Oh, that's amazing. I can't thank you enough. It's wonderful news. Am I pushing it to ask if we could move in before Christmas?'

'No problem and don't worry, it will be affordable. If we start with a short let, say six months, till you sell yours?'

I rub the side of my temple. 'But what if it takes longer? I can't keep shifting the kids about, it's not fair to them.'

'Understand, but let's not worry about that now. First things first, did you speak to Wellers yet?'

'No, I haven't had a chance.'

'Ah. You've a lot on your plate, I can give him a call if you like?'

'Oh, would you? Please Dan if you could that would be wonderful. Thank you. George is my priority. I'm a bit out of my depth. Tom used to do everything like that you see.' *Why on earth did I say that? Makes me sound pathetic.*

'Not a problem, you get off to your boy. Oh, and nice photo by the way, and a pretty good article.'

The moisture dissipates from my mouth. The magazine article, I'd forgotten all about it.

'I — I, haven't seen it yet. Sorry, Dan, I don't mean to be rude but – I have to go and thank you. At least

I've had one good thing come out of the day.' Dan chuckles.

'If a chat with me makes your day, we should do it more often.'

A light blush warms my cheeks. 'Don't be facetious Dan Mayne,' I say a grin lifting my cheeks, 'you know what I meant.'

'Yes, okay relax, no worries.' Call me tomorrow, now you have my number. And I hope George is better soon. Bye.'

I'm okay I tell myself. George will soon recover, and we will have a fabulous new home. I can't help the warmth of gratitude spreading towards Dan. He has been incredibly kind and now I know he's single, he can flirt with who he wants, but maybe not too often. I think I've been naive. My life isn't exactly packed with male experiences. I've only ever been with Tom, but we do have more in common than I expected. We are both single parents and care a lot for our families. I think he's more vulnerable than he lets on. An un-invited thought pops into my head. When exactly did Tom and I last have sex before the revelation? I refuse to call it love making. Six, or eight months? If Dan was feeling sexually frustrated, I can empathise, but I refuse to become another notch on any man's bedpost.

37

'Well, isn't that typical?' I say. 'An agent from Lansley's just called with a four bed cottage to let. He says the markets on the turn. I hope that means Darwin House sells quickly.'

'I've everything crossed for you. We can put up with each other for another few weeks,' Jenny says, leafing through a glossy magazine. 'Sorry I didn't mean that the way it sounded. I'd like you to stay a few more weeks…If you could.'

I study her, it's such an odd remark to make. She looks back at the page she has open but not before I see her quivering bottom lip. I decide to make light of it.

'I know you, madam, you're going to con me into doing your Christmas shopping. Or making puddings or something. You can't con a conner.'

'No chance, I'm buying Dan's ready-made. Better than mine any day,' she says. 'Anyway, where was it?'

'It's Evelyn's holiday cottage.'

'Ha-ha be careful what you wish for.'

'Too right, A short-term solution but at what cost? Can you imagine being beholden to Evelyn Grainger? That's not a comfortable place to be. I mean, could you trust her not to use her spare keys and go nosing through anything private, like bank statements?'

'Or your knicker drawer.'

'Oh per…lease. Anyway, the work on the house is almost finished and I can be shot of the place. It feels empowering. Like painting over graffiti. Fresh paint and a fresh start. No more milk-cart gauntlets. The right side of the railway gates, and no bloody answer machine blinking at me when I get home. I'll be free to do as I please. I'll be happy to leave Jack in charge as we'll have close neighbours in case there's an emergency.' My hair falls across my face, I scrunch it back with one hand. 'Must get this cut,' I say. 'Do you know Jen; I was married longer than I was ever single. Frightening. New Year, I'm going to re-hash my skills, in readiness for a career. Though it'll still have to fit in around the little ones, but that's not forever. So, what are you up to?'

'Me?' Jen says, pointing to herself. 'Yoga at ten, nails at twelve, doctors at three. Oh, and divorce lawyer at four.'

'Yeah right. Every marriage has its rough patch, your twenty-one years is three sets of seven-year itches. You'll make it.' I tug at my sleeves. 'So, Doctors, what's up?'

Jenny sits forward tucking her blouse into her waist band.

'Can't win, can I? Between yours and his nagging. I thought I'd get a check-up. Told you, the menopause thing. I can't sleep, sweats, stuff like that, probably need HRT then I might stop being a class A bitch.'

'You're not a bitch silly, but I have been worried about you. I know that was you at the hospital. I saw your car as well.'

Two pink spots appeared on Jenny's cheeks.

'Can't fool you, can I?' she says tapping her nose with a finger. 'I was seeing someone.'

'Who?'

'Not telling.'

'You're not having an affair?'

Jenny throws back her head and roars with laughter.

'No, I'm not. One man pawing at me every five minutes is enough, thank you. I'm just going through the midlife thing, all lumps and bumps and hormones. Have you seen the size of my bum lately? Cellulite like a foam rubber mattress. Flipping change of life.' She walks over to the mirror examining her face.

'Here turn around.' I pull a serious face. 'I see. Uh huh.'

'What?'

I step back. 'Nothing, just checking.'

Her eyes widen. 'What for?'

'Thread veins, hairs growing on your chin.'

'And?'

'Nothing there, not even a ginger one. Still stunning. Come here, let's have a hug.' We entwine each other, rocking sideways like a silly dance. 'Say after me- I am sexy, I am beautiful.'

'I am fat and constipated.'

We pull apart laughing. 'Right go on, get going. I'll cook dinner tonight and you can relax in bubbles while I do it.' I tap her bottom. 'No more glum thoughts. Get thee behind me oh menopause.'

Jenny shakes her head, a swathe of russet hair swinging around her shoulders. 'I love you Grace La - Denning.'

'Careful. Almost lost your best friend status. Grace Lane has left the building,' I yell at the ceiling. 'And I love you too. I could never, ever, have got through all this without you. The only way is up.'

'Pet shop boys or Yazoo?'

'Who cares.'

38

The magazine article has certainly produced a positive response. Jack is the first to say that most of his class seemed to have read or heard about it, and all the ribbing and jibing has stopped. It's wonderful. Overnight the sniggers and whispers behind my back are no more. Everyone wants to congratulate me. Alice is the only one put out.

'It's all pages of you and words. We should all have been in it, like in *Hello*. I could have worn my blue party dress and had makeup put on me. We could have sat on Aunty Jenny's sofa, with me at the front and the big ones standing behind. This is boring,' she stomps off. 'I don't understand what all of the fuss is about.'

My orbit has changed on its axle, my life shows a glimmer of hope. We'll be moved in well before Christmas. Dan has kept to his word, and Eric Weller is marketing our former home. I'd emailed Tom to ask what he wanted from the house, saying I hoped he wouldn't make things difficult, and that I wanted everything to be amicable. I was greeted by a wall of silence.

My heart went out to George. Despite my numerous messages about our son, Tom made no contact.

The last I'd seen of him was that day at the golf club. George had shrugged off my fibs and didn't seem too bothered. His expedition to the hospital has brought him out of himself. He's more confident and the bed-wetting stopped. Perhaps five days away from his siblings had given him a chance to grow a little.

Hauling a stack of newspapers into the back of my car, I'm perturbed to see Robin hovering in the open garage door. He's beckoning. Hissing my name in an exaggerated tone.

Oh God, what now?

I blow out an elongated breath. No matter how hard I try to expunge the memory of Robin's wandering hands, it flashes through my consciousness. His eyes dart from the side of the house and back to me nervously.

'What's up?' I say coldly. He leans towards me conspiratorially.

'It's Jennifer. You must have noticed. She keeps vanishing and won't say where she's going. I caught her crying the other night and when I asked what was wrong, she screamed at me. I can't seem to do anything right. She won't even let me, you know,' he dropped his gaze to his hands. 'She doesn't want me near her. I think she's having an affair. I thought she might have told you.'

I tilt my head. 'Robin, you are unbelievable. Just because Jen's off sex, doesn't mean she's having an affair. Perhaps she's worrying about something?'

'Like what? She has all the money she needs. A lovely home and Lucy to do all the running around with the kids and organise the household. No, it's not that, there must be someone else? Are you sure you don't know? Please, don't lie to me, I know I upset you when I…, well anyway. I am sorry for that, but you would tell me, wouldn't you?'

I give a small shake of the head.

'Robin firstly, not all women are designed for domestic bliss and secondly, having money to spend on yourself is not the grounding for a happy wife. Or willing to jump into bed at your behest. Christ Robin, I know that from experience. That does not mean she's having an affair. Have you tried talking to her about it?'

'She says nothing's wrong; she wants some space. Women say that when they have a bit on the side, don't they?'

I flinch at his crudeness. 'I wouldn't know about that, but if you are asking if Jen has told me about her 'bit on the side', then the answer is no. And I have no doubt that if she were, I would probably be the first to know. Man up, Robin. Give her what she wants, a bit of space, and I am sure she'll swing back to norm soon enough. Take her out for a meal somewhere quiet. You must stop obsessing about everything, Jenny must find it exhausting.' I'm about to walk away but hesitate. 'Personally, I think it's been a bit much, having the five of us under your feet, once we're out of the way, I'm sure things will get back to normal.'

He looks like a small lost boy, hands in pockets, shoulders hunched.

'Thanks, Grace, I hope you're right. I do love her — very much.'

For once driving to my former home isn't a worry; it's all good positive stuff, unlike Robin and Jenny? I've been so preoccupied; I've failed my friend. As soon as we have moved out and into our new home, she'll be my focus. I suspect the menopause story is to put me off the scent. Jenny's hiding something, but I doubt it's a lover.

There are two cars parked on the driveway. One's Dan's and I presume the other is Eric Weller's. Dan made introductions, greeting me with a kiss on both cheeks. I don't mind, I'm less wary of him now. Eric wears a deerstalker hat and tweed jacket, he's a tall but rotund gentleman.

'Good timing Grace, Eric may already have found you a buyer.'

Eric blows out his ruddy cheeks.

'Now let's not get too excited, it's only a viewing.'

A viewing – a twinge of hope.

'Well, it's a start,' I say. 'Are they local?'

Eric scratches an itchy nose with a bent finger.

'No. Have you heard of the Black Nails, Blue Souls?'

'Er no,' I say, grinning at the name.

'Me neither, but my granddaughter tells me they are,' he raises his fingers to mime inverted commas, '"super sick". Which apparently is a good thing? Anyway, their agent is coming down from Manchester to have a look and see if the house has the potential.'

'For what exactly?'

'A recording studio. If the barns can be converted to the right acoustics,' he scratches his head, displacing the deerstalker. 'The house will need some changes internally and possibly an extension. He was talking about the possibility of a residential music academy as well as a place they can comfortably stay between tours. Well, that was the conversation anyway. The location would be good, no chance of complaints from disturbed neighbours.'

'Better not tell Jack, Grace, you'll have him camping out, he loves his music.' Dan adds. I'm conscious of him watching me while Eric and I converse and try to ignore it.

'And good of you to give him somewhere to practice, once again Dan, thank you.' His eyes seek mine and briefly lock but the flutter in my gut is a little disconcerting. I'm the first to look away. 'Well, I'll leave you to it. I've come to do some more packing. I see the skip's arrived and there's enough junk in this house to fill a few of them.'

Eric doffed his hat. 'I'll be in touch Miss Denning. Thank you for the instruction.'

'You came highly recommended. I'll cross my fingers on the viewing and please excuse me. If I don't make a start, the movers will transfer everything.' I head upstairs with a roll of black bags, aware of the conversation continuing without me. I can't stop grinning like an idiot. Dan's becoming a bit of a Superhero and not just in Jack's eyes. The more I see the more trusting I get.

But I don't believe in fairy tales and Prince Charming just yet. He could still turn out to be the Big Bad Wolf.

39

There's a frisson of excitement between us as my family load into their respective seats and buckle up. George is the last to clamber onboard. He's still moving with caution following an argumentative conversation with Alice, who had informed him that if he split his stitches, his guts would drop out and as they were 100 metres long, no one would be able to get them back inside. I tried to appease his fear, but Alice had embellished the facts, making George wary.

'Right, off we go then on a new adventure.'

'Hardly that,' Melissa offered haughtily.

'Come on Lissy, don't be such a damp squib.'

'What's a squib?' says George.

'I've no idea, it's a sort of a...'

'Spoilsport,' Melissa offers.

'Yes, that's it, Melissa's right. I have to admit, I'm never sure if it's a squib or a squid? Squid would make more sense as its wet under the sea, so it would be damp.' Melissa exhales heavily.

'Well, Becky Greenway's Mum says —'

I catch her eye in the mirror 'Can we please have one day without the sayings of Evelyn Greenway. She's not the world authority on everything.'

The car falls silent, the atmosphere unreadable. I'm hoping they'll love the house as much as I do and despite Melissa poo-pooing the idea, it is a new adventure. A new start. Somewhere without Tom's stamp on it.

Alice offers a 'Wow' as I unlock the front door. A stampede of children push past. George at the rear. My hand rests on the banister listening, squeezing my eyes shut in silent prayer. My heart sings as a chorus of "*bagsy*" comes from above. Doors and cupboards open and bang. Strangely, there's no arguing. Melissa reappears at the top of the stairs grinning. She scoots down the stairs arms outstretched. I step back to catch my balance as Melissa lunges in for a hug.

'Oh Mum, I love it. Sorry if I was a bit negative earlier. It *is* a new adventure.' I pull her head into my chest. So, prayers do get answered. I don't trust myself to speak. Melissa pulls away grabbing my arm. 'Come on Mum, show me the rest.' We wander from room to beautiful room. Even though the sky is a murderous grey outside, the rooms are bright. I can't stop smiling as my daughter bossily says what furniture should go where. We reach the lounge, stopping so abruptly we bump into each other dumbfounded.

'Oh goodness,' I say, overwhelmed.

'Oh Mum, it's beautiful. What a wonderful surprise, and its enormous.'

'It's not me. I didn't do this,' I say as we move forward in unison.

An enormous Christmas tree partly dressed stands in the alcove. The same place it had probably been placed for many Christmases before by Kate and John.

Melissa flicks the light switch and what seems like a thousand white fairly lights swim before our eyes.

'It's so beautiful I could cry,' Melissa says moving closer.

I can envisage Dan sitting in a chair by the fire, a brandy glass catching the light from the grate, a shadowy image of Kate and her husband. Leah playing with a new toy on the rug with her father.

Melissa, still holding my arm urges me forward. The reflection from the blinking lights are twinkling in her eyes. It's the best surprise ever.

'Look Mum there's a message.' She removes the envelope propped between the branches, and hands it to me. Inside is a handwritten note.

Dear Grace

I know it's traditional to bring flowers or wine as a house-warming present, but I thought this might be a bit more useful.

I hope you and the children will be happy here and make your dreams come true. You deserve it. It was always such a happy home. It needs some laughter again.

Merry Christmas,

Love Dan and Leah xx

Reading the note – the appreciation of the gesture floods my body with a deep emotion. The gratitude spreading like tendrils, warming me. I gulp a breath. Such kindness signals hope. A lone tear balances on my lashes. I brush it away.

'Who is it from Mum, Aunty Jenny?'

'No, it's from Dan. What a lovely thing to do.'

'I liked him before. Now he's like Father Christmas,' Melissa says.

'You met him?' I say confused.

'Yes, loads of times. Remember we did a school trip out to the farm to see how things were made.' Of course, I'd forgotten. It was pre-headlines, in another life. 'He stopped me one day when I was out with Becky to ask if we were all alright and to ask how you were – said to call him if ever we need help. Didn't I tell you? His sister's nice too.'

So, apart from George, three out of four of my children think he's a good bloke, amazing.

'I hadn't planned on a tree this year; unpacking was going to be a big enough challenge but—' Alice rushes in jumping up and down, squealing with delight.

'It's the biggest tree I've ever seen. Can we decorate it now?'

'When the removers come with our things, or we could get new ones…'

'With a fairy in a pink dress and chocolate money?' she says with a toothy grin.

'Tell you what, us girls will go to the grotto at the garden centre and you can choose the fairy.'

'Yeah!' Alice shouts, jumping around on the spot. 'This is the best Christmas *ever*!'

Jack appears with George. His eyes meet mine.

'Love it Mum, great house. Everything's going to be good here. I can feel it.' He puts his arm around George's shoulder, 'And us men have got one end of the house as a girl free zone, haven't we mate?' Jack ruffles his little brother's hair. George immediately smarms it back into place.

'Yes, no girls allowed.'

'Not even me?' I say playfully.

39

'Yes, you can Mum, cause you're not a girl.'

Before I can dwell on that one, Alice retorts, 'Good, no smelly boys in our bathroom. Mum, can we go outside and explore?'

'Yes, just don't bring muddy shoes back into the house,' there's a chorus of '*we won't*'.

My face aches from grinning. It's all coming together. I fold Dan's note, tucking it in my jeans pocket. For some reason it felt too sentimental to discard. It was so unexpected, leaving me juggling my emotions.

I discard the measuring tape on the bedroom windowsill to answer my phone.

'Hi, Jen.'

'How's the house move going?'

'So far so good. The kids love it, and Dan arranged for the most beautiful Christmas tree to be set up as a surprise, such a kind thought.'

'Sounds like he's wooing you.' She said in a sing-song voice.

'Behave. He's just being kind. There's no sign of the removal men yet. Right now, it's the calm before the storm but...'

'Funny you should say that. That's why I was calling. I thought I should warn you.'

My stomach drops. 'What?'

'It's that old devil Tom, not the nicest guy in the world but he has his followers and a fan base.'

'So? And more to the point, what's it got to do with me?'

'I have a feeling you are not going to like this my lovely, but I've heard via a friend that he's signed to do a new sort of game show.'

'Game show?' I echo nausea building in my gut.

'Mmm, it's called *Dish the Dirt*. It's a cross between those old programs- Big Brother, Jeremy Kyle, and I'm a Celebrity. Not sure of the format, but they started filming a few weeks back. Are you still there? There's a strange echo.'

'Yes, I'm still here. Can we stop him? I mean, I presume I will be the subject of the *Dirt* he'll be dishing?'

'We don't know that, but it's a possibility. However, the TV Company won't be that stupid, they'll have had their own lawyers vetting it, but I'll make a few calls.'

A dragon's breath of loathing rises in me.

'Christ Jen, why does he have to keep hurting me? Doesn't he realise it has a roll-on effect on our children? I wish he'd drop dead and leave us alone! Is there anything we can do?'

'Possibly. I've an idea but I may have to call in a few favours first. Look, I'm sorry to load this on you. Don't let it ruin Christmas. If my idea comes off, we could essentially stop this show before it starts. No promises, I'll tell all once I've got my ducks in a row.'

Even the background noise of my kids laughter can't kick away my downward spiral. This house was to be my shining light. My emblem of a fresh start. Exhaustion crushes the air from my lungs. Will I ever be immune to Tom's actions?

40

Lucy's back from her round of family goodbyes before she sets off travelling in the new year. She's been amazing doling out tasks. Alice labelling the names of the rooms on *My Little Pony* post-it notes, so the removers know what goes where. George had done his bit by marking the packing cases. Tom's belongings I left in the barn at Darwin. I'd messaged his agent that they'd be there until the end of February when the Black Nails, Blue Soles took ownership.

Everything had gone without a hitch, only our possessions from Jenny and Robin's remained. This was our last night. In the morning, we would permanently move into our new home democratically named High Five House because there are five of us and to high five meant something good. So, High Five House it was.

It was drizzling with a fine rain as I pull into the drive and give a low moan, Robin is hovering in the open garage door. My body aches from lugging stuff up and down stairs. I'm craving a bath, food, and a good night's rest, in that order. Robin waits for my kids to go inside. He's waving a piece of paper. With a heavy heart I join him.

'Look, see. I told you. She's having an affair. This proves it.' To my embarrassment, his face crumples and he starts sobbing.

'Oh, Robin I'm sure that's not right.' He holds out the paper and I take it.

Robin, I'm sorry. I must go away for a few days. Cover for me with the kids. I don't want them worrying. Say I've gone to a spa or something. Love Jenny x

It's a strange note and I can understand him being upset. I should comfort him, but what with his dripping nose and a saggy dribbly mouth, I don't feel able.

'I don't think she's left you, and the note ends love Jenny and a kiss. If there were another man, she'd hardly write that. She's just gone for a few days. Look her car's here. It's a bit odd I admit but Jenny can be a bit spontaneous. There'll be a simple explanation.'

Robin lifts his head. 'Do you think so Grace, honestly? You don't think she's left me for someone else?'

'No, I don't. For one, she loves you, and she wouldn't do it to the kids. She says a few days, not forever. She asks that you cover for her. She wouldn't write that if she'd left you. So, a few days, probably Christmas Eve. Come on Robin pull yourself together. Perhaps it's a Christmas surprise she had to go somewhere to get.'

Robin nods sulkily. 'Like where?'

'I don't know. Greenland, the North Pole, New York.' He grabs my hand with both of his.

'Oh, thank you Grace, I hadn't thought of that. She's been behaving weird lately. I didn't know what to think.'

Neither do I. Our evening glass of wine and gossip had stopped weeks ago. Conversations were short and sweet, and she remained tight-lipped. I'm as confused as Robin.

'You know how impulsive she can be. It won't have occurred to her that she's scared you stiff. Go in now, it's freezing out here,' I say bossily, 'and I'm starving. Lucy has a big pot of chilli on the go. She's amazing and Jen knows she's left you in safe hands.'

He produces a handkerchief from his pocket and blows. We go inside, with me praying I'm right about Jenny's absence. Why didn't she tell me her plans when she rang earlier about Tom's new show? I've been so wrapped up in the move that I haven't been there for her. Would I have noticed if there was a man in the background? Have I missed something more sinister?

41

I can't believe we've accumulated so much living at Jenny's. Jack has taken a study day off to help me. I follow him up the stairs with the last of the bags.

'Happy?' I say.

'Defo, Mum.'

I'm beyond proud of the way he's become, even though it was Tom's dalliance, for want of a better word, that was the catalyst.

'You've been such a help, thank you.' He puts the bags on the bed and shrugs.

'I told you I'd help more, and I will.'

'We are a bit of a team, now, aren't we?' I say, nudging him playfully.

'Dan says I'm a good team-player. I don't think of it at home, at work its more obvious.' He busies himself as we start placing socks and pants into drawers.

'Well, I know I couldn't have got through this without you. So, thank you.'

We have done as much as we can, so I head into town for some last-minute Christmas shopping, listening to the radio playing festive tunes. My thoughts flip between what the hell Jenny's playing at and Dan who I'd badly misjudged. Apart from a text with Ted the builders phone number, I haven't heard from him, and I'm mildly disappointed that he hasn't phoned or popped in, as he lives so close. Twice I'd rung to thank him for the Christmas tree, on both occasions it went to voicemail where I was forced to leave a message or appear rude for not acknowledging the gift.

Three hours later, with my feet aching, the car is loaded with food and gifts. I pull out into the late afternoon traffic. The streetlamps glow a sulky orange through the drizzle, which isn't robust enough to warrant my windscreen wipers, but thick enough to blur my vision. The rhythm of the traffic is frustrating – handbrake off, move a car-length, stop, repeat. I'm approaching the six-exit roundabout when the traffic comes to a standstill and my phone breaks into jingle bells. I groan, someone's changed my ringtone, probably Melissa. 'Damn,' I curse because my handbag is on the back seat. Flipping my left indicator, I pull into a side road. The ringing stops, then starts again. Twisting awkwardly, I reach it.

'Jenny,' I breathe a sigh of relief.

'Grace, thank God you picked up. I need you. Please you must help. Can you come and get me?'

'But where've you been? Robin's worried sick. We all are. Where are you?'

'Please Grace no questions, I'll tell you when I see you.'

'But—'

'Just come, please don't make me beg,' she chokes on a sob, that alarms me.

'Okay, okay, no more questions. Hang on.' I rummage in my bag and find a grocery receipt and a pen. 'Right, ready, where are you?'

Alert and worried I punch the address into the Sat Nav. Questions swarm like gnats on a summer's eve. Jenny's always so upbeat. I've almost never seen her cry. I'd noted that her speech was slurred but there's no good surmising, in twenty minutes the mystery will be solved. What has Jenny got herself into, and what is she doing in a hotel?

It was the sort of place that had great soft furnishings, but bad room service. Off the beaten track, and if you wanted to have some "afternoon delight", then Grace supposed it would be an excellent venue for the purpose. The gory pattern of the wallpaper below a chipped dado rail screamed 1990's. I trudge the endless corridors pushing through unforgiving fire doors until I reach Room 401, tap lightly on the door and wait. After a protracted pause I knock again, this time I can hear movement over the hum of a TV set. The door opens and I gasp.

'Jen, what on earth — what's happened?' She falls into my arms sobbing. I crab-walk her to the bed and set her down. Her body trembles against mine. I lower her to the bed and pull the chair out from under the desk-cum-dressing-table for myself. Jenny talks and cries at the same time.

'I'm sorry, I thought I could do this on my own. Robin is so… so bloody useless. He wouldn't be able to cope.'

Oh, God. It is another man. No, he won't be able to cope.

'I can't think of many men who would.' She looks up, her eyes puffy and bloodshot. 'What? It's not their bloody body, is it?' My eyes narrow. Something about this conversation is going terribly wrong. I sit back and shut up, watching my dear friend's face crumple under the ugliness of tears. 'He's not the one having to strip off every five minutes and be pulled about by strangers.' I raise my hand.

'Darling. Stop there. I've no idea what you are talking about. Explain what's going on. If you're having an affair and he pulls you around, why are you putting up with it?' Jenny blinks rapidly, her body trembling. I plonk down beside her and pull her to me. It takes a second before I realise the tremor is the result of near-hysterical laughter. She crosses her arms over her chest, hands resting on her shoulders, rocking herself. Her face is puce with laughter and tears. Then I notice something that scares me.

'Jenny the bruises on your hand. What has this man done to you?' She stills, dropping her chin to her chest, and mumbles something incoherent. 'Say that again, I couldn't quite hear you.' She lifts her head and turns to me with eyes that are full of fear. I catch my breath.

'It's cancer Grace. I have cancer, and I am fucking terrified.'

I can't speak. My own hot tears run down my cheeks. We cling to each other until exhausted we fall back onto the bed. I prop myself against the headboard, she lies on the bed beside me, her head resting on my lap. Stroking her hair brings comfort to us both. I open my mouth, saying the most stupid things.

'You know Jen, I'm glad it's only a bit of cancer, both Robin and I thought you were having an affair.'

She hitches up the bed, a small smile tweaks her lips.

'I knew you were the right person to call. That's why I hid away until after the biopsy. Robin would have gone to pieces and so would the kids. They're not as resilient as your lot.'

A displaced hair has attached itself to Jenny's eyelashes. I set it free.

'So that's the mystery of the hospital cleared up. When Robin said he suspected you were having an affair. I began to think the same. But why didn't you tell me? Why did you go through this alone? I could have supported you. Am I such an awful friend that you couldn't trust me with your secret?' I'm crying again. I'm a horrid person, and after all she's done for me. She must be so scared and I've been all take, no give. I sniff and blow my nose. This is her time not mine. With a fresh tissue I blot her face, as if she were one of my children.

'Now have a good blow,' I demand. 'I'm *so* sorry that you didn't feel you could confide in me.' She looks at me through the corners of her eyes.

'I was going to when we had lunch that day, but Tom had dumped on you and I thought I was imagining the lump and it would go away.'

'But it didn't.'

'No and the more I read about it I scared myself, then when the results came through, I didn't believe it. Complete denial. I thought I'd get a second opinion, so I went to London.' She takes my hand in hers. 'I couldn't lay this on you. You had enough on your plate, what with SF, the press and then the Matt thing. I didn't want to tip you over the edge. And then of course there was Hannah and how hard she fought but still lost her battle. I didn't want to see the fear in your eyes. I'm sorry.'

I throw her a look of disdain. 'Silly stupid girl, I'm very cross with you. You know how much I love you, but you don't play fair. It's okay for me to dump on you, take over your home for weeks on end – you help me deal with every bit of my crap, but not yours? Fine bloody friend you are Jennifer Maxwell.' Jenny's eyelids droop with exhaustion.

'I've had a lumpectomy,' she indicates to her left breast. 'The tumour was large but contained so they tell me, but we have to wait for the histology report to see if they got it all and what grade it is. They checked the first four lymph nodes to see if it's spread, they say it hasn't, but they do that don't they? Let you get stronger so you can cope with the bad stuff.' She pulls back her beautiful red hair, wincing as she tries to grip it with both hands. God don't take her too. Give me the strength not to fail her. She's not Hannah, it's different, please. 'It's funny what goes through your mind. All those Les Dawson sketches I watched as a kid, where the word cancer was only ever mouthed. Now I know why. I had the surgery on Monday. I just couldn't face telling anyone, seeing the fear in their eyes. Robin, poor love, I know he's not everyone's cup of tea and such a worrier, but I wouldn't change him for the world.' She dangles her legs over the edge of the bed. 'So, I left a note. It didn't occur to me that you'd jump to the wrong conclusion, and I think the chances of anyone finding old Leftie here a turn on is quite slim, don't you?'

'You named it Leftie?' I grin, amazed by her mirth. 'Not Burt and Ernie, Leftie?'

'Well, I sort of feel all sorry for it. It's like the odd one out —'

'Stop right there,' I say. 'That's the old Jen's humour, and that's what'll get you through it. I can't imagine what it's been like. Old Leftie here has given us a whole lot of trouble, but I think we can help him get a bit of a fight going on, don't you? Now let me help you get dressed and get out of here and home to your family.' We stand facing each other, Jenny shakily offers me a one-armed hug. 'I'm scared Grace.'

'I know you are, but let's not think the worst. The lymph nodes thing is good news, isn't it? When do you see the consultant next?' She bites her bottom lip.

'New Year's Eve. Good timing huh?'

Jenny is waiting in the car. I enter the house first, to pave the way, hoping that my beaming smile looks more natural than it feels. Robin, Todd, and Lily are watching a film together. I feign an excuse to get him on his own. Surprisingly, although genuinely shocked, he doesn't turn into a blubbering jelly as expected.

'What should I do Grace? I feel dreadful that she went through this alone, but I don't know how I should react.'

'You'll find a way. There's no rule book for this one.'

'Have they talked mastectomy?'

'I don't think so, well she didn't mention it. She's scared Robin.'

'Me too. Bloody hell! Cancer! No wonder she didn't want me near her. I should have guessed.'

'Why? You're a vet, not an oncologist.'

'True. But what's the prognosis, did she say?'

'Not really.'

'Oh God Grace, I can't lose her.' He runs his fingers through his hair. 'God, what shall I tell the kids?'

'I think that's a discussion you need to have with Jenny. You don't want to frighten them unnecessarily, but they need to know something. Be more positive, it's what she needs. Millions of women survive this, and it's a good sign that it's not spread. She said the lymph nodes were clear. Look I'm no doctor. Jenny probably knows more than she's said so far. It was hard enough for her to tell me, it's you she needs to share this with. She needs you to be supportive.' Robin rolls his shoulders and gives a slight jerk of his chin.

'You're right, and I won't let her down. Where is she now?'

'In the car. Perhaps we can sneak her in, so that the two of you can talk before you tell the kids?'

'Good idea. Will you keep an eye open and give me time to get her in?'

'No worries, now go, the engine's off she'll be getting cold,' he slips by me. 'Oh, one more thing,' his head inclines sharply. 'Don't look so worried, she's given it a nickname.' His face can't hide his impatience.

'What?'

I tap my chest to demonstrate. 'The bad one, she calls it Leftie, her little joke. It might be good to adopt it as well, rather than saying, well you know.'

He nods and rushes from the house to Jenny. I fulfil my part by distracting the kids in order to buy Jenny and Robin some private time. I'm aware that my own children must be wondering where I've got to and make a quick call to Jack and get him to order pizzas. Now we have neighbours close-by, I don't mind so much that I'm not there, he is old enough to be responsible. The excitement of having a takeaway delivery will cause a stir as it had never been possible before. Simple pleasures I think berating myself for feeling smug while Jenny's two sit happily watching a movie, outside Robin and Jenny share a painful reunion and an uncertain future.

I'm tense, my neck's stiff, a headache threatens. I rub my neck and massage the pinpoints of my skull, trying to alleviate the sensation. Will I always be wrestling with guilt? It's almost second nature nowadays. Guilt, for not being at home right now with my children, preparing for Christmas. Jenny's words, and the acknowledgement that I never talk openly about Hannah –because her death had been too painful. It's time to change. Celebrate the twenty-five years she had lived. I realise I've been shut down emotionally for far too long, refusing to even mention her name – turning the radio off if Hannah's favourite song played and hating the smell of freesias. That's enough now. Time to look ahead not back. I'm done with this horrible year. The new one will be different. It would be lucky 13, not unlucky. 2012 had given her a rough ride, but that was almost over, Grace Lane had been a push over. Grace Denning will be the one doing the pushing.

42

Christmas came and went in a flurry of light snow and three happy children. My fourth, Alice, I'd painfully watched race around checking the garden and garage, ever hopeful that Daddy had arranged for Santa to bring a pony. There was a full melt down at the realisation he hadn't.

The New Year starts with high winds and never-ending rain. Thoughts of Dan slip in uninvited. I had hoped he might call in, or that we might bump into each other in the rounds of Christmas drinks parties. Perhaps I read it wrong. I'm no expert on romance. Was his gesture of kindness just that, and the heroic character in my head my own invention?

I toyed with the idea of taking the children away for a few days before they started back to school on the tenth of January. Some winter sun would be nice. I trawled the internet on my new laptop, a Christmas treat to myself; and I was silently chuffed that I wasn't a dinosaur after all and had set it up myself. I think I've just found somewhere ideal when Melissa wanders in and drapes an arm around my shoulders.

'Are we going away?'

'I thought we might, a week at the most before you go back to school.'

The smoothness of her skin nestling against my neck makes me close my eyes, enjoying the tender moment between us.

'I was thinking Gran Canaria. It's only a four-hour flight and good winter weather. Look at this one. Clubs for the little ones, activities for you and Jack.'

'Looks epic – three pools.'

'And a water park nearby. Something for everyone.' Melissa squeezes me and kisses my cheek. 'What's that for?'

'Because you're a great Mum and I love you. It's been a horrid year what with Dad, George, Aunty Jenny, but I love this house and I think it'll be a lucky one for us.'

I swivel to face her. 'I could hug the bones off you. When did you become so aware?'

Melissa shrugged. 'Perhaps I'm growing up.'

'Perhaps you are. Thirteen soon. Right, lets book it.'

Pleased with myself, I attack the papers from the box file that contains things from our old pinboard and what was left behind the toaster. Leafing through I discard pre-Christmas appointments but halt, fingering the invitation to the Chartley reunion. The date delayed due to crucial building works and a request for donations. It would be great to catch up with my old dorm mates and see how their lives had panned out. Would Cassie have a brood of children? Dear tiny, mousy Sophie, Maureen's lackey, and what of Maureen? Well, that was a question and a half. She was earmarked as the one to succeed, she had the looks and determination, I'd be surprised if she'd not flourished into a modelling career or married a millionaire. Chartley was going to be one hell of a party. Silly how at the time I'd thought my life mundane. LWT (life without Tom) had changed that. I wonder if any of the girls read my magazine article?

The journal, a present from Jack, lay beside the invitation. The cover faux silk in vivid colours. I pick up my pen and write:

LWT 2013 New Year's Resolutions.
Stop thinking about Dan Mayne
Keep up the gym.
Take up another sport, perhaps tennis or golf.
Learn a new skill – tap dancing, pottery, photography.
Learn a new language.
Don't neglect your friends.
Do something scary.
Think more of others.
Stop blaming Tom.
Stop thinking about Dan Mayne.

I don't have to add stop smoking, I'd done that, giving up was easier than expected and now I only drink in moderation, something else I have SF to thank for. A tingle of excitement runs through my veins. Two thousand and thirteen would be my year. No more being the victim.

The holiday had been my best idea yet, but it was good to be going home. Jack helped me load the luggage into our car. My other three settle into their seats and fall asleep as I drive and for once, Jack doesn't switch on the radio.

'Great holiday Mum. Thank you.'

'Aw, Jack that's nice. Thanks'

'Just think,' he says. 'When we get home- no electric milk-floats or railway gates to cross. I can bike to sixth form, even the little ones can walk to school.'

'Yup, I'm so looking forward to a fresh start. Not just school runs, but activities and clubs will be a piece of cake now we're living closer to everything. We can all move on.'

Jack was thoughtful. 'Mum?'

'Yup.'

He hesitates. 'It'd be fine by me if you started dating. I mean you should get out and enjoy yourself.'

I reach across and squeeze his knee.

'When did you grow into such a lovely young man, with such empathy?'

'S'pose, working at the farm I had time to think. I enjoy it, we start work again next weekend. I want you to be happy and you're not too old.'

'Thanks,' I say, giving his knee a playful tap, 'but I'm not quite ready for dating, although if someone nice comes along in the future, then so be it. First, we all need to settle and have less turmoil in our lives.'

'Will Aunty Jenny be ok? I mean, not like Aunty Hannah.'

'She'll be fine. Not everyone dies if they have cancer. Hannah was one of the unlucky ones. Hers was a rare form, and very aggressive. Jenny's isn't like that.'

'I liked her – Aunty Hannah I mean. I remember she tried to teach me the piano. I was crap.'

'Thanks, Jack.'

'What for?'

I turn slowly into our driveway.

'Bringing Hannah to life. We don't talk about her and that's my fault. From now on we will. I was so sewn up in my own grief, I didn't realise anyone else missed her too.'

'Missy and I often talk about her. The little ones don't remember her, but she was great fun.'

A warm cosiness fills my heart, not just from my locked-up memories, but my children feeling it's the right time to be honest and open. I cross my fingers. I want it too.

43

Jack rouses the young ones from the car, waking Melissa too. I unlock the front door, stop and inhale the gratifying aroma of baking flooding my nostrils.

'Something smells good,' Melissa says, struggling to get her suitcase over the threshold. 'I bet it's Lucy. Great I'm starving.' Sure enough, there are cakes cooling on the rack and a lasagne and salad in the fridge.

Once everyone's fed I call Lucy to thank her, but the phone rings out unanswered. I hang up before it goes to voice mail. A few moments later my phone rings and expecting it to be Lucy seeing a missed call, I put it to my ear without checking the screen.

'Oh great,' I say. 'Thanks for calling me back. I wanted to thank you for everything. The kids have brought you back a little something and I was wondering what you were doing tomorrow. If Jen can spare you, come for supper. I promise I'll do all the cooking and you can sit back with a glass of something stronger than your usual coffee.'

'Mm, not sure, coffee is my usual, but cooking me supper sounds a magnificent idea.' I jerk my phone away reading the screen.

'Dan?' I say flustered, as something akin to butterfly wings flutter inside my ribs. 'Sorry, I thought you were someone else.'

'Obviously. So does that mean I don't get supper?' His voice does something strange to my insides and the sensation is alarming in its rareness. He's snuck into my thoughts on many an occasion while I lounged in the sun. My cheeks grow hot and all sensible conversation escapes me, I flounder for something witty to say.

'Maybe another time. We've just returned from holiday. I haven't unpacked yet and I need to catch up with ironing the children's things for school.' *Boring, boring. Next, I'll be telling him the oven needs cleaning.*

'I'll hold you to that. So, nice holiday? Plenty of white bits? Just teasing. By the way, sorry to hear about Jen. How's she doing?' At last, something we can talk about without me sounding inept. I want him to keep talking; the warm, cosy feeling in my gut is addictive.

'She's doing well. Getting stronger. Robin's taking her away once she's finished her treatment. I think they all need it. Cancer takes its toll on everyone in a family, not just the one who has it.' He makes a strange sound followed by silence. 'Hello Dan, are you still there?'

'Yes, sorry, miles away.'

'Sorry it's me, I do drone on.'

'No, you don't.' His voice has lost its humour. 'Now why did I call? Oh yes, Leah's birthday. I'm stuck with organising a party at very short notice. I have no idea who should be there or how to go about it. Kate took care of that sort of stuff.'

I smile at the thought of him being less self-assured than usual.

'Do you need my help?'

'Nice of you to offer, but I have it all sorted, I think. Well, I cheated. I have no idea what eight-year-olds do at parties, so I booked an entertainer. All I need are some guests. I can't find the address book, Flora's put it somewhere. Do you have details for Olivia, Lily, Maxine, and Freya. Goes without saying that Alice is invited. It's Saturday.'

'Lovely, and yes, I'll text them over. What time, and does it have a theme?'

'Three-thirty, and yes it does. It's a catwalk party. Red carpet, pink lemonade, hair, and nails and all that stuff. My sister's idea, apparently it's the "done" thing in the US. That's what I meant about the entertainer. It's a woman and her team, not my idea of entertainment. It's like a red-carpet pageant. Not that I understand any of it.'

'Sounds wonderful. She'll love it. What can Alice get her?'

'Nothing, nothing at all. She's already been spoilt to death. I got her a pony, which she has yet to meet. I must admit, I can't wait to see her face, I love surprises. So no presents. Save your money for Alice's next birthday bash, you'll need it.'

Is it that I'm tired from the journey that makes me so sensitive or the way he says it that makes me bristle. Does he think we're on the breadline now that we've bought the house? My nose twitches with aggravation.

'Dan, I may be a single mother bringing up four children but I'm not destitute. I can afford a birthday present for Leah. Tom robbed me of my trust, not my bank account.'

'Whoa, whoa, stop there. Where did that come from? I'm sorry you got the wrong end of the stick. I wasn't insinuating you're a charity case, merely that Leah will be overrun with gifts —' 'One of which will be from Alice. I'll text you the numbers. Now if you don't mind, I must go.' I cut him off before he has time to reply. 'Bloody man, who does he think he is, and why do I let him get to me?'

<h1 style="text-align:center">44</h1>

Tom hadn't made contact at all over Christmas. Instead, he sent an envelope with cheques made out to each child. Jack's is still in the envelope, and I suspect that's where it will stay. I wish I were rid of Tom, our divorce proceedings drag on, with him running up my bill by arguing every point.

My phone rings again and this time I check the screen.

'Happy New Year,' Jenny yells.

'And to you, my lovely.'

'Mind you after last year's debacle, it couldn't be any worse.'

I cross myself. 'Don't tempt fate.'

'Rubbish. Anyway, the reason for my call. The idea to stop Tom's show in its tracks is gathering momentum…'

'You haven't told me what your idea is yet. Should I be worried or excited?'

Jenny trills a ladylike laugh. 'Be patient, I will reveal all, but I thought it would be better to get Kellan from KIT involved. It was her idea, and she has the contacts. I can't take all the credit. We talked about it when I was in London. She's been doing a feasibility study. She's going to call you to get some dates pencilled in. She'll come here. Any excuse to get out of London.'

'Jen, this is all smoke and mirrors. Where exactly do I fit into this?'

'Be patient.'

'Easy to say but I'm nervous at what you're plotting. How are you anyway?'

'Still sore, glad I can shower again. Everyone is less panicked and Robin gets *Man of the Year* award. He's been brilliant. I should've had more faith in him. He didn't fall apart, and it's made us both stronger.'

'I'm glad. You two are forever.'

'I hope so.'

'Believe it. I was going to call in to the surgery for a chat with him today. Alice keeps on about a dog. I'm not keen but I wanted to ask about breeds etcetera.'

'Oh, deep joy. Get another cat, they don't need walking and bury their own muck. Enjoy.'

'I will.'

'Oh by the way, have you heard the caravan park thing went through planning? Evelyn will be livid.'

'Anything that annoys that woman is good in my book,' I laugh.

Robin's surgery is reasonably quiet. He discusses the road and safety of the animal first. Jen was right, it is a bit of a responsibility. I'm about to leave when out of the blue, Robin says he's seen Tom.

'He was a bit down actually. Said how he'd missed the kids at Christmas. Also, how he'd mucked up and said some nasty things. The pub thing. He wanted to hurt you because of the row you had at the house. He knew that Jack would never forgive him. I think he meant it. He seemed quite sincere.'

'I don't want a war with him, and if he had wanted to see the children over Christmas there was nothing stopping him. It's this quiz thing that worries me.'

'Yes, Jenny told me. It's a worry. I suppose, I mean, you never know the way these things work out, do you?'

'Well as long as it doesn't affect our lives, I don't care how he earns a living.'

'I think he misses his job. He said what he did was— —'

'Part and parcel of it? Yes, that was his excuse for multiple adultery. I told him that the Mutiny on the Bounty excuse about bedding tribeswomen didn't wash with me, and he wasn't Fletcher Christian. Sorry, Robin. I don't wish him a bad time. He did that for himself. It's his loss. I can't feel sorry for him.'

I'm surprised to get a phone call from Kellan. Yes, I've met her on many occasions and each time she made me feel frumpy. She is everything I'm not- tall, slender, olive skinned with huge almond eyes. She always looks as if she'd climbed off the catwalk. I'm even straightening my skirt just saying hello. We exchange niceties about our respective Christmases then switch to Jenny.

'I know. Robin says she's hardly left the house since Christmas,' I say, feeling guilty that I'd abandoned her by going away.

'Did you speak to her today?' she asks.

'No. Not yet.'

'She's had good news. Her tumour's been downgraded to two, so no need for chemotherapy. Seven weeks of daily radiotherapy, though. Lucy's made up a rota to take her. Can you believe she wanted to drive herself each day?'

'Yes, I can,' I say, feeling miffed that Kellan heard the good news before I did and now I'll have to pretend I don't know so that I can be excited when Jenny tells me.

'That's why I called. I think by now she may be up for lunch, and it's easier to discuss the project face to face.'

'Ah, so I'm a project now, am I?'

'Definitely. I'll text you some dates.'

'We'll work around you as the only working girl among us.'

'Ah,' she says mysteriously. You never know, things may change on that front. But that's enough of a teaser for now. I've a meeting in ten, but I have to say that I think we have something special for you.'

Alice has at least five strops while getting ready for Leah's party. Thankfully Melissa comes to my rescue and takes over 'the what-to-wear' drama, leaving me to panic over my own outfit. For some reason I want to look especially good today. Some reason? Who am I kidding? The last two occasions Dan set eyes on me I looked a wreck.

I choose a pale blue silk top, my vintage Chanel bouclé jacket, tan trousers, boots, and add a string of pearls for good measure.

I'm appraising my look when Melissa brings Alice in for inspection.

'What do you think, Mum? Alice, give us a twirl.'

She's created two fine plaits from her forehead and pinned them with a sparkly comb at the back.

'Goodness, is that lipstick?' I say.

'It's lip gloss Mum. It is a catwalk party, remember? And look,' Alice comes closer, her eyes revealing a light brushing of gold eye shadow.

'It's lovely. You look like a princess,' I say.

Alice beams. 'Lissy is brill at it. You should let her do yours.'

'Yes, come on, Mum, you always do the same old thing.'

I laugh. 'No way. You'll have me looking like a rock chick.'

'No I won't…promise.'

'Go on, Mum,' eggs Alice.

Melissa returns carrying an eye shadow palette and several brushes.

'Now sit back and sit still.'

'Bossy boots.' Reluctantly, I sit on the stool and close my eyes.

'No peeking till she's finished,' Alice adds.

Melissa's touch is light.

'Right, you're done. Look at me, so I can see if they match. 'Mm, pretty good, you look more like Aunty Hannah.'

I swivel my knees to face the mirror.

'Oh my goodness,' she's right, I can see Hannah in my reflection.

'Like it?'

'Love it. Smokey greys. I would never have tried that combination. Clever girl. How did you learn all that?'

'YouTube. You can learn anything on there, and I want to be a make-up artist when I'm older.'

Alice frowns, examining me closely.

'Hum, pretty good for a Mum. Now you might actually get a boyfriend.'

'Alice Lane,' I exclaim in fake shock. 'You're a cheeky monkey and I do not want a boyfriend.'

Is that a truth or lie?

45

I'd never been to Brackton before. Yes, I know it's a large country estate but the length of the driveway from the road to Brackton Hall was at least half a mile. Rhododendrons flank our route on either side. I can only imagine what they look like in bloom.

To my left, rising above the hill are woods, the silhouettes of bare branches are like lace against the winter sky. An involuntary shiver ripples across my skin. The leafless trees remind me of *Lord of the Rings* when the trees start walking down the hill. Further along an army of apple trees are ranked like a massive army, ready to march down the valley towards the river.

My nerves are getting the better of me, even though I like what I see when I periodically glance at my reflection in the rear-view mirror. But am I ready for this? Dan's absence has made me keener to see him, especially now I know he's not an unfaithful husband. But now I'm here I feel silly, unprepared. My car glides around a tight bend and through another gate where an ancient stone wall encircles the homestead.

'What a lovely house,' I say.

'Not as nice as ours,' Alice says unbuckling her seatbelt, 'and it smells of beer or something funny.'

I grin. 'It's Cider Alice, a drink they make from apples.' My breath whistles at the house. Brackton Hall stands tall and regal, hewn out of local stone. The entrance is flanked by four columns supporting the portico entrance where stone steps jut forward. I can picture servants living in the roof quarters and ancient callers arriving in horse-drawn carriages in ball-gowns, swishing up the elegant steps. This is a different world that makes me feel almost shrunken.

Claire Taylor's Subaru pulls up beside us. Alice clambers out to greet Bryony who is balancing a brightly covered gift tied with lilac ribbon. She, too, is wearing makeup and a little tiara is perched on top of her sandy locks. I hand Alice our gift, and the two excited girls race toward the entrance. Claire locks her car and comes to greet me, arms open to pull me into a hug.

'Nice to see you and looking so lovely. Is that a Barbados tan you're wearing?' she says.

'It's not. I fancied a bit of sun but couldn't face a long-haul flight. We went to the Canaries. Close enough to get the benefit, without the effort.' We stroll towards the entrance, our girls already pressing the doorbell. My insides jitter. *Why do I feel so nervous? This is ridiculous.*

'I can empathise with that. I love the Caribbean but detest jet lag, and if he's not a dirty word, then Tom deserves a medal for the distance he travels to work.' She touches my arm, 'Sorry, that's insensitive of me to mention him.'

I square my shoulders. This is something I'm becoming accustomed to.

'Yes, you're right, and not in a proper aircraft either, no free drinks or duty free.' My voice squawks higher than I meant it to, Claire throws me a questioning look.

'Oh, and by the way, loved the magazine article.' She slows her pace. 'I thought you were very brave to do it.'

I shrug and Claire steps ahead of me climbing the stone steps, the massive oak doors swinging open. Dan appears in a crisp white shirt and jeans, looking hunkier than ever. Alice and Bryony push past him with excited squeals.

'Ah, my two favourite fragrant ladies of the parish.' He starts to bow, and Claire thumps him affectionately on the chest.

'Fragrant indeed Daniel, you're incorrigible.' I watch her raise her hand to his hair and brush something aside. 'Apple pies?'

'Mini ones, and sausage, apple and sage rolls to help the adults soak up the wine.'

'Oh, very Delia.'

'I taught her all she knows,' he says, his eyes not moving from mine.

'Course you did.' Claire tinkles.

'Grace, how lovely to see you.'

I'm on a lower step, so he towers over me more than usual. I look away, and when I look back our eyes snag each other's. Claire's still babbling away.

'Whatever you say, Daniel Mayne. They sound as yummy as you smell.'

'Well, I can't have my guests drunk and disorderly and taking advantage.' His hand trails her arm as she steps over the threshold, mumbling something. He turns his head toward her retreating back. 'I resent that. I'm not a womaniser,' he says, returning his attention to me. My legs refuse to climb the next step. 'Flirt indeed. Rubbish, I only have eyes for one woman.' He lowers his voice seductively. 'Isn't that right, Grace?' His words bring heat to my cheeks. I'm no good at this and he's practised. It terrifies me.

'I wouldn't know,' I say a little curtly, feeling a mix of annoyance and attraction, knowing I'm not going to stay and watch more of his performance with the village mums.

'What time shall I collect Alice?'

His brows fold. 'You're not coming in for a drink? But the kitchen's full of adult company if you want to avoid the squeals of excited little girls. And my cooking's legendary. Please, Grace, stay.'

'I'm sure it is,' I say. 'Sorry, I have to be somewhere.' *Anywhere but this close to you.* His shoulders sink. Am I imagining the sadness in his eyes? I push the thought away. 'Thank you, but no. I must get back. Six okay, to pick her up?'

Dan's frown settles above the pleading look in his eyes. He clears his throat.

'Make it seven. The grand finale will have finished by then.' I turn to leave. 'You're not still cross with me, are you? I didn't mean to —' I didn't want to drag up that conversation again but feel I must say more.

'Of course not, and Leah's very lucky.' *That sadness again, tangible this time.* His gaze settles somewhere over my head, mid-distance.

'Families have to pull together.'

It's not what I expect him to say, and now he's turning away from me, closing the door. Should I? I take a step down, then up again. *Best to leave.*

***

I mulled over my decision not to join the adults at Leah's party the rest of the weekend, unsure if I'd made the right decision until an excited call from Jenny tells me I simply have to join her and Kellan for lunch. She won't explain why but from the tone of her voice she's excited.

The Country Club is quiet, but it is a Monday. Kellen pokes at her poached salmon. Not a split-end or chipped nail in sight, nor an emerging spot on her chin, just perfection.

'Well, the question is, do you think you can do it?'

I shake my head with vigour. 'Absolutely not. I'm not like one of those celebrity women on lunch time chat shows who bounce off each other and I've never interviewed anyone in my life.'

'That won't be a problem. They'll coach you, and you'll be scripted. Look, it's just an idea and the fact is that Tom's lot have the run on us with his show, it might not be a goer anyway. It may all come down to budgets in the end. Come to the meeting and at least listen. It could do you a lot of good. A whole new career.'

'I don't know that I want a new career.'

Jenny narrows her eyes. 'Fibber. This was going to be your New Year's goal. Your trouble is that you've let Tom undermine you for so long, you've no idea what you're capable of.'

I try to deny it but sound like a mewing kitten. Kellen piles on the pressure.

'I bet you'll have a great screen presence, and people naturally warm to you. Don't say no, give it some consideration.' We briefly lapse into silence until Kellen fills the void. 'You're looking good, Jen, all things considered. How's the treatment going?'

My attention turns from my delicious Seabass to Jenny, who shifts position.

'Fatigued but determined. The ginger biscuits help with the nausea, a bit like when you're pregnant. Anyway, let's stop talking about it, it's so boring. I'd rather get caught up in someone else's drama. Grace, you'd be mad not to do it, I'd jump at the chance of my own TV show.'

'I said I'd think about it, stop running ahead. And it's not a given, it's a pilot. Tom made several of those that came to nothing. I'll probably go to the meeting, so no more pressure. Let's change the subject. Tell Kellan about the holiday you've booked Jenny.'

'You booked; you mean. Quite the holiday planner. Grace has been amazing. I didn't want to fly for hours on end, and Malta's a short flight. And she's altered all my favourite clothes. I couldn't face clothes shopping too- exhausting. I'm sick of the inside of my own home and even sicker of hospitals.' She grins at her own joke. 'You know what I mean. I don't want to be reminded of Leftie here, every day and that's another reason you should do the show. I need something to keep me going. I'll be your solicitor, PA, your hanger-on. You can take me to the studios with you, moral support and all that. Call it convalescence.'

'We'll see. You've sprung this on me. Let me take it in before I commit.' I examine my fingernails, cop a load of Kellen's and hide mine in my lap. This conversation's making me weary, and I wish I'd not had the pâté as a starter. I'm feel sluggish. A good run later will clear my head and help me slay a few dragons to-boot. Jenny catches my eye, a slow smile of gratitude spreads across her face and I reciprocate. No words are needed. It's over- the fear, the anxiety; my dear friend is not going to die a young death. Her *I Will Survive* ringtone now holds even more significance.

'So, here's to a great holiday and no more treatment!' I chirp, raising my glass of sparkling water.

'Fingers crossed, just drugs and six-monthly checks and I should be good to go.'

Kellen puts her cutlery down. 'That's wonderful. I'm so happy for you, and is Robin more understanding now, about what you went through?'

There's a beat of silence, Jenny reaches over and gives my hand a squeeze. We exchange a look. One that says 'It's all okay'. She mouths *sorry* and I know instantly that she's referring to Robin's behaviour that night. I give a slight nod in appreciation. It's done, it's past. I want to forget the bad.

Jen wrinkles her nose. 'Mm, sort of. He's very keen to show me that he's not put off by Leftie, but I'm not ready to like it myself yet. You'd think that six weeks of radiotherapy, where every day I strip to the waist and get my tits out – in front of total strangers – would make it alright, but it doesn't. I still can't look in the mirror with my top off, but I'm sure that will pass.

Anyway, enough talk of tits and love lives. What's going on with you, Kellen?'

'Normal work-work, but I have actually sold myself on this idea, and I think Grace should do it.'

I groan, pressing my face into my hands.

'I thought I'd asked you to drop it. Give me a chance to consider it at least.'

Kellen pushes. 'First thoughts though?'

'Well, it's a stupid idea, I couldn't possibly do it, but the premise – wronged or betrayed women and their lives after, all sounds, well, a bit needy.'

'Not at all,' Kellen says, pouring water into her glass. 'It's not designed to be sensationalism, it's serious journalism.'

'Hardly,' I quip. 'I read the outline. I mean, one husband ran off with that MP, what's his name? Bushy eyebrows was in the cabinet for a while god knows which PM was in place. Anyway, him. Another murdered his next-door neighbour when she threatened to tell his wife about their affair.'

'Bloody hell. Sounds fab, I'd watch it.' Jenny says taking my hand and giving it a squeeze.

'Oh, come on Jen, I've no experience of any of it. I'd look a right prat.'

'No you wouldn't, you have street cred. You have compassion and empathy. I think you'd be brilliant. And- what a turnaround, you'd become a celebrity! That would upset old SF and serve him right.'

'Stop it, Jen,' I say. 'I have no wish to become famous.'

'You don't get it, do you?' she says shaking her head. 'You already are. Tom made you a celebrity by what he did. You can become the champion here, not the victim. For goodness sake, just do it?'

46

I'm busy making a *Tin Man* outfit for a reluctant George, who didn't want such a major part in the school production of *The Wizard of Oz*, but I'd agreed with his teacher that he needed a little more pushing to the forefront. I study him carefully reading his lines. His small his fingers shakily tracing his progress, his fear is evident. Still a little boy even at ten, he was maturing later than his elder siblings. My hand brushes his talc soft cheek. The interruption makes him falter.

'I'll give you a hand with those lines when I've finished this,' I say, finishing my journal entry, I'd got into the habit of recording my thoughts each day. George nods, biting his lip with concentration. 'If I read the other parts, you can read me yours.' He frowns, resting his chin in the V of his hands.

'There's an awful lot of them.'

'I know love, but it will be easier if we do it together. Tell you what, I'll make us some hot chocolate. That always helps make things easier.' I'm waiting for the kettle to boil when I hear the landline ring.

'I'll get it,' Jack shouts. A moment later he appears at the kitchen doorway. His face expressionless but his eyes are cold with what I perceive to be hatred.

'What's up?' I say.

'It's him.'

'Who?'

Jack harrumphs, curling his lip. 'Father of many. He wants to speak to you.'

I sense George's eyes on me and even though my guts strangulate, I try to act normally.

'Okay fine. Jack, will you make some hot chocolate for us all? The kettle is about to boil.' I make my way to the study and pick up the receiver from the desktop.

'Yes Tom, hello?' I say, not sure of how to behave, but I'm not expecting the vitriol that comes down the line.

'Grace, what the fuck do you think you're doing?'

I gasp. 'Don't you dare speak to me like that. *What* are you talking about?'

'Trying to take the fucking limelight, and don't say you don't know what I'm talking about. I've heard about this stupid idea for a chat show. Let's make one thing clear. *I'm* the celebrity in the family. No one even knew who you were until—'

I dig my nails into my palm. 'Until what Tom? You got caught out? Well, if that's how I got *my* celebrity status, I have you to thank for it, and by the way, I hear you have a part in a new game show. Now, what was it I heard? Jeremy Kyle meets Big Brother, or I'm a Celebrity, or some other trite title? Well, thanks for that one. I would have hoped that you'd have some consideration for our children after what you've put them through already.' I prop my hand on my hip. 'Tell you what, I'll make a deal with you. You pull out of your show, and I won't do mine.'

It's a second or two before he replies. I'm not sure if it was my words or retaliation which softened him.

'Look Gracie, let's not fight; you don't want to do that show and have all the fuss it'll bring. On the other hand, it's what I do.'

'Is it Tom? Or is it what you used to do? I hear Channel Four shelved your series?' I say it cruelly, but I feel like gloating, it feels good to have the upper hand for once.

'That's not permanent, it's just till things calm down.'

'And you think publicly trashing our marriage will help, will it? Tom – you're an idiot.'

His voice not so sure of itself raised an octave or two.

'You don't understand the pressure I'm under – financially.'

'Financially! How's that then? I've asked for minimum maintenance. It's not us demanding your money. It would appear I can earn quite a lot myself. We're not the ones leaving you short. You could have saved a fortune in solicitor's fees if you hadn't been so pig-headed.' I realise I'm shouting and worried that George will have heard one half of the conversation. 'Look Tom, for the kids' sake, I want us to be civil.'

'Me too Grace, It's just I'm having a bit of trouble with some of the radical bodies.'

'What are you talking about? Who?'

'Save the Children for a start. They think I should support the other fourteen financially.'

I lean against the wall. 'You mean your jungle kids? And I think you'll find it was seventeen last count.'

'I'm contesting three of them.' He says it as if three fewer made his crime less worthy. 'Seriously, this could ruin me. Grace, Grace? Are you listening? It's ridiculous, you agree, right? If you drop the chat show stuff, then mine can go ahead, and I can get them off my back.'

Bile bubbles in my windpipe. The wound inside me poked raw once again. It's incomprehensible that I once loved this stranger. That we shared dreams, made love and babies together; the last obviously not so important to him as it was to me. I clear my throat, my head suddenly clear.

'It seems that you know even less about me than I you. Do you actually give a shit about our children?'

'Calm down, of course I do.'

'Liar. I left you dozens of messages when George was in the hospital. You didn't even bother to call back. Not one phone call Tom, not one. He could have died for all you cared. We all could've. Well, if you want to go ahead and do your stupid show and humiliate us further, go ahead. Until you called, I wasn't even sure if I wanted to do mine. I haven't even signed a contract, but now I think you've helped me make up my mind. So, I tell you what Tom, we'll both do our shows and see which does best in the ratings. As for the other problem you have, well as the saying goes, you made your bed so you can lie in it. Goodbye, Tom.'

I replaced the phone on its cradle and pull the socket from the wall, feeling a stronger person than five minutes ago. *How dare he tell me what I can and can't do.*

In the kitchen, Jack pumps a fist. I gather he caught some of the conversation. George, owl eyed with apprehension, is pale. I paste on a smile, a signal that all's well. Even though I have rats gnawing at my ribs.

'Right, Tin Man. Let's get this show on the road. We'll show them what having a heart looks like.'

***

I slept well last night and with the kitchen to myself, I'm doing some baking when Melissa bursts through the door with such force I almost drop the bowl.

'Mum, you are never going to believe this!' Melissa waves jazz hands at me. Her eyes sparkle with mischief. 'You'll never guess, it's brilliant. Well not for Becky, but … Becky Greenway's mum —.'

My face morphs into a distorted scowl awaiting the delivery of the thoughts and times of Evelyn Greenway.

'Do I really want to know?'

'Oh, you bet you do,' she says.

'Go on then, I can see you're determined. What's she said now?'

'It's not what she's said Mum, it's what she's done.' I mime a yawn while my daughter takes a pause for effect. 'She's only been having an affair.' I blink, did I hear right? 'And you'll never guess who with… only the milkman!'

'No!'

'Yep, Becky's Dad had the trots or something. He went home and found them doing, well you know. Becky says that's why the milk-float was always in the way. It took him so long to do his round because of stopping off at Becky's house. Can you believe it?'

Our laughter bubbles to a pitch. I'm actually holding my sides. My mobile is doing a vibrating dance on the counter.

'Bet that's Aunty Jen.'

I pick it up, 'Bet is off, its Jenny.' Melissa raises a palm and scoots out of the back door.

'Well, well, well,' she says.

'Yup, unbelievable.'

'Ah, you heard then.'

'Hm, Melissa almost burst a gut.'

'What a hypocrite though. It's time she got her comeuppance. After all the things she's had to say about everyone else over the years, and there she is banging the milkman. Robin says what's his name, Charles, is-'

'Craig,' I corrected.

'Knew it was a C, damn brain doesn't work since the treatment, well that's my excuse and I'm sticking to it. Well, he's kicking her out. I hear it's not her first time.'

I giggle. I can't help it. 'I just can't imagine her doing it. I don't mean doing it but *doing it?*'

'Mm handcuffs and whip, the lot.'

'No!'

'Course not,' Jenny snorts. 'I made that up, but she could have been. And if I'm to take over her role as village gossip, I may as well have some artistic licence. Do you think it will be in the Parish magazine?'

'Well, if it isn't it will be the first edition this year that hasn't had her bloody name in it. It takes me out of the spotlight for a while. Yesterday's chip paper or whatever.'

'Does that mean you're not going to do the show?'

I roll my eyes at the question. 'I haven't made my mind up yet, but I have agreed to go back for further talks. Personally, I think they want a celebrity to do it, Davina McCall was mentioned, but we've a second meeting scheduled for next week, so let's wait and see.'

'Is it both sexes you'll be interviewing?'

'Don't know. Why?'

'Just thinking, Craig Greenway could be a guest.'

'You are impossible.'

'I know, but you love me?'

'True.'

***

The fallout from Evelyn's affair, brought both good news and bad. The good being that I no longer have to listen to her third-hand philosophy and that the milk-float was no longer a traffic hazard. Someone tipped the dairy off about the debacle and they replaced Evelyn's lover with a new milkman. One who kept to schedule. The bad news was that Craig Greenway refused to honour the various financial school funding commitments Evelyn had made; announcing to anyone who would listen that she had made a mug of him once too often. The upside, or the downside, depending on your point of view, was that Tom stepped in with his wallet instead. All hail the conquering hero. It makes me wonder who's keeping him up to date on village gossip, someone obviously is.

47

The oval table at one of ITV's many meeting rooms is full. With my nails shellacked and newly tinted hair I feel alive and excited. I can do this. Although removed from my comfort zone, I join in discussions about pilot shows, legal obligations, formats, and the merits of a studio audience — or cosy one-to-ones. I'm alert and give concrete answers to all their questions. My previous anxiety melted away and the idea of doing this show grows in momentum; especially when they mention the fee and the ability to support us all with money earned – not drip fed. Independence.

'So, Grace,' Gilbert, the thin-faced director says. 'It looks like we have a show. I'll get the contracts drawn up for your solicitor to go over. Welcome aboard.' There's a peal of applause and chairs scuff, signalling the end of the meeting.

'There's one thing,' I say. I'm aware of eye-rolling and huffing but this is important to me. 'I don't want to be billed as Grace Lane. I want to use my maiden name.' Sneaking a glance at those edging to get away – the ones who wore their tablets and laptops the way others wore shoes and ties, I forge on. 'If I'm going to carve out a career in TV, it won't be on the back of Tom's name.

Gilbert lifts his glasses, pinching the bridge of his nose. 'Nonsense. It could help in the ratings.'

'No Gilbert, I'm sorry, it's a deal-breaker. Grace Lane doesn't exist anymore. I can't help what the reviewers will say, no doubt I will be called the ex-Mrs Tom Lane by many.'

Gilbert purses his lips. 'I suppose it won't hurt. It's a pilot for God's sake, the whole thing might not make the six shows. If it makes you happy, Grace Denning it is.'

The day is fast approaching for filming. Even though I'm a bag of nerves my head buzzes with excitement. In preparation I've had another makeover, losing several inches of hair to a ruffian style that I can't get used to I keep flicking my head, expecting my long bob to flip across my shoulders, and jar each time I catch my reflection. That's exactly what I'm doing when Alice comes up behind me.

'I'm bored, can I have some friends around to play?'

'Mm, next week's half-term we can do it then.'

Alice crosses her arms stubbornly. 'Why not today?'

'Because it's too short notice and I have things to do. Anyway, who would you like to invite? As there's no school, you could have a sleepover. How about that?'

Alice crushes against me, hugging my waist.

'Can I? A proper sleepover?' Her plaits dance with excitement.

'Course you can. Now let me guess who will be coming, Er, Leah and Fleur?' Alice nods, against my hip.

'Can I call them now?'

'Yes, here.' I hand her the leather-bound address book. 'Put it back on the hall table when you've finished.'

Alice pulls over the stool and makes herself comfortable.

'Not too long chatting, mind. Phones are not free, remember?'

I'm unloading the dishwasher when Alice stamps into the kitchen with a long face.

'What's up love, you look like you've swallowed a bumble bee?'

Alice sidles onto a kitchen chair, unamused. 'That's a silly thing to say. I'm not a baby anymore. Leah's not there.'

'Well don't worry, you can call her later.'

'No silly. She's not there because she's gone to America. The old lady says she doesn't know when she'll be back. Now I can't have a sleepover.'

'Do you mean Mrs Taggart, the housekeeper?'

'Yes. She's gone to see her aunty in America.'

'That's nice for her, isn't it?'

'No, it's horrid. She didn't even tell me.'

'That's not nice Alice. Her Auntie Kate's been very unwell. Leah's probably gone to cheer her up.'

'S'pose so. Can I have a biscuit please?'

'No, it's too close to lunchtime.'

I shouldn't, I know, but the words jump out. 'Alice, do you know what Leah's Mum's called? It's an innocent question.

'Yes, her name's Maggie and she ran away.'

My scalp itches. 'I think you may have got that wrong, sweetheart.'

'No. I haven't. Leah told me. It's our secret and you mustn't tell anyone. Her mum's called Maggie and has black hair down to here,' Alice indicates her waist. 'I saw a picture. Alice keeps it in a box. Maggie is a free something.'

Free loader, I wonder. 'Spirit? Is that what you mean, a free spirit?'

'Yes, because she's not dead like the holy spirit, or ghosts or anything, just away.'

Raised voices filter in from outside, distracting us. Jack has kicked a football into a tree and is trying to free it with the aid of the clothes prop. George is weaving around, arms outstretched ready to catch it. Alice is off her chair and in the garden in seconds, leaving me greatly confused. I call Jenny.

'Jen, hi, it's me. What do you know about a Maggie and Dan Mayne?'

'You pick your moments, I'm making pastry. Hang on.' The sound of a tap running fills my ear, followed by a clunking of pans. 'You reminded me. Here I am, slogging over a hot stove when I could have bought one of Dan's cook-chilled ones instead. Right okay, Maggie? Maggie Beaumont, yes, I remember her. She was a year younger than me, had amazing hair, bit Kate Bush. Very sporty – horses, County show. That's where they met, I think. We got invited to the evening ball. Maggie didn't mix in my circles, but I do recall her out riding with Dan a few times. Why?'

'Something silly Alice said. That she's Leah's mum?'

'Hum. I must have missed that bit of gossip. But possibly, I'd never thought about it. Why, is she back?'

'No reason, just wondering.'

'Of course you were, and if I was single so would I. Dan always had a housekeeper, Scottish, bit of a gossip but nothing on Evelyn Greenway, and the child, Leah, lived there most of the time, but I used to see Kate in the playground occasionally. So, come on, why the sudden interest in Dan the man, and Maggie. I haven't seen her for years by the way.'

'Curious that's all. How come you know all the dirt on everyone, and I don't?'

'Because you were once the wife of a prominent TV shagging bastard. Living in a rural settlement, who never lifted her bum off the seat of the Range Rover when collecting her kids. Whereas I was a playground groupie. Well, strictly speaking Lucy was, but she was great at recounting the details.'

'I didn't have time to park and chat, only pick up and drive onto the next.'

'No excuse now though, better location and thanks to Evelyn, the milk-float's long gone.'

'True,' I say, clocking a cheer from the garden.

'So, come on, give, you have the hots for Dan, admit it.'

'Don't be daft. I don't have the hots for anyone. No time, what with my new career. I've exchanged Tom's fan club and newsletter for a Blog. It's not live yet, thank God. I think I'll have to enlist Jack's help, I'm such a dimwit with technology.'

'Nah, they'll have a marketing department for that, you'll just have to come up with ideas. Anyway, when's kick-off? I saw it advertised last night, exciting.'

'Scary more like. Can't believe I'm doing it, *and* TV puts pounds on you, so I'd better get to the gym pronto. Catch you tomorrow.'

'Oh wait, I remember now,' Jenny says. 'Maggie's parents were cattle breeders, Aberdeen Angus, over near Hicksmore Ley. Robin knew the family well. Old money. Anything else you need to know?'

'No, and don't go building this into more than it is.'

'Of course not.'

'No meddling. I was only asking because of Alice.'

'Course you were.'

'Jennifer!'

'Just kidding. Now back to my very own humble pie.'

I hope my interest hadn't piqued Jen's infamous meddling. So Alice had been correct, Maggie was Leah's mother? In which case, where was she? Perhaps I'll drop it into the conversation next time and see what reaction I get. Or perhaps not. Maybe I'm a bit too interested in Dan's private affairs. I haven't seen him since Leah's party. I presume he's in America too.

48

Arriving on set early was a good idea, I want to feel at home in the swivel chair and become more familiar with the autocue. My water glass has been replenished twice already and after half an hour in make-up I don't recognise myself beneath the thick matt foundation that makes my skin taut and heavy.

On the rail are three outfits but I think I'll settle on the simply tailored blue dress, which compliments my new deep chestnut hair. *If he could see me now* I think, then realise he soon will. Along with millions of others, and I need the bathroom again.

Returning to the set, the clock ticking – mouth as dry as a box of sawdust and floaters whizzing around my eyeballs. I have imposter syndrome big time and I'm convinced I'll have to rush off with the trots when the cameras roll, as my stomach churns like a cement mixer.

All I have to do is be truthful. Oh God, what have I done? I can't do this. I must tell them now before I make an idiot of myself.

I'm gripping the prompt sheet in case I get stuck, but my hands are shaking so much the words blur. I glance hopefully at the lighting man.

'If I bribe you, can you cause a blackout if it all goes wrong?'

'You'll be fine once it gets going, adrenalin will pump in and it will all seem natural,' he says without meeting my eye.

'I think I'm going to be sick.'

'Now that'll make interesting watching,' he says with a cheeky wink.

'Oh God, what have I done? I shouldn't be here.'

'Don't think about it luv, forget everyone else. I'm Mick. Pretend it's only me and you'll be fine.'

'I'm not that good at pretending.'

'Honest, trust me, you'll be great,' he says.

I close my eyes and tell myself all I need to do is stick to the format. The show's airing after the watershed because of the adult content. It will be okay, I chant as a chap in headphones approaches.

'Now how we feeling? Ready? Just a couple of microphone checks and we'll be good to go. Okay?' I pull a smile so taut I worry my makeup will crack.

'Too late to make a run for it, I suppose?'

He shakes his head showing uneven teeth.

'Yep. The doors are all locked – no way out.'

'Bugger.'

'Just think,' he says checking his clipboard, 'Naomi Banks. Poor cow, she's brave.'

On that we were both in agreement. I'd been surprised when I was introduced to Naomi in the green room earlier. She was stunningly attractive, with an hourglass figure and legs to die for. I tried my best to cover the ground with as much empathy as possible. I wanted to bond with her. The briefing notes made me squirm through pre-show meetings. I'd never met anyone whose husband had been caught doing disgusting things to a sheep, in broad daylight. Compared to my own humiliation, it was mega. What Tom had done was bad enough and I know that like me, Naomi will have been judged on her sexuality and ability to keep her man happy. But sheep? Yes, I'd laughed at the Wellington boot jokes over the years, but this was different. This woman had suffered through her husband's court appearances, jeers from the gallery, neighbours and so-called friends crossing the street and letters from weirdos.

Naomi is brought in and miked up. While sipping water from her glass the tremor in her hand slops water on the floor. My heart and my hand go out to her. I place my hand over hers as the countdown starts.

'Don't worry, I know how you feel. Let's do this together.' The music fades, camera one is on me. *Remember*, I tell myself *it's just Naomi, Mike, and me. I'm doing this not just for myself, but for everyone who's ever been betrayed by some intolerable situation.*

My voice is calm and clear.

'Welcome to *What a thing to find out*, a new and exciting programme that gives the other side of the story a voice. The truth, not a tabloid version. Not a trial by public eye. Thank you for coming on the show Naomi. Firstly, as you are aware, I have been on the receiving end of what it's like to be thrown under the bus for the scrutiny of every man and his dog.'

Naomi's right knee jiggles under her silk trousers. I briefly recount a little of my own experience, relaxing as my confidence grows.

The interview goes smoothly and before I've realised it, I'm thanking an eloquent Naomi and hearing *well done* in my earpiece. My chest swells. There's no doubt in my mind I've found something I'm good at. It was like breathing in air in a pine-forest. Dipping in a cooling sea in summer. The buzz tremendous. No more to do now but sit back and see what the ratings say.

***

Jenny waves the box of chocolates towards me.

'No ta,' I say, pushing them away.

Jenny selects another chocolate wrapped in silver foil.

'What time did you say it was on?'

'The same time it was when you asked me before, after Big Brother,' I say, and the sooner it's over the better, I think.

Jenny and Kellen arrived an hour ago for moral support. It occurred to me that half the village would be glued to the box to watch Tom. Had Dan watched my programme I wondered, unsure if I wanted him to or not. Was he back from America yet? Alice hadn't said. I wouldn't admit it out loud, but there's a lot to like about him. In fact, I'm beginning to admit I quite miss him.

We all sit forward as the music starts. I grit my teeth. Tom's show is not at all what I expected. He and the other so-called contestants went through a succession of challenges. Except they weren't actual challenges, more like, I can top your story with one of mine. The questions were naff, the answers doctored, and a studio audience heckled.

'I actually feel a bit sorry for him.'

Jenny taps my knee. 'Grace Lane – you can't.'

'I can, and it's Denning, not Lane. He's obviously been set up as the fall guy. It's humiliating. I'm glad the kids are in bed.'

'He must be desperate. He'll be on that cheque-book programme next,' added Kellan.

'Blankety Blank.' Offered Jenny. 'My granny liked that.'

'Not sure, I'm more sort of a *Southbank show* sort of a girl,' Kellan says.

I wish they'd shut up. 'Shush! I'm listening.'

Jenny hurls a cushion at me I fend it off.

'But it's pretty bad TV, not even sure if I follow it.'

'Because you keep yakking. I'll explain. At the end of the programme the contestant with the fewest votes has to do a forfeit. The audience pick it from a pre-defined list using secret buzzers. The opponent can play or nominate.'

The dark side of me almost cheers when Tom is nominated. His look is salacious when he sees the near naked dancer who will take him off stage and teach him some racy dance moves, later to be per-formed live on the show. It's seedy. I drop my gaze to the carpet feeling uncomfortable.

'OMG. Tom never could dance. He tried his best but failed miserably. He's got no sense of rhythm. This will be a car crash.'

'Can't wait,' Kellen says yawning. 'I mean who actu-ally sits up and watches this sort of inane stuff anyway?'

'People on night shift.' Jen says through a mouthful of praline.

The adverts seem eternal before the smug faced presenter announces Tom's routine. They'd dressed him in a matador outfit, complete with cape. The audience are laughing at him, not with him. He can't hold the beat or remember the steps, he tries to make it funny and go along with the laughter but doesn't pull it off.

'I can't bear it. Enough.' I grab the TV remote and switch over. Watching Tom's humiliation gave me no joy. It was such unpleasant viewing that I vowed never to watch another.

49

When the Postman's van arrived, I didn't expect him to produce a sack full of fan mail. I've enlisted Jenny's help and my kitchen table is awash with envelopes.

'Right,' Jenny says. 'Let's get organised. I'll split them into two piles, one each and from that, into smaller ones. Lovelies to reply to, here,' she labels a yellow posit note and sticks it on the table. 'Next, begging letters.'

'Begging letters? I've not won the lottery you know.'

Jenny scrunches up her nose, 'I know, but there's bound to be some. There's always the odd one who thinks because you're on the telly you're loaded. And this pile is for the crazies.'

'I think you are enjoying this a little too much Jennifer Maxwell. How many are there anyway?'

'Eighty-six. Ready, Steady, Go.'

An hour and a half later the categories have expanded to include marriage proposals and requests to open fetes.

'Jen, I can't believe the nutter pile is the biggest. There's one here from a lady who wants to know if I'll help her choose wallpaper, and another wants advice about next door's dog who growls at her when she's hanging out the washing. What have you got?'

Jenny clasps one to her chest. 'I can beat those hands down.'

'Stop laughing. You're enjoying this, aren't you?'

'Yep.'

'Come on show.'

'Sure?'

'Yep, sure.'

With a flourish of hand, Jenny lays a photo on the table.

I screech with horror. 'No, oh my God.'

'Do you think he's cold? I mean all that snow and just a bobble hat.'

'Was there a letter attached?'

'Shouldn't think so, it looks too small to attach anything to.'

We both explode into fits of giggles and place the image face down on the table. I leave her opening the last while I put the kettle on and rustle up a snack to keep us going.

'Boy, you have some strange admirers…actually, I take that back, do you remember a Sophie Coggan? Says she went to Chartley with you? That right?'

I peer over her shoulder and take the pink pages from her.

'Sophie, yes, bless her.'

Jenny rests her chin on her fist, frowning.

'Why bless her, what was wrong with her?'

'Oh, nothing. She was very nice but innately naive. You know the sort always keen to please. Helpful, sweet girl.'

'Sounds a bit ditsy. Sorry, that's rude of me. She was your friend.'

'Sophie was a bit of a worrier. There were four of us who shared the same dorm. Cassie, myself, and Maureen. Maureen was a right cow. Sophie was terrified of her. I wonder where she is now.'

'Her address is on the letter.'

'Doh! I meant Maureen, nutter. She was stunningly beautiful, Mediterranean looking with a fab figure. Father was in the army, Major or Colonel, something high ranking. She was a bit tight-lipped about them, and they never attended open days or even Graduation day I recall.' I perch my bottom on the edge of my seat to read the letter from Sophie properly, while Jenny reads the last few. I put the letter back in its envelope. 'Can't wait to catch up at the reunion. That's if it takes place.'

'I thought it had been and gone?'

'No, the building's falling apart. I had a letter asking for a donation but the amount they're after is staggering. They're trying for a lottery grant but there's a big deficit. Shame, it's been pushed back twice now. Some ceiling collapse or something. Now that I'm not a fat grey blob, I can't wait to meet them all again.'

'Fat grey blob? Huh, you never were that. SF stripped you of your own identity. That was the problem.'

'Mm could be. Well, I've found it now and loving it, and I meant to say- Alice keeps asking who or what SF is.'

'We'll tell her?'

'Oh yes, course I will. Alice, SF is a nickname for your father, shit face to be exact.'

'Yup, I see your point,' she says spearing a cherry tomato. I'll be more aware around the kids and keep *Shit Face* just for us.' Jenny holds out two envelopes. 'Two more each and it's job done. Then we can draft a standard reply and add a line to personalise it.'

'What would I do without you?'

'Hum, tricky one that. Find a man? How is Mr Puff Pastry these days?'

'Stop it,' I warn, knowing it won't make a spot of difference once Jen gets an idea in her head.

***

The TV series has gone well, there's one last episode to air and I'll miss it. There'd been discussions on a second series, the ratings claimed an outstanding following, but cutbacks and advertising sponsorship put it on hold for the time being. I've had little time to dwell on Dan or the mysterious Maggie.

For me the TV exposure opened many doors, I found myself invited to grand events, even award ceremonies where I gawped at handsome A-list film stars. My confidence growing along with my celebrity status. I'd even taken part on a quiz show unfazed by the live audience. My life has a glow of expectation helped along by spring's bursts of sunshine sweeping across the patio and into our kitchen. Outside, the birds are busy choosing mates and building nests. Their chirping makes my chest rise with expectation of new life.

Occasionally, I drive past Darwin House and smile when I see straggly groups of fans camped out by the new high electric gates that the Black Nails, Blue Souls, had installed. No one would be going through their dustbins in a hurry.

Its Alice's eighth birthday on Saturday and the weather forecast is good. There hasn't been time to plan anything fancy. It would have been easier to hire a party planner, and while my purse has the necessary funds, I've taken Alice to far too many of those types of parties; where the parents can't be bothered to put in some effort and write a cheque instead.

Alice has changed her mind five times on the theme for her party but has finally decided on a barbeque and cowgirl party. I've rung through my order to Matt's farm shop. I'm planning to marinate a few skewers of chicken, cheese, and nibbles for the inevitable grownups, who would expect a drink and something to soak it up with, as they pick holes in my décor and discuss the cleanliness of my cloakroom. Driving the familiar route my thoughts trail back to Leah's themed catwalk party, with a pony to be envied in the paddock. I suppose it was the best Dan could do under the circumstances, but what exactly were the circumstances? Alice had mentioned Leah a few times, so I knew they were back, and Leah had returned the crayoned acceptance card filled in by Dan.

A niggle of annoyance that I can't justify keeps returning. One minute I can't get rid of him, now it's been weeks since Leah's party and it's like I've been cheated. Or is that down to my lack of experience that reads more into his attention than existed, that I'm too embarrassed to admit even to myself?

Bloody Hell.

I engage my brakes to avoid killing two of Matt's cows, who stare at me before continuing at their own pace across the road.

'Christs sake. Poop all over the road why don't you.'

I'm looking out for Matt, instead it's a stranger who closes the gate. He raises a palm of thanks in my direction and I wonder who he is. With my route clear I drive the fifty or so yards to the entrance and pull up in front of the barn conversion that has become a busy farm shop. Matt has extended his range of products since I was last here, from butchery to eggs, vegetables, fruit, condiments, chutneys, and jams. There were also meringues, home-made cakes, biscuits and fancy types of crisps and breads, and naturally Dan's 'With' range. I fill my pull-along plastic trolley and collect my meat order before stepping to the till area, where I recognise the plump ginger lady who serves me from school, her daughter is in Melissa's class.

'Hello, Mrs Lane. Saw you on the telly, my John and I loved it. Our Annie says Melissa's proud as punch of you and rightly so. Happy in the new house are you – settled in?'

'Yes, all settled in thanks. Does Annie like their new teacher?'

'She does indeed. Did you hear about Miss Walker? Such a shame. And now, well, so many young deaths. It's a sad week for the village.'

I have no idea what she means, Miss Walker died before Christmas and certainly wasn't young. The woman behind me tutted. A queue is building behind me.

'Very sad, well, must go.' I leave feeling happy that I hadn't been subjected to innuendo or searching looks, just normality. Bliss. Weighed down with my purchases I struggle towards my car.

'Hey Grace. Let me help you with that.' Matt's strong hands take the weight of the cardboard box I'm balancing, allowing me to divide the hefty carrier bags between both my hands.

'Thanks. Yet again you come to my rescue. I see you've taken on some new labour?' Matt frowns. 'The cowman. I haven't seen him before,' I say.

A smile creeps from the corners of his mouth and all the way to a twinkle in his eyes.

'Well, it only goes to show how quiet gossip is without that Evelyn. Actually, he's not my cowman.'

I open the boot and he places the box inside.

Straightening, he turns to me. 'Carl's my partner… my life partner. Well, that's what I'm hoping. We're getting on well. He moved in two months ago. He's from Edgecombe, I used to go over there for a beer some nights, less gossip and stares than in the local, after the, well you know. Daft really, but if it hadn't been for what Tom did and the fallout, I'd probably have stayed in the closet and died a lonely old man. Sorry—I didn't mean to say what he did was a good thing.'

I laugh, happy for him. 'You don't need to be sorry. The reality is I've a happier and more fulfilling life too and I no longer have the ghastly gauntlet to run. The kids have more friends around. In fact, the house is hardly ever empty. We have a happier life and I love our new home. So in a way, he did us both a favour.'

Matt scratches at the dark stubble on his chin. 'Well, if you put it that way. Oh, and I managed to watch your shows, Carl recorded them for me as they were shown past my bedtime, I'd never make it up for milking if I watched it live. Great show, makes you think yourself lucky somehow, if you know what I mean?'

'I do. It was fun to make, but hard to listen to. I had to learn not to let the emotion get to me. Not easy at times. Anyway,' I step forward and kiss his cheek, 'I'm glad you're happy and it's all working out for you.' I clamber into my car. Matt rests his hand on the roof.

'What's all the shopping for anyway? Having a dinner party?'

'Birthday, Alice is eight, or should I say going on twenty-eight. The theme is cowgirls so nice easy catering- sausages, burgers, and beans for the kids. Most of this is for the grownups, but I have a guilty secret. Do you think I'll get away with passing off Dan's sausage rolls as mine?' My hand searches out my car keys that have managed to slip to the bottom of my handbag.

'Unlikely, they're a best seller. Dan's done well, adding to his cider and apple juice range.'

'Shush, don't tell anyone, but I only recently found out that's what he does. Even with my Jack working there. I must have been living under a stone or something. I'd no idea what was going on, I must tune into my nosy side. I thought for ages that Kate was his wife, I'd never make a detective. I'm so glad she was happy to sell, I don't know how she could bear to leave it.'

Matt sniffs, his gaze straying over the roof of my car.

49

'Devastating, about Kate. Lovely person.' Dread hollows my stomach. 'It must be awful for Dan trying to carry on for Leah's sake.'

A cold lump settles in my throat. It was the way he'd said *devastating* that sends splinters of shock down my back.

'What's happened?'

'Sorry Grace, I thought you would have heard. Kate died, a week ago, awful. They had so much faith that the treatment would work. Sad, too young to die.'

'I knew she was ill,' I say my eyes tearing. 'I thought she was getting better.'

Matt draws a stone towards him with his shoe.

'It was kept under wraps, so it didn't reach Leah's ears, but when Kate got sick, America had the best treatment available. Dan managed to get out there with Leah to say goodbye. Dreadful. God knows what he'll do, it's tough bringing up a child on your own.'

'Yes,' I say, recalling what Dan had said all that time ago.

'Poor Dan. Perhaps Leah's mum will pick up the slack, muck in a bit more.'

'Unlikely. Dan went through the mill at the time, bloody gossip about him and Maggie Beaumont, and him keeping the child.'

'You knew her?'

'Yes, not well, mainly from farming bashes, very pretty lady, nice but a bit like a feral cat roaming around. I mean, never settling, not close or anything like that.'

'No, I understand.'

A Volvo enters the yard looking for somewhere to park.

'Look, I'll go. I'm losing you customers.'

Matt waves me out as I digest the sad news about Dan. He'd kept all that to himself and there I was thinking nothing but bad about him. That's what he'd meant about families, he and Kate were very close. I wonder if there's anything I can do to help, not a grand gesture, I remember how intrusive that had felt when we lost Hannah. Perhaps I can have Leah over to play after school. Give him a break while he's grieving, but then Leah will be too, she'll probably want to be with him. I'm ashamed to have tagged him a womaniser. He's no gigolo. Just a nice guy bringing up his daughter. The urge to go straight to Brackton Hall and offer some comfort is strong, but also wrong, that would be more about my need to see him than his need to see me. I can justify it by saying I've lived his pain by losing Hannah. I sniff away a need to cry. It's not my grief, even though it feels like it. I'm disorientated, overwhelmed by being so happy living in what was Kate's happy place. And Dan, no wonder he'd been quiet showing me the house. Knowing his sister wasn't coming home and negotiating my rental at a time when it must have been so hard to discuss. The feelings I'm experiencing are powerful. Question is, why do I care so much? Because that information leads me down scarier paths, that I don't think I have the nerve to wander down.

I'm in the huddle of parents in the playground waiting for Alice and Leah to appear. Eventually Alice comes into view, dragging her school bag behind her.

Her wispy curls held back with a sugar-pink headband. She sees me and waves, I spot the gap in her teeth and wonder what drama this created for her teacher. Alice drops her bag at my feet, tilts her head back opening her mouth.

'It came out. See.'

'So, it did. Did you lose it?'

'No silly. Miss, put it in a tissue in my lunchbox.' I scan the stragglers but don't spot Leah.

'Darling, where's Leah?'

Alice shrugs. 'She didn't come to school today.'

Of course, she didn't. Disappointment edges in. I so want to help, be useful. On the one hand it's nothing, on the other it means everything.

50

Ear-piercing squeals threaten to shatter every window in the house and that's with only three of the little darlings, there's another seven due. Jack and Melissa are overseeing games in the garden with George's help although he looks terrified at the prospect of having to talk to Alice's friends. I'm proud of my children, Jack has taken on the duty of barbequing the sausages. The doorbell shrills.

'God help me,' I mutter, wiping my hands on a tea towel before going to answer it. Jenny bursts in waving a bottle of champagne, closely followed by Lucy.

'Mwah, Mwah.' Jenny air-kisses loudly in my ear. 'Let's get this open and start celebrating.' She leads the way and Lucy and I follow back to my kitchen.

'This is supposed to be a kiddie's party,' I say scornfully.

'It is, but we're celebrating, aren't we Lucy?'

Lucy grins broadly. 'If you say so Jen, but not for me, I'll be the designated driver.'

Jenny has found the champagne flutes and is uncorking the bottle when the doorbell rings.

'I'll get that,' Lucy says, 'then I'll help Jack and Melissa in the garden.'

Lucy vanishes from sight, returning with four more children, two mums, and a dad. I busy myself being hostess to the adults, offering nibbles and pouring drinks. Claire Taylor's next to arrive and I'm disappointed to see she has Leah with her. The child is pale, clutching her Betty-Jean doll. Quashing my disappointment I take Leah and Bryony by the hand into the garden where Lucy is organising some game or other, and return to make small talk with our guests. A break in the proceedings by *Mr Chocolate Chops* the clown, who produces chocolate bars from burst balloons, allows me to slip to Jenny's side.

'So, champagne? What are we celebrating?'

Jenny links her arm through mine. She's smiling but there are tears in her eyes. I take a breath wondering what's coming.

Jenny shakes her head. 'No. No, nothing bad. I got my six months all clear. My Oncologist is very pleased with me. Phew, I can't tell you how I feel. I know I've a long way to go but being classed as in remission, well, it calls for champagne,' she shakes her head. 'Look at you. Don't you dare start blubbing Grace Denning, I'm still in a highly emotional state myself.'

I swallow back my tears and throw my arms around her.

'Enough, I can't breathe.'

'I don't swear often, but that's effing fantastic. We must celebrate properly. This calls for something special.'

'Mm, like a spa weekend.'

I shake my head laughing. 'You are incorrigible. Anyway, I can't do a weekend, unlike you, I'm a single mother.'

'It's all sorted. Lucy will stay here with yours, mine have Robin. Make the most of it, she's leaving next month on her travels. We've been so lucky that she's hung around all this time but she needs to move on, and we can understand that. So as of June, she's off. First stop Hong Kong then over to Oz. She has a cousin living in Melbourne she'll stay with and then they both go off to Bali.'

'Lucky-old her.'

Claire joins us and I'm desperate to ask how Dan is. Claire would be the one to know. At a break in the conversation I'm about to ask how he's coping since Kate's death, but realise that doing so would be insensitive in front of Jenny, who's flying high on positivity. I leave them with Claire congratulating Jenny on her good news and set about organising the birthday cake and candles. The party goes well. Only one child was sick, and Jack didn't burn either the adults kebabs or the cowgirls sausages. The wigwam cake is awkward to cut but no one seems bothered. Tired little people begin to leave clutching their goody bags and I breathe a sigh of relief. My face aches with smiling and I'll be glad to relax with my own glass of wine.

Dusk is approaching. A succession of comings and goings and the party ends and somehow I missed Claire leaving with the girls. I've just waved off Lily and her dad when there's another rap on the door. I open it and gasp as Tom puts his foot over the threshold.

'What the…. What are you doing here?'

'That's not very nice Gracie, how about a kiss for your husband.'

'Ex-husband. What do you want Tom? You can't just come barging in whenever you feel like it.'

'But it's our Alice's birthday. She'll want to see her Daddy.' He schools his face into a pouty-mouthed expression.

I'd love to slap the face off him, but his now smug expression says that was exactly what he wanted. Any excuse to be the victim. George appears behind me, his lip quivers as Tom lunges forward to hug him. George looks at me with eyes appealing for help. Tom squats down in front of him.

'How are you then, Georgie boy?' He says, aiming a playful punch at George's tummy. 'Oops, perhaps not. Still a bit sore are you old chap?'

'That was four months ago,' I want to add *not that you cared* but don't. George is already wary and backing away out of his father's reach.

'George, why don't you tell Alice that Daddy's here?' Relief slackens his jaw and he scurries away.

Tom curls his lip. 'See you're making a mamby-pamby out of him. He always was a wimpy kid. He needs to man up.' He looks around. 'Beautiful house, did Dan buy it for you?'

I force my fists to stay by my sides and grind my back teeth in a snarl.

'This is my house. I bought it.' I'm aware my children are in the house and lower my voice to a menacing whisper, 'George will grow up more of a man than you ever were. Thankfully, he won't, in fact never did, have much of your influence. So no danger of him becoming a despicable excuse, like you.' Tom blinks, the confidence and swagger subsiding. If only I'd been more like this in our marriage.

'Steady on Gracie. No need for that, I was only playing.'

'Daddy!' Alice flings herself at him. 'You came, you should have come sooner. I had a brilliant party.'

'Did you Princess? I like your cowgirl outfit. And what do you think I've got for you?'

Melissa appears, leaning against the doorway, arms folded. No words are needed, her expression says it all. She makes no attempt to move or speak. Their eyes briefly meet. Tom's drop away but only for a second.

'Hiya Lissy.'

She remains mute and he gives in, easily returning his attention to Alice.

'So, Princess, what do you think I've got for you?'

Alice's eyes twinkle as she bounces on the balls of her feet.

'A pony! You got me a pony!' She makes for the door. 'Where is it, can I see?'

Tom grabs her arm, laughing. 'No sweet pea, it's not a pony. They cost lots of money.' He reaches into his pocket and produces a fifty pound note.

Too much cake and chocolate takes its toll. Alice's face turns red, I brace myself for her meltdown.

'You promised, you said I could have one for my birthday.' Tears flood her eyes.

'Next year baby. They cost a lot of money and Daddy has to get a new job.' Alice backs away into my hip and the floodgates open.

'You said you'd get me a pony for *this* birthday, *this* one.'

50

'Well maybe next year Princess, Daddy has to get lots of money together to buy something as expensive as a pony.'

Alice juts out her chin. 'Liar. I can't have a pony because you have too many children. That's why you have no money. I hate you.' I try to calm her but she rushes upstairs sobbing.

Melissa pushes herself off the doorframe.

'Well done, Dad, you just ruined my little sister's birthday.'

'I'll go after her,' he says, his hand resting on the newel post.

'No, you won't. You'll leave. Now!'

Tom looks at his shoes, up the stairs and then to Melissa, who is holding open the door.

'Lissy's right,' I say. 'You've already ruined her birthday. You're not welcome in this house and certainly not uninvited. If you want to have access to any of your children, I suggest you speak to your solicitor. It can easily be arranged.'

His eyes are slits of contempt as he leans in. His breath is sour with stale beer and coffee.

'You've done this, you've turned my children against me,' he growls.

'No, you're wrong. I haven't said a disparaging word about you. In fact, I don't even mention you. Out of the mouths of babes Tom, Alice is her own person, she tells it like it is. If you'd been home more often you would have learnt that about her. If it's in her head, it comes out of her mouth.'

His shoulders sag. He straightens his collar, clicking his neck.

'This isn't the last of it, I want to see my kids.'

'And you can- once a week, once a month, whatever you or they want, but by arrangement.' I notice his pallor a putty-grey, the puffiness under his eyes, and thread veins spider his cheeks. He blinks an understanding and turns towards the door, placing the banknote on the hall table.

'Give this to her when she's calmed down.'

'I'll see she gets it. Now please go.' The weight of the day dominates. I push the door to and hear voices, one Tom's. I peer at the shadowy figure approaching in the half-light. Tom produces a loud fake guffaw and shouts over his shoulder at me.

'No wonder I wasn't welcome. Expecting lover-boy, were you?'

The unmistakable voice of Dan replies gruffly as he comes closer.

'For Christ sake. Grow up man. I'm not in the mood for you. Leah left her doll, that's all I'm here for.' He strides past Tom. 'Sorry to disturb you. Leah left Betty-Jean and she can't sleep without her.'

This isn't the confident, outgoing Dan full of quips and innuendos that I know. He's like a dejected shell. Empty. His collar stands oversized around his neck. I beckon him in, arguing in my head whether a hug would be appropriate. He looks like he needs one.

'Probably in the Wigwam,' I say. 'Come through, I'll get a torch.'

'No need, I can find my way around this house even in the dark.' He edges past me, goes through the kitchen and outside. Unsure what to do I wait for his return, absorbing his words. Of course he didn't want to come here. This had been Kate's house. It must feel like a kick in the teeth to be reminded. He reappears, his shoulders filling the doorway, carrying the ragdoll with its yellow plaited hair in his hand.

'Found her, thanks. Sorry to disturb you.' My fingers twitch with the need to touch him and recognise his grief.

'No worries.' His strong fingers caress the head of the rag doll. 'I'd offer you a drink but I expect you have to get back.' I can't pretend I don't know. 'Dan, I'm so sorry to hear about Kate.' He blinks at the mention of her name.

'Thank you. Yes, it's hard. Well, must go.' He waggles Betty-Jean. 'Mission accomplished and all that. I'll see myself out. I'm sure you have plenty to do.'

'And he was gone Jen, just like that. He looked so sad, so… sort of shrunken.'

'Poor guy. I remember they were very close., unlike my disjointed relations. They were on the same wavelength. I'm surprised you never met her.'

'Not really, considering my incarceration on the —' I tweak my fingers to quotation marks, '"Settlement", It's amazing I got to meet anyone from the area at all.'

'So, what are you going to do about it? Dan, I mean. You obviously have the hots for him.' She tilts a brow, daring me to deny it.

'I do not have the hots for him. I feel sorry for him that's all.'

'Yeah, and my mother was Doctor Who's sister, from Mars. Admit it Grace, you have a weak spot for him. It's a bit of a giveaway, the way your eyes light up when you talk about him. Look, he's sad and lonely, you're sad and lonely. It makes sense to me.'

'Stop matchmaking, I've enough on my plate.'

'But you are entitled to some dessert every now and then. Seriously Grace, you're a free woman to do and see whoever you like, and you have to admit Dan is pretty gorgeous?'

'Well?'

'Well nothing. Take the bull by the whatsits and get a life.'

'I have a life, and it's a great one.'

'Be even better with someone to snuggle up to on a chilly night.'

My face cracks open in a grin.

'You're not wrong, but the timing is — well, let's wait see what happens. He's got a funeral to get through yet.'

'Will you go?'

'No of course not, I never knew her.'

'But to support him?'

'No definitely not. I'll leave the poor man the privacy of his own grief. It's not the right time to force finding out if we have a connection. Perhaps it's all in my head.'

51

My appearance at the garden centre caused a flurry of interest. I've been stopped twice and asked if there will be a second series of *WATTFO*. I explain that I have signed for another but filming won't start until late autumn, and puff out my chest at the warm sensation of achievement at having my own career. A long time ago, when Tom first became a TV celebrity his ego was almost suffocating, it makes me more determined to play the whole thing down. But it had its advantages, I'd once mentioned at a celebrity dinner that Jack and Melissa were both X-Factor fans, and free tickets arrived for the final. They'd been beside themselves with excitement. I was looking forward to attending a garden party at Buckingham Palace.

I wonder what my mother would say if she knew what I've achieved. My early years with Tom were tough financially but in those days Tom had my back when my mother phoned, slurring bible quotes and hatred.

I fill my trolly carefully, checking heights and flowering seasons. Rows of shrubs progress to rose bushes. I'm after four with fragrance. A weeping standard catches my eye. It's purple edged, fading to a light shade of peach, with an almost red centre. The label makes me sigh. *Kate's Cloud.*

***

Dan answers the door holding a half-eaten sandwich. His expression reads both surprise and embarrassment. I mirror the latter.

'Grace.'

My tummy shifts at the sight of him.

'Sorry, I… should have rung first. If you're busy, I can come back another day.'

'No, no, it's fine. Been trying out some new ideas for party food. I just popped into the house for a bit of lunch, something plain and ordinary,' he waves the sandwich as if to confirm his statement. 'It's nice to see you,' he steps back, 'do come in.'

Tempting as it is I decide against it, not wanting to intrude.

'Er, no I won't hold you up.'

'You're not and now that you're here let me show you around. Have you seen our packaging plant? Sorry, daft question, no you haven't and why would you want to?'

'I'd like that if you have time, but I'm disturbing your lunch—'

'You're not disturbing anything. Let me get rid of this.' He wipes his mouth on the back of his hand abandoning the food on its plate. 'I haven't much of an appetite of late. I could do with an opinion from someone who can actually taste their food. Everything's like cardboard to me lately.'

I want to say I understand, that it had been the same for me when my sister died, but I detest it when others hijack your grief, attempting to top it with their own.

'I don't know if mine are that sophisticated, but I'll do my best.'

We step across the courtyard to a low, white building.

'Most of my food is quite humble. Pies and Puds for the can't be arsed, or mums in a rush.' He opens the door standing back to let me in. The homely smell of baking fills the air. White coated workers wearing blue hairnets look up from their tasks. 'What's your thing, sweet or savoury?' Before I can answer, he takes two packages from a shelf and tears one open, shaking out a folded white coat. 'I should have warned you. Sorry about this but we have to cover up. Not exactly glam, but necessary. I promise not to laugh if you don't.' He holds out the coat and I slip my arms in then puts on his own, handing me a blue hairnet. I groan.

'Thank God there's not a mirror.'

'No room for vanity in here. Not that I'm implying you're vain, honestly.'

We slip on elasticated overshoes. 'I feel like I'm at a crime scene not a kitchen,' I say.

We walk through bottling and production. The pungent smell of cider making me heady, and on into baking where the delicious aroma of ginger and cinnamon fill the air. 'Apple and rhubarb pies,' he says, pointing to a glass-doored industrial oven with revolving shelves.

My mouth waters. 'I couldn't work here; I'd be the size of a house.'

'You'd soon get used to it, and lastly, our research kitchen. We move into a tiled area where unfamiliar machinery stands on the worktop.

I point to one. 'What on earth is that?'

'A crispness tester.'

'I think you're winding me up.'

'Not at all. I test all sorts. Even lipstick.' I pull an *oh yeah* face. 'Honestly. Right, if you were a woman in say, Dubai, you'd need a hard based one that won't melt in the heat, but if you live in Alaska for example, you need a lipstick that won't freeze and become too brittle to apply. It's the same with pastry – not a temperature thing, but how long it keeps it crispiness after baking. Twenty minutes in the oven at one ninety is good, twenty-five it becomes too dense and will fall apart when you cut into it.' He moves along to an area with covered bowls and containers and opens one. 'Here try one of these, designed to pop straight in.'

He holds it to my mouth, and I allow him to feed me. The soft pad of his thumb brushes my lips it's all I can do not to groan with pleasure.

'Salmon dill and watercress.'

'Mm, delicious. So, what are you researching? Tastes perfect to me.'

His hand returns to my lips, wiping away a stubborn crumb with his thumb. Heat races through my torso; I look away hoping he would put the flush to my cheeks down to the warmth of the ovens.

'Things like how fresh they keep, which go best together. Will the Boursin cheese in the puff pastry stay fresh? No soggy bottoms. I want to do a Thai range as well but some of the ingredients won't chill well. And the mini steak and bell pepper fajitas are topped with a lime sour cream. Should that be in a squeezable package and added after the cooking process? Sorry, I'm boring you. I get very passionate about my food.'

'Not at all, I wondered what you did all day.'

'Apart from chasing beautiful women around you mean.' He says from behind, helping me out of the white coat. I remove the offending hairnet and zuzz up my hair.

'Or coming to my rescue on how many occasions? I've lost count.' Sneaking a sideways look I notice the set of his jaw and realise that it's taken some effort for him to joke.

'So, have you a name for the new range?'

'No. It needs to be in line with the others. I haven't got that far.'

'What like? With Guests, With Friends, With Wine?'

'Very good. Kate came up with the 'With' branding, it was so simple, she would've liked *With Friends.* I might just use that.' We leave the kitchens and stroll to my car.

'I didn't ask why you'd called. Sorry, I just bamboozled you with my business.'

'Not at all, I found it fascinating. I dropped by with a little gift that's all – for sorting out Darwin and High Five House – as the kids have named it.' We halt whilst I locate my car keys. 'What you did, with the Christmas tree, was special. It was what we needed, something to give us a bit of hope that our new home would become well, just that. You gave us Christmas. It was a lovely gesture. Very kind.'

'My pleasure,' he said, his eyes focusing above her head.

Dare I hug him? He looks so vulnerable – no I'm intruding – time to go. I trail around to the rear of the car and open the boot, struggling with the heavy ceramic plant pot, pulling it closer to the tailgate.

'Here, let me,' he says. I step away and he takes the weight of the potted tree and places it by the stone steps. I waffle.

'It's a weeping standard. It should be okay in that pot for a couple of years. I saw its name and thought of you.'

He stoops silently to read the tag that's flapping on its string in the breeze. His voice is thick with emotion as he reads out.

'Kate's Cloud. I—.'

His face falls. Oh God, what have I done, I shouldn't have come. I turn away, I can't bear to see him like this. The tailgate is still open, I shut it and walk to the driver's door. He's still staring at the label.

'Right, that's it, mission accomplished. I must go. Bye Dan, I'm sorry for your loss.' I say it briskly, business-like. Keen to allow him his grief in private I swing into my seat and start the ignition, roughly throwing the gearstick into reverse. My eyes sting with suppressed tears and the fear that I've made things worse. 'God, why did I think that was a good idea?'

I can't stop thinking about his sadness. Perhaps he was beginning to recover and my gift made Kate's death raw again. I'm tempted to call Jenny but don't, knowing she'll tell me I'm being over-sensitive.

The din of my children returning from school interrupts my musings. There are vegetables that need chopping, washing that needs sorting while helping Alice build a pyramid for her Egyptian school project and....

Melissa slouches into the kitchen skirmishing for food. I relieve her of the biscuit tin.

'Dinner won't be long.'

'I know, but I'm hungry now. Does everything have to be run to a timetable?'

My ringing phone halts further argument. Is it really that time of the month again when Melissa turns into a screeching banshee? I roll a satsuma across the worktop in her direction and pick up my phone.

'Hello, Grace speaking.'

There's a beat of silence. 'Grace, it's Dan. I wanted to thank you for the rose tree. You must have thought me rude.'

I give up a silent prayer. 'No Dan, not at all. In fact, I was worried that I'd made things worse. Upset you.' There's another pause and the sound of him clearing his throat.

'No. It was a lovely gesture. I know you never met Kate, but it was the sort of thing she would have done. Grace, I've been a bit of a recluse and seeing you has made me want to snap out of it.'

Before I can think of a reply he carries on.

'I saw your programme. It was excellent, you came over well.' A change of subject, was that good or bad? I can't decide. 'Are you doing another series?'

'Yes, later this year.' I try to make my conversation light. 'I wouldn't have thought that was your sort of viewing.'

'I watch anything nowadays. Oh, God, I'm sorry, that sounds so rude, it wasn't meant to.'

My laugh sounds contrived. 'I know what you meant, so no stressing.'

'Phew. Thanks, I have a habit of saying the wrong thing to you. What I mean is it's a very caring show about people's indignities. It's time the press were taken to task.'

I hear the ping of a timer and imagine him in the testing kitchen.

'Has it unleashed new career opportunities? I mean, will you be the next Oprah?'

'I doubt that. I'm just enjoying it at the moment. It's what I needed. Something to get me off the round-about I was stuck on.' I catch my reflection in the hall mirror. A warm feeling sits between my ribs as I realise, I *am* more confident. 'But I must tell you, I was surprised to be invited to be on, or is it in? I'm a Celebrity Get Me Out of Here.' The sound of Dan's laughter is music to my ears.

'You're lying? Never.'

'No honestly. They needed some Z list celebrities. That includes me. I'm not doing it, though. Hearing Tom rant on for years about how manufactured it was, and I couldn't eat a —'

'Grace,' he interrupts, 'I need a plus one. Will you accompany me?'

It's so unexpected I wonder if I heard right.

'A plus one. Sounds fun. I'd like that, but where and what sort of function?'

'Nothing flashy, dinner at a friend's house. It's their first time entertaining.'

'Okay. Do I know them?'

'You do. Matt and Carl. I think we might be their trial run.' The familiar confidence of him is remerging. 'It'll be an early doors sort of affair, due to the commitments of a dairy farmer. Suits me, I'm not one for late nights nowadays.'

'Me neither, I can't even remember when I last saw a New Year in. So, when is it?'

'Saturday the ninth, six thirty for seven. Gives you a few days to organise your tribe.'

'Ouch, Dan. No please – wrong choice of words. That's a Tom-ism. I prefer brood, gang, clutch, anything but —'

'Sorry. Yep, I get the picture. Pick you up at six, if that's not too early?'

'Lovely, thank you. I'll look forward to it.' We say our goodbyes and I hug myself. I'm going on a real date with Dan the man. I give a silent air pump.

After dinner and buzzing with pent up energy I go for a run. While my feet pound the grass track my thoughts take a mental check. I'm ready for this and today I experienced a different side to Daniel Mayne, one that is sensitive, kind, and passionate. Passionate about both his family and his work. It's an attractive combination. Will this date be the first of many?

52

I've never been inside the farmhouse before. The solid building with its five front facing windows and flint walls. If I'd expected bachelor messy, I was wrong. The smartly coordinating furniture and decor of black, grey, and white is interspersed with the odd silver or pewter piece of abstract art and is striking. Introductions made, Carl leaves us to prepare drinks and Dan follows, leaving me alone with Matt.

'Well, what do you think?' he says, beaming with pride.

I wave my hand around the room. 'About Carl, or this?'

'Both. I'm so happy Grace.'

'And you deserve to be,' I say, lowering myself to the middle of a soft leather sofa. I catch a waft of scent from the tall white lilies placed in an elegant grey vase.

'You're our first guests. We thought we'd pick with caution, we are delighted Dan asked you. You look good together.'

I eye him suspiciously. 'Nothing to do with you two trying to play cupid I suppose?'

'Whatever gave you that idea?' he says, winking.

'Matt Barton! You did!'

'Well, someone needed to push you two together. It was Carl's idea.'

I shake my head. 'Incredulous.'

'Come on. You're both right for each other. You've both had a rough time. A little love wouldn't go amiss.'

Dan and Carl enter laughing, bearing oversized glasses of gin and tonic with strips of cucumber inside the rims. Thank goodness our conversation ends as I'm terrified I'd agree with Matt.

'Just friends.' I say quietly.

'Then make it more,' he hisses back.

Carl distributes the drinks.

'Time for a toast I think.' Matt says, moving to a spot that once held a mantelpiece, but now houses a log-filled opening in the wall. He raises his glass. 'To new beginnings and absent friends.'

Dan raises his glass towards me. 'To new beginnings and good friends.'

'Enough with the toasting,' Carl says, setting his glass on the black slate coaster. 'I've got to nip to the kitchen and see to my soufflés. It's all the pressures of cooking for a MasterChef.'

The comment was aimed at Dan who chuckles. 'Nope, merely a self-taught cook and lowly Cider maker.'

'Wonderful, and we must talk cheese later. I want Matt to produce his own.'

Matt gives an exaggerated sniff. 'Is that burning I can smell?'

'Christ.' Carl rushes out of the room. 'Only joking,' he calls out after him. 'Sit down Dan, you tower over me.' Matt rises and Dan takes his place next to me.

The heady smell of his aftershave is still fresh in my senses from our car journey. His hand rests on the soft leather beside mine. It would be so easy to take his hand and entwine our fingers.

'So, how's Leah doing, and you for that matter?'

'Oh, little girls are quite resilient, thanks Matt. I think it helped that Kate was away for so long, she got used to not having her around. As for me, still feeling a bit lost. Our parents died in a sailing accident when we were in our teens so we only had each other, and then Leah came along of course. I don't think either of you were living here then.'

Matt nods. 'So, what now, any plans?'

'No, I'm playing it by ear. Trying to be a better Dad. It may have been easier if I'd had a boy. Little girls are like aliens at times. Sometimes I see glimmers of Maggie and it scares me stiff.'

Relief centres me. So Maggie wasn't a secret he'd hidden from me. Her name just never came up in the few conversations we'd had.

Carl flits in then out of the doorway.

'Table, now, before the damn things sink.'

We drink our glasses dry and follow Matt into the dining room that is aglow with candlelight. This room is more as I'd imagined the farmhouse to be. The dark oak furniture is covered with tealights and a candelabra with tall ivory candles is the centrepiece at the table. Talk about romantic. A quiver of warmth rides down my spine.

'Who's the one with the interior design flare,' I say, taking the seat that Dan is holding out for me.

'Carl. He's a decorator.'

'I heard that, Mathew,' Carl says, handing out mouth-watering soufflé. 'Decorator indeed. I'm an interior designer. Well, I was, till I fell for this great hunk and ended up herding cows.'

'So, do you enjoy any of it? Farming, I mean. The soufflé is excellent by the way,' I say.

'Not at first. Me mammy was born on a farm, but I didn't know one end of a cow from the other. Then this great lummox caught my eye, and how could I refuse such a lovely man. Anyway, excuse me for asking—'

'If you must excuse yourself first, don't.' Says Matt. 'Just eat.'

'Listen to him. You're too buttoned up for your own good Matthew Barton.' Carl addresses me. 'If I left things unsaid, we wouldn't be sitting here now.' His look confirmed their meddling.

'Now, excuse me for asking the obvious, or perhaps the not so obvious.'

'Or perhaps the outright nosy,' Matt offers, but Carl waves away the comment.

'But are you two finally going to get your act together?'

I chased the last morsel of soufflé around the ramekin with my spoon and swallow deeply as Dan takes my free hand under the table and squeezes it, turning my insides to mush.

'This is officially our first date,' Dan says. 'Although Grace will probably disagree and say it's not a date at all. She's made me work hard to pin her down. I think local gossip may have given her the wrong impression. I'm a lamb in wolf's clothing, and I'm happy to play the long game. That's if Grace wants me to?'

I look at Matt and Carl who stare back expectantly.

Is that angels I hear? The shift to a relationship is a surprise: a welcome one that makes my heart sing.

'Talk about being put on the spot. I'm not sure what he means. We've both had a lot going on in our lives. Moving to a new house, children, the TV show, all that and worse, a bereavement.' My turn to squeeze his hand. 'Personally, I felt like I was running down a steep hill, unable to stop.'

Dan lifts our joined hands to the tabletop and I catch Carl nudging Matt.

'And I've been too wrapped up in myself. Kate wouldn't have wanted me to wallow and if she'd met Grace, I'd have got a lecture. Kate was incredibly bossy – with me anyway. She always said I picked unsuitable women as an excuse not to marry them. I think she'd have approved of this one. He lifts our clasped hands to his lips. 'Anyway, thanks for inviting us.' My heart clicks a little faster and my cheeks flush, but I'm bolder now and the wine gives me courage.

'Yes, thank you. It's actually quite nice to be with Dan in a controlled environment.'

Carl's feigns disgust. 'Controlled? Not here dear, only utter abandonment.'

'Will you stop trying to take the limelight. Let Grace finish what she was saying.' Carl threw Matt a spoil-sport face.

'Yes, please go on, I want to hear this myself,' says Dan. 'She makes me sound like an unexploded bomb or something else, as dangerous.'

Wriggling my hand free I link arms and rest my head against his shoulder. It feels decadent but natural.

52

'He's not the gigolo I had him down as. I've learnt more about him in ten minutes at your table than I have in the last eight months. Perhaps he is a little less *wolf* than I first thought.'

Carl begins collecting plates. 'Matt, I need some help in the kitchen.'

'Ah, yes right.'

I will myself to breathe. The setting is intimate under the bewitching glow of candlelight.

'Carl's not backwards in coming forward, is he?'

I giggle. 'Subtle as a – as a –'

'Brick?'

'Yep, that'll cover it.' The proximity of his body next to mine is awakening feelings of arousal, denied for so long. I sit up straight and fold my napkin.

'Thank you for agreeing to come, and what I said earlier — my intentions are entirely honourable. I'm fond of you Grace, I've admired you from afar for years.' He turns inwards toward me, his eyes reflecting speckles of candlelight.

'God that makes me sound ancient,' I say, locking eyes.

'You know what I mean,' his tone is serious. 'I'd like to see more of you. I'm in no rush, let's just play it by ear, see how we get on. I don't want to scare you off. You tell me when, or if, I start pushing my luck. Or perhaps my intentions are unwelcome. What do you think?'

'I think we feel the same and you're beginning to grow on me, especially now I know it's a wool coat not a fur one you've been hiding,' I say.

He throws his head back and roars with laughter.

'What have I missed?' Carl asks, placing an enormous leg of roast lamb on the table.

'Mind your own business,' Matt says, laying down a dish of cauliflower and broccoli cheese. 'That's Carl's problem, hates missing anything, he's so nosy. Bad as that awful Greenway woman. Brilliant she eventually got her comeuppance.'

'Why, what happened?' Carl asks, spearing the lamb with a carving fork.

'See what I mean?' Matt says, shaking his head, 'he must know everything. I'll tell you later. The food's getting cold and some of it's still in the kitchen.'

Carl frowns, then shouts orders. 'Roast potatoes? gravy? Now? While I carve.'

'You're so bossy sometimes,' Matt says, getting up.

'That's what you love about me,' Carl says.

Matt stops in his tracks. 'Whoop-whoop get you. You really are GP tonight.'

Carl waves away the comment and continues to carve.

Dan looks from Matt to Carl and back.

'Well, I'm certainly seeing a different side to you Matt, but what's GP?'

'Going Public,' they chorus.

Carl points at us. 'Your turn next.'

'We're in no rush are we Grace?'

Our eyes are drawn to each other's. A tingling sensation I don't recognise that's both warm and intimate and long lost since my student days when I first met Tom. I moisten my lips to speak.

'No rush at all, but can we talk about something else more serious please?'

'Like what?' says Carl.

'Like how you get your potatoes to roast like this? They're, delicious.'

The three men chuckle and the evening passes with anecdotes and happy chatter. The predicted thunderstorm rattles overhead as we say our goodbyes and make a run for the car, squelching our way into our seats. Leaves, dust, and debris take flight. A wooden pallet that was leaning against the barn took off, crash landing near the gate. Dan swerves to avoid it.

'Christ this is going to be a rough trip,' Dan shouts in my direction.

The howling wind whistles so loudly we can hardly hear ourselves speak. I screech like a frightened child when a tree branch lands on the bonnet. Dan applies the brakes, gets out and shifts it, the wind and rain ruffling his hair.

The windscreen wipers fight a losing battle against the downpour. Raindrops run races down Dan's face making me wish I could magic up a towel. He sits forward, his knuckles bleach white in the darkness as he grips the wheel. The car headlights barely break into the gloom. The landscape is intermittently silhouetted with each bolt of lightning, then blackness. Paper, twigs, and undetectable items batter the vehicle. I've never been so pleased to see the lights at the end of my drive.

I mouth. 'Coffee?'

'No thanks.' He shouts over the din, 'Inviting as it is, think I'd better get home. Leah hates storms, if she wakes, she'll need consoling.'

'Understand,' I say pushing the car door open, fighting the force of the wind. 'Thank you for a lovely evening.' I blow him a kiss and back out of the car and get a further drenching before I can unlock the front door.

Dan waves, turning the car towards the gates. I huddle in the porch until the glow of his tail lights vanish.

Inside I strip to my undies and dump my wet dress in the utility room then climb the stairs, calling out goodnight to anyone who's still awake. Only Jack replies.

My wet hair sends a river down my shoulders. I should be freezing but as I towel my hair I'm filled with a luxuriously warm sensation of everything good between Dan and me. We've moved mountains tonight.

Dry and snug under my duvet with a banshee of a wind whistling around the eaves of the house. I have my phone by my side hoping Dan will call with a last goodnight and re-live the warmth of his strong hands and softly spoken words.

Are we falling in love, I hope so?

53

Dan didn't call. I presumed Leah had been unsettled by the storm but I can't help humming as I'm packing my children's lunchboxes, I can feel Melissa's eyes drilling into me.

'Good evening was it, Mum?'

I try not to smile through my reply. 'Yes, it was. Very nice. Matt's friend is an excellent cook.'

'And? What about Dan? Is he very nice too?'

She cocks her head, a glint of teasing in her eye.

'Oi, cheeky.'

'Half the girls in my class had a crush on him when I was in the other school.'

'Really?' I say, trying to sound only mildly interested. Thankfully I'm distracted by Jack tapping on the window. 'What on earth are you doing out there? You'll be late for college.'

He gestures to the trampoline caught high up amongst the trees.

'It's stuck fast. I think it's torn,' he says.

'Alright but come and have some breakfast. I'll think of something.'

'The fire brigade,' offers George helpfully. 'They get things out of trees.'

'Yes, cats, not trampolines silly,' Alice says, dipping a toasty soldier into her boiled egg.

'Look, let's not worry about it now, it may fall out of its own accord,' I say.

'My tooth's all wobbly,' Alice says, pushing the loose tooth forward with her tongue to demonstrate.

'Goodness Alice. You're keeping the tooth fairy busy and stop doing that. You'll make it sore and bleed.'

'Perhaps I shouldn't go to school, just in case.'

'Nice try, but no.'

***

With the house to myself I set about the weekly bed change, my attention firmly fixed on the look I'd seen in Dan's eyes and wandering to more intimate thoughts, which were halted by the phone's interruption.

'Is that Alice's mother?' The voice held a Scottish brogue.

'Speaking?'

'I'm Flora Taggart, Mr Mayne's housekeeper. I wondered, was he still with you?'

I frown. 'No. No, he's not. He dropped me off about ten-thirty last night?'

'I see. I'm a wee bit concerned. He didn't come home and that's unusual especially as there was a storm, Leah hates them.'

An icy chill runs through my scalp. 'So, he didn't call or anything? Sorry, stupid question, if he had you wouldn't be phoning me.'

'I don't want to alarm anyone, it's just most unusual.'

'No of course, but it's understandably a concern.'

'Do you think I should call the police?'

I'm distracted by someone rapping on the front door.

'Flora someone's hammering on the door. It might be him.' I rush down the stairs and yank it open. Matt's grave face meets mine. I look at the phone in my hand as he steps past me. 'Mrs Taggart, can I call you straight back? I'll just be a moment?' I don't wait for her to reply as Matt reaches out, clasping the tops of my arms.

'Grace, I'm sorry. It's not good news, there's been an accident. It's Dan. He's alive, but severely injured.'

No, it can't be true. My legs buckle and Matt lowers me to the bottom stair.

'Looks like he ran over a fallen branch and it flipped him into the ditch. He's conscious but injured. 'Sorry, but I thought I should come and tell you.'

Tremors run through me but deep inside I'm numb, this can't be happening. Matt squeezes himself in beside me and takes me in his arms.

'Are you sure he won't die?' I sob. Matt hands me a hanky to wipe away the snot and salty drool. 'Where, where are they taking him?'

'Cambridge, I should think. It has the best A&E; they airlifted him so he should be there by now. Can I make you a cup of tea or something?' I struggle to my feet.

'Oh goodness Flora, I must ring her back.'

'That can wait a minute,' he says, guiding me to the kitchen and forcing me to sit. 'I'll give Flora a call while the kettle's boiling.'

Resting my head on my arms I stare through the gap at the floor.

'He mustn't die. Please God. Do something. And what about Leah, poor love. First Kate now Dan it's too horrid.' I gasp in a breath ready to fill the split second where my breathing was suspended and shudder.

'The police have called in on Flora now. Dan was able to ask someone to contact her. So he can't be that bad if he can be thinking about passing messages on.'

'He must have been there all night. What time did they find him?'

'Not sure. I got a call around six-thirty asking to bring my tractor to pull a four-by-four out of a ditch. I'd no idea it was Dan until I got there. Postman in his van discovered him.'

I get up unsteadily and go to the boiling kettle ready to busy myself and make tea.

'Here, I'll do that.'

'No Matt I'm fine, honestly. It was the initial shock. I need to think what I can do that's practical to help. I can pick Leah up from school, it's ballet tonight, she'll be with Alice anyway. Will anyone have told her?'

'I doubt it. It's still fresh news.' We sip our tea and I realise this is almost a déjà vu moment, except this time there's no cat for Matt to bury.

'I don't know what to do for the best. I'll ring Mrs Taggart back. I mean, I'm not family or anything, I can't just butt in, but I want to help.'

'Tricky one, but I'm sure you'll think of something,' he drains his mug. 'I need to be getting back. Carl got the morning milking by default. I'll never hear the end of it, and he has a hangover.' He scratches the back of his neck. 'What a shame after such a lovely evening too.'

'It was, yes, thank you again. I'll have to reciprocate once Dan is better.' I suck in my lower lip to ward off another round of tears. 'He will get better won't he Matt?'

'Yes, I'm sure he'll be okay, but are you? Can I call someone – Jenny? I don't want to leave you on your own or, you can come back with me if you like?'

'Thanks, but I'm but made of tougher stuff than I used to be.' He wraps his arms around me and rocks me in an embrace. 'Thanks Matt, this cuddling lark is becoming a bit of a habit. I'll be fine, you get back to Carl.'

My heart squeezes when I go to call Flora back, she doesn't pick up and the sound of Dan's voice requesting I leave a message brings a lump to my throat. I mumble a few words to say I'll pick Leah up with Alice later. The phone rings while I'm showering, by the time I'd turned off the water and grabbed a towel it stopped. I have a new voice message.

'Hello, its Flora here, sorry I missed your call, I was on my mobile. It's very kind of you to offer help with Leah, but I have it all in hand. Thank you very much anyway.'

I sink onto the side of the bed. The message feels like a shun, leaving me feeling rejected and empty. I want to help but wonder if Flora blames me. If he hadn't been out in such weather, he would have been safe. As far as Flora is concerned, apart from Matt and Carl, we are nothing more than acquaintances. I have to back off but it's hard. I want to be involved and I crave news.

54

Sleep escapes me. I'm up before sunrise, exhausted and feeling desperate for an update on Dan's condition. Frustrated, I ring Cambridge hospital, but as I'm not a relative they were unhelpful. While my children banter over the breakfast table, I decide to ring Flora again.

'Hi, it's Grace. I rang to see how Dan was.'

'Thank you yes, this phone has not stopped ringing. I feel like a message machine, but the latest news is good – well, better.'

'Sorry, I didn't mean to —'

'No, of course, don't worry. I was going to call you myself later.'

'So, how is he?'

'He'll live, that's the good news. He's broken several ribs, fractured his pelvis and has a badly fractured leg, the rest is minor cuts and bruises. Thankfully no internal damage.'

'Thank God. Is he up for visitors?'

'Not yet. They're keeping him sedated so no visitors for a day or so then family only, for the moment. He needs rest.'

In the background, I hear Leah's chatter. 'Can I help at all with school runs, play dates?'

'Thank you, but we're fine.'

'Well, if anything changes.'

'Yes, yes.'

I detect Flora's eagerness to end the call and quickly ask if she'll let me know when I can visit.

'Yes, I will. Thank you for calling.'

The cogs of my brain run into each other. Family only. Well surely that's Leah, Flora and probably Kate's husband. The tone of an empty line registers how I'm feeling – disconnected.

The weekend looms ahead, I try to make plans of how we will fill our time. With Jack at rugby then a party, Melissa on a sleepover, it's only George and Alice.; so I decide a trip into town and the cinema would be a good distraction. Leah wasn't at school last week and news of Dan's accident has been relayed around the village. Desperate as I am for an update, I don't feel I have the right to keep bothering Flora.

The three of us settle in our seats armed with popcorn and blue slush puppies. It's soothing to hear the happy sound of my children's giggles. Strangely, I feel sad for Tom; missing out on so much, but then he always had. There'd been a hiatus from Tom's solicitors. Alice's party was the last contact we'd had from him.

Film over, I cling onto Alice and George, shuffling towards the exit, our speed determined by the crowds. The crocodile line bends to pass through to the stairs and I'm sure I see a glimpse of Leah, walking beside a tall, slim man. I get a better look as we descend the stairs. It is Leah. But who's the man with dirty blond, shoulder length hair with her? Surely not Kate's husband?

The man stoops to speak to Leah and I glimpse a wispy beard. I lose sight of them as the red carpeted corridor curves, meeting another. George is dawdling, and they are too far ahead to catch up. Outside I blink in the brightness and search the crowd. Then I see them waiting by the kerb. Before I can guide us towards them, a battered camper van pulls up to the pavement. Leah and the man get in and the van drives off. How weird. Perhaps he was one of the estate workers?

I recount the description to Matt when we call into the farm on the way home. It is evening milking and George and Alice watch, fascinated. Carl makes them stand behind him, as the cows exit the milking stalls and pour into the yard. George shies back, Alice holds her hand out to a cow who stops to sniff it cautiously. She pulls a face.

'His nose is all runny, that's yucky!'

'It's a cow, they're girls not boys,' says George.

'How do you know? They might have some boys.'

'You're a numbnut.'

'Well, you're a poo pants.'

'Girls are cows and boys are bulls,' Carl says halting the dispute. 'Hey, anyone want an ice cream from the shop, once I've got the cows back in their field?'

'Yes please.' They chorus and follow him.

I tell Matt about the man with Leah at the cinema.

'I don't recall anyone like that up at Brockton, but they come and go. Land workers are transient. But there's no way Flora Taggart would let her go off with anyone she wasn't sure about. She guards that child with her life.'

'Yes, that's what I thought. So, have you had any more news on Dan?'

'Mine's probably about the same as yours. Recovering slowly, but I can give Flora a ring if you like. She shops here often and I know her quite well. Or you could pitch up at the hospital.'

My jaw drops. 'I can't do that.'

'Why not? Who's to say you can't? I doubt he has a stampede of visitors,' he nudges me. 'Go on, be bold. I'm sure seeing you would hasten his recovery.'

'I'll think about it, and thanks for letting the kids watch the milking.' I go to leave but he stops me.

'Grace, you two were starting something. Anyone can see how you feel about each other. Put your mind at rest, go and see him.'

We stroll towards my car. 'Think about it, the worst that can happen is you get sent away.'

'I'll give it some thought I promise, but the only people who know us to be a couple is you and Carl. He may not have wanted to go public just yet.'

'Look, both of you've had a rough time. You deserve some happiness. I bet he's dying to see you but can't contact you. He may not have his mobile or can't get access to a phone.'

'I hadn't thought of that. And hospitals are fussy about using mobiles, aren't they?

***

The children are back at school. This is my first opportunity to get to Dan. I take care with my makeup, check visiting times, and enquire which ward he's on. By the time I reach the hospital car park my nerves are churning my insides and doubts slip in. What if he doesn't want to see me? Then I think about the conversation we had that night at Matt's and realise that I'm being stupid.

After trudging miles of corridors to the Orthopaedic ward, I eventually reach a central nursing desk. The six bedded wards are to my left, I use the hand sanitizer and go in. Several beds have the curtains pulled, I step back outside looking for a nurse, but they all appear busy. I spy a whiteboard with bed numbers and names of patients. Bed 3C Daniel Mayne. A flutter of expectation tweaks the corners of my mouth.

In the first bed is a man with a plastered leg raised on a pulley. The second has the curtains pulled, as has the third, that is Dan's bed. I'm unsure what to do. I can't knock on a curtain or just walk in; it could be embarrassing for us both. The remaining patients all have visitors. I take a seat near the wall and wait, noticing movement from behind the curtain that doesn't reach the floor. I stare, unbelieving of what I'm seeing. A pair of woman's sandaled feet with toes painted a fluorescent orange – definitely not a nurse.

I flounder at the sound of Dan's voice, behind the curtain.

'Still as beautiful as ever.'

I gasp.

'And still those lovely soft lips, Dan, I'd forgotten that.' a woman's voice purrs.

My muscles are rigid, I force myself to stand. My foot catching the edge of the chair leg with a clatter. I stumble, heart pumping, but make it to the doors without falling. They bang together behind me. Dodging porters with trolleys and patients in wheelchairs, I run full pelt.

Outside, I fold forward, resting my hands on my knees while my heart jackhammers my ribs. Sweat slicks my top lip. My anger vibrates like a spin cycle. I was right after all, he's another cheating, lying, git just like Tom. I'm tempted to go back, pull open the curtain and slap his smug face, injury or no injury.

'I'm not going to let him make me another a victim!' I say out loud. A woman approaching the entrance grabs her child by the hand and hurries past me, shaking her head. I'm muttering and sobbing as I locate my car. An elderly gentleman stops to enquire if I'm alright. I nod my thanks. As further insult, the bag of cherries I'm carrying slips from my hand. I watch as it lands on the tarmac. The dampness where I'd lovingly washed the fruit for him splits the brown paper bag. The shiny red globes roll freely like marbles under neighbouring cars. I wrench open my car door and slide behind the wheel, hurling my handbag to the rear passenger seats. The sound that escapes my lips sounds inhuman. Raw, burning anger has me hammering my fists against the steering wheel.

'Fuck, fuck, fuck him. The cheating lying shit bag. He walked all over my emotions, and I let him. Of course he had other women.' I rub at my cheeks with the flat of my palms. He's just like Tom, a serial liar, who can't keep his hands to himself. I reach for a pack of tissues from the glove compartment, realising my stupid dreams of happy ever after are trashed. Leah and Alice sharing a room. Jack and Dan watching rugby.

'What a fool I've been. No more cheats and no more fucking liars.'

I swear an oath not to ask Jack about his job or Alice about Leah. Today I've had a cold hard lesson –a bitter pill that felt like one of my mother's slaps, over in an instant, but the sting lasts forever. Why do I attract liars, am I so unlovable?

I'm in a mood for days. It's impossible to forget what I heard and saw. I can't switch off, I torture myself, arguing inwardly between head and heart. It's an effort not to be short with my children. I cancel coffee mornings – lunch dates, even Jenny. Instead, I hammer my body at the gym, praying for the pain to go away. What doesn't help is the anniversary of the day Tom made us headlines.

The start of the school holidays is only days away. I'm in panic mode. Alice will want playdates and sleep overs involving Leah. George supplies the answer.

'Mum, can we do something for the holidays?'

'We always do something. Perhaps we can find a treasure hunt. I expect there's one going on somewhere.' He pulls a face.

'That's for babies. I'm too big for that. All my friends are going away. It's going to be boring.'

He sounds like Jack at a similar age, but Jack liked sport, unlike George who prefers reading or drawing. I take his face in my hands fighting the temptation to spit on my palm and flatten the stubborn clump of hair that stands out on the top of his head.

'Let me have a think about it and see what I can come up with.'

'Thanks Mum. Something really cool.'

'Yes I promise, something fun.' I'm rewarded with a hug.

'You're the bestest Mummy in the world.'

'Thank you darling. I try.'

With the gauntlet laid I have to come up with something to suit everyone. Half an hour later we are booked for a holiday park adventure. Something for everyone, clubs, activities, canoeing, laser combat, quad biking, and pony trekking. I wonder if I can still ride a bicycle or even a horse. Even if I fell off it couldn't hurt as much as Dan's betrayal.

***

The holiday is wonderful. Unbelievably there are no arguments, everyone has something they wanted to do either as a group, or alone.

Melissa and I had a spa for some girly time and I managed at least one activity with each of my children. Since the day we arrived I had left my mobile in our cabin, only checking each evening for missed calls but apart from Jenny there were none.

We have just returned from canoeing, everyone is chilly. Waiting for our ready meal to heat up I use the time to check my phone. There's one missed call and a voicemail. Tapping 901 into the keyboard I nearly drop it at the sound of Dan's voice.

'Grace it's me. I finally got hold of a new phone. I've been calling the house but no reply, so I guess you're away with the kids. I was hoping to see you now that I'm on the mend. I'm a bit bashed about and have a few bits out of action, but overall, I'm lucky to be alive. Flora told me you offered help. Thank you. So, when am I going to see you? You'll have to visit my bedside, but I promise you'll be perfectly safe.' There's the hint of a chuckle. *'Bye for now. I miss you.'*

I snort with disgust. 'Does he actually think I'm that much of a pushover?' I delete the message and the number. How dare he think he can just keep stringing me along like a bloody yoyo. I refuse to become part of his harem and wonder how many stupid gullible women there are?

'Damn you, Dan Mayne.'

***

'Mum, can we go to the holiday park again next year? It was a smashing holiday.' Alice is helping sort holiday photos. 'Much better than going to boring Somerset with your pony, like Leah. Not like us, we did everything.'

At the mention of Leah, I pick up a slightly askew photo Alice had taken of George on the climbing wall. Melissa came up with the idea that they all had a disposable camera to record their activities to make a family album.

'So, do you want Freya over for a sleepover?'

'No, she's had a holiday with her mum, now she's gone sailing with her dad.' Sliding into the seat next to Alice I select a photo of Melissa, looking remarkably like Hannah at the same age. 'That must be very bor-ing, being on the sea all day. Not as good as kayaking and not nearly as exciting as our holiday. Her daddy races boats. Who wants to be wet all day?'

Freya's parents had an uneventful divorce, unlike my own virulent one. I suspect dissing Freya's holiday is more to do with the fact that she had a daddy who kept in touch and openly cared about her. Whereas Tom sent a gift of overpriced confectionary without a message. Predictably, Jack said we should throw it the dustbin, dashing my hopes that his hatred for his father would fade. I was hoping they would each find their way to forgive Tom and keep in touch, I didn't want them having regrets when they got older.

55

A full scale shouting match has me making for the kitchen. Jack is leaning in wagging a finger, his deep voice booming at Melissa.

'Not this year. I don't care what Mum says,' Melissa screeches back, her face is flushed with indignation.

I place myself between them. 'Melissa, stop shout-ing.'

'Yeah, stop yelling Melissa.'

'Jack, stop winding her up.'

'But- '-'

'But nothing. What's going on?'

'I'm *not* sharing my birthday with him,' she growls. 'I want to do something on my own.'

I close my eyes momentarily. They both share the same birthday and until now joint celebrations.

Jack leans back against the sink, legs crossed at the ankles.

'That suits me — my mates won't want to be around stupid girls anyway.'

'Stop.' I say, raising my palm. 'Jack, what do you want to do for your birthday?'

'Why ask him first? That's not fair!'

'Lissy shut up. You'll get a turn.'

'There's a gig on in Cambridge and the band want to go and see what the competition's like.'

'Competition?' Melissa sneers, 'You wish.'

'I said be quiet, Melissa. Let him speak.'

'Well, that's it. I want to go to the gig,' he drags his floppy fringe from his face.

'And Melissa, what do you want to do?'

She has her hands on her hips. 'Well, I don't want a stupid party with him.'

'Did I say you had to?'

'No, but we usually do.'

'Well, not now you're older.'

Jack punches the air with an ear cracking. 'Yes.'

Melissa turns on the charm. 'So lovely Mummy, can I go ice skating first then for pizza? There will be five of us, possibly, six max.'

It is the first time they have wanted to do things without me and although that's sad, it's also good for their confidence.

'Right Jack, yes to the gig, but you will be on the last train home and no alcohol, understand?'

'Yup.' Jack sidles up to me kissing my cheek. My nostrils react to the overkill of aftershaveaftershave, and I sneeze.

'Melissa. Five, and no more. I won't be able to fit you all in the car.'

'We can go on the train. It's not fair if Jack's allowed and I'm not.'

'That's the deal and Jack's going to be seventeen.'

'It's not fair.'

'Take it or leave it.'

The hall landline rings, I expect it to be the nuisance caller who always hangs up if the children answer the phone.

'Hello.'

'Hello Grace, it's Dan I —'

'Bloody cheek.' I say, cutting him off. I'd already rejected several calls on my mobile, now this. Why doesn't he give up? Isn't one woman enough for him?

'I'm going to the farm shop everyone, so no more arguing. I won't be long.'

Carl waves as he herds his cows across the road. I wave back and decide to wait for his return, so much has happened since I last saw him. As I park outside the farm shop I'm met by Ida Murphy and become embroiled in a lengthy conversation.

'It's the pain you see, I can't get a decent night's sleep. I've even bought a new mattressmattress, but it doesn't help.'

I zone out of the conversation as Matt approaches.

'Good morning, ladies. Beautiful day, isn't it?' Ida thins her lips and doesn't acknowledge Matt's presence.

'Sorry, I have to go now, as a matter of urgency.'

I'm amazed at the speed she gets into her car with such a bad back.

'That's odd,' I say, giving Matt a peck on the cheek.

'Not really. I do it on purpose, if she doesn't like what I am, she can shop elsewhere.'

I'm aghast. 'You think she left because you joined us? That's ridiculous.'

'It's not, she's homophobic. I think she expects to get Aids or something being near me.' Matt chuckles. 'Ignorant woman.'

'And a hypochondriac to boot.'

'That'll be it then – she'll be spraying herself with disinfectant as soon as she gets home.'

Matt bends to pick up some litter the wind has carried in. We walk together towards an industrial-sized green bin where he deposits it.

'So how are you and the kids, alright?'

'Great thanks, and you and Carl? I waved at him earlier.'

'He makes me the happiest man alive. I had hoped you'd drop by and give me an update on you and Dan. Have you gone public yet?'

I look away; Matt touches my arm.

'Hey, what's up, you had a row or something?'

'No, nothing like that,' I say, swallowing back my hurt.

'What then? We thought you two were so well matched. What's happened?'

'I was right first off. I should have stuck with my initial impression. Dan's a rat, he's seeing someone else. Luckily I found out before anything got serious. I think he saw me as a challenge.'

Matt scratches an earlobe. 'Well, he had us fooled. The way he was looking at you, well, that and what he'd said. That's out of order Grace, I'm sorry. Is it anyone I'd know?'

He reaches for a metal basket from the stack.

'I've no idea. I haven't actually seen her.'

'Then it could just be gossip, we're all victims of it, unfortunately.'

'No, I heard them. When you said I should visit, I did. The curtains were around the bed, but Dan already had a woman with him.'

'Perhaps it was a nurse and you were mistaken,' he says tilting his head to one side.

'Not a nurse,' I quote, '"I'd forgotten how soft your lips were Dan", or something similar.'

'What! No, that's awful.'

'I got out fast before I made a fool of myself. He's tried to call me since but I don't want to know. One cheating git of a man is enough to last a lifetime. I'll not be taken for a fool twice.'

He shakes his head sadly. 'I'm surprised at Dan; I know he likes to play the womaniser card but it's mainly blagging, his heart and soul are into that little girl.'

I glance at my watch, I'm due to meet Kellen for lunch.

'Hmm, and bigger girls too it would seem.'

The weight of Matt's hand on my arm is comforting.

'Come on Grace, bitter and twisted isn't your style. I hope it's all a misunderstanding.'

'Unlikely. I'm beginning to think I'm cursed. I've given up on the idea of love. It's not for me apparently.'

56

I received my Decree Absolute ten days ago. I haven't quite got used to being single. It feels strange after so many years of being a wife.

Living so close to local amenities, I often allow George and Alice to go to the post office cum corner shop. It's a five minute walk without any roads to cross. I'm always anxious until they return, but they must be allowed to develop some independence.

Alice has gone to pick up her comic and calls out that she's back but doesn't join me in the kitchen. There's something about the tone of her voice that's off. My hands are covered in suds, I rinse and dry them.

'Alice. Come into the kitchen and I'll make you a milkshake.' I'm aware of the soft thud of footsteps running up the stairs. My mind races with fearful scenarios. Has someone approached her and scared her?

Alice is sitting on her bed, her magazine held open covering her face.

'Alice, did something happen?'

The comic stays gripped in position.

'No.'

'Then why didn't you answer me?'

'Didn't hear you,' she says with a catch in her voice.

'Don't fib. Put the magazine down. Now, what's up?' I take the comic from her. 'Oh Alice, you've been crying. Did someone hurt you?'

Alice launches into my lap gulping great sobs. Has someone tried to do something to my baby?

'Please, darling, tell me.'

Alice lifts her head, her little face twisted with emotion. 'It's Dad, he got married again and she's got three children already. Now I'll never get a pony. He has too many children – seventeen and three makes twenty. I don't even know what number I am.' She scrunches up her small fists. 'I hate him.'

I hitch a nervous laugh. 'Alice, who told you this?'

'The ladies in the shop were talking about it.'

'Darling, I think you may have got this wrong. If Daddy were getting married again, he would have spoken to us about it.'

'But it's in that magazine – the one they have in the hairdressers and one of her kids was bridesmaid. I saw it,' she cries. 'It's not fair. I thought I was his favourite. He's horrid, and I hate him.'

Another bout of sobs rack through her small ribcage. I rock and hug her close, disbelieving of what Tom has done. It takes ages to calm her, wash her face, smother her with kisses and hugs and tell her she is special and very much loved. After her favourite milkshake and more cuddles, she begins to recover.

'What would you like to do tomorrow? I have to work a bit in the morning, but if you want a playdate with Freya, we can have her over'

Alice shakes her head. 'She's going to her auntie's. Can I call Leah?'

There is no reason to disallow it or to upset Alice further.

'Alright off you go then, but no talking for too long, okay?'

Is Alice right? Only one way to find out. I Google Tom Lane. The hairs on my neck bristling. She had heard correctly. Tom has married a leading TV presenter with two sons by her first marriage and a daughter by her second. In an instant I understand the rush to wed. Tom's game show flopped. It appears that even the demographic who once watched trashy expose-type shows have more taste, so I doubt Tom married for love. More likely this woman can further his flagging career.

Tempted as I am to call him and berate him for not telling his children first, it's not worth the breath. That's Tom all over. Alice's discovery forewarns me that this might raise some press attention again.

When everyone is home, I relay the news of their father's nuptials. George, as usual, is the only one not to verbalise his opinion. He tucks into his bangers and mash with his typical vigour while Jack and Melissa sit solemnly.

A nerve beats out a rhythm near Jack's left eye.

'I just hope this doesn't get us in the papers again,' he says.

Melissa clatters her cutlery.

'Well, I never want to see him again, and I'm never going to get married. Most men are the B word.'

To my relief, Alice doesn't enquire what that means.

My bed is a tangle of bottom sheet and duvet. I spent a disturbed night dreaming of tabloid headlines: *Serial Father of Twenty; Jungle Tom and his Tribes.*

The following day, the media has moved on to a madman shooting at cars from a motorway embankment. Someone else's misery – yesterday's news.

Excited squeals from the hall announce Leah's arrival. Both girls come rushing up the stairs and vanish into Alice's bedroom. My arms are full of laundry that I clasp a little tighter when I see a woman with a mane of dark curls in a long floral dress, placing jars of jam onto the hall table from her tapestry bag.

'Ah, you must be Grace.' She proffers a delicate hand and I readjust my bundle of washing to shake it. Her many silver bracelets jangling together that break the silence. 'I'm Maggie. Flora's visiting her sister so I couldn't ask for your phone number and Leah was desperate to see Alice. I hope it's convenient.'

Jenny's description – likening Maggie to Kate Bush, was spot on. A heart-shaped face below tumbling locks of coal coloured hair. Generous lips and huge expressive eyes. There isn't a trace of makeup, but her overall beauty is blemished by weathered skin that has seen too much sun.

'We brought you some of Flora's plum jam. I hope you like it. Dan says it's even better than his. It's nice to meet you.'

'Yes, and you.' So this is Leah's mother. It's like an ambush. I have no choice but to be hospitable. Maggie is back in Dan's life. It was her he was kissing at the hospital. I'm rigid with jealousy. 'Would you like tea or coffee? I'll just get rid of this laundry.' I lead the way to the kitchen wondering if she knows the way as well as me. 'So, how's he doing?'

'Just water, please.' Maggie pauses. 'To tell you the truth, I'm worried about him.'

We sit opposite each other and I'm trying to find a reason not to like her, apart from the fact that Dan has got someone new. It's worse she's his former lover and mother to his daughter. How could I *ever* compete with that?

'I thought he was out of danger and recovering.'

'He is, physically. It's emotionally, he's not himself,' she makes a fist and bangs her chest. 'It's in here.'

I flush with irritation. I've known her five minutes and she's instigated a cosy chat about Dan. Perhaps it's her way of warning me off.

'I don't know what you mean?'

She smiles at me, her eyes searching mine.

'Sorry can I offer you a biscuit, or I have some ginger cake?' Any excuse not to look at her.

She shakes her long curls. 'To be honest, and please excuse me if I have this wrong as I only have Flora's word to go on, but I think it's you.'

I look directly at her. 'What? How? I don't think so. We've had a coffee once, and that was a disaster, and then dinner at mutual friends the night of the accident. We hardly know each other.'

'That's enough for Dan. He'll have admired you from afar a long time before plucking up the courage to ask you out. Flora told me he was the happiest she'd seen him in ages the night before the accident. Singing as he got ready, face like Batman's Joker- that sort of thing. When he didn't come home, she hoped it was because he'd finally fallen in love.'

I stutter to find a suitable reply. 'Maggie, to be honest, the Dan you describe is alien to me. The Dan I know is a flirt. A ladies' man.'

'Right on all counts, bar the ladies' man. He's a harmless flirt, a born romantic. There were only two women in his life — Kate and Leah. Me for a bit but never seriously.'

My hands tremble, I put my glass down for fear of dropping it.

'But you had a baby together.'

'An accident, a flip of nature and bad birth control on my part. I was never born to be a mother, but I don't believe in abortion either. I like to travel, get up in the morning and go. I collect waifs and strays along the way. I'm a bit of a free spirit always have been.'

'But you're back now. The time might be right for the both of you.'

Maggie's face splits into a roar of laughter.

'There will never ever be a time that's right for Dan and me.'

'But you came back.'

'To sign legal papers that makes Flora Leah's guardian in instances like this. I am still her next of kin, after Dan. I'm not that heartless, Flora has my number. I stepped in as a friend.'

'But Leah – you're her mother.'

'No, I'm Maggie. Kate stepped into my role and now she's gone…'

She gives a shake of her shoulders.

'I leave for Holland on Tuesday, but let's get back to Dan. The only visitors he's had are Flora and his friend Claire. He could do with a cheer up and I think you're the person to do it. That's if I've got it right.'

I'm afraid to answer.

'Give it a try, make him happy. He deserves it, and from what Flora tells me, so do you.'

'I don't know. I-'

'Grace, give him a chance.'

We talk for over an hour and hug goodbye like old friends. I wave her off and close the door, elated as Maggie's words take shape. Is Maggie's hunch right? Could Dan be in love with me?

<h1 style="text-align:center">57</h1>

The desire to rush to Dan's side is unbearable but self-doubt hangs like wet washing, warning me to be cautious. I steel myself to wait until Monday when the children will be at school and Jack at college.

Flora Taggart smiles then gives a knowing nod that brings colour to my cheeks when I drop Leah home. I don't mention Dan. I can't even enquire on his well-being, I'm in a time slip until Monday. Driving home the car is filled with Alice's constant chatter. I zone out of most of it until she mentions Maggie.

'What was that sweetheart?'

Alice huffs and crosses her arms.

'Mum, it's rude not to listen when people are speaking to you.'

'Sorry love, I was concentrating on the road; we don't want an accident, do we?'

'No, we don't. We were talking, Leah says she wants a proper mummy like you, and I want a daddy, a proper one like Dan. One who lives at home and gives cuddles and pocket money.'

'Not to mention ponies?' I say, containing a grin.

'Well that too, but more important is him living with his family. I don't like Freya's daddy, and he has a wife, so that counts him out.'

'What brought this conversation on about needing a new daddy – or mummy?' I add hastily.

'Well, I did think you could have guessed, what with Dad choosing a new wife who will probably have a zillion more babies; and Maggie who's not a proper mummy, even if she does let Leah paint her toenails and have a henna tattoo. Leah says she's yippy.'

'I think she means, Hippie.'

'That's it. Although she did grow Leah in her tummy, she's not a proper mummy because she lives in a camper van and goes where the wind takes her.' I get a vision of a mast and sail attached to the roof of a camper van.

'You think I should get you a new daddy?'

'Yes, but we should all choose,' she pauses. 'Like on X-Factor.' I turn into the drive and talk of new daddies.

Melissa tuts, her expression sour. 'Mother, do something about Jack. He has a woman in his room.' Alice pushes past. 'Oh, let me see.'

I grab the hem of her jumper to stop her. 'Alice, no. He's entitled to his privacy.'

'You wouldn't say that if I brought a boy home.'

'That's different Madam, you're only fourteen.'

Jack's face appears at the top of the stairs; his cheeks flushed. I hope it's with embarrassment.

'Hi Mum, Livy came round to look over our playlist, she's going to be our vocalist.'

'No need to explain, Jack. It's perfectly alright to have a friend round. Just let me know next time.'

A slim, dark-haired girl with hair almost to her waist and a band of green ribbon tied across her forehead, appears beside him. She gives a little wave.

'Hello Mrs Lane.'

I notice that her wrists are covered with beads and bits of leather and try not to stare at her mature bust.

'Hi there. Nice to meet you. I'm about to make dinner, would you like some, or a drink of something?' Anything to entice them downstairs.

'No I'm good thanks, Mum will be here to pick me up soon.'

I'm getting a stiff neck staring up. 'Okay fine, have fun.' Do I mean that? It's only when I hear a husky female voice singing that I begin to relax.

I'm preparing tea when the doorbell rings. Keen to see who the owner of the dark-haired beauty is I race Alice to the door. The face of Claire Taylor greets me.

'Claire, this is a nice surprise. Do come in. How are you? Coffee? Wine?'

'Coffee, please. I can't stay long; I came to grab Olivia and head home.'

My eyes widen. 'Livy? That's your Olivia?'

Claire takes off her jacket and hooks it over a chair.

'Yep, grown too fast for my liking, but she's a good girl. Music mad – sees herself as the next pop idol. I wouldn't normally let her go to a boy's house without vetting them first, but your Jack's such a lovely polite lad, it felt safe enough, and you have to start trusting them sometime, don't you?'

I remembered my own raging hormones at the same age. I'm hoping that Tom's copulating monkeysmonkeys' video has given Jack enough information to make serious choices.

'Yes, I suppose so.'

57

Claire's eyebrows shoot skywards. 'Grace, they know much more than we did at that age, believe me.'

'You're probably right. So, how's Dan doing? I take it you've been visiting?'

'I have. He asked if I'd seen you. Nice if he had more visitors, he's a bit down in the dumps.'

'To be expected for such an active man,' I say, head down making coffee. The image of Dan being active takes me to places that shouldn't be in my imagination. 'I mean, he must be bored stiff.'

'Yes, I expect so, it's going to be a long job. They're moving him tomorrow to St George's; to an orthopaedic specialist unit. He needs some bone grafting and they're the best apparently.'

My pulse picks up pace. 'St George's, where?'

'Tooting, London. I won't be able to get there so he'll be on his own. Such a horribly bad time, can you imagine? Losing Kate and now this, God knows how they got hold of Maggie. I expected her to be living in Morocco with a commune or something.'

'I quite liked her, she popped in.'

'Well, I suppose not everyone's cut out for motherhood, at least Maggie was honest enough to give Leah up. Between Dan and Kate, Leah has had a loving family.'

As if on cue, Jack and Olivia wander in. I focus microscopically on Jack, relieved that I can't detect anything untoward and I give myself a virtual slapped wrist. I must learn to focus on real problems, not invented ones. News of Dan being moved has left my nerves jangling. Knowing the truth I feel ashamed of my behaviour and worry if I've missed my chance of happiness?

58

'Jack! Turn that down!'

Jack rolls onto his back and presses the remote.

'Sorry Mum, too loud?'

'Mm, a bit. I must pop to Aunty Jenny's; George is on a sleepover and Freya's mum will drop Alice back by six. Can you hold the fort?'

'Yep. Oh, did you hear about Dan? They're moving him to London. Hope he's not gone long. He's funny at work, knows loads of jokes but don't ever ask him to sing, it's dreadful. Anyway, yup, no worries. Say hi to Aunty Jen.' There it was. Another vision of family stability. Jack enjoying Dan's company and two things I didn't know about him – he tells jokes but can't hold a tune. Before I drive off I ring Claire and get Dan's new number, feeling mortified that I'd deleted it as well as hung up on him.

***

Todd opens the door wearing a bored expression.

'She's in the kitchen,' he offers without being asked.

'Thanks, Todd.' Jenny is chopping garlic, she looks up and beams.

'Hello, this is a surprise.' I hang my arms around her neck, avoiding several inches of sharp steel and a garlic infused sleeve. 'What's that for?'

'I missed you, that's all.' We disengage and she plants a kiss on my cheek then steps to the sink, lathering handwash and rinsing.

'You could always move back in. Or have you got your eye on a position in a certain manor house? Wine, coffee, tea, gin?'

'Jenny, stop it,' I giggle. 'But I have news about Dan.'

'Then sit. I need details.'

'Damn you, Jenny. Why are you so ruddy nosy?'

'I was born that way; I should have been a detective or a spy. Come on girl, give.'

Jenny listens from the beginning. Kind enough not to point out my downfall being trust issues.

'And your plan is? You have one, right?'

'Well, I need to phone him first, put things right.'

Jenny claps her hands. 'And then?'

I stare at my lap. 'I don't know, I haven't thought that far.'

'He may, of course, be totally pissed and decide to cut *you* off for a change. You do realise you could have blown it?'

'Oh God, I hope not. I've been so pathetically stupid.'

'Yup agreed. Right, here's what you do- phone him. Whichever way it goes, good or bad. Then, tomorrow you go to London and see him. No matter how angry he is on the phone, face to face will melt him. God, I'm loving this already, it's like a film.'

'Jen,' I say blowing up my fringe. 'I wish I were you.'

'No, you don't, you'd be stuck with Robin – bless. If you want it bad enough, you can do it.'

***

With the door closed firmly against intrusion I arrange myself on the corner of the bed, my phone slick with sweat from my palms. The phone rings twice then goes to voicemail. I ring off and stare at the screen. This is an emergency. The man I love is lying hurt in hospital. *Shall I send a text?*

'And say what?' I'm wearing a hole in the carpet from pacing. I could send him a photo. The nice one Lissy took of me in the kayak. I fall on the bed and stare at the ceiling. No, that's far too naff, he'll think I'm bonkers. 'Come on Grace, you're not a kid. Phone back and keep trying. He'll see the missed calls.' A mental clock suggests my time is running out. The automated message clicks in, I hold my breath then my words escape in a whoosh.

'Dan, hello, it's me. I'm sorry I didn't take your calls. I've been stupid. Maggie came to see me. We need to talk. I can hear you saying you've been trying to, and I'm sorry. Claire tells me they are sending you to London. Ring me when you get this. Bye.' Should I have said bye love, or blown a kiss? I bang my fists together. Why am I still holding back?

I'm still awake at two am. My message unanswered. Dreams chase me from a fitful sleep. Discarding my fears of rejection, I focus on being there for him. Google gives up the number for St George's Hospital, Tooting. Frustration of being put through to too many wrong departments rises my pounding blood pressure. My nerves are shredded by the time I'm finally told he's still en route. I beg the person to say I called. By two thirty I've cleaned every conceivable part of my cooker. I try again. Yes, the message has been delivered. No, I couldn't talk to him, he was being assessed and prepped for theatre. I'm told to call back at six. I do. He's still not back on the ward. I nibble my thumbnail, desperate to hear his voice. In my mind our relationship has leapfrogged ahead. Nine, ten, eleven o'clock passes. I give it one last shot.

'Hello this is Grace, I phoned earlier. Is Dan Mayne back from theatre please?'

'Are you a relative?'

'Er. No.'

'Then I can't pass on any information. You'll have to contact a family member.'

'But he doesn't have any, only a housekeeper and a daughter who is eight years old.'

'Just a moment.' I hear papers being thumbed. 'What did you say your name was?'

'Grace Denning – or Lane.'

'You're not listed.'

'No, I won't be —'

'Then I'm sorry, I can't help.'

I yell 'Noooo' as she hangs up, and stare at the hand-set. I go outside and yell at the cawing crows in the Oak tree to shut up, go back inside and phone Brackton Hall. It goes to voicemail. I recall, Flora is at her sisters', and I don't have a phone number for Maggie. There's only one thing to do. Go to London.

59

I've woken with a stiff neck and a sore throat, praying it's the result of too much wine and sleeping with my mouth open and not that I'm taking germs to a hospital. George brings me back to the now by edging up to me as I'm chopping fruit for lunch boxes.

'Mum, can I tell you a secret?' he asks from behind a cupped hand.

'Yes George, I promise I won't tell anyone.'

'Not even Alice?'

'No, not even Alice.'

'I have a girlfriend, she's called Molly.'

Oh, bless his heart. I squeeze his shoulder.

'That's a lovely name, is she in your class?' George checks the room, his expression serious. 'It's okay they can't hear.'

'We sit next together. She brings me things.'

'How lovely,' I say in hushed tones. 'What sort of things?'

His huge eyes reflect the pleasure behind his glasses. 'Sweets and a cupcake.'

'That's nice, and did you give Molly anything?'

His eyes dart towards the group at the table, 'My banana.' I can already hear the snort of laughter from Jenny when I tell her.

'What are you whispering about?' chimes Alice. 'It's rude to whisper, Mum, you said so.'

George's eyes dart between us.

'I know,' I say 'but sometimes we don't want to blurt things out. It's not kind.'

'Like when he wet the bed or pooed his pants?'

'I didn't Mum. Tell her I didn't.'

'Alice, that's gross and your brother hasn't done either of those things, now eat up or you'll be late.' Loading the dishwasher, I wish I could be a child again. I'd willingly have shared my banana with Dan Mayne.

The second the front door shuts behind my children I rush into action by checking London train times. I feel light of foot and my heart beats that little bit faster. I'm going to see Dan. I change the dial on the radio to Golden Hour. This is more like it. I'm lost in nostalgia. A lovesick teenager once more, listening to music from my youth and first boyfriend. Patrick Kenny, with a twinkle in his eye and Northern-Irish accent, I thought him the sexiest boy alive. What happened to him I wondered. Chartley was co-ed. I hoped he'd be at the reunion so I could see the adult version.

Bruce Springsteen breaks into *Dancing in the Dark*; a tune that makes me crank up the volume and dance madly along the hall with complete abandonment screeching –

'Messages keep getting clearer, dah-da-dah.

Take a look in the mirror, la- la- la.

You can't start a fire. Can't start a fire without a spark.'

That was it, there was a spark! She and Dan could start a fire.

With feet pounding the floor, arms punching the air and hips grinding I dance with fervour, but something is amiss. I slow, listening. The doorbell. Breathless, I tug the hall door shut to muffle out the music. A slim figure is visible through the side panels. I open the door to see Maggie on the doorstep.

'I thought I was the only Springsteen fan left,' she says smiling.

I stand back to let her in, catching sight of my sweaty, red-faced self in the mirror and run my fingers through my scruffy locks, attempting to make myself presentable. We traipse into the kitchen and I kill the music.

'I think there's still a few of us left. Coffee?'

'No thanks, the camper van's loaded and we're off now that things are more settled, but I had a sudden urge to say goodbye before I set off to catch the ferry.'

We stand facing each other, Maggie's petiteness makes me feel cumbersome.

'That's right you said, Holland wasn't it? So, when will you be back?' Maggie grins, revealing deeper sun lines than I noticed before but on her they look charming.

'I never know. I'll get off the boat and then decide if it's left or right. Jed's my latest stray; I may let him choose. I recall the man with the dirty blonde hair I'd seen at the cinema with Leah. 'Or I might go it alone.'

I'm fascinated by her wanderlust. 'Don't you ever get lonely?'

'Never. I was more alone than I can ever describe living in a huge stack with cooks and chauffeurs, and parents that hated each other. Every time Dad took a new lover, Mum got a new piece of jewellery. It was crazy.'

'And you don't miss any of it?' She doesn't hesitate. 'I miss some of the people, the farm hands, the gardener – Robert, who taught me how to grow things, but nothing else. I can only wear one pair of shoes at a time, drive one car, and I hate champagne. What's to miss? Anyway, enough of that rubbish. I called to say that Dan's in St George's. It's open visiting now. He needs something to look forward to and I know you're that something.'

'How can you be so sure?' I say, my fingertips tingling.

A purple varnished nail taps the side of her nose.

'Sixth sense. That and the fact that he chewed my ear off talking about you.' She takes a folded slip of paper from her pocket and holds it out. 'Here, this is the ward number. He might even be in a private room by now. Please call him. Don't miss a chance at being happy Grace, you both deserve it, and Leah needs a woman younger than Flora in her life. Now I must be off.'

A rush of sisterly love so absent since Hannah revisits me as Maggie pulls me to her, smothering me under a mass of black curls. I hug her back like a conjoined twin. The emotional bond fixing itself as I breathe in the smell of something familiar – Patchouli oil. My eyes shut to the memories of Hannah.

'Take the love that's being offered Grace. It needs a place to bloom.' We fade away from each other, arms dangling, empty. 'I hope we meet again. You'll go to him? Promise?'

'I promise,' I say, our eyes both glistening with emotion. I lean against the door frame, watch Maggie walk towards the orange camper van. She climbs in shouting something through the open window.

I step forward cupping my ear, 'Sorry, I didn't hear.'

'I said, great moves by the way.'

I laugh out loud. 'How long were you there?'

'Oh ages, almost the whole track.' Jeb starts the engine, toots the horn and drives away.

Maggie's bond stays with me, it's magnetic. No wonder Dan fell for her. Time to keep my promise.

'Lucy, hi it's Grace. I know you're due to set off on your travels but I wondered if I could beg one last favour. I need someone to stay overnight to keep an eye on my lot. Jack and Melissa would be okay to leave, but not the little ones. You see, I have to go to London.'

60

Dear Grace,

Thank you for replying to my letter, I was excited to receive it. I've watched every one of your shows and can't wait for the next series. What a shame the Chartley reunion got put back. I'm thrilled at the prospect of us all being together again.

I haven't been able to catch up with the other two yet, Maureen changed her name to Mia and was living in Sardinia. She was always so beautiful and mysterious. I wonder if she'll come.

I was married and I'm now a widow but that's a long story. All I can say is, you won't recognise me now. My luck has changed in so many ways. Please give me a call if you have time, number below.

I put Sophie's letter back in its envelope. The countryside whizzes past in a blur of greens and yellows. The carriage sways slower and grazing cows make me think of Matt and his newfound happiness. I dare not imagine my own.

The letter from Sophie is nice, just like she was. She used to remind me of a lively puppy with big trusting eyes—always willing, never down, smiley, but painfully plain. I wonder what she meant by saying I won't recognise her. She was the shortest girl in our school, no amount of hair colouring or restyling can change that. It's interesting that Maureen calls herself Mia now. No surprise there. She was bound to change her name to something more exotic. Will the pull of old friendships be enough to make her attend the reunion?

The vista outside changes, hamlets meeting villages and villages, towns. As the train turns into the terminus fellow travellers shuffle out of their seats, gathering up their belongings. Outside the skyscraper towers make me shiver.

My hotel is a tube ride from the hospital. A pinch of something akin to guilt catches me by surprise. I'm only a few stops from my mother but have no intention of visiting her. There's no bond, only blame and harried conversations. She has no interest in my children and I can't recall if she ever met anyone but Jack. Tom called her bitter and twisted, one thing we both agreed on.

There are some things that scare me- wasps and swimming in deep water, but none compared to the fear that my words of apology to Dan won't be enough.

I check into the hotel and freshen up before taking the short walk to the underground. Then stroll from Tooting Broadway to St. George's Hospital, following the signs to the Orthopaedic Trauma Unit with my stomach doing flips and jitters of apprehension.

The nursing station is unmanned. I don't feel I should go delving through unmarked doors, so I wait. The sound of wheels on rubber makes me turn.

'Be with you in one minute,' a male nurse says with a smile, securing the medication cart. 'How can I help you?'

'Can you tell me where Daniel Mayne is, please?' He moves to the nursing station and taps into a keyboard.

'Ah yes, transferred from Cambridge.' I'm studying his face and watch his smile fade and the frown appear. 'Ah, sorry. He's already gone to theatre.'

I'm hammered with crashing disappointment.

'Can I wait?'

He shakes his head.

'When he comes out of theatre, he'll go to high dependency unit for at least forty-eight hours. No visitors. I'm sorry.'

I can't hide my disappointment. A wetness skims my cheek. My hopes are dashed. I'd built myself up to making things right, now it can't happen for days.

'Is there any chance I can see him any sooner?'

'I'm sorry you've had a wasted journey. Would you like the number of the HD ward? At least they can tell him you came.'

My shoulders sag. It's better than nothing. I nod a thanks. 'At least he'll know I tried.'

I buy a takeaway coffee and find a bench in the hospital grounds. I'm not sure what hurts more; the emptiness inside me or the pain in my heart. My gaze sweeps across the hospitals façade with its many windows, wondering if the man I love is behind one. With a sigh, I turn my phone back on. I'll have to go home and wait, I'd better ring Jenny and tell her.

'No way are you coming back. I don't care if I move into your place for a month Grace Denning, this is your life we're talking about. A few nights without their mum won't hurt your kids. I'll speak to Lucy when she gets back from the dentist.'

'But I can't stay in London. What if it's days and days?'

'So what if it is? When did you last have any time to yourself?'

'But what will I do?'

'You can stop being such a wimp. Take in a show, go to a gallery, a spa, feed pigeons. It's ruddy London, not Beirut. Now man up.'

'Well, if you're sure.'

'Grrrr, bloody hell, Grace. You sound like you're asking for permission. Just do it. As long as you speak to the kids and explain. What did you say to them about London?'

'I said I had people to see.'

'Well, that's true.'

'I know, but I can hardly tell my own kids that I've finally worked out I'm in love but may well have blown it and come to beg forgiveness.'

'Don't see why not.'

I shake my head fiercely. 'Because Jack and Melissa may understand, but not George and Alice.'

'Okay, gone to visit your mother.'

'I *never* visit my mother.'

She curses under her breath. 'I'm trying to help?'

'I know.'

'Okay, got it. You're seeing people about the show format. We could hint at the next series and some pub-licity.'

'I don't enjoy lying.'

'It's not a lie, more a bendy version of the truth. I'm hanging up now before you can invent more excuses. Bye.'

Back at the hotel, I swap my heels for flatties.

'Are you planning anything special now you're staying longer?' The young man with the Australian accent inquires, tapping the keyboard at his computer.

I take a moment to reply. 'Yes, I'm going to take life by the horns and give it a damn good shaking.'

'Sounds exciting.'

'It is. I hope I haven't missed a genuine opportunity though.' He gives me a quizzical look. 'I've several days before I find out. Wish me luck.'

'Of course.'

'Thanks, I'm going to need it.'

***

It's weird wandering the streets of London alone, but the guilty pleasure of time is luxurious. The hospital has given me an update based on the fib that I'm Dan's fiancée. The lie is a brave one that I hope won't backfire on me, but I could hardly say I'm his sister. My heart gave a barrel roll when I say the word fiancée.

There's something I hadn't planned on doing but exiting Richmond station, I head to the flower stall that's been there forever. They don't have any sweet peas, so I settle on cornflowers, heady scented phlox, and white pom-pom chrysanthemums. None as good as sweet peas that always bring memories of Poppa, who grew showers of them on trellises against his garden shed.

I cross the road, passing the Orange Tree pub where I'd watched fringe theatre in the upper rooms on hot sweaty nights with Tom, then an aspiring but untalented actor.

The bus stop isn't far. From the top deck of the bus I appreciate the beauty of the Thames, with fond memories of watching the boat race with my father. We reach Mortlake where I get off and make my way to the cemetery. The gravel paths criss cross. The last time I came here was to bury my sister. Mother was inconsolable, with no thought for anyone's grief but her own. I remember how hollow I felt; numb yet raw.

I'm searching for a tree on a boundary – the grave is three rows down in a family plot.

William John Denning (Poppa), devoted husband of Betsy Denning

Father of

Richard Peter Denning

Father of

Hannah Rebekah Denning

The headstone is black marble with gold lettering. It strikes me how both Hannah and dad would have hated its gaucheness, and why no dates? The grave was a puddle of mud, wooden planks, and fake grass at their funerals. I'd implored my mother to place Hannah with our dad and Father Murphy's intervention made her see sense. The more I look at the ugly stone, the more I wonder why there aren't any dates or ages and why is Grandma Betsy's name on the stone? She didn't rest here. She died in the blitz. There was a crater where the house once stood, nothing left to bury.

My attention turns to a vase of flowers; they are only a day or two old but there isn't room for mine. I feel bad about removing the blooms but take them to the bin provided and refill the vase from the tap. Squatting down, I arrange my flowers.

'Huh. After all this time, you bother to come.'

Goose pimples race up my arms. The voice- hard, cold, menacing, and unexpected, spooks me. Graveyards are not the best place to start hearing voices. I spring to my feet, shading my eyes from the sunlight.

'Mum?'

'Who else do you think would come here every Wednesday for seven years?' she snarls. I'm shocked by her appearance. Her hair is a dirty white, greasy, and unkempt. Her skin, sagging in jowls below her chin, has an unhealthy pallor. When her thin lips part they reveal a missing tooth, the next a jagged fang. She steps closer, levelling me with her bloodshot eyes. She's drunk as usual; I can smell it on her. 'Seven years without my Hannah and you, an uncaring daughter.'

Thoughts and emotions trip over each other. I hadn't planned on this meeting, but I won't back away from it either. I glance away from the face I can't honestly say I love. Love has to be earned.

'She was my Hannah, too.'

My mother grunts.

'The headstone, there are no dates. Why?'

Her voice is ice. 'Nice of you to notice.'

'But why?'

'I don't need reminding of the years that robbed me of my husband and daughter. Not that you care, living in your fancy house. The great TV presenter. All I've left is a block of marble and a rundown house.'

Heat rises, boiling, bubbling through my sternum — filling my skull. My lips part and the words I'd always locked inside me spew out.

'That's crap. It's all in your head. Is it any wonder? You drove Dad away with your religious claptrap and too much altar wine. You used God to punish him for Hannah. She had cancer, he didn't give her that. You hated Dad because he was a loving man.'

Her eyes narrow to deep dark slits. 'Love.' She rolls the word over her remaining teeth. her lips twitching into a sneer. 'Don't speak to me like that, you little bitch.' She raises her hand to slap me but changes her mind. 'I didn't drive him into that whore's bed.'

'You may as well have. He left you with your cold heart for a warm one. Someone who appreciated him, who was kind. When you confronted her, that was it. You drove him into such a rage that night, he drove like a madman to console her. You killed him with your tongue lashings and stony heart, and I know what that feels like.' I firm my stance. 'You hate me because I look like him, and loved Hannah because she didn't. Do you know how hard it was to love you?' A flicker of something gleams then fades in her eyes.

'You were always a troublesome child. Only Poppa and your father understood you.'

My legs jerk and twitch. I inhale a breath so deep I expect my feet to rise from the ground. Black thoughts travel like scum to the surface.

'I loved them, too. You shut me out and when Hannah got sick-'

She waves away my words. 'God took Hannah because of him, as punishment.'

'And you wished it was me.' I say calmly. There's no attempt at denial. She spits out her venom through taut, vengeful jaws.

'And you married a man just like him. Couldn't keep it in his trousers.'

I step into her space. My face is within an inch of hers.

'And you were pleased to see me go. I understand now why I let Tom boss me around, and why I was so fucking compliant.'

Shock registers on her face like a slap at the use of my profanity.

'I feel sorry for you. I thought, no, I hoped you'd mellow in your old age, learn how to be happy and want to know your four beautiful grandchildren.'

Her voice is a hiss. 'You moved away. Was I supposed to come crawling? Living with that smarmy Roderick's son. Him having all those heathen black babies. Disgusting. And you like a sow, delivering him child after child. That's what ruined your life. Don't blame me.'

Her hand moves under her jacket. I catch sight of her rosary, it sickens me. I reach out and shake her by the shoulders.

'Why do you wear that thing mother? God won't want you in his house. You have a cruel soul.' My arms drop to my sides. Enough said. I walk back to the headstone, bend, kiss two of my fingers and touch their names. 'Goodbye, my lovelies, I won't be back for a very long time but at least you all know I'm happy.' Hurrying away, I almost collide with a boy on a bicycle. He swerves last minute hitting one of the many waste bins. The contents- dead flowers, cellophane bags, oasis, and fake ribbons, spew across the path.

'I'm sorry. I had to hit it or crash into you,' he says red-faced, righting the bin. I smile at him. He's young, perhaps ten or eleven, his eyes fearful that he's in trouble.

'Don't worry no harm done. I'll clear it up,' I say.

'Thanks,' he mumbles, clambering onto his bike and scooting off.

I look about me in disbelief at what I'm seeing. Amid the detritus there's a bunch of sweet peas, some still in bloom. Kneeling, I select three stems of still fresh flowers, their delicate scent tickling memories. I glance skyward whispering a thank you to the clouds before unzipping my bag to look for something to wrap the flowers in. I come across the booklet *"Information for visitors to St. George's"* and lay the blooms safely inside its pages. When I get home I'll dry them ready to place in frames and display on our family gallery. One for Poppa, one for my dad, and one for Hannah.

61

I approach the nursing station straight backed and confident, far removed from the person who'd stood there three days earlier. I can hardly contain my excitement. A nurse gives me directions.

He's asleep. I'm not disappointed. It's an opportunity to study him unabashed. I gently pull up a chair and ease myself onto it. His chest rises and falls in a calming rhythm. There's something wonderful about taking in his every close detail. His shadowy lashes look mink-soft against hospital-pale skin. I can't help but wince at the healing scar arcing over his right ear. The generous lips I so desire to press against mine. His chest is a stubble of regrowth against yellowing bruises; nicks and scratches mar his gym-toned shoulders. A seatbelt burn runs across and downward, disappearing under a V of downy hair that I have a strong desire to run my fingers through. My cheeks tingle at the strength of my imagination.

A tea cart rattles its way into the ward, I jolt back in my seat. Dan flinches and opens his eyes; his head is turned away from me.

'Tea? Sandwich?' The ward assistant asks.

'Yes, tea, thank you.' Dan croaks, his voice gravelly from sleep.

'You want one, lady?'

I shake my head.

Dan swivels to look at me, his eyes sparkling with surprise. A smile breaks across his handsome face, sending pins and needles to my heart. 'You came?'

'Yup. Followed you up and down the country. You were difficult to keep up with.'

The assistant places the cup and saucer on the locker and moves on.

Dan tries to sit. 'Sorry, you'll have to help me. I can't bend either leg yet.' His hand feels around for the bed controller. I get up to help as the head end rises and assist him, restacking his pillows until he's comfortable. 'Would you mind sitting down? I'm getting a stiff neck.'

'Ah, so bossy,' I say, lowering myself onto a plastic chair. He takes my hand, threading his fingers through mine then raising them to his lips.

I gulp at the intimacy.

'I'm so glad to see you, Grace. You can't imagine what I thought when you wouldn't take my calls.'

He looks too exhausted to take the entire explanation. There will be time, later, when he is stronger.

'I suppose I overdid playing hard to get,' I say.

He grins, his eyes crinkling into fine lines at the corners, staring into mine. 'Well, can you desist now? I'm not in the position to come and find you.'

'I will explain but not now. When you're better. I got the wrong end of the stick. I was stupid and I'm sorry.'

'Me too. I know I said we could take our time but —'

'But nothing. You get better. It will be fun finding out about each other.'

'So, you're in it for the long haul?'

'I am.' He's staring at my mouth. We inch together but then he jerks away, looking over my shoulder.

'Oh no, not now. Please,' he cries, his features buckling as he slams his head back against his pillows. Two porters pushing a trolley approach. 'Come on guys, give me a break. Not now. It's visiting time for God's sake.'

One smiles, exposing a pickle-stabber of a tooth. 'Sorry, mate. You're off to X-ray.'

'Can't you come back later?'

'No can do. We have to stick to our list.' He pulls a folded paper from his chest pocket to confirm it.

The shorter of the two men lines up the trolley then tugs the bed covers, exposing Dan's legs. I wince at the sight of the metal clips piercing into his flesh- taut, shiny, raw, and swollen. Yellow iodine drives across purple, blue, and green damaged tissue. I bite my lip, determined not to grant my tears their freedom.

'I'll wait outside,' I say, 'while they get you out of bed. I'll walk down with you.' Our fingers uncurl and I experience a sense of loss.

'Thanks, it's agony when they move me.'

'I'd hate to see a grown man cry,' I say with a wink. 'See you in a minute.' Outside I rub my cheeks, I could so easily have lost him.

The trolly carrying Dan comes through the double doors. It's difficult to walk alongside. I have to keep dropping back as the oncoming traffic of people on crutches, screaming toddlers, and folk in wheelchairs come towards me. We slow at the entrance to the X-ray department.

'Will you wait?' He says over his shoulder.

I glance at my watch, my face a grimace of apology.

'Dan, I'm afraid I can't. I'll ring, okay? Every day – twice a day. I promise.'

He raises his hand.

I watch until he's no longer in sight before I walk away.

***

The journey home gives me time to dwell on the hand that fate has dealt me. If Dan hadn't had the accident, I wouldn't have come to London, and I would never met my mother or been able to tell her what I'd festered about for so long. I'm not the same person who got off the train. I'm a changed version of me-stronger, more confident, and in love.

I remember the sweet peas and open my bag to lift out the booklet. The compressed flowers are a representation of my history and a banner to my future. I truly believe in signals. Who put the flowers in my grasp? Was it a fluke? Dad or Hannah? Whenever I question myself, they will remind me of the day I became my true self.

62

'When's he coming home?' Jenny asks, stabbing a mushroom with her fork and popping it into her mouth.

'Wednesday,' I say. 'Claire's journeying down to get him. I wanted to go myself, but we're filming right up to Saturday. Actually, Kellen,' I say, moving on my chair, 'I don't believe I ever thanked you.'

'Nothing to thank me for. You did it all on your own.'

'But the show was your idea, your contacts. You made it happen.'

Kellen smiles warmly in acceptance.

Jenny pushes her plate away.

'God, I'm stuffed. I can't afford to put on an ounce. I'll become even more imbalanced, and the dreaded check-up's looming.'

I sip my water. 'I'll come with you?'

Jenny shakes her head. 'And do Robin out of seeing my surgeon again? I swear he's besotted. He goes all boyish in her company. She makes you look plain, Kellen.'

Kellen ignores the backhanded compliment, resting her chin on a curled fist.

'How long does the reconstructive surgery take?'

'Depends, probably no longer than forty-eight hours, if Leftie behaves himself and drains quickly.' Jenny pulls a face. 'Sorry, that sounds gross. I've told Robin this is going to cost him a fortune in expensive lingerie once I have a matching pair again. Oh, and talking of tits, anything on old SF?'

'Thankfully not. Sad for the kids, but I for one am glad the drama's over.'

Jenny pulls a mischievous face. 'So, back to Dan, I need filling in. I've ogled him from afar, he's gorgeous. I don't suppose there's been any opportunity for sex yet, but spill. Is he a good kisser?'

I groan. 'Jen, you're incorrigible.'

'And you're blushing.'

I poke my tongue out at her. 'The accident was eight months ago. Then three more operations and extensive rehab to get him walking since then, so unless you count very public hospital visits where its nigh on impossible to snog the face off a man in a wheelchair.'

Jenny turns to Kellen 'Unbelievable. What is this girl like?'

'You mean you haven't even kissed?'

I sigh.

Jenny turns to Kellen. 'Unbelievable. What is this girl like?'

'Hey. There's no rush. It'll happen when it happens.'

Jenny makes an *I give up* face. 'Well, when you said you weren't rushing things, you weren't joking, were you? This romance is slower than War and Peace.'

A waiter approaches with three flutes of champagne. Kellen raises her glass. 'I thought the occasion needed marking. A toast to tits and kisses.'
Jen and I dissolve into fits of giggles.
'To tits and kisses,' we chorus.
'With knobs on, for Grace?' Jenny snickers.

EPILOGUE

Dan's due in twenty minutes. He's kept to his word and not rushed me, although that hasn't been difficult as his road to recovery has been a long one. He was adamant that our dinner date would be on hold until he could walk unaided.

I'm fizzing from head to toe and keep checking my watch. My stomach clenches with what I hope is nerves and not an untimely tummy bug.

The phone rings, Jack beats me to it. My breathing stalls. Is Dan calling to cancel? Jack bellows Melissa's name over the landing. Not for me then. I put on my coat and then take it off again. I don't want to that look too keen. Who am I kidding? We're both well past dating games. On second thoughts, if he does come into the house the children will gawp and embarrass us both. Coat on it is. Headlights arc across the windows then sweep across the driveway. Brake lights glow red.

'And breathe. One, two, three,' I open the front door. The driver's door opens and Dan's long legs appear, followed by his suited body. My heels click on the pathway, he limps around the car, opening the passenger door.

'I like a lady who's on time,' he says, kissing my cheek.

I breath in the lathery lemon freshness of his cologne. 'Mmm, you smell good.' He breathes into my ear.

'Likewise, kind Sir,' I say playfully.

Dessert wine is something I usually avoid but Dan is insistent. We share desserts and sip smooth Sauternes.

Dan's an excellent raconteur and it's fun getting to know each other, but I have a niggling sense of foreboding. I'm convinced that the jokey mood pre-empts a more serious conversation. A lull as we eat confirms this.

Dan sits back in his chair, takes his napkin from his lap, folds it and places it back on the table.

Nerves force me to fill the void. 'I've had a lovely evening Dan, thank you. I don't think I've laughed as much in ages.'

He has a pensive look as he reaches across the table and takes my hand. 'It's you that needs the thanking. God, you've been patient. If Kate had been alive, she'd have taken her tennis racket to my head. She was a great girl.'

He breaks off as the waiter brings coffee and pours. I'm willing the man to hurry up.

'You must come and see the rose bush. Leah chose a spot for it on the terrace so we can see it every day. It was a lovely idea.'

'I'm glad you both liked it.' *Bugger, I interrupted.*

There's a pause as Dan stares into his coffee cup. 'I feel lost without Kate. She was my rock, though bossy. I miss that. I'm a bit like a duck without a pond. She was a great problem-solver and even though she was undergoing treatment, we'd still Skype every few days and I'd offload any issues that cropped up with Leah; Kate always had a solution.'

He takes a sip of coffee. 'When Maggie announced she was pregnant I wanted to do the right thing, but Kate talked me out of it. I'm glad she did, as by Maggie's own volition; she'd never have made a mother let alone a wife.'

I sense it's okay to comment. 'She left, and you were okay with that?'

'Yes. I wasn't in love with her or she me. She was crazy and fun to be with, but it would never have worked. She had itchy feet, always wanting to be on the move. I had to run the farm. Thankfully, although strong-willed, Leah hasn't as yet shown many of her mother's characteristics.'

'She certainly has less hair.'

His forehead crinkles. 'Thank God for that. It took me years to master plaits. I bet the village gossips had plenty to say when Maggie turned up after the accident. She always gave everyone plenty to talk about.'

'I met her, twice. I liked her.'

'Yes, who wouldn't? But wild, restless, full of energy and idiotic ideas. I can't believe I went along with her demands.'

I flatten my lips and throw him a quizzical look. 'Demands?'

'Yes, she made a few stipulations that I agreed to. One was that Leah call me Dan, not Dad. Maggie stayed long enough for us to register Leah's birth, then left.'

A lone tear slides its way over my lower lid. It's the thought of her walking away from her baby.

Dan notices and leans forward, blotting it away with the pad of his thumb. 'No need to cry, it all worked out well. I didn't mean to tell you all this. I'm usually less verbal on matters of the heart, but I wanted to explain, put things right.'

I take a tissue from my bag and blot my face. 'It's sad. Not what I expected.'

'I'm not the gigolo you had me marked down as?' He lifts his hands, depicting a banner. 'Local playboy, lock up your daughters.' His grin and bravado are short lived. 'So, that's it. Now you know, and before you ask – yes, there have been others. Of course there have, but no one that I wanted to commit to. That is, until I met you.' His hand rises, running his fingers through his hair.

The telling has tired him. I stand up. 'Come on, let's get the bill and get out of here. I think you've done enough soul-baring for one night. Is Leah at home?' Dan's brow cords.

'No, she's on a sleepover at the Taylors'.'

'Good. Then can I come back for a nightcap? Don't look so surprised.' *I can't believe how brazen I'm being.*

It takes a moment for him to stand, his legs clearly stiff from sitting. He takes a sidestep, moving away from the table and holds his arms out. I willingly slip into them.

He breathes into my hair, pulling me closer. 'Thank you.'

The other diners fade into oblivion. It's just him and me. 'What for?' I sigh, my hand cupping the nape of his neck.

'I was talking to Kate, not you.'

I pull back far enough to meet his eyes.

'I told her everything about you,' he says, his eyes melting my soul.

'And?'

'She told me to stop running.' His eyelids close and I want to kiss them. 'Grace, I think I'm falling in love with you.'

My heart gives a kick. 'Think? You're not sure?' I tease.

'Actually, I'm positive.'

'Thank you.'

'What for?'

'Loving me.'

'Ah, that was the easy bit, convincing you was the hard part.

'Thank goodness for that.' My grin's so wide it pulls on my cheeks as my heart beats in a tap-dance. 'Can I be so bold as to ask… are you a good kisser?' I feel his chest rise against mine, his fingers sliding into my hair to tilt my chin.

'I'll let you be the judge of that.'

Our lips meet- soft, sweet, and yearning. Lost in the moment, neither of us care we are standing in the middle of a crowded restaurant and that our first kiss is so public. We have found each other, and love will deal with anything that gets in our way.

Other Books by this Author

The Woman I've Become.

The Chartley Girls Series

The Girl on the Hill.

The Chartley Girls Series

Accident of Fate.

First of the Liam Riley Duo

Accident of Birth.

Second of Adam/Liam Riley Duo

SUE MACKENDER took up a career as an author after twenty seven years in the recruitment industry. Selling her businesses in 2007 gave her the opportunity to write her first novel *Accident of Fate.*

The Woman I've Become is Sue's forth novel.

Sue lives in a pretty village in Surrey with her husband David. She has three sons, seven grandchildren, and a great granddaughter and regular visits from one of her three sons's chocolate Labrador's Rollo.